ANTHRACIS

ANTHRACIS

A MICROBIAL MYSTERY

Millicent Eidson

Maya Maguire Media - Vermont

DEDICATION

For public health veterinarians and One Health allies

ENVIRONMENT

Bacteria hide out, lie dormant in the soil, cocoon a few inches deep. Humans are irrelevant—not important to survival at all.

Fifth plague of ancient Egypt. Known to Homer in The Iliad, 700 BC, and Virgil. Contributed to the fall of Rome.

Shapeshifter microbe, invisible underfoot. Sporulation—circle the wagons, hunker down, pull in. Form a hairy fringed enveloping membrane and an amazingly resistant coat.

Capture the essence on a photomicrograph? Look empty, play dead.

But all the ingredients of life slumber inside. What else can endure extremes of temperature, chemicals, and irradiation? Passive survival, up to two hundred fifty years in South Africa by carbon dating.

All living things want to multiply, so infection inevitably happens. Death often follows. First degree murder requires deliberate and premeditated killing. Not specifically the intent.

But take them out?

Sure, with indifference. And a helping hand is always nice.

ONE

Two young, damaged people, more than a hundred miles apart in different states, paused under meager piñon pine shade to inhale superheated air and admire the stark high mesa beauty. Each was lean with bronze skin and shoulder-length, glossy, black hair. Maya Maguire's was bound back into a perky ponytail and Danny Koopee's was tied off at the base of his neck. Summer of 2018 was the hottest on record. When they removed hats to fan their necks, the sun sizzled as it absorbed into their scalps.

In Keams Canyon, Arizona, seventy-five miles west of the razor's edge border, Danny Koopee didn't know he had played his last song. Next to the sheep he protected, he reached for the water bottle to wash away dizziness, a headache, and visual distortions in his left eye.

After swiping a hand on the sweat beading his ruddy forehead, he propped his guitar against a log and vomited blood on his white Nikes. "Masauwu," he muttered, then collapsed unconscious into the saffron soil, the weight of his body splintering Korina wood and snapping steel strings.

Typical of monsoon season, the late July towers of darkening clouds promised respite from the energy-sapping sun and searing heat. But they also posed a threat. As Four Corners' natives, both travelers grew up with the knowledge that flash flooding could overfill arroyos, wash out roads, and sweep people away to a watery death.

Fifty miles east of the New Mexico-Arizona border as the raven flies, Maya pressed her long, piano-prodigy fingers into the burning pain of her lower back. With only five seconds between thunder booms and lightning flashes, she picked up her pace along the well-marked trail to the Chaco Canyon parking lot and willed herself to slow down her breathing.

A third, even more broken soul glowered a hundred feet away from Danny. Concealed behind an aromatic juniper, the witness finished his scribble, closed the wrinkled brown notebook, and slipped it into his leather shoulder bag. The bleating herd backed up as he toed the Hopi boy's body with a worn cowboy boot.

Two sheep were down. One was dead that the kid had opened up, putrefying organs crawling with flies. The odor was enough to gag a maggot. A second one lay twitching under a creosote bush, sporting a double set of horns. Aberrant, just like him, and he stroked its neck.

Animals suffered too much on behalf of humans, but there was nothing he could do this time to help. As monsoon rain stung his arms, he tossed a cigarette butt to the earth and pivoted for the nearest road.

TWO

First munth
Mother gave me this direy for my birthday
    this iz my 1 entry
She sayz I am growing up almost 5 feet tall
Hope I can rite when I want
not practis with this
            The Lord had the Negro remain on earth
                 for the devil to work with.
Our Profit sayz we practis this in church school

I wanna take care of animalz not go to school
I nevr seen a Negro are they devilz?
Brother Jacob iz 4 and copez my work

Direy iz goldn like earth. Angel Moroni on cover
Mother rote my name there

I love Motherz hair. Motherz never cut hair
need it long to wash Fatherz and Jesus feet

THREE

Sciatica streaked down Maya's right leg from the harrowing Sunday drive in monsoon storms between Chaco Canyon and Santa Fe. As she opened the state health department door, she verified the time—7:45 AM, another fifteen minutes to spare. First day on the first real job. Important to keep emotions from mucking up intellectual function.

She slipped into the restroom to armor for battle. Pulling a brush from her purse, she formed her hair into an orderly wave. Earrings of black onyx, a protective, warrior stone, complemented the opaque depth of her eyes. No eyeshadow for her tapered lids. With smooth, featureless skin except for one small mole near her left eye, she never plastered on facepaint. Flattening folds of a navy skirt and blazer, she inched out into the entrance foyer.

"Dr. Maguire for Dr. Grinwold." Her voice was feeble—she was always shy with new people.

An older dark-haired woman behind the lower level front desk hesitated. "Did you say Maguire?"

Maya inhaled, calming an immediate defensive twinge. She should have learned to stifle her instinctive reaction to everyone's confusion between her Irish last name and Chinese heritage.

"I'm the new Epidemic Intelligence Service Officer from the Centers for Disease Control and Prevention." She projected more confidence. "I met him at the April conference when assignments were made."

The secretary guided her down the hall to the office of the State Epidemiologist. Middle-aged, with wisps of brown hair combed forward over his pale bald forehead, he wore the same plaid, used-car salesman's jacket that her EIS classmates mocked during his presentation in Atlanta. She shifted on the guest chair, grateful to work with a physician who completed the same CDC training program.

"You're finally here." Dr. Grinwold shuffled folders on his paper-strewn desk. "Make sure Stephanie has your number. With our limited resources, the EIS officer always needs to be reachable, even if you're only a vet."

Ouch. Her colleagues warned being a veterinarian in the human medical world would be a struggle. She bottled up her thoughts and maintained a placid exterior. *People won't have time for you if you are always angry or complaining.* Her astronomer mom addressed all problems with a Stephen Hawking quotation. Hawking was a genius to write *A Brief History of Time* in spite of paralysis. No one was allowed to give into weakness.

Her new boss tossed a page titled *August 2018 Meeting Schedule* across the desk and picked up the phone. "Stephanie, show Dr. Maguire her office."

With a narrow view of brown dirt and yellowing lawn edge through the high windows, she stretched to her full height beneath the low-angle morning rays. New York's noise and masses of people had overwhelmed her during Columbia University's Master of Public Health degree. A work assignment back home under spacious skies was a dream come true.

Stephanie handed her a map. "I circled City Hall—don't forget voter registration. Our November election will have important races."

"Maybe next week you could get me up to speed on those?"

"We have two years working together, and I'd like to be friends," Stephanie answered. "Let me know how I can make your time filled with good memories."

After the visit with their grouchy gringo boss, Maya's heart rate slowed in response to the secretary's Spanish accent. Stephanie could help her integrate, not just inhabit New Mexico. During Maya's formative years in Arizona, having older Irish American parents isolated her from other dark-skinned kids at Flagstaff schools.

She had no recollections, only photos, of the run-down Chinese orphanage. Raised by a white family, she didn't notice race in the mirror as an adult. But she was still self-conscious with other penetrating eyes.

. . .

The iPhone rang as she pulled a steaming pot pie from the microwave. Her mom's imperious tone filled the kitchen. "Maya, glad I caught you. We freed up our calendars to help you unpack."

"I'd love to see you both, but I didn't move much stuff. Gotta go, see you on Labor Day?" She dropped the phone and a wash of guilt flooded to her toes.

She understood her parents' solicitousness. On a balmy spring day after kindergarten, she wandered one street over on her banana bike. At the same time, according to the police report, a sixteen-year-old in a Ford pickup headed home from driver's ed class. The car phone his parents recently installed rang. His knees held the steering wheel while he searched for it under his book bag. As he felt its bulky rectangular shape, a loud thud vibrated through the truck frame.

When the vehicle was found at the auto repair shop the next day, he complained to the cops, "I never saw her, she came out of nowhere."

Maya, tossed in the air like a rag doll, lay moaning on the asphalt. Right leg projected at a strange angle, blood oozed from a massive gash, and jagged thigh-bone protruded from the muscle. The boy flipped out and fled. When she closed her eyes, her grandfather's misty ángel beckoned her to fly. Within fifteen minutes, a neighbor spotted her hemorrhaging out on the street.

Following a lengthy procedure to stop the bleeding and plate the femur, she awoke in the ICU to see her parents crying and laughing. One week later, with unbearable pain despite a morphine drip, the surgeons realigned her shattered pelvis with a second operation.

Three weeks in the pediatric ward, then recovery at home and missing the last month of school. The year of post-traumatic stress disorder therapy, new family pets, and piano lessons when she could sit again helped her refocus from chronic pain and fear. But many ordinary life activities and human interactions still triggered a heightened fight-or-flight instinct.

Flashbacks to those twenty-year-old scenes always intensified her anxiety. After slipping on silk pajamas, she brushed out tangles in her thick hair. Should she call and apologize for the hasty hang-up? Instead, she crawled into bed and drowned out the whooshing heartbeat with her favorite Broadway album on the iPhone.

Like the *Hamilton* lyrics about hurricanes and yellow skies, her memories were plagued by brief flashes of golden sky and empty street with dulcet bird songs before the truck roared away and she lost consciousness.

. . .

Dr. Suzanne Jaworski of the Epidemiology Workforce Branch checked in from Atlanta on Wednesday. A dentist, the CDC field supervisor was reputed to be a supportive coach for the non-physician EIS officers.

"Good morning, how is it today in God's country? What are you working on?"

Maya leaned her elbows on the desk. "Orientation—I don't know if Dr. Grinwold is confident of my abilities."

The Long Island accent was abrupt, but reassuring. "You won't be siloed. They're short-staffed."

CDC ranked the assignments in deciding which ones to fill. New Mexico had gone several years without an EIS Officer, and it would be a disaster if she gave a bad impression of the placement.

She took a sharp breath. "Summer's busy for infectious diseases. They'll put me on the consult team soon."

The phone resonated with keyboard taps before Dr. Jaworski continued. "I'm checking for Epi-Aid requests. Those are from other states for assistance in their outbreak investigations."

Maya hoped her mild complaint about the slow start wouldn't trigger relocation. With school pressures behind her, a steadier pace would be wonderful.

. . .

She tapped her iPhone and checked messages. 7:30 Friday, August 3. As she grabbed a consultation notebook, the desk phone rang with the first call of the day.

"I went to Harvard," a physician said. "We got stool results a hell of a lot faster than you."

Dropping an elite school credential had the opposite effect on Maya. La invidia, the envy, was anathema to the locals. Shouldn't act like you're better than anyone else.

The phone jangled again within minutes of persuading the Albuquerque lab to expedite testing. "Is Dr. Grinwold there?"

Dr. Jaworski's sharp tone triggered lightning across Maya's nerves as her Atlanta supervisor continued. "Presumptive anthrax in a sixteen-year-old Hopi sheepherder. The Nation is within Arizona, but tribal sovereignty requires a federal epidemiologist on the investigation team."

Maya sank to the chair as her vision turned black. After 9/11, anthrax was mailed in letters to senators and reporters, but that was decades ago. She sat more erect. Never admit panic attacks to colleagues.

"Sorry, I only learned a little about anthrax in vet school."

Dr. Jaworski rushed on. "Find Fred and call me."

When Maya joined Dr. Grinwold on his speakerphone, Dr. Jaworski filled them in. "The boy collapsed last weekend and is hospitalized in Phoenix. Initial lab tests indicate *Bacillus anthracis*, but we'll confirm. With many possible sources including bioterrorism like 2001, we need a diverse team."

Dr. Grinwold drummed his sausage fingers. "What's the implication for us?"

"Indian Health Service requested a CDC Epi-Aid. Maya's the nearest Officer."

As his heavy weight twisted in the roller chair, he bellowed. "We've had her less than a week."

The voice from the speaker was curt. "Fred, EIS Officers must be available for Epi-Aids."

His wrinkled scowl pinned Maya to the seat. "Fine, but bring her back as soon as possible."

"Agreed. I'll email details and an airline ticket from Albuquerque."

Slamming the phone, he yelled out the door. "Maya's flying to Phoenix. Drop her at the airport shuttle bus."

She trooped behind Stephanie down the hall with a sharp pain between her shoulder blades. No chance to decline even as her mind raged that she had no idea what she was doing.

. . .

After the short flight, an Indian Health Service driver picked her up from Sky Harbor. Within minutes, the sedan came to a halt at the Phoenix Indian Medical Center front door.

A clean-shaven Hispanic man stepped forward, wide smile matching the brilliance of his white military uniform. Only an inch taller than her five-and-a-half feet, the officer reached out to shake her hand.

"Dr. Maguire, I'm Manolo Miranda. Thanks for coming quickly."

"Miranda? You know who you look like?"

"*Hamilton* fan?"

He chuckled as they broached the sliding doors. "Might be a distant cousin, we're not sure. I don't mind getting mixed up with a genius who writes hit Broadway musicals."

"How about growing up as a Chinese Maguire?" she asked, now

enjoying the incongruity. The physician's exuberant greeting relaxed her from the hurried trip and anthrax dread.

"You can share that story later." His attitude became formal. "Let's check on our patient. Unconscious, critical condition."

They donned masks, gowns, and gloves in the antechamber to the Intensive Care room. Cloying material hugged every inch of her body and her warm breath was captured in the mask. "Biosafety level three?" she asked. "Are we at risk?"

"Anthrax isn't contagious person to person, but negative pressure will keep anything hazardous from escaping."

"I checked while waiting at the airport. No other recent cases."

"Just the guy from 2011 visiting parks in the Northwest. No one discovered how he was exposed—a major mystery." He elbowed open the door to the ICU room.

Uncertain what to say, Maya stared at Danny Koopee. His yellowed skin and black hair flashed in vivid contrast to white hospital bedcovers, and intensive care equipment dwarfed his thin frame.

Ventilator sounds made her weep inside, as she wondered about his family. The heart monitor's steady beep-beep echoed the pulsating whoosh in her ears during a panic attack. She tightened her muscles, trying to regain control.

This was the real world, school over. She turned away and pinched the gown to ease space next to her body, hoping to cool down. "As a veterinarian, I'm not sure how to help. Are there family members I could interview about the herd?"

Dr. Miranda nodded. "His Dad might drive down tomorrow for the weekend."

Determined to keep up with her colleague, she asked, "He's jaundiced, right?"

"Yup, liver enzymes are elevated. Also, he has internal bleeding with a drop in hemoglobin, hematocrit, and platelet count."

Her stomach churned—the odors, sounds, and body close enough to touch were too vivid. Thick tubes dripped white, viscous liquids from Danny's chest and abdomen, while smaller lines transported fluids and blood into his arms.

"He has respiratory distress and a blood infection," Dr. Miranda said. "His father found him and rushed him to the Hopi Health Care Center, then they flew him here to Phoenix on Wednesday. I'm surprised he's lasted this long."

Her voice was faint behind the mask. "Why are you thinking anthrax?"

"The lung changes and gram-positive streptobacilli in his blood. Sputum and cultures were negative, but antibiotics could mess those up. Any idea when your CDC lab can weigh in?"

"Atlanta started confirmatory tests," she said. "And they're discussing antitoxin."

Suddenly she was back in her five-year-old body, trapped in the hospital for weeks, leg suspended in the air. As the old break throbbed, she leaned on the lone chair.

"You okay?"

Dr. Miranda's voice snapped her out of the memory. He released Danny's hand and guided her by the arm to the changing room. His steady dark gaze triggered a hormonal punch, or stress.

"Get some rest. I'll check with you tomorrow."

She ripped off the claustrophobic personal protective equipment and took short, hot breaths on the walk through the outdoor parking lot. As the car headed away from the medical center, she spotted a bank digital sign.

The driver wiped his neck with a red bandana. "7:30 PM and it's still 111°."

Scalding heat, an Arizona teenager with anthrax, an appealing IHS doctor—not what she envisioned on Monday as the new CDC epidemiologist assigned to New Mexico.

Out the window, purple, pink, and yellow bands slashed the western horizon, and orange clouds dripped like a Dali painting.

. . .

Attempts to relax in the Phoenix hotel failed. Danny's image punctuated bouts of interrupted sleep. He had resembled a frail child, not someone hardy enough to live outdoors, managing a sheep herd. Was he the index case for a larger outbreak?

The iPhone jarred her awake from a recurring nightmare of monstrous, swerving vehicles.

"This is Manolo." His voice was tense. "Danny died, and his family reported dead sheep. We'll pick you up at four-thirty." Prying her eyes open, she checked the time, 4:05 AM.

During the ride to the hospital, she rolled down the window to energize with refreshing air. A dull whir from cicadas mating was the only sound. When she joined Manolo at the autopsy suite, they donned PPE again.

"We had a long night," he said. "Never get accustomed to losing patients so young."

Her instinct was to reassure him. "It's devastating news, but I know you did everything possible."

He opened the door. "Let's get in. They've started."

A pathologist had sliced Danny's skin with a long, Y incision from each shoulder and down to the pubic bone. Although Maya had assisted in animal necropsies, she was surprised to be invited to a human autopsy. So she stayed silent and watched.

The naked body and smell of bodily fluids triggered a wave of dizziness and nausea when the pathologist's electric saw buzzed through the ribs. She inhaled the odor of burning cartilage—good thing she didn't consider pathology or surgery as potential careers.

After the abdomen was open, an assistant removed the organs as a group and placed them in a stainless basin. Small, dark red spots covered fluid-enlarged lymph nodes, lungs, and abdominal organs. Bloody and pus-filled thick fluid adhered to the cavities. While the assistant weighed each organ and collected samples, the pathologist removed the skull's crown.

"The black hemorrhage on the brain is called cardinal's cap," Manolo said.

Maya swayed with sleep deficit and the shock of seeing Danny dissected. One minute alive and struggling, opened up like a dead cow the next. Unlike last night, she didn't find a chair to lean on.

How was Manolo so stoic? He never had an anthrax case before. But then she saw the hollows under red-streaked eyes. Maybe it got to him, too.

"I know you're not done, but we've seen enough," he told the pathologist and turned to Maya. "Let's step out."

In the anteroom, she lowered to the bench and tore off the protective wrappings.

He deposited his gown in the waste receptacle. "Your lab just called mine. They employed a test which detects anthrax lethal factor, one of the toxins excreted by the bacteria. It was positive, and fits with these results."

She had hoped their initial guestimate about anthrax was wrong. Even with the lab confirmation, she struggled to accept it. "Human infections are so rare. Did you say there are dead sheep where Danny was found?"

"The U.S. Department of Agriculture requested your assistance in checking them out."

"But as an epidemiologist, my clinical experience is minimal. I expected to collect data, not perform anthrax field work."

"I can talk with Danny's family and check for suspect cases, but can't help the USDA. I'm not the veterinarian—you are."

Although his tone was impatient, his expression remained calm. "I'll notify the state health department and tell them to let us manage public release. Get a couple hours rest, so we can head north at midday."

Her pulse quickened at the chance to read up and counter a brain fog about the disease in sheep.

"Veterinarians working with infected animals are recommended for pre-exposure prophylaxis," he said. "Won't be effective immediately, but you should start it."

"Did you get it?" With multiple surgeries, she didn't have a fear of needles, but had not heard there was a vaccine. "Are there any side effects?"

"I'm not handling animals, and patient exposure isn't a risk. The nurse will give you the list of adverse reactions, including the usual pain, redness, and swelling."

"You don't need to persuade me," she said. "I'm a fan of vaccinations. Anything to decrease my anthrax anxiety."

A moment of silence, then he said, "Pregnant women have some vaccine risks."

She flashed hot in an instantaneous reaction to the intrusive comment. "Not a problem. Direct me to the clinic and I'll see you at noon."

As he pointed down the corridor, she spun on her heels and left him behind. She understood his clinical concern, but he wasn't entitled to her sexual history, or lack of it.

FOUR

<u>Oktobr 15 2001</u>
Mother sayz Mormons kicked us out so Utah could becum state
No TV here but hurd rumorz of big thingz in outside world.
Planez hit buildingz, poizun letturz

<u>Nov 3</u>
Mother drillz me to spell rite and sneeks me books
Teenz sposed to be adults and more smart even if no school

Today we fix Profit stone fense
Friend John sayz kid shot himself after unlawful sex with Profit
Whatever that meenz
John iz full of shit   Not sposed to cuss, but he iz

FIVE

The bank sign across the road changed from 119° to 120° as Maya wilted under the hotel lobby overhang. When the SUV arrived, Manolo leaned over to push open the passenger door. Climbing in, she avoided his eyes, embarrassed about her reaction to the predawn vaccine pregnancy warning. Chalk it up to long hours and pathogen unease.

"Can you forgive me for being short this morning? I'm feeling out of my element." She brushed perspiration from her face and gulped water from her bottle. "How do you cope with this heat?"

With the vehicle on cruise control as they drove north on I-17, he cranked the air conditioner up another notch.

"I've been in Phoenix a year, and we get temps over a hundred almost half the time. But growing up in NYC, we had high nineties with a hundred percent humidity. That was rough."

Maya rotated her neck, attempting to relax. "Columbia's MPH graduation was in May, so I escaped the City's hot pavement this year. I just moved back to the Southwest after CDC training for a month in Atlanta—that was unbearable."

"Climate warming and weirding." He turned his head with an amiable smile. "We need to adapt, right?"

"I reduced my carbon footprint for two years in NYC by walking and mass transit." She gazed out at the dusty hills, punctuated by gigantic, vertical arms of saguaro cacti. "At least we're carpooling today."

Manolo hit the radio power button and drum beats of *Doesn't Matter* by Christine and the Queens vibrated the dash. Maya tuned out the depressing lyrics as she flashed through an internal slide show of Danny's autopsy images. She experienced grief when losing animal patients, but the species barrier provided some distance.

Even without responsibility for Danny's care, his death hit hard. Sometimes her obsessive attention unraveled a solution, but not this time. So she refocused on the scenery. With glimpses of Manolo's intensity maneuvering around trucks, she was still adjusting to how much he looked like Lin-Manuel Miranda.

Entering Black Canyon, he turned off the music and interrupted her efforts at distraction. "So what's the Chinese Maguire story?"

She stretched her legs to the floorboard. "My parents are Irish Americans who settled in Flagstaff before my adoption. In eleventh grade, we moved to Denver."

"Any time for hobbies?"

"Piano." But it wasn't entirely accurate, with almost no practice during nine years of college.

Manolo braked for an 18-wheeler challenged by the steep hill, then carefully passed to the front of it. "Viviendo en Arizona y Colorado, ¿hablas español?"

Way too long since high school Spanish. "No recuerdo mucho. Mi pronunciación es terrible." She spoke the words with a halting cadence. Embarrassed by her own accent, she didn't say his was easy on the ears.

"Tu español está bien," he answered with an encouraging smile. "Where did you go to vet school?"

"Colorado State in Ft. Collins."

He nodded. "For me, the Uniformed Services University provided officer's salary, including residency and infectious disease training at Walter Reed. I needed a change of direction, so came out here to the Indian Health Service."

"Well, the uniform suits you." She regretted her remark and turned away, fingers wrinkling the fabric of her dress pants. "Public

Health Service was an option for me, too, but I got more flexibility joining CDC as a civilian." She had flunked the military's health exam—another item of personal history he wasn't entitled to.

"PHS and the Indian Health Service are great for me." He yawned, covering his mouth. "No debt, and I contribute leadership for system changes."

Mid-height piñon and juniper forest replaced the desert scenery as road signs announced Camp Verde. "Mind driving?" His eyes were surrounded by slight lines and droopy eyelids. "I'm beat."

Anticipating the driver's seat, she dialed down her vehicle-associated anxiety. Lack of control—at the mercy of fate or other people's stupidity—was intolerable. Manolo pulled into a gas station and topped off the fuel while she bought a soda to get caffeinated.

As she started the SUV, he leaned against the passenger door jamb and pulled the white uniform cap over his eyes, then shifted several times in the seat before dozing off.

With only the noise of the engine and passing vehicles, Maya ran a hand through her hair, scratching her scalp to settle down her brain. She turned the radio to a classical music station and tried to avoid distressing over anthrax. Her left foot tapped the floorboard in frustration—not enough time for research and preparation.

In Flagstaff, she turned into a Circle K for another break and he stirred awake. "Nap hit the spot, thanks. How are you doing?"

"Arm's a hair sore from the vaccine."

"Can I check it?"

The skin of her upper arm tingled as his fingertips gently lifted the short sleeve of her shirt.

Heart racing, Maya reflexively nudged his hand away. "Just pulling your leg, I'm fine." Physical contact beyond shaking hands was awkward for someone who never dated.

Manolo opened his door. "Let me grab coffee. Want me to get you anything?"

Averse to coffee taste, she shook her head. When he returned, she had moved to the passenger side.

"The clinic's on edge." He slipped his cell phone into one of the cup holders. "They might have another patient connected to Danny, so we can't stop again."

Maya's radar amped to maximum. If there were more cases, the expectations to handle it increased for her as representing CDC. "Details?"

"When we get there."

After pulling out on I-40, he resumed casual conversation. "Where do your parents live now?"

She hesitated. Why did he hold back on what he learned on the call—not trusting her as a partner already? But she pushed aside the angst to go with the flow. "They retired back in Flag when I graduated from vet school. No reason to stay in Colorado when I left for NYC and grad school."

The tall, dark green ponderosa pines faded in the rear window as the landscape transitioned to high desert with ocher hills and fewer cacti. One marker pointed toward Apache Death Cave and Canyon Diablo, and he waved at the sign. "Been there?"

"Apaches murdered Navajo families, then hid out in a cave. Other Navajos set fire to smoke them out and killed them. White settlers tell stories of ghostly groans and footsteps. There are still fights over who belongs on this land."

"¡Dios mío! Morbid family tourist attraction."

Visiting there had been too scary, but anxiety was always bottled up, even from her parents. "Speaking of family, Mom'll be mad that I'm not stopping in Flag. She's worried about the demands of my first job."

The SUV decelerated as he exited the interstate. "You're probably not used to dying patients."

"Not people, especially one with his whole life ahead of him."

Within an hour on the two-lane road, they approached a T-intersection and Manolo turned right at the Second Mesa Post Office toward First Mesa. After passing a modern housing development, they parked at the Health Care Center. The desert hardscrabble retained the heat, and Maya took a deep breath of the thinner, high altitude air.

In the conference room, an older short-haired Hopi woman in a white coat shook their hands. "Manolo, thanks for coming. Maya, I'm Humita Nampeyo, the medical director here."

She turned to introduce the tall, tanned Anglo behind her. "This is Dave Schwartz, Area Veterinarian in Charge from USDA's Animal and Plant Health Inspection Service."

"Dr. Maguire, I'm grateful for another vet on the case." Lanky and lean, he appeared to be in his early thirties. "When they called about dead sheep, I drove from Albuquerque. The Arizona State Veterinarian is tied up so you've got me. The animals are inaccessible by vehicle and we need to go on horseback. Can you ride?"

Her eyes widened. She hadn't worked with a horse since vet school. "Not super experienced but I know how."

"We have café food and rooms to sleep," Dr. Nampeyo said. "You two start early tomorrow. Manolo, Danny Koopee's father is now ill and hospitalized here. The Tribal Council is distressed that you informed the state health department. I need to caution you about public comments."

Her voice became more agitated. "Danny's death and any others may raise questions about our quality of care and reduce our level of support."

Manolo opened his mouth to speak but Dr. Nampeyo raised her hand to cut him off. "We don't want to get labeled, like hantavirus and the 'Navajo flu.' I realize that was almost thirty years ago, but people have long memories and resentments."

With a respectful expression, Manolo continued his interrupted response. "When investigating cases, we talk to people who might go to the press. Anthrax has never been reported from Arizona, so we need to discover and prevent what's causing this."

While the physicians remained in the conference room for case surveillance plans, Maya swallowed a yawn and joined Dave for dinner. They shared an order of fry bread and he told stories from his college days at Texas A&M. As they neared their rooms, he drew out an article from his bag. "A little light anthrax reading before bedtime."

. . .

Despite restless sleep in a dormitory-style bed, Maya awoke at six and donned a dark green Colorado State University sweatshirt and jeans. More alert with a steaming cup of tea, she joined Dave in his vehicle.

For a moment, she forgot their mission with the cloudless sky tinted a brilliant cerulean-pink-orange. As the pickup began to move, the cool morning air refreshed her skin. After passing the Keams Canyon Shopping Center, they headed northeast on a well-graded dirt road and pulled over to the shoulder where a stooped Hopi man in a navy shirt and blue jeans waited with three saddled horses.

Her heart broke to encounter the saddened, deep-set eyes when he introduced himself as Danny's grandfather.

"I'm so sorry for your loss." She bowed her head and tried to bond with him through good memories. "Someone mentioned your grandson was an accomplished guitar player."

His voice was deep. "It helped him pass the time. Michael Jackson was his hero and he memorized all the songs. We found out about Jackson's Neverland Ranch and what he did with the boys there. I tried to guide Danny along a healthier Hopi path."

He shrugged, appearing disgusted with his grandson's affinity for the tainted pop star. Perhaps he thought Danny's death was a consequence of deviating from the spiritual road. The elder held her horse, but Maya needed a boost from Dave to swing her leg over the saddle.

In the lead, Mr. Koopee and his Palomino snaked down a rocky trail toward the canyon bottom. They forded a trickling stream and trotted up the forested eastern slope. Entering a cottonwood grove, Maya spotted two dozen animals with long coarse wool and black, tan, or white faces and legs. Some lounged in the grass but others bolted. The trio dismounted and Mr. Koopee tied up the horses.

"What breed?" she asked as they donned white paper coveralls over their clothes along with masks, boot covers, and gloves.

"Navajo-Churro, adapted to our climate. Sturdy—good for meat, dairy, and fleece."

An animal writhed with convulsions off to the side and Dave parted the thick fibers to place a stethoscope. "Foaming at the mouth and respiratory distress."

Uncertain how to help, she extracted a pen and pad from her pocket to take notes. He pushed aside the sheep's feces-encrusted tail to insert a thermometer in the rectum. "106.9°, very high fever."

Nearby they spotted a deceased black-fleeced ewe with a double pair of horns and a bloody nasal discharge. Maya easily moved its limbs. "How long has this one been dead?"

"I saw it earlier but had to get back for an update from the hospital," Mr. Koopee answered. "Timothy buried another one the day after he found Danny. It had been cut open. He thought Danny had been curious about why it died."

"This one should have rigor mortis," Dave said. "Could be plant or chemical poisoning, or another infectious disease. But sudden death with no rigor mortis fits with anthrax. When was your grandson here?"

"He took care of the flock on weekdays. Timothy took over on weekends. My son had business Saturday so didn't return here until late Sunday. A flash flood made it hard to get through." A small rusty cloud formed when Mr. Koopee kicked at the dirt.

"My grandson needed a day off now and then. But Timothy said he'd be fine out here an extra day. More quiet time to write his music."

"Let's catch them for checkups." Dave said. Maya waved the sheep one-by-one toward Mr. Koopee, who restrained them by the neck. Dave reported the temperatures to Maya and used his stethoscope to evaluate each animal's heart and lungs.

"Four are febrile, tachycardic, and tachypneic. Is that what you have recorded, Maya?" He turned and translated for the herd owner. "These sheep have fever and high heart and breathing rates."

"We can't do a field necropsy if we suspect anthrax." She glanced up to Dave for confirmation as he paused, hands resting on his hips.

"You can take blood samples from this dead one and the one with convulsions. There are stains to identify the spore capsule." He withdrew a needle and syringe from his case. "I'll extend the neck. At least it won't be moving." He gave her a sardonic smile.

She struggled to feel the jugular vein with her left hand through latex gloves and thick wool that needed shearing. Practice on larger, live shorn animals at vet school wasn't enough help. Every time she drew back the plunger, the vessel shifted under her fingers and the syringe was empty. On the third attempt, her right hand shook and the needle slipped all the way through the skin into her left index finger.

"Fuck it, girl, don't they teach you anything in Colorado?"

Dave dropped the body and ripped off her glove. Then he squeezed her finger and it oozed a drop of blood.

Woozy, she sank to a large rock while he shuffled through his kit. The sight of blood, even her own, didn't necessarily trigger panic. But some diseases were transmitted by needle sticks. She recalled vets getting brucellosis when vaccinating cattle.

He swung back with disinfectant and a bandage. "Probably not a transmission route for anthrax. But I'll follow protocol and file a report."

She donned a fresh glove before passing him a new needle and syringe. "I'll defer to the superiority of an Aggie."

"Now you're talkin'. Let me handle the pointy part." After hitting the vein easily, he repeated the process with Maya holding the sick ewe.

Next he shoved paper towels into the dead ewe's mouth, nose, anus, and vagina, and finished by duct taping a garbage bag around the animal's head. "Don't need an anthrax leak."

He sank to the ground under the deep cottonwood canopy and invited Mr. Koopee and Maya to do the same. "Did you read the USDA article I gave you?"

Quick review of the details in her mind before speaking—still embarrassed about the debacle with drawing blood. "Ten states with livestock anthrax outbreaks, often preceded by drought and higher temps. None in Arizona, and mostly cattle, not sheep."

She drank from her water bottle, glanced at the grotesque dead animal, and continued. "Infected cattle shed spores into the earth where they stay for decades. Climate change can promote soil getting stirred up."

The back of her neck prickled. Was she at risk from the soil, in addition to her clumsy accident? It was too early for her vaccination to help. "Animals or people breathe in spores or swallow them. Inside the body, they become activated bacteria making lethal toxins. Monsoon floods reduce blowing dust, but scour up deeper dirt."

"This isn't one of the 1800s cattle drive routes like in Texas where we've had problems." He ran fingers through dusty, light brown hair. "Mr. Koopee, was this flock vaccinated?" The older man answered no.

"Cattle have been raised in the area so there could be spore releases," Dave said. "Low mortality here, so low-level risk."

Perplexed by his conclusion, she glanced over at their host, torn about disagreeing in front of him. "Danny died of confirmed anthrax and the animal he opened up could be the source." She swallowed hard. "His dad might be the next infection."

Annoying flies buzzed around the animals. Dave jumped up and offered Maya a hand. "I'd feel safer if we burn and bury the sick and dead sheep. Mr. Koopee, we can't save this one that's down. Can I euthanize it?"

The Hopi elder nodded. Dave took out the euthanasia solution and injected it. He gave Maya the stethoscope to verify the animal's death, then asked her to use paper towels and a bag over its head like the first one.

Still flustered about not hitting the vein, she wracked her brain to remember something useful. "In vet school I learned about quick lime for inactivating spores."

Dave shook his head in disagreement. "A Canadian study found quick lime—calcium oxide—might preserve anthrax spores instead of killing them. I'll dig a pit and locate the buried sheep that was cut open. Mr. Koopee, can you find a pack mule to transport wood and hay? Plus an ax and more shovels."

"Trading post will have what you need."

"Maya, you go too." Dave tossed her the keys. "We need the blowtorch, diesel fuel can, and ammonia disinfectant."

Back at the vehicle, she dismounted with Mr. Koopee's assistance, then organized the supplies and called the clinic.

"Manolo, hope I'm not interrupting you."

"Hola, Maya, I examined Timothy. We don't think he's infected with anthrax."

She leapt down from the truck bed landing in a pirouette, followed by regret for the impulsive move as her upper thigh throbbed with pain in the area of the metal pins.

"Can't wait to tell his father." Crouching over, she gripped the phone and kneaded her leg.

"Timothy is diabetic and incredibly stressed," he said. "Single parent, three young kids. He was on his way to Phoenix but got news of Danny's death and collapsed. No fever or elevated WBCs, but I took serum for anthrax antibodies."

She sighed. "Not as lucky here—some symptomatic sheep. It might take a *Hamilton*-sized effort to sort them out."

"Lo siento." His laugh acknowledged her reference before his voice was solemn. "I'll call other providers who might see patients."

"Use a sensitive case definition that includes different forms of anthrax including cutaneous," she said, "even though Danny didn't have that form. Then get more specific with lab tests to rule it out."

"You mean skin lesions that might fit with anthrax exposure, too? Good idea, I'll expand our search. Hasta luego, mi amiga."

Mr. Koopee released a cautious smile when she told him about his son. A muscled young Hopi man led a gray mule with oversized, fluffy ears. The animal resembled a cartoon caricature loaded on both sides with wood and a hay bale in place of a rider.

When they rejoined Dave near noon, she was saddle sore and sweaty. "Sorry, can you give me a hand off?"

She was chagrined to need his help again. The news from the hospital energized everyone and they finished the hole quickly, piling hay and wood at the bottom.

Dave had found the buried animal and dragged it over with the other two. Shoving the carcasses into the pit, they spread more flammable materials on top.

Mr. Koopee rounded up the flock, guiding it on horseback toward the trading post. Once the riders were out of sight, Dave poured diesel over the area and lit his blowtorch. The funeral pyre exploded into five feet of flames.

They stretched weary legs while relaxing against the grooved trunk of the largest cottonwood. Lowering face masks, they guzzled water to counteract warming temperatures and burning flesh.

She pulled a granola bar from her pocket. "This was in your truck."

He bumped her hand away. "Not hungry."

"Too squeamish to eat while steeped in spores?" She broke open the package and did a long toss into the bushes. "People food for the rock squirrels." Only minimally protected with one vaccine dose, accidental ingestion of any anthrax was too terrifying.

The pit continued to smolder as he tossed in more logs. "How didya end up in EIS?"

"Like my classmates, I initially focused on clinical practice." With weeks in the hospital as a child, she was motivated to help animals with illness or injury, but the truck that haunted her sleep and imposed residual anxiety was too personal a reveal.

"My first epi course opened up the bigger picture and the teacher connected me with EIS officers."

"No regrets about public versus private practice?"

She shrugged. "Too soon to say."

The investigation petrified her, unsure about her contribution. "Did you do clinical work?"

"Almost didn't make it through vet school, so I went with my ranching background, just horses and cows. But getting knocked around is hard on the body. My wife's from Albuquerque and I didn't have any family left alive for me to stay in Texas."

Someone so young with no relatives? "I feel lucky to have mine, even if they're still too much in my life."

"It's been better in New Mexico. I can put the Texas deaths behind me." After fingering an inner pocket, he proudly produced a photo of two little girls on horseback.

"Emilia begged me to take a USDA job closer to her kin now that we have kids."

With the fire out, they stretched stiff muscles and collected soil samples where the sheep had been bedding, eating, or drinking. He poured disinfectant over the cremains and they filled the hole with dirt. Hours later, sweat dripping despite the higher altitude, they pointed their horses westward toward the increasingly colorful sky.

"At least we had a spectacular sunrise and sunset," he said as they admired the view. She envied his ability to adapt and enjoy the moment.

Mr. Koopee met them at the truck. They sealed boots in plastic trash bags for cleaning and dropped coveralls, masks and gloves in a separate bag for disposal. Before arriving at the health center, Maya called for someone to open a back door so they could head straight to the showers. The clinic director messaged that her husband would transport them at eight to a home-cooked Sunday night dinner.

· · ·

When Maya joined Dave and Manolo in the lobby, she hoped the loose black pants hiding a bruise on her inner left thigh didn't look too wrinkled.

Manolo was the most relaxed since she'd met him. "Finally something to celebrate. Nobody has suspicious signs of anthrax, and Humita said you got the sheep rounded up."

A chunky, fortyish Native American opened the hospital front door. "Hello, everyone, I'm Juan. Dinner's ready."

The Ford Fairlane crawled up a narrow dirt road toward three treeless, rock-and-adobe mortar villages clinging to the top of First Mesa. Their host drove past the few homes of Hano to Sichomovi. A pack of midsized, lean dogs barked and danced as the trio climbed from the car.

"Our home only dates from the 1600s," Juan informed them.

Inside, her nostrils were tickled by the smoky patina staining the white kiva fireplace in the corner, unlit in the summer warmth. The thick adobe walls, small windows, and prominent pine vigas supporting the ceiling gave the room a comforting, cave-like feeling.

Humita greeted them in a flowy, yellow pantsuit. "It's too late, or we'd walk you up the road to see the thousand-year-old homes in Walpi. No utilities so they're mostly used for ceremonies and dances."

Steam rose from a colorful platter that Humita set on the hand-hewn table. "These are sweet blue corn tamales called Somiviki." She poured ice tea and ladled black beans.

As they ate, Juan described a gallery where he carved and sold katsina dolls representing Hopi ancestor spirits. "The Katsinam arrive at dawn with gifts, and all the new brides are given a blessing. At this time of year, the Katsinam are in the San Francisco Peaks near Flagstaff."

He also had katsinas for sale in the nearby modern hotels. "New developments are controversial. Preserving the land as it is versus economic progress—an old conflict."

Humita was relaxed and gracious in hostess mode, thankful the outbreak seemed under control without additional political or public fallout.

"It's important that we handle this ourselves, without a whole swat team from your National Center for Emerging and Zoonotic Infectious Diseases descending on us."

Maya grabbed her phone. "I'll share your concerns with Dr. Jaworski, my CDC supervisor in Atlanta."

Dave chimed in. "We'll check on the sheep before I drive back to Albuquerque tomorrow. Maya, would you like a ride to New Mexico?"

Her eyes darted to Manolo. She regretted not having more time to work with him. Did he appear disappointed, too?

"Unless you require more CDC assistance . . ." With his silence, she turned back to Dave. "Sounds reasonable."

Manolo carried plates to Humita's kitchen. "After this meal, I'll sleep so well I won't need my backup driver."

So he didn't think she was good for anything else. "Sorry I couldn't give you a hand with case finding."

"Dave needed your help," he replied. "You all had a strenuous day."

"Maya hung in there, considering she's not ranch-raised," Dave said. "We'll get a well-earned rest tonight."

. . .

Following the emailed warning to Atlanta, overworked muscles forced her swirling brain to shut down for a welcome night's sleep. She woke up only once, and prayed Danny's case was just a one-off.

The next morning, Manolo had left for Phoenix when she met Dave for breakfast. They drove to the confinement pen and checked each animal.

"Healthy." He clapped her on the back. "Let's stick with the samples we took yesterday."

He navigated the two-lane highway to Gallup within two hours, then she dozed during the final stretch to Albuquerque and arrived back in Santa Fe by shuttle at five o'clock.

When she climbed into bed, her internal hardware radiated agony as punishment for the strenuous investigation efforts. Perhaps if she admitted her childhood surgeries, she could have avoided the field work. But she would have lost face, and a chance to make a difference.

Labor Day was still a month away, but compensatory time for the weekend effort could allow a longer Flagstaff visit. A family reunion in her beautiful western hometown nestled at the base of the San Francisco Peaks would offer refuge and renewal.

She maneuvered the heating pad under her lower back, pressed the button for high, and opened the *Hamilton* album on her phone. Drifting off, she realized that despite her challenges, like Aaron Burr she wanted to be in the room where it happens.

SIX

<u>May 2 2002</u>
Some familez moving to Texas
Father said we are safer staying here.
Mother wants to escape Fatherz wife 3
she tried to smother me when I was a baby.

Profit told Father that Mother must lern her duty to bless
her husband every day of her life.

SEVEN

"Four hits on my samples," Dave reported on the call a week later from Albuquerque. "All three ill or dead sheep and one soil sample from that wider sandy spot under the biggest cottonwood. Thanks again for your help."

Maya's heart began to race, but she tried to view the results in a positive light. "I guess that confirms a natural source for Danny's death."

"Appears so. Our team will spread more disinfectant and fence the area to restrict access. His dad is out of the hospital and I told him to keep the flock confined until the end of this month."

She pressed her palms to her eyes. It was over, almost. "When does this go public?"

"Tomorrow, they were waiting for results. You should alert your bosses that our names could be included. I know they don't like surprises."

Although he was older and more experienced, it seemed like Dave respected her as a colleague, despite her slipup taking the blood sample. As she set down the phone receiver, her parents' fighting about skipping school grades echoed. Her dad worried about emotional readiness but with Maya's massive reading advancements during the accident recovery, her mom suggested skipping first grade. Then she lobbied for high school after seventh grade and a three-year bachelor's degree.

Had her dad been right? Functioning at the same level as older

EIS classmates was a challenge. A mosquito horde buzzed in her brain. *You can't do it.* She waved at her ear, swatting the pests away before anyone detected a flaw.

Dr. Grinwold seemed disinterested when she swung by his office to update him on the anthrax results. But on the phone, Dr. Jaworski was enthusiastic.

"You helped confirm the first anthrax in Arizona. I heard compliments from our sister agencies about your contribution."

Sister agencies? USDA could be grateful for the assistance, but maybe Manolo had also put in a favorable report. She had zero contact with him following the Keams Canyon investigation of Danny's death.

The feedback from her Atlanta supervisor reminded Maya that she hadn't talked to her grad school mentor since the move to New Mexico. The phone was answered with the husky voice of Faye Simpson, NYC's Public Health Veterinarian. Maya recalled blue-veined, wrinkled hands laced through a reddish-gray pixie cut while the older vet lounged in her chair, feet up on the desk.

"Kiddo, how the heck are you?"

"Hanging in."

Not entirely true. She'd been draggy in the week since the field work. But they wore protective gear, so infection was unlikely. Refocusing, she asked, "Any deaths in the City from the heat waves?"

"Interns are looking at heart disease, kidney failure, and birth defects." A slurping sound emanated from the speaker. "None of the new ones have your statistical acumen."

Maya's shoulders straightened with the affirmation. If only she could replicate her internship success during the CDC assignment.

"I miss your big datasets in NYC. Yesterday I crunched the numbers for an office potluck with fourteen people, showing salad was the norovirus source. The lady who made it was embarrassed, probably fecal-oral hygiene problems."

The drinking sounds continued. Faye was known for multitasking and never taking a break. "Big things and little things make it exciting.

Had a couple more *Anaplasma* cases in Staten Island from ticks. One's a senior with severe peripheral neuropathy. People freak out about Lyme, but don't know about these more obscure diseases."

"No *Anaplasma* here." Maya closed the office door and mimicked her mentor, slipping her feet up on the plain prison-constructed desk. "We have anthrax in Arizona, but nothing like your 2001 powder in the mail. A Hopi boy died after exposure while sheepherding. USDA got positive sheep and soil samples. My first Epi-Aid."

"Challenging way to start." Faye's voice sounded concerned. "How did it go?" She was the only professional contact Maya had trusted with the history of her childhood hit-and-run accident and panic disorder.

"I saw the boy before he died and witnessed part of the autopsy." Maya's eyes teared up, and she grabbed for a tissue. "I had to use cognitive therapy to avoid passing out."

"Pace yourself. You don't need to be all things to all people."

Maya swallowed her tears and tried to muffle her coughs.

"Any chance you're coming down with something?" Faye asked.

"Just worn out from the field trip to the canyon where he collapsed. Not adapted to that much horseback riding and hard labor in recent years. And now a slight respiratory infection." She left out the needle stick. No need to admit all her failures.

Faye's voice rose higher with concern. "Did they vaccinate you? I remember the vaccine having some serious side effects, especially when given to Gulf war soldiers."

"Got it right before the possible anthrax exposure, but this feels more like a cold. I looked up the vaccine when I got back. There was a bad adjuvant during those years, but not now. This isn't anything. Don't worry about me."

Faye was silent, then said, "Find a psychologist there, a local sounding board. Anxiety can lead to paranoia. The counselor can help you sort out which of your reactions are reasonable. And use your medical insurance. Get checked out if you don't recover quickly."

"I'll think about it." But she wouldn't pursue the recommendation for therapy. Even acknowledging its need might lead someone to doubt her acumen. "I miss interning with you, but love getting back here to the Southwest."

"Miss you too. Take care of yourself and keep me in the loop."

Back on her computer, Maya checked again for anthrax and needle sticks. Panic was associated with hypochondria, and she had looked for information after returning from Arizona. If she'd been vaccinating the animal for anthrax when her hand slipped, there might be a problem, but not for drawing blood.

She pressed on the finger. No pain, no redness, no pus. Nothing indicated the cough was related to anthrax, but checking her temperature daily couldn't hurt.

A light knock, and she switched off the screen before opening the door to the friendly greetings of bubbly Stephanie and Erika, the willowy, blonde surveillance coordinator. "Want to join us at Santa Fe Indian Market on Saturday?" Erika asked.

Maya perked up, looking for ways to fit in. "I'd love to."

Danny's death and the additional test results were released the next morning. Low enough in the food chain, she didn't handle media questions. With the Hopi teenager as the first U.S. inhalation case since the 2011 tourist, 'Anthrax in Arizona' was the top story on regional TV stations and newspapers. A few climate change demonstrators picketed the State Capitol building in Phoenix, but authorities reiterated that Texas had infected cattle most years, so a single human infection wasn't unexpected.

· · ·

Narrow streets around the Santa Fe Plaza, lined with adobe buildings, were restricted from car traffic and jammed with artists' booths and pedestrians. "This show's a hundred years old and there's a thousand artists," Stephanie said as they hopped off the bus.

Maya was captivated by the striking contrast of walls and roofs glowing golden against the bright blue late summer sky.

Her respiratory symptoms were improving and she was no longer anxious about anthrax. Then she remembered her visit to First Mesa. "I met a Hopi artist who makes katsinas."

"Let's see if he has an exhibit here." Erika located Juan Pantewa and his booth number on her phone's digital map. They worked their way through the eclectic crowd with women of all ethnic groups in bright, solid-colored blouses, wide patterned skirts, and heavy Navajo turquoise and silver jewelry.

"Maya, great to see you again. Humita's still coordinating the fallout from your trip." They listened as he did an engaging spiel about katsina history for a dozen potential customers.

"Our spirit dancers give the katsinas to kids at special ceremonies." Juan focused back on Maya. "Any particular one you like?"

The carvings were so imbued with spirit, she wondered whether one could help her cope with health problems, but the price of her favorite was seven hundred dollars.

"Can't afford it today, but this is beautiful." The one-foot tall doll had a white face, green neck ruff, black and orange eyes, nose and ears, above an equally colorful skirt. It was of painted wood except for feathers in the hands and head between black-striped white horns.

"Mountain Sheep or Ram Katsina. Have fun looking around— not just southwestern traditional artists like me. Couple hundred different tribes from all around the country and Canada."

Near a hotel, Erika admired silver masks with haunting, blue jeweled eyes made by a Haida-Cree. Stephanie ogled a pair of Kiowa high heels overlaid with tiny, multicolored beads depicting a Native American woman. Maya's final favorites back at the Plaza were huge Taos metal animal sculptures.

They feasted on young dancers more colorfully attired than Juan's katsinas while sampling lamb stew from a curbside vendor. As throngs of people crammed the small central area, Maya felt hot and hemmed in. Aligning her breaths to the calming chanting and clinking bells on the dancers' ankles seemed to help.

On the return bus ride, Erika stretched out in the window seat. "We're happy to have you on board. How do you like the job?"

A woman friend to confide in would be wonderful, but she hardly knew Erika. "Dr. Grinwold always seems remote and irritated."

"Don't take it personally," Stephanie answered from across the aisle. "I've worked with him a long time, and he's on the gruff side but worse lately, not sure why."

Erika kicked the empty seat in front of her. "Patriarchal society, cowboy heritage."

"I hate to admit it, but there's Hispanic machismo, too," Stephanie said.

Maya's eyes flitted around the partially full bus. Locals, tourists, or something in between, like her? Anyone listening? "I was spoiled by my NYC internship. Plenty of women in leadership positions."

"Didn't the women's rights movement start in New York— Susan B. Anthony and Elizabeth Cady Stanton?" Erika made a sudden shift on the bus seat. "I should move there. Sometimes I feel like a piece of meat."

Despite Erika's rage, no one looked in their direction. All lost in their own conversations.

"Most of our coworkers are fine, but a few of them—let me know if you ever feel pressured," Erika said.

The mellow mood from the entrancing event was disrupted. Perhaps all places had hidden hurdles, even a state as beautiful and outwardly welcoming as the Land of Enchantment.

Maya pulled out a tissue to blot her nose and drank water from her bottle to soothe the sore throat. Summer cold, nothing to worry about.

· · ·

Two weeks later, Stephanie greeted Maya at the front door of the Epi Office.

"Want to join us at Zozobra tonight? Another local tradition, a giant swaying statue of Old Man Gloom. We drink and eat and sing until sunset, when the mob screams 'Burn him, burn him!' and we light him on fire."

Hesitant, Maya hugged her body. Although she'd recovered from the Arizona trip, her unease with the Indian Market crowd would be magnified by drunken mobs at night. If older people like Stephanie were going, it might be all right.

"I'm headed to Flagstaff tomorrow to see my family for Labor Day, but if I'm not out late and don't drink, I could join you."

"We'll touch base to work it out. By the way, Dr. Grinwold's looking for you."

He paced impatiently in front of his desk. "They want you again. Two new anthrax cases were confirmed."

Shaking her head in disbelief, Maya took notes as he continued. "Southern Arizona. One's a minister, the other a Tohono O'odham Nation artist. Atlanta wants you coordinating with USDA."

Stephanie drove her to the shuttle. "Too bad you'll miss the chance to ignite all your troubles. If you think of any glooms to burn up, we'll write them down and slip them into the special box at the bottom."

Maya wanted to torch her pieced-together pelvis and panic disorder. After twenty years, why couldn't she leave all that behind? Instead, she told Stephanie, "Put one in for me about grumpy bosses."

Stepping off the bus in Albuquerque, she spotted Dave leaning against a support column, smirking like a younger version of the movie star Sam Shepard.

"I guess we're both valuable commodities," he said. "Don't know if the southern Arizona cases have a livestock connection."

They worked so closely in northern Arizona, could she admit her concerns? "Danny Koopee and these new ones are in opposite ends of the state. You mentioned climate change and heat could be an influence, but just a month apart? It's suspicious."

From Sky Harbor in Phoenix, they were picked up by Dr. Ben Smith, the Arizona State Veterinarian. The African American, taller than Dave and appearing to be in his late forties, helped her up into the back seat of his gigantic SUV.

"Apologize for the size of the vehicle—not comfortable in anything smaller. And I didn't play basketball, although they sure pressured me to do it at school. Too uncoordinated."

So many people faced stereotypes. She got the smart Asian one. Academic work was easy, but she was overwhelmed by everyone's automatic high expectations. Scrutiny and pressure to measure up were primary panic triggers.

Maya left a phone message for her parents as Ben began the drive south on I-10 in Friday holiday rush hour traffic. His eyes darted between mirrors and over his shoulder. A motorcycle cut in front and he braked hard to miss it.

"Can you please be more careful?" Her words slammed out and woke Dave up from the front seat.

"Girl, what's your problem?" He snapped the question and lowered his cap against the slanting sun rays.

"I'm sorry." Remorseful for shouting at an older superior, she added, "Just a jumpy passenger here, Dr. Smith. Too much coming at me all at once. I promise not to be a backseat driver."

Ben's neck muscles flexed. "Kid, I'm trying to get to Tucson Medical Center quickly. And I've never had an accident in thirty years of driving." His fingers lifted from the steering wheel in a slight wave. "We're all antsy with this anthrax."

She played a mindless solitaire game on the iPhone to keep her eyes from the traffic and brooded over missing the long weekend with her parents.

They'd waited until their forties to begin a family. When starting the adoption process, Tom Maguire, genial Irish Protestant, was an administrator with Northern Arizona University's Office of Emergency Management. Barbara Robinson, Irish Catholic, graduated from the University of Arizona's prestigious astronomy program and became a Lowell Observatory research assistant.

Work gives you meaning and purpose and life is empty without it—

another one of her mom's Stephen Hawking quotes. Perhaps that had been their sole focus when young.

"I never get a night out for dancing," a friend's mother had whined. Her own mom never complained, even though she danced in her youth and drove Maya to lessons until the accident. Then they focused on getting her to walk again, and enjoyed long strolls on Flagstaff trails. Her dad also walked her to school on his way to work, until her mom switched to the night shift so she could drive Maya to the more distant middle school campus.

The glowing lights of Tucson interrupted her mental meanderings—she had missed the sunset. As they pulled into the mixed complex of modern and stuccoed buildings, the bright blue metal saguaro cactus on the TMC sign glowed in the headlight reflection.

When they arrived at the ICU, Ben asked for Janey Johnson, the Pima County Health Department's epidemiologist. Sitting outside the observation window, the energetic young woman updated them on her case.

"Reverend Sophia Tompkins has been in and out of consciousness, so no exposure history. Thirty-five years old, minister for the Unitarian Universalist church on the south side of town."

"You don't mean the Moonies?" Maya smirked. "My folks told me about them. Korean Unification Church."

"No, UU is a legitimate, mainstream faith with origins in several denominations. It's socially conscious, which could play into the source of her anthrax."

Maya took notes as Janey described Sophia's fainting on the pulpit. She vomited when the congregants brought her to the bathroom. As they supported her on the office couch, she was perspiring and confused.

They thought it was heat exhaustion with summer temps exceeding a hundred. But her daughter said her mom felt lousy for a few days. With Sophia's lack of awareness of her surroundings and difficulty in breathing, the administrator called an ambulance. The

ER exam documented fever and increased heart rate, respiratory rate, and blood pressure, so she was admitted into the hospital.

Through the ICU room window, the minister's eyes glowed darkly red, and chest sounds gurgled from obstruction and secretions in the larger airways. Janey shared the chart.

Arterial blood gases confirmed Sophia wasn't getting enough oxygen. X-rays indicated infiltrates consistent with pneumonia. Blood cultures after antibiotics showed no growth, but a nasal swab detected *Bacillus anthracis*. Then a chest tap tested positive and antitoxin was ordered from CDC.

"She's not doing well," Janey said.

A chest tube drained bloody liquid, similar to what Maya had seen with Danny. "Fluid's putting pressure on the heart, with abnormal rhythms," Janey added.

"We heard someone's raised a concern about a possible connection between her anthrax infection and the church?" Maya asked.

"Maybe like your Hopi case, from soil? The UU congregation puts out aid for migrants. Much of the border is Tohono O'odham land, with wildlife refuges on both sides. Seven thousand migrants died in the last two decades, primarily from dehydration. The groups leave caches of water, food, socks, blankets, and first aid."

"You really think the Reverend's anthrax is soil-related?" Dave asked. "Does anyone know where she was? Any sick or dead animals to give us a clue?"

"No animals, and soil will be hard to assess," Janey answered. "On public land, it's illegal to leave anything for the immigrants. The refuges specifically forbid using their property to aid and abet the criminal act of sneaking into the U.S."

"The church might be afraid to talk about it," Maya said.

Janey nodded. "Activists were arrested, with potential penalties of twenty years in prison."

Look for patterns, Epi 101. "Is there a Tohono O'odham case? That could help us narrow down the Reverend's exposure."

"Out of my jurisdiction." Janey shrugged. "He's hospitalized in Sells—Indian Health Service."

Maya's pulse increased with a legitimate reason to reach out. "I don't know which IHS district that is, but I can ask Manolo."

"Does this hospital have anthrax vaccine?" Dave asked. "If we're headed to the field, Maya should receive her second dose."

"We won't get more done tonight," Ben added. Maya was zeroed in on the human cases and forgot he was there before he spoke up.

Janey directed her to an exam room for the vaccination and agreed to contact the church about the Reverend's distribution of supplies.

With another sore arm, Maya headed out of the hospital into the cool evening air. She rubbed the back of her neck, gazing north to the Catalina Mountains and the clear, sparkly sky.

"Kinda surprised to see so many stars from the city," Dave said.

"Tucson has regulations to reduce light pollution for the Kitt Peak Observatory." She turned to Ben. "My grandmother lives here. Could you swing through a fast food joint and drop me at her place?"

He let her out at the apartment complex. Maya's maternal grandfather had died ten years earlier and Martha Robinson, at age ninety, lived near the Catholic high school where she taught math for thirty years.

"Sweetie, why are you here? Come in." The tiny, hunched woman stretched up to envelop her granddaughter. With neat white hair in a bun, she was dressed in a long, embroidered robe. A pudgy black cat with emerald eyes rubbed up against Maya's legs, and she bent down to stroke its silky fur.

Her muscles relaxed, an innate response to the purring animal. "Grandma, I'm so happy to see you. I have a work assignment in the area. Can I sleep on your sofa?"

"Sandra, take the night off." Her grandmother patted the arm of the middle-aged home health aide. "I'll be fine with my Maya."

Sandra opened the sofa bed and Maya located linens in the closet.

Hypatia, named in honor of the first known female mathematician, was no longer a kitten but darted in and out of the sheets, paws outstretched, hampering the process. Maya changed into a golden silk shift and rested on the sofa bed next to her grandmother's reclining chair. Hypatia snuggled close and kneaded her hand. While Maya finished her fish sandwich, slipping slivers to the feline, her grandmother spilled the latest *Bachelorette* news.

"Becca got engaged." The narrowed, indigo eyes shifted to Maya. "When will you find your true love, little one?"

"If I don't have time for TV, I don't have time for that either. Let me help you to bed."

She verified the oxygen supply in the bedroom was working for her grandmother's chronic obstructive pulmonary disease and rotated the baby monitor dial. After closing the door, she curled up under the covers with Hypatia on her feet and found Manolo on her iPhone contact list.

"Maya." One word, just her name—his warmth and optimistic joy floated across the miles.

Nudging the cat aside, she adjusted her legs to a less painful position. "I'm working on anthrax again and one patient is Tohono O'odham. Can you connect me up with someone in Sells?"

"You got him." His tone conveyed gentle mirth at being able to surprise her. "Already here. This hospital isn't the Phoenix district, but Tucson doesn't have an ID specialist."

She stayed in professional mode. It didn't matter who she worked with from IHS. "Can you tell me about the patient?"

"Basketweaver, forty-one. Last weekend he got low-grade fever, chills, sore throat, headache, tiredness. A day later, he had dry cough, chest heaviness, shortness of breath, night sweats, nausea and vomiting. He came in for a checkup and they admitted him."

She remembered he'd been confirmed with anthrax. "Lab work?"

"WBC slight left shift and elevated liver enzymes. X-ray showed widened mediastinum, pleural effusion, and enlarged lymph nodes.

Blood cultures grew *B. anthracis* so they adjusted the antibiotics. Respiratory distress is being treated with diuretics, corticosteroids, and periodic chest taps. He hasn't needed a drain yet."

He paused to catch his breath. "Are you on the Tucson case?"

"I'm waiting for information on her group's humanitarian efforts down there," she said.

"Maybe both patients were in the same place?"

"Unlike Keams Canyon, nobody's mentioned animals as sentinels for the location. I'll ask Dr. Smith if the land is used for livestock. We'll stop by tomorrow and see how our cases are linked."

"Hasta pronto, Maya."

"Buenas noches, Manolo." She wondered why disembodied voices on the phone sometimes were more intimate than being face-to-face, especially when sitting in bed. Distracting thoughts— her sole focus should be on not letting PTSD hold her back at work. Tossing the phone on the bed covers, she spooked the cat to the floor.

"Hypatia, want to join me in the shower? It always makes me feel better."

The cat hissed from beneath the kitchen table. "I really wasn't threatening to throw you in the water. And I'm sorry to disrupt your normal routine so much. I'll make it quick, then we can settle down for a cuddle."

EIGHT

April 2, 2003.
Jacob bugs me, following along on builds.
He is 8 and always drops tools
I know how to drive a backhoe and earth mover
I can do concreet, sheet rock, trim and doors

Mother said nothing more important than family
and I should watch out for him
Should help me with animals horses, cattle, and sheep,
but hes scared of them
Scared to get up high too. Little chiken shit.

May 17.
Baby sister died last week of FUMARASE DEFICIENCY.
Mother wrote it for me.
Wish I had more school so I know what that is
John says its from marrying with family

Yesterday Mother left to visit cuzzin in Saint George.
Not shur when she cums home.
Profit said Father should go get her
she will be punishd for disobediens
This is not first time she escapd.
Hope he doesn't wash out her brain or chop off her head.

NINE

"Why did Mom and Dad move to Denver?" Maya wiped up spilled grease from the fried turkey bacon at the electric stove top.

Her grandmother shifted the walker aside and settled into the plastic kitchen chair. "Flagstaff wasn't a big enough pond. You were a precocious teenager, halfway through high school at fourteen after skipping two grades."

The older woman sipped the hot tea and honey that Maya poured into the crochet-cozy covered mug. "Funding exploded for emergency management. Your dad got a promotion at the Denver Federal Center and they increased college savings."

Maya forked the bacon to a plate except for scraps dropped to the cat bowl for Hypatia, who stood on hind legs with front paws against her calf. "Colorado isn't a hotbed for astronomy like Arizona."

"Barbara didn't find work but drove you to piano lessons and recitals. Eventually she landed the Chamberlin Observatory job. Bit of a step down, but she was fine with that."

Maya hurried to finish breakfast and clean up the kitchen, while ruminating about the tradeoffs her parents made. They started their marriage in Flagstaff, years before deciding to adopt. Clearly it was their heart-home because they returned when she left Colorado. Was she appreciative enough of their sacrifices?

She alleviated her guilt with a phone update to her parents, then called Dave, gave her grandmother a squeeze, and exited with a playful tug on Hypatia's tail. She tried to put her mind in anthrax mode while perched on the concrete stoop, admiring the early morning cloud shadows dancing across the Catalinas.

When her colleagues stopped to give her a ride, Dave directed them to the UU church with information provided by Janey. The matronly administrator fluttered around the chaotic office.

"If Border Patrol finds these locations, they'll throw supplies away, or use this map to arrest us. We act on our faith by helping desperate people. The government asylum process doesn't work well, so immigrant families take chances to get somewhere safe."

On his chair, Dave pitched forward, elbows resting on his blue jeans and fingers knotted. "You're putting out caches, regardless of consequences?"

"Reverend Sophia is our inspiration. She and her daughter Cecilia were named after women important in religious education. She's a single mother and wants to set a stellar example."

Maya rubbed at a fingernail. Dave's body language communicated too much negativity.

"My mom is the same with me."

She smiled, hoping to get on the older woman's good side. "In my public health work, we keep our information confidential. We won't show your aid locations to anyone."

The administrator glanced from the two men to Maya and handed her the map.

Back in Ben's SUV, they headed south for a short time on the interstates before turning southwest on the Ajo Highway. It narrowed into a busy two-lane road cutting through the green palo verde and black mesquite trees. Lines of electrical poles marched like ramrod soldiers, breaking the blinding blue of the sky. Bright patches of Mexican Bird of Paradise flowers provided a red-yellow counterpoint to the dull roadsides.

Maya alerted Manolo they were on their way and chatted with Ben from the back seat, relaxed with the less stressful traffic conditions.

"For Danny's infection, the sheep were sentinels for contaminated soil, but we don't have any animal connection with these cases. Any livestock where we're headed?"

"Mostly range cattle," he answered. "Anthrax is a cattle disease, so we should find it on the ranches, Bureau of Land Management land, or in the Tohono O'odham Nation if there's a risk—although animals are dispersed until roundup."

In less than an hour, she noted the greener hills of Kitt Peak. "When I was a kid, we stopped at the observatory on visits to my grandmother. Mom practically lived here as a UA astronomy student. Their nighttime Milky Way programs are the best."

Tiny worry lines creased her brow after the Kitt Peak turnoff when they were slowed by a roadblock. Cars headed northeast were stopped, but they were traveling southwest, so the uniformed agents scanned the interior and waved them on.

"CBP—Customs and Border Protection," Ben said. "Looking for undocumented migrants and drugs."

"Our Church of Jesus Christ of Latter-Day Saints brings faith to other areas including Mexico," Dave said. "But like my wife, whose Spanish ancestors have been here hundreds of years, we're only in favor of *legal* immigration. Open borders are a disaster—can't help everybody."

Ben drummed his fingers on the steering wheel. "My Baptist church helps immigrants, however they got here. And my ancestors came as slaves. Does that count in your book as legal?"

"Who pays for schools and health care overrun by illegals?" Dave glared at Ben across the front seat. "Not the liberals from out-of-state."

"I agree with Minister Sophia," Ben answered. "My religion is more dogmatic than hers, but we still believe in helping those in need."

Feeling her skin flush, Maya tried to placate her veterinary colleagues. Even loving arguments between her parents triggered anxiety.

"My family jumped through a lot of hoops to bring me here legally. But I saw very different conditions and Communist oppression when I went back to visit China. I can understand the urge to escape here."

Dave didn't back down. "Got a short fuse from lack of sleep. Noisy police copters scanning Tucson neighborhoods with floodlights make me *really* want to live here."

She was relieved when Ben dropped the subject with Dave's admission of insomnia. Southern Arizona was on edge with media uproar about immigrant children in detention camps. Workers were charged with sexually assaulting teenagers at a Phoenix contract facility. Everyone had a strong opinion. It was all too close to home.

Ben focused on driving and within an hour and a half of leaving Tucson, they parked next to the small white Sells Indian Hospital with two lonely palm trees out front.

Short time to reach another world of stark beauty with a sparse landscape and breathtaking, huge sky. Maya was imprinted with taller vegetation in northern Arizona, so this expanse was alien and blinding. While shading her eyes with one hand, she texted Manolo.

His white uniform gleamed even brighter against the intense skyline. He shook all their hands and hers sparked at his touch. In the hospital room, he introduced his patient, propped up by numerous pillows. The beaming man was hefty enough to fill up most of the bed, and multiple family members were jammed in on both sides.

"We considered transferring Mr. Felix to Tucson but as you can see, he's recovering nicely," Manolo said.

She cleared her throat and resolved to be assertive. After all, she represented CDC.

"Mr. Felix, we're trying to find out about the risk from anthrax in soil. A previous case in northern Arizona was a teenage sheepherder." His relatives' expressions changed to dismay and fear.

"Our tests confirmed anthrax up there in the animals and soil," Dave said.

Ben jumped in. "Is your family involved with any livestock?"

"No, we're not." A tall woman holding the patient's arm answered with a prickly tone.

"Thanks," Ben said. "I'll contact the Livestock Inspectors to see if anything's been reported. Dave, you want to help?"

Maya exhaled and reconnoitered. Perhaps they were too abrupt and alarming in the face of Mr. Felix's poor health. But she was unsure what to do except keep going. She dug in her bag for a state highway map and held it up.

"Unfortunately, we have another anthrax case nearby, someone leaving humanitarian supplies for the immigrants. You and this other person might have been in the same area."

"I'm Terroll's wife," the woman said. "We're caught in the middle. Our homes are broken into and cars stolen by illegals. And the Border Patrol arrests us because we're brown like them. Our tribal lands extend into Mexico, but they make it difficult for us to visit family there."

"I feel bad," Terroll whispered. "Six dead bodies a week."

"We understand why the churches want to be involved, but they're outsiders, they don't have to live here." Mrs. Felix glanced down at her husband. "Let's step outside and talk about it."

Manolo found a small table in the cafeteria. Maya placed the map facing the woman and again took the lead.

"Are there any specific places where your husband has been here in the Baboquivari Peaks?" She pointed to the west side of the Buenos Aires National Wildlife Refuge next to the tribal lands. "This is one of the routes used by immigrants heading north, unless they run into La Migra." She didn't admit that she usually heard it as Chinga La Migra or Fuck the Border Patrol.

"My husband's a basketweaver," Mrs. Felix said. "The baskets started out for food and wine but became our primary art form. We use native plants like yucca, devil's claw, and beargrass. Weavers buy grasses at our co-op but Terroll likes to do things old school. He goes out to gather them himself."

"Any specific spots he's been to in the last two weeks?" Maya brought out a couple of brightly colored pens and laid them on the table to mark the indicated areas.

"Terroll's been all over. He knows this land like the back of his hand and doesn't use maps." Mrs. Felix's voice wavered, then went on. "He's self-conscious about not reading. Looking at this map won't help you. With one of our young sons, he just explores on horseback or ATV."

Disappointed that she couldn't get common locations from both patients, Maya thanked Mrs. Felix before she headed back to her husband's room.

"Lo siento, querida," Manolo said.

I'm sorry, dear one—Maya was startled by the affectionate expression, unsure of its connotation.

The Ag vets sidled up with more discouraging news. "No sick or dead cattle to help us pinpoint a problem," Ben said.

"The inspectors could be afraid we'll impound the animals." Dave scuffed his boot on the linoleum.

Feeling the tension rise again, she tried to redirect them to a plan. "We couldn't find out locations for Mr. Felix, but the UU map of their caches is specific. Why don't we take samples there?"

Ben and Dave agreed with her proposal, and Manolo stayed in the hospital to keep on top of any potential cases.

"Cuídate," he whispered in her ear as he gave her a brief squeeze goodbye. Take care.

This time, she didn't flinch. "Y tú."

. . .

Replenished by hamburgers in Sells, they headed east on the Ajo Highway, this time slowed with vehicles questioned by the border patrol. She shifted in the back seat and fretted about CBP's reaction to an Anglo, African American, and Chinese American with mysterious sampling equipment.

She'd read reports of young Chinese women smuggled across

the Canadian border for the New York sex trade in massage parlors. The stern Anglo agent looked her over and scrutinized their IDs. When asked why they were in the area, she jumped in and said they had visited a patient in Sells. They were waved through.

Ben drove back toward the Tucson suburbs until Sasabe Road, Highway 286. On the clear, hot day, he successfully navigated all the dirt roads on the Reverend's map. The headquarters building was marked on Maya's iPhone to the south. Realizing they wouldn't get approval for sampling without showing the church map, all agreed not to request a permit. If an officer stopped them, she would say they were on the way to the office. Not technically a lie, because some of the roads were on the way.

"Masked bobwhite quail—that's why they established the refuge." She scrolled her iPhone screen. "But little success at bringing the birds back north of the border."

"People yes, birds no," Dave replied with a provocative look toward Ben.

Overspread with grasses, oaks, mesquites, and piñons, the landscape was more verdant than she expected. Nothing like the desert except for tall, spindly ocotillo stems. And towering above, the eight-thousand-foot-high rocky pinnacle of Baboquivari Peak.

The Reverend had marked seven caches on her map. Dave collected soil samples at each one and Maya took photos for their records. Two areas with plastic water bottles, a blanket, and snack bars were intact and undisturbed, apparently not discovered yet.

Brown Canyon, filled with eighty-foot-tall Arizona sycamores, was the one area she hoped to revisit someday under less stressful conditions. The huge, dusky cottonwoods had hefty trunks with thick, deeply lined bark. In contrast, each sycamore had multiple white trunks with smooth, thin bark—a Cézanne painting of flaking white, brown, and green. Tracks from wildlife indicated they took advantage of the shady protection.

Trash tarnished the sandy and rocky rivulets, and torn candy wrappers appeared fresh. She rubbed hands over goose-bumped, bare arms at the idea that someone might have passed through just the night before. Did they make it to safety?

"This area has more than just trash from the minister's cache," she called out to Dave and Ben. "They probably lightened their loads for a final dash past La Migra on the Ajo Highway. Or they got scared and left in a hurry."

She reverently held out a well-thumbed, moldy Bible with the name 'Ramirez' and 'Mi Dios Es Grande' scripted inside the front page. After setting the book into the dirt, she poked through photos of boisterous families having joyful meals around the table, kids mugging for the camera. Colorful Batman LEGOs were broken apart with sand kicked over some pieces.

Rescue these lost possessions from their gravel grave or respect their final resting place? She reluctantly set the Bible back down. Honor the goal of a refuge—leave everything as you find it.

They finally gave up on the seventh site at sundown. Tall, slate monsoon clouds moved in from the west, although none had released their watery bounty in the refuge.

She asked Ben to pause the SUV so she could hop out to enjoy the moment. The slashes of cloud color pierced by the hulking height of the natural monolith made a memorable picture.

While rubbing her lower back, she clambered up into the vehicle and set the iPhone on the seat. "Dave, we have to stop meeting like this, sunrises and sunsets."

For the first time, his voice sounded tired. Of the three of them, he spent the most time scrounging down in the dirt for his samples.

"We're working too hard. Got to get back to eight-hour days."

Ben apologized for the plodding pace as he carefully guided the SUV to the highway, making sure it didn't bottom out in the sand, leaving them stranded. The area only got more dangerous with nightfall.

Maya recalled the murdered southern Arizona rancher found near footprints tracked to the border, and migrant children dropping dead of heat stroke forcing parents to leave their bodies.

Back in Tucson, wearied and famished, they stopped at a Mexican restaurant—blue corn chicken enchiladas with sour cream, her favorite food. Ben again swung by her grandmother's apartment.

"Another night in the Old Pueblo, dear?" Her grandmother headed to the green velour sofa where Hypatia snoozed. Maya's mind flipped through images of the abandoned items in Brown Canyon.

"Grandma, when I was young, we joined other families to celebrate Chinese New Year's and the Dragon Boat Festival. Dad mentioned it helped parents bond over the challenges of multiracial families."

"It was hard for your mother when people stared. They got it from Chinese people, too. At one of those New Year's performances, a man asked if you knew you were adopted. You were four years old. How could you not know?" The older woman shook her head.

"They tried to keep me involved in Chinese culture, but sometimes I tuned it out. A few parents talked about red threads. Could you remind me about that?"

"Ancient Chinese lore and adoptive families believe there are invisible red threads of destiny connecting people across the continents," her grandmother said.

"Like we were meant to be together?"

"Your Chinese papers say you were found on the orphanage doorstep at noon on February 14, 1993. Staff thought you were brought there within a few hours of your birth, and they assigned it for the records at eight o'clock. Your mom and dad thought Valentine's Day was a perfect remembrance of their love for each other and for starting a family."

"Isn't eight the luckiest Chinese number?"

"Yes, a propitious omen. On February 13, your mom finished an astronomy meeting in San Diego and headed to Balboa Park just before four. She relaxed on a bench in the beautiful grounds and her ears picked up a baby's cries, but she couldn't see one. After getting the adoption papers, she calculated the time zones and realized it was eight o'clock February 14 in China when she was on that bench. She heard a baby crying at the same time you were born and brought to the orphanage. Did she hear you?"

"Grandma, what a great story—how come Mom doesn't talk about it?"

"Sweetie, she's a scientist, doesn't believe in mumbo jumbo. Too spooky for her to admit. And she didn't want you worrying your birthday here was really the thirteenth, which happens to be our unlucky number."

Maya helped her grandmother into bed, then tossed and turned, the cat avoiding the turmoil. Links across the miles, invisible red threads. They connected her to the people walking at this moment to find a safer environment, along the same earth she had collected earlier in the day. Her adoption gave her a secure life in the Land of Opportunity. She prayed those walkers didn't disturb an invisible, biological enemy, slumbering in the soil.

TEN

Jan. 20, 2004.
Profit, Seer and Revelator, President of the Preesthood expelled
Father today
Gave Mother to anothr husband
Didnt know you could marry your uncle

He said Father was not keeping her from wicked path
They found books behind her bed, but not my diary
Our family of 5 girls, me, and Jacob are moving
Fathers 2 other wives and 15 children assigned to othr elders
Now I have new brothers and sisters.

April 29.
Mother cries a lot.
We don't know where Father is, but we have New Father.
Today while we put roof on home,
stupid friend John says Mother is wicked
When I hit him he fell off. We all fall off a roof some time.

ELEVEN

"I guess we're such a good team, we can wrap up this anthrax quickly." Maya stretched tired legs on the back seat of the SUV. The air conditioning provided soothing solace compared to the heat and mental challenges of the previous two days along the Mexican border.

As Ben navigated the holiday weekend traffic of the Tucson-to-Phoenix interstate, Dave turned from the front passenger position.

"You're right," he said. "The Hopi boy and the two down here didn't take long. Like the cattle cases in Uvalde County, Texas, these appear to be background soil-related incidents."

She'd been optimistic with her earlier joke about their rapid success, but innate hesitation and worry crept back in. She rubbed hands over her face. "For Arizona, this is all new, plus a dead teenager."

"And anthrax is the gift that keeps on giving," Dave said. "Once in the soil, it tends to stay there."

"At least we don't have animal problems here," Ben said. "I need to plan for the Arizona National Livestock and Horse Shows."

Dave had a puzzled expression on his face. "Not 'til December. Working on it already?"

"Largest show in the Southwest." Ben shifted his outsized bulk and stretched back to scratch his bald head. "Gotta make sure it's safe."

"Dr. Smith, I swear we won't dump any more anthrax on you."

She silently prayed to keep her promise when saying goodbye to Ben and boarding the plane to Albuquerque with Dave.

At the Santa Fe shuttle stop, Stephanie reminded her of the annual effigy burning. "I put in your Zozobra gloom about grumpy bosses and it went up in flames. No more trouble from Dr. Grinwold. Join us at a Labor Day picnic tomorrow?"

Maya admired Stephanie's ability to bounce back after her husband's death from lung cancer the previous year. With no children, she threw herself into work and social activities with colleagues—a role model for the single life. But Maya declined the invitation.

"Sorry, spending entire day in bed. See you bright and early Tuesday. Dr. Grinwold will be thrilled I only missed one day in the office."

. . .

September in Santa Fe was a magic month with crisp, brilliantly blue days. Yellow swatches made a Monet canvas of the mountainside. Each aspen tree extended its roots underground and popped up another white-barked trunk, painting entire hillsides with trembling golden leaves.

Even the roadsides glowed like impressionist masterpieces. Carpets of asters created resplendent purple paths, intermixed with swaths of yellow daisies, along the dirt backroads and the interstate. Maya inhaled the clear, cool air and was gratified to be back in the high-altitude community.

On September 10, Dave called with lab results. "One confirmation from Brown Canyon. Texas has a new procedure to reduce other environmental contaminants when anthrax spores are scarce. It's more sensitive than prior methods."

"So that was the only contaminated spot?"

His voice was cautious. "Soil testing is hit or miss, but storms can concentrate minerals in potholes and help spore survival."

"For an update on my end—Reverend Sophia had a remarkable

recovery and is home with her daughter. Plus, she went alone to stash the caches, so no more exposures to investigate."

"Unconscionable taking the risk as a single mother," he said, "doing illegal activities after others were arrested for something similar. This is all coming out tomorrow in a joint release including the U.S. Fish and Wildlife Service, since it was their property."

"Any anticipated blowback?" Maya sagged to the chair, remembering the promise of confidentiality to the church administrator.

"I could be up the creek for sampling on a federal refuge without their approval. Hell, even though I've only been with the feds for a couple of years, it won't be my first reprimand for pushing the envelope. You know, ask for forgiveness, not permission."

She wondered how to develop his relaxed attitude. "Is Reverend Sophia going to be arrested when this becomes public?"

"I gave my word not to broadcast our source, but whatever happens, she brought it on herself."

. . .

None of them anticipated how much they had flouted protocol. Following the press release, Dr. Grinwold tersely ordered her into his office. Stephanie's burning of the gloom didn't work.

With a brick-red face and flared nostrils, he put Dr. Jaworski on speaker. The CDC supervisor was tense. "Dr. Schwartz took blame for your unauthorized soil samples on a federal refuge, but you helped him and didn't check first. This wasn't an emergency. You should have asked for approval."

Her vision turned dead of night—about to faint. She lowered her head into her hands and pressed on her temples. Damned panic disorder. *Go the hell away. I'm sick to death of you.*

"I'm sorry, I truly am. We didn't know the patient outcomes, and they could be the tip of the iceberg. If I needed to share the cache map with anyone, the church wouldn't give it to me."

"It's fortunate you're a civilian rather than Commissioned Corps.

The Uniformed Services are much more militaristic in their chain of command," the sharp disembodied voice warned.

Her supervisors dismissed her and she dashed back to her office, locking the door. She sank to the worn carpet. *Second grade teacher passes out paste for project. Try to help—grab extra jar, teacher boxes ears. Race to bathroom stall, shaking, sobbing, 'til Assistant Principal comes.*

She shook off the vision and rose from the floor, then settled into the chair and scrubbed her face with a tissue. Another flash of memory—Indian Health Service was Commissioned Corps.

"Ma-Manolo." Holding the phone to her ear, she was barely able to squeak his name out. "Are y-ou in trouble?"

"Matter of fact, I am." His voice was surprisingly complacent. "But us Puerto Ricans are a bit rebellious."

"Are you trying to cheer me up? You shouldn't be punished for our decision."

"I'm using the 'not on the scene' excuse for all it's worth. But I knew your plan."

"I feel awful." With one hand entangled in her hair, she pulled hard to distract her brain.

"You figured out where both cases probably were infected, and they can take control measures," he said.

Remembering the warmth of his hug at Sells Indian Hospital, she held her shoulders. "I couldn't live with myself if anything bad happened to you."

Subsequent calls verified Dave and Ben also in a holding pattern. She collapsed in the office chair and dialed her NYC mentor. The gravelly voice brought back memories of success, not failure.

"Kid, if I counted the number of times I stepped on toes, I'd run out of fingers."

"Faye, you're just trying to make me feel better."

"I can see this situation is discouraging, and your health issues make it difficult to roll with the punches. I admire Dr. Schwartz for taking the blame."

"He and Dr. Smith have families to support. It would kill me if they lost their jobs over this. I was the one who suggested we do the sampling, even when the second case couldn't confirm he was in the same locations."

"Can't imagine it would go to that extreme."

. . .

Faye was right. None of them were fired, but she and Dave received letters of reprimand for their federal employment files. The Governor summoned Ben to his office for an official dressing down.

The Fish and Wildlife Service considered enforcement against the UU church for violating rules about leaving humanitarian supplies in a federal refuge, but government attorneys decided against bringing charges. Perhaps they rebelled against a stupid policy or took pity on a mother who could have died. Or they didn't want bad press. Whatever the reason, Maya was grateful.

Dr. Grinwold promised CDC he'd instruct her about chain of command and keep her under closer supervision.

Midafternoon on September 21, she saw an announcement of a climate change rally. She was still discomfited by Dave's confidence the anthrax cases were just weather or climate-related. Remembering the Hatch Act named in honor of a New Mexico senator, forbidding federal employee political activity, she caught Dr. Jaworski in Atlanta working late.

"Glad you're checking. If Fred agrees, you can stop by the event on your own time. Just don't let people think you represent us or the state health department."

The next day, she observed from the sidewalk as the chanting protesters marched by. Numerous senior citizens carried signs, but the loudest shouts came from the kids, whose existential fear was palpable. Would Earth still be a livable planet when she was old and gray?

. . .

With cool October temperatures, she put anthrax and a warming world out of her mind. Color spread down from mountain aspens to the cottonwoods lining river valleys and dry washes. Although she missed the splashy red of New York and New England maples, she prowled through narrow Santa Fe streets taking photos of the brilliant yellow and orange leaves contrasted against tan stucco walls and spectacular crystalline blue skies.

On October 7, Stephanie swung into Maya's parking lot at 5:30 AM to share the drive to the Albuquerque mass ascension of more than five hundred hot air balloons.

Noisy, bright bursts from propane burners provided welcome warmth as they wandered among the colorful nylon envelopes painting the grounds. Rose-streaked gray clouds hugged the horizon behind a pink pig, green Yoda, and Darth Vader vying for space overhead, as zebras, launch coordinators in black-and-white striped outfits, choreographed ascension of the next wave.

"Dr. Grinwold smiled at me once this week." Maya studied Stephanie's honest face while handing her hot chocolate. "Do you think he's forgiven my southern Arizona snafu? Or he's happy with my summary of the foodborne outbreaks this year?"

"Not sure, maybe both?"

Maya stretched and finally relaxed during their stroll through the colorful balloon-spattered field.

. . .

A sense of harmony with her boss didn't last. The next day, Dr. Grinwold took a call from his Arizona counterpart and called Maya to his office. Erika had gossiped about the two State Epidemiologists' alcohol-fueled conviviality during annual Border Conferences. While keeping her breathing steady, Maya prayed she hadn't made another major mistake.

"We let Pima County and you handle the minister," Dr. Nancy Bingham said. "However, we have new anthrax cases and I'm getting involved. Don't know what's going on, but we need Maya again. None of us were thrilled with what went down earlier, but I'll keep a tighter rein."

Her New Mexico supervisor slammed a folder down on his desk. "She might as well be assigned to Arizona for all the work she's doing for you. What is it this time?"

"Cutaneous anthrax, unlike the three previous inhalation cases. Two kids, a nine-year-old Hispanic boy from Holbrook and a seven-year-old Navajo girl from Ganado."

Maya stood next to the speaker phone. "Any connections?"

The voice of the middle-aged woman sounded baffled. "Are you familiar with Holiday Home in Flagstaff?"

"No, I haven't lived there for eleven years." Tiny tremors of apprehension tickled the back of her neck as she admitted any lack of knowledge.

"It's a theme park featuring exotic animals. Both kids were there before their skin lesions. Ganado is about fifty miles east of Keams Canyon and Holbrook is about eighty miles southwest of Ganado. There's probably another common exposure between them or with Danny Koopee." Dr. Bingham sounded like she wanted to discount the Holiday Home theory.

"Is USDA involved?" Maya asked.

"Dr. Schwartz from their Albuquerque District. He's on their shit list from your border escapade, but all is forgiven when they need him."

When the call ended, Maya jogged back to her office. Then she chugged water to calm her nerves and called him. "Is it a jinx for us to work together again?"

"My wife accuses me of spending more time with you than with her," he joked. "You should move in with us to avoid all those shuttles between Santa Fe and Albuquerque. You can interest our girls in piano instead of video games."

"The Navajo girl's hospitalized in Gallup and the boy's in Flagstaff."

"Animal Welfare Act requires inspections and a Class C license," he said. "Holiday Home's paperwork indicates occasional issues with animal housing and safety."

. . .

He picked her up at the Sunport shuttle and they drove west on the interstate. Midday at the Gallup Indian Medical Center, they were surprised to find Manolo.

"How'd you get here from Phoenix so quickly?" Dave asked. Maya avoided eye contact, still embarrassed about the unapproved sampling.

"IHS doesn't budget for too many specialists, so you're stuck with me again. But you vets are a bad influence."

Assuming he was insulting them, she tensed. But his merry eyes belied the sober words.

"Vet students think they'll be alone or in a small practice, like James Herriot." Dave laughed. "We're a lot more independent and ornery."

She shook out her limbs from the long drive. How could they joke about the bureaucratic nightmare? In the pediatric ward, the hospital was using contact precautions, so they put on gloves and gowns.

Two frantic young parents cornered Manolo as they entered the child's room. "She's been here a week, will she get better soon?"

"Let me check." He picked up the girl's swollen right hand and Maya crowded close behind. There were multiple lesions on the fingers and palm. The centers were depressed, and most had formed black scabs. Several encompassed an entire finger. All the surrounding tissue was crimson and inflamed. "How are you doing today, Gloria?"

"Pretty good?"

He checked her chart on the computer screen. "She's had twenty-four hours of normal temperature. Let's sit down to sort through how this happened, and figure out a plan."

Leaning close together, they scanned the record. Gloria was

lethargic a week after Labor Day, then developed pus-filled pimples on her fingers and hand. As an outpatient, she was prescribed a topical antibiotic and corticosteroid to reduce inflammation. A few days later, when the swelling and reddening worsened, she was hospitalized.

"For the cellulitis, they started her on floxacillin through her intravenous line," Manolo said. "They added erythromycin the next day."

"When did they get test results?"

"Lesion swabs were collected for the hospital lab. *Staphylococcus aureus* and a *Bacillus* species thought to be a wound contaminant were isolated. A photo of her finger looked suspicious for anthrax and the gram stain was compatible, so they sent the specimen to Phoenix where we confirmed it last night."

He went back to the medical record. "They already switched to intravenous penicillin for six days, so only two more days to finish." Turning to the parents, he touched the arm of the father. "I'll consult with the attending physician but the lack of fever is a promising sign."

As the child's eyes welled up with tears, he reassured her. "Gloria, we hope you can go home soon." The family appeared to be relieved by his soothing voice.

Maya noticed the family name on the screen. "Mr. and Mrs. Begay, do you have any ideas on how this might have happened?"

Both shook their heads. "We thought about the Hopi boy when they told us anthrax," Mr. Begay said. "But we didn't go to Keams Canyon."

"A colleague mentioned you went to Holiday Home outside Flagstaff," Maya said.

"Yes, two weeks ago. Gloria loves animals."

"What did she do with them?" Maya asked.

"Feeding and petting 'em. You can walk into the reindeer pen and feed leaves to other animals through a fence." Mr. Begay looked to his wife for support.

"Elk, bison, musk ox, and yaks," she added.

Dave took notes and compared them to his copy of the USDA license.

"Piggy!" the little girl chimed in.

"She loves that pig who follows commands to spin and sit," her mother said. "There were also bunnies and chickens. We have livestock through our extended family, but Gloria likes the exotic, North Pole-type of animals."

"Was she bitten by any of them?" Maya knew how often animal bites spread nasty diseases.

Mrs. Begay turned to her daughter. "Did any of those animals at the Christmas farm bite you?" Gloria shook her head.

Dave verified that the family didn't know of illnesses or deaths in their own animals, then Maya said goodbye. "If you think of anything else, let Dr. Miranda know."

Manolo followed them to the hospital entrance. "I'll leave the field work to you two again. You can do all the fun stuff and get in all the trouble."

"We're doing it by the book this time," Dave said.

"I don't know how much this petting zoo is patronized by Native Americans," Manolo said. "I'll call our regional facilities while I'm here. Cutaneous anthrax is a new wrinkle."

"Most frequent type in endemic areas," Dave pointed out.

After shaking Dave's hand, Manolo gave Maya a hasty hug. "If I don't answer, leave a message. I might be tied up reviewing infection control. Need to be ready for multidrug-resistant bacteria."

In the parking lot, Dave winked and opened the passenger door with a flourish. "I think that dude might like you."

She reinstalled her hair tie tighter to corral the heavy weight. Whether what he implied was true, she didn't know, but the comment was troubling. The last thing she needed was a colleague sniggering about her personal life.

TWELVE

<u>May 2.</u>
Sister Emily married New Father today.
Shes only 13.
Doesnt matter hes already married to Mother.
John says the Prophet has 42 wives so no one notices
one more or less.
You need at least three wives to get into Heaven
John is fucked up. I hit him in the nose again.

<u>July 13.</u>
One of Prophets family said he raped him.
Is that same as what happened to Boy who killed himself?

<u>Sep 10.</u>
John got caught with old Walkman.
Prophet says when you enjoy the beats,
your enjoying Spirit of black race.
John got kicked out like Father.
He knew we can't have those things.

But I'm gonna learn as much as I can.
Unlike Mother and John, I'm smart enough not to get caught.

WILD

Any animal will do. Doesn't take much, maybe only ten spores. First activation—awakening. The microscopic covering mottles and breaks down.

But with spore death comes transformation and germination, just like a seed, once inside the warm mammalian body. Swell up, happy to be alive. Extend a short tube, rod or filament. The thick coat releases life to blossom, but with some protection from a vegetative cell wall.

Wild creatures are prevalent and free-ranging. Their unfettered emancipation allows the bacteria freedom, too. Once inside, multiply in the lymphatics and spleen, then overwhelm the blood stream during the final hours.

Humans try to keep track, but they only really care about other people. Mostly they miss the natural cycle entirely.

THIRTEEN

After forty minutes of country-western radio, Dave adjusted the volume. "Should we stop and check out Gloria's homestead?"

The southern Arizona fiasco had Maya second-guessing her decisions but she waved him on. "Head to Flag for our next patient."

Realizing she sounded abrupt, she was chastened by her sharp reactions to her colleagues. She made a long unhurried stretch of her arms to the cab ceiling. "If we were off the clock, I'd recommend the old Hubbell trading post near here. Beautiful Navajo rugs and baskets."

"New Mexico's enlightened me about Native American history and culture." His hooded hazel eyes were locked on the highway. "I think we can learn something from other people, but there's still clashes and strained relations, the way I was raised."

"Does that make for tough Texas Thanksgiving dinners?"

The planes of his face firmed up like hardwood. "Nobody left to do them."

She squinted with a sudden memory of Keams Canyon, where he mentioned having no family. But his voice was calm, even proud.

"Heritage includes German Democrats who became Republicans. LBJ did anything legal or crooked to make south Texas a better place. Still have conservative values about hard-work, frugality, self-sufficiency."

"I understand. People are too quick to classify others as the enemy."

"Abortion determines a lot of political attitudes. Between my Mormon background and Emilia's very active Catholic faith, we can't vote for anyone who supports it."

She bit the inside of her mouth, uncertain how much to share. "I was thrown away 'cause Chinese women have no reproductive freedom. If they were wealthy, my father would have forced sonograms and abortions on my mother until she had a son."

His bronzed cheek twitched, but he didn't respond. She didn't know what else to say. China's one-child policy had horrific outcomes, including spelunkers tripping over dead baby girls in caves. Many things had to go right for her to avoid those fates. Her skin vibrated with an involuntary shiver.

Refocusing on their shared task, she checked her phone for the time. "The home environment could be important for these two kids, and cases are classified by home address. People worry about Lyme locally, even though there's often travel history to other infected areas."

"Do you think the anthrax cases were exposed to it somewhere else, like Lyme Disease?" he asked.

"I don't know." She kicked off her black pumps and wriggled her toes. "This whole outbreak has broken all the rules."

. . .

Back wracked with spasms from the long drive, Maya stepped out of the truck at Flagstaff Medical Center as the sun dipped behind the ponderosa pines. While donning gloves at the entrance of the pediatric room, she blanched at the sight of the boy's disfigured, swollen face. Raised red and purple borders circled profuse milky blisters. Tar-black scabs pockmarked his lips. An oxygen mask eased his breathing and his thick distended neck belied the thin frame.

Both lymph nodes below the chin were enlarged—all those lymphocytes fighting the infection. His dark eyes swept between them, pleading for help. He lifted a hand in greeting, his small fingers taped, probably to prevent scratching.

She patted his arm. "Hello, Rickie." She turned to the thirty-something parents, a dark-haired couple who appeared overwhelmed with fear. "Mr. and Mrs. Sanchez, I'm Dr. Maguire from the CDC and this is Dr. Schwartz from the USDA. We heard your son was diagnosed with anthrax yesterday."

Without Manolo around to handle the child and his parents, she was doing better than anticipated. Swallowing before speaking, she tried to stay upbeat and supportive.

"Dr. Schwartz has a lot of experience with anthrax from Texas. The cutaneous or skin type is the mildest form. Rickie will receive great care."

But twenty percent of cutaneous anthrax cases died. She pushed it to the back of her mind. It wasn't her role to mention that, and she needed to get the family focused on his exposure.

Flustered, she turned to Dave, then back to the young couple. "We're here to find out where Rickie got anthrax."

The parents mentioned seeing press about Danny's death, and were unsettled about any possibility their son could suffer the same fate. In recent weeks, none of them had been to areas with other cases, or around livestock. Like the Begays, they didn't mention the petting zoo unprompted.

Maya recalled kids in NYC who developed kidney failure with *Escherichia coli* infections from a county fair. Getting up close with unfamiliar animals was fun, yet risky. Most people never worried about it. When asked about Holiday Home, their trip was a week after Gloria had visited. If something happened there, it wasn't a point source, single-day event.

Mr. Sanchez said the petting zoo was a dusty outdoor pen with about a dozen animals of all ages and sizes, and visitors walking freely among them. The adult reindeer had antlers, larger on the males. Injury waiting to happen, even if no infectious diseases.

"Staff helped Rickie put a carrot in his mouth to feed the moose while we took a picture," Mrs. Sanchez said, "but he got saliva on his face. We didn't see restrooms nearby, so he wiped it with his sleeve."

Dave shifted weight in his seat, looking undecided about saying something. Maya took the lead at ending the interview.

"Here's my card if you think of anything else. We'll visit Holiday Home and check it out."

They exited the hospital into the chill, dark night. Ominous clouds hung over the mountain peaks.

"Too soon for snow, but could have a storm," she said. "What was that reaction back in Rickie's room?"

"Who on earth lets their kid feed a carrot to a moose with his mouth?" he vented. "Except for experienced people managing reindeer as captive livestock, no one should be up close and personal with those kinds of animals."

His expression was shadowed, the dim parking spotlight haloing his body from behind. Surprised by his incensed reaction, she recalled the intensity of his disagreement with Ben about immigrants.

"When I was twelve, my family took me to China. At the Chengdu reserve, I held a baby panda while they took pictures. It gnawed on my hand because it was teething. Do you think they were bad parents?"

"No comment." His clenched jaw indicated he was still annoyed. Maybe he dreaded their Holiday Home inspection.

"Was it a culturally important experience?" he asked.

"Yeah, it's something I'll never forget."

He regained control and shared his enigmatic cowboy grin. "Let's eat. I'll be a good boy for once and contact my superiors. We'll both get out of the doghouse."

She directed him to an affordable café her family enjoyed. He wolfed down a bowl of beef stew and wiped his mouth.

"So you'll pass up one of these hotels to stay with your folks?"

"I never ask for housing or food reimbursements for my family visits." Concerned about the implications of malfeasance, she squirmed in her seat.

"Any other relatives in Arizona to see on our next joint excursion?"

"I hope there isn't another one." She crossed her arms for emphasis. "If this is background soil contamination, these cases will stop when the snow comes. Whatever weird is happening in Arizona shouldn't continue, right?"

He plucked at his bushy brown eyebrows. "Arizona's been walloped with global warming and some areas won't have much snow. But anthrax waxes and wanes. We'll get the wane part soon."

. . .

She saluted him as the porch light flickered when she knocked on the door of her family's downtown apartment. After the door opened, the truck roared away.

"About time you showed up. Where's your friend?" At six-feet tall, her mom's authoritative heft filled the doorway, with her dad behind, clearing his throat.

Flushing at the implied criticism, she hugged them hello. "At least I made it before Columbus Day. You'll meet Dave tomorrow. He's worn out from the long drive and headed to crash at a motel."

Her dad took her bag to the small guest room, then brought out ice cream and blueberries for dessert.

"This outbreak has been scary," Maya said, eyes going to the floor. "Especially the Hopi teenager dying."

"We're proud of you, but worried, too." Her mom's freckled cheeks flamed.

"My decisions can have life-or-death consequences. And I've made mistakes—pissed off my bosses already."

"Find out what they want and need," her mom warned.

"It seems there's no perfect answer, so I have a hard time knowing what to do."

"I'm happy CDC has people doing the job like you, who are intelligent and have a conscience," her dad said.

"It's definitely using all of me, more than I have."

"Just keep plugging away, one foot in front of the other. You'll get it done." Her dad gave her a reassuring squeeze, and they all turned in. The wind and thunder roared in the rare early autumn storm, but she fell asleep quickly.

. . .

"Come share breakfast," she told Dave at seven. "Dad makes wicked pancakes."

Topped with blueberries left over from dessert, the pancakes filled them up. Dave regaled them with stories of his daughters.

Did her parents feel the grandkid pull? But she planned to follow their example and wait until her career was established. They should understand it was way too early to be thinking in that direction.

The conversation switched over to anthrax. Her parents knew about the previous cases, but Dave didn't mention details of the new ones.

"Most people aren't aware the spirochete is worldwide," he said. "Infected cattle in western states, wood bison in Northern Alberta and the Northwest Territories. Other infected wild herbivores include deer, llamas, giraffes, and hippopotami."

"Hippopotami." Her parents laughed at the sound of the plural noun.

"Outbreaks in African game parks, too. Carnivores have no symptoms but shed spores in their feces. Big cats, bears, raccoons, mink, and badgers."

"Heavens, that's a lot of animals," her mom exclaimed. Maya was impressed at the facts on the tip of his tongue. He was relaxed and friendly as he played the expert with aplomb.

"Just two years ago in western Siberia, there were twelve hundred reindeer deaths when a heat wave thawed long-frozen carcasses. Spores at the surface infected new reindeer, plus some nomadic herders. Burning the bodies led to wildfires. They ended up vaccinating hundreds of thousands of reindeer. There was one human death, a little boy."

Her parents were no longer laughing. "I don't like you working with such a deadly disease," her mom said.

"I'm vaccinated and careful. Thanks for breakfast."

Heading out the door, she chastised him. "Too much information. You scared them."

Seeing him frown, she directed his attention to the drive up Mars Hill Road. "I could walk this one blindfolded. Mom worked ahead at the Observatory."

He pulled over halfway to the top at the gaudy, evergreened sign for Holiday Home. They walked through the red, ski chalet entrance festooned with huge antlers on the roof. He had planned the early arrival to see the lay of the land before any crowds.

The middle-aged Santa-clad owner was defensive and hovering. They followed him through the Toy Tunnel, an underground cave with gifts for purchase. When outside again, sizable open pens with covered sheds offered shelter at night or in bad weather. Santa's elves scurried ahead, cleaning up gloppy, malodorous animal feces that flowed out after the previous night's storm.

Dave requested a list of animals from Santa to match against information on the USDA license, then called Maya to the side of the reindeer corral.

"Comparing their permit to what's here, we're missing two juvenile reindeer born last year and one adult female."

He led her out, studying the area map. "The moose that slobbered on Rickie should be here, but it's not."

The reindeer and moose pens were on the outer perimeter. An eight-foot high chain link fence topped with barbed wire separated the corrals from the ponderosa-dotted open landscape. No homes or commercial buildings, just tall trees and grassland, spread up the browning hillside.

Santa had run out of patience. "What's going on?"

Dave didn't reveal the cutaneous anthrax cases. "There have been concerns which we're investigating. Looks like you're missing the moose and three reindeer. Where are they?"

Santa harrumphed. "Sold 'em."

"Get me the paperwork," Dave said.

After a few wide-gaited steps toward the office, Santa gestured to an older female elf, and agitated whispers followed. "Sparkle tells me they're over here." He pointed to a huge, disturbed mound of dirt in the corner.

"Damn it! You can't hide something like that. Dig them up, so I can take samples and find out what killed them." Dave whipped out his cell phone while the worker elves powered up a backhoe and removed the soil covering the animals.

Santa was talking on his phone, too. Dave ordered Maya into the pit with the rotting carcasses. They completed sample collection, then he answered another call and took her to the side.

"We're going to let them stay open but restrict public contact."

"You can't be serious."

She used a hushed but steely tone, conscious of Santa and the elves on the other side of the pit, scrutinizing them. "Two children with anthrax, and the animals they touched are dead. You have to shut them down."

A couple months earlier, with her rookie blood draw mistake in Keams Canyon, she didn't talk back when he chewed her out. But experience bred confidence.

He reached for a rock and flung it at the fence. "We don't have lab evidence these pit animals had anthrax, and Santa cornered his Congressman. The live ones aren't showing signs of illness and we don't know where your kids got it."

She fumed several feet away as he gave instructions to the owner.

"You can remain open pending my test results, but I want no animal contact. Place barriers to keep the visitors from getting close to the pens. Cover up the pit and make sure no one goes into the moose pen. Someone will stop by to make sure you're in compliance."

As Dave peeled out of the parking lot, Maya called Dr. Bingham. "Can I update you on Holiday Home?"

The older woman's response was disturbing. "Flagstaff Medical Center just reported Rickie Sanchez died of toxemic shock."

On speaker phone, they got the news at the same time. Maya tried to control her reaction and voice as she updated their findings and the plan.

"With USDA needing lab confirmation on the animals to use their permit to close Holiday Home, are there any state health regulations that would apply?" She glanced over at Dave's rigid posture and stern countenance.

"I'll talk to the lawyers about a public health order." Dr. Bingham ended the call.

Maya slipped the phone into her bag and stared out the bug-splattered passenger window.

"I told Rickie's parents he'd be okay," she said in a strangled whisper.

They were silent for the rest of the long drive home.

FOURTEEN

<u>Jan. 1, 2005.</u>
Going to dedicate new temple on ranch in Texas.
Mother is antsy like she wants and doesn't want to go.

<u>May 7.</u>
Temple looks like palace.
Lots of free labor to build monster near nowhere.
School for younger kids so they can learn religion and math when not working.

Pretty orchard with fruit trees.
Better land for livestock and I'm learning a lot,
castration, insemination, helping cows and mares give birth.

Maybe become vet someday. What kinda schooling do you need for that?

FIFTEEN

A physician assistant ending a shift at 1:03 AM on October 9 saw a black Mustang with a throbbing engine and broken rear tail light roar up to the front door of Phoenix Children's Hospital emergency room, according to the detailed medical records Maya reviewed a few days later. The passenger door flew open and a booted foot propelled a tiny, blonde seventeen-year-old out to the asphalt.

The PA rushed her inside. Vomitus and feces soaked the clothes, so they changed her to a hospital gown, hooked up IV fluids, and strapped her down to prevent a fall from uncontrollable limb movements as her body thrashed about. Feverish, she was incoherent and couldn't provide her name.

A nurse wrote notes in the electronic chart about track marks with blisters on the lower neck above the clavicle and the left leg behind the knee. After spotting reddened gums, he asked her if she was doing horse. The girl nodded.

By the next day, she was calmer, but developed a throbbing headache and severe cough. Most of the skin on her thigh was blackened, and one of the fluid-filled blisters was the size of an orange. Both of her breasts were bright red and swollen, with linear extensions to the upper arms.

Already diagnosed with heroin withdrawal, on October 12 the state lab found *B. anthracis* on a blood culture. Surgeons removed the infected skin tissue from her thigh, leaving a gaping wound. As darkened blisters spread on the leg, the surgery was repeated. Then she developed pneumonia and needed chest drainage. Jane Doe still provided no contact information, and no one visited during her care.

Another chart recorded a primary care physician meeting his thirty-three-year-old patient in the lobby of St. Luke's Medical Center in Phoenix on October 10. She was accompanied by her aging mother and three unkempt, frantic children.

The doctor suspected his patient had deep vein thrombosis following heroin injection into the right elbow. Since January, he had treated her for multiple drug dependencies and hepatitis C viral infection.

For the previous few days, she had progressive swelling, reddening, and pain in her arm. When she began to shiver with fever and swelling spread to her torso, she called the PCP. At an outpatient visit in the morning, he noted blistering around the area of injection and ordered hospitalization.

The PCP shotgunned laboratory tests to identify a bacterial source for the infection. On October 12, he received state laboratory results reporting elevated anthrax antibody titers confirmed with polymerase chain reaction of skin lesion material. He shared the diagnosis with his patient's mother by phone and requested that she stop by the hospital to visit her daughter. The notes indicated that she never showed up.

A forty-seven-year-old undocumented Honduran with bad teeth arrived at Phoenix Mayo Clinic Hospital on October 11, according to a third record sent to the health department. In front of an intake clerk, he pointed to a swollen and reddened heroin injection site on his left arm, and was admitted with nausea and shortness of breath. Staff noted his history of cocaine and alcohol abuse, as well as his taking of methadone as oral replacement therapy. He also reported a previous diagnosis of hepatitis C and cirrhosis of the liver.

As his breathing problems worsened, the patient was moved to the ICU where his condition deteriorated. On October 12, he died of septic shock with multi-organ failure and massive internal hemorrhaging. PCR testing that evening confirmed *B. anthracis* infection.

. . .

Dead moose, reindeer, and animal pen soil from Holiday Home were announced as positive for anthrax in a USDA press release early on October 11. State attorneys considered a public health order before the attraction chose to close in response to panic created by the publicity.

A part of Maya wanted to slip Dave a smug "I told you so," but her mixed feelings about confrontation kept her from making the call.

Two days later, she pulled on boots for a hike with Erika's family at Bandelier National Monument north of Santa Fe. As she headed to the apartment parking lot and her car, the iPhone rang—Dr. Grinwold about Arizona heroin users.

"I think you're Joe Btfsplk. Anthrax keeps stalking you. No one knows what the hell is going on with all these Arizona cases in different parts of the state, and you damn well better work it out before it pops up here."

On the Sandia shuttle to Albuquerque's Sunport, she answered Erika's call. "Where are you? We've got a kid racing around the living room, wanting to get out of the house."

"Sorry, Erika, I don't know whether I'm coming or going. Dr. Grinwold's ordered me back to Arizona for some strange anthrax cases that have something to do with drugs."

Her colleague's voice became more sympathetic. "No problem. Need me to help with anything?"

Maya figured she should lead with conviction. "I've got it under control. There's time before the flight to review the case records they sent. Go have fun with Kyle."

She arranged for the Arizona health department to pick her up when she landed at Sky Harbor, then did an internet search on her phone. Joe Btfsplk was a cartoon character with a perpetual dark rain cloud over his head. Did her boss really think she was the world's worst jinx?

On a holiday weekend, the downtown Phoenix street was deserted when the contact tracer parked across from the tan stucco and glass Department of Health Services building. Maya's finger swiped to the weather on her cell. A hundred degrees in October? The asphalt shimmered and occasional palm trees broke the monotony of the pale blue sky.

Several nurses and epidemiologists worked the phones in the otherwise empty offices, and Dr. Bingham, the plump, mid-fifties State Epidemiologist, rounded them up for an impromptu meeting. "As most of you heard, the laboratory confirmed three heroin-associated anthrax cases, one deceased."

With graying short brown hair and reading glasses dangling from a chain, her gaze focused on Maya. "Dr. Maguire, your first task will be to create a database for the information from the case records." Maya nodded before Dr. Bingham continued.

"This anthrax source has never been documented in the U.S., so there will be a lot of eyes on us after the press release tomorrow. Over a hundred injection anthrax cases were identified in Scotland and Germany starting in 2009, with others in Denmark and France."

Maya raised her hand. "In the European outbreak, they don't know how the heroin got spores?"

"The drug was Afghan or Pakistani origin. When transported to Turkey, it was contaminated with goat-strain anthrax, perhaps when they wrapped it in goat skins for trafficking. Or they cut the drugs with bone meal to maximize profits. For our infections, we have no idea at this point."

"I can stop by the hospitals to talk with patients and families to find out more," Maya offered.

Dr. Bingham shook her head. "With heroin as the source, I'm anticipating more cases. County health is following up. The database is your priority for tracking and analysis."

As the setting sun turned the white office walls a yellowish hue, the team was sent home to rest with a plan for expanded case surveillance through hospitals and urgent care centers the next day. A nurse dropped Maya at the same hotel where she stayed for their first anthrax fatality, Danny Koopee.

She unpacked her clothes and reflected on the August night when she met Manolo at the Phoenix IHS hospital. There was no connection between Native Americans and this new cluster, but she piled pillows on the hotel bed and stretched out to call him.

"Maya, ¿cómo estás?"

"I'm in Phoenix. We have three heroin-associated anthrax cases. One's only a teenager, and another was an undocumented immigrant who died day after admission." She recalled the images included in the medical records. Sprouting goose bumps as she glanced over her notes, she twisted the blanket higher.

His voice sounded alarmed. "I remember similar cases in Europe, but never here. Are you burning the candle at both ends?"

"It was a long day getting here from Santa Fe and starting the investigation." The cookie from the front desk beckoned on her night stand. "No time for lunch."

"Querida, let me take you to dinner."

She blushed and hugged legs to her chest, glad he couldn't see her reaction. She hadn't intended to lead him into the invitation.

"Está bien." Wanting to continue the intimacy of their conversation in Spanish, she searched her memory. I'm hungry. "Yo tengo hambre."

"¿Qué quieres? ¿Mexicana?"

"Sí, por favor."

. . .

She paced the worn flowered carpet until he pulled up to the glass lobby doors in a vintage, red Corvette.

"You dressed for my car, querida." He held the passenger door open, smiling at her sleeveless red sheath.

His casual appearance in a forest-green shirt and blue jeans enhanced her relaxed mood. She'd never seen him out of his official summer whites.

"I didn't take you for a Corvette kind of guy."

He closed her door and jogged over to the driver's side. "Could be the DNA, Latinos like showy cars."

On a Saturday evening, the small diner was crowded but the host shook Manolo's hand and guided them to a cozier table toward the back. With the restaurant's stereotypical Mexican décor, she was grateful there weren't mariachis. Romantic singing guitarists would have been too much.

While waiting for their food, she gave him details on the anthrax cases and he promised to manage IHS notifications and surveillance.

"Let's not talk disease during dinner." He clinked their salt-rimmed margarita glasses. "Tengo algunas preguntas."

"I'll try to answer your questions, as long as I don't drink too many of these."

She returned his toast. Why did he look like a Broadway star? One sip of the margarita and she was already tingly.

He leaned back in the chair. "You have an unusual name. Where did it come from?"

"Dad was out-of-state after the adoption paperwork was sent to China. He thought of role models and remembered Maya Lin. As a Chinese American college student, she designed the Vietnam Veterans Memorial in D.C."

"That's why it sounded familiar. And your mom was fine with his decision?"

"She had scrutinized books with baby-naming rules, like two syllables are best and no difficult spellings. When he came home and mentioned Maya as his first choice, she turned pale and opened her list. My name was at the top. They never talked about it again."

"One of your favorite family stories?"

"My dad thinks we were fated."

The friendly auburn-haired waitress brought their chicken flautas, and his expression turned deliberative.

"Do you ever wish you hadn't been given up for adoption?"

She squirmed and rubbed her thighs, undecided whether to be exasperated at such a probing, personal question.

"When I was little and had a temper tantrum, I threatened to find my real parents. A Chinese boy plotted an escape for us to get married in China."

"Your first boyfriend. Whatever happened to him?"

"The preschool teacher told us to shut up and take our naps."

His appealing smile broadened.

"My folks suggested I write notes to my biological family when I missed them. The letters weren't mailed—we don't know who they are—but it offered a way to express my feelings."

"Gotta give 'em credit." He clasped his hands behind his neck. "Seems like a smart thing to do."

She briefly closed her eyes. "During a China visit at age twelve, the poverty, begging, and unhealthy environment were right there in my face. I felt blessed to be an American, and never threatened to run away again."

"I admire you for coming to terms with that."

Uncomfortable with too much focus on her origin, she switched gears. "So, what's the Dr. Miranda life story?"

Moving empty plates to the middle, he glanced at his watch. "Let me take you to dinner again tomorrow and I'll share my dirty little secrets."

She rose from her chair, realizing she was drained. "Sounds like a plan. Muchas gracias."

"De nada, mi amiga." Just friends.

. . .

A staff member from the health department picked her up at seven in the morning. She reflected on Manolo's quick embrace when dropping her at the hotel the night before. Nothing too unusual. Friends hugged too.

Dr. Bingham greeted her in the Epi Office. "Use this workstation and summarize drug-associated anthrax. Present it at our ten o'clock meeting, and we'll finalize a press release for noon."

Maya dropped into the computer chair and held her head. Familiar weak-at-the-knees reaction. Too reminiscent of Columbia University when the room turned black and she fled at the end of her thesis defense.

But admonitions from previous therapy flitted in. Running away from stressors didn't help. She had to lean into fears and build up confidence in facing them.

By midmorning, Dr. Bingham ordered to work two dozen staff members from their three-day weekend. One hand anchored to the podium and her knee on a chair, Maya steadied herself before summarizing injection or skin-popping as a new route of exposure to anthrax. She explained how bacterial multiplication could lead to a fatal blood infection and how toxins could stimulate an over-reaction of one's own immune system.

A few in the audience gasped at the gruesome photos of blackened, necrotic skin, and she responded to her butterflies with a swallow of water.

The State Epidemiologist reminded the staff that they should use their expertise in working with persons who inject drugs. Targeted outreach could help identify early anthrax cases.

No additional ones were reported by day's end but the Public Information Officer handled a steady stream of inquiries. Dr. Bingham gave a short interview to a local TV station and allowed them to take background video footage of staff working on Sunday. Maya helped Atlanta with CDC notification to other states. At sunset, Dr. Bingham told her to take time for dinner and recovery.

She called Manolo to let him know she was free. Anticipating heat, she again chose a sleeveless dress, this one an indigo blue which brought out the shine in her hair.

"Up for a longer ride?" He held the door of the Corvette.

Her heart skipped a beat with a momentary twinge of distress. What did he mean, exactly?

"We're heading to Paradise Valley. It's cooler tonight, so we can eat outside."

Without workday commuter traffic crowding Phoenix streets, they parked at the Milagro Inn within twenty minutes. He cupped her elbow as he led her to the restaurant patio, where abundant shade tree limbs were punctuated with miniature white lights. A hidden blue lamp illuminated a central fountain, with tiny water droplets cooling the surrounding air.

The perimeter alternated prickly pear cacti with old, wooden barrels containing bright, multihued annuals. At the horizon, the setting sun splashed the western sky with a rosy tone and cast a golden glow on Camelback Mountain to the northeast.

They settled into comfortable equipale leather chairs and she exhaled in carefree contentment after a sip of the refreshing Riesling. Small lanterns lit each table. She glanced up at the darkening sky and shimmering farolito imitation candle lights lining the Inn's adobe parapet.

"I can't imagine a more beautiful setting." Concern about the enticing mood crept in like a centipede. Her mind crushed it under foot.

"Stuffed squash blossoms with cheese and chorizo—very tempting." He read from the menu, appearing to dare her to be similarly bold.

"I'll be crazy too and order fish in the desert. Can't pass up the halibut."

Orders placed, he toyed with the fingers on her right hand. "Anything new I should know?"

She didn't withdraw, the light contact providing courage. "I gave my first anthrax presentation and it was very difficult." In response to his curious expression, she gulped and continued.

"I have panic disorder and anxiety since a pickup hit me on my bike when I was five. A neighbor found me. I was in terrible pain, unable to walk." Her breath caught at the memory. "I almost died, and had several surgeries."

Trusting him enough to reveal her secret was a surprise. "Since then, I have multiple panic triggers. People focusing on me is one of them."

His warm, dark eyes opened wider. "I never would have guessed."

Unable to bear him concluding she was incapable of performing her work, she ignored her unsettled stomach and returned his gaze. "Mom quotes her favorite astronomer, 'Quiet people have the loudest minds.' Maybe that applies to me."

Leaning over her fingers, he gave them a brief kiss on the knuckles. "I like you just the way you are."

Startled, she eased her hand away.

"But if you're self-conscious about someone staring," he said, "it's too late. You're the most beautiful woman I've ever seen, and I can't take my eyes off you."

Her toes curled up and knees drew together. He must be teasing. No one ever said anything like that before. She scoured the outdoor seating area for their waiter and spotted him bringing the plates.

"We were supposed to talk about you tonight," she said with a shy smile.

The waiter delivered the meals during a slight pause in conversation. To avoid endless discussion of national politics, she elected on a local focus.

"Your new home state is changing. Tomorrow Phoenix and Tucson celebrate Indigenous Peoples Day. It's nothing like when Mom and Dad were in high school with the right-wing John Birch Society and Mafioso boss Joe Bonanno living openly in Tucson."

He offered his fork with a bite of squash blossoms. "There's a legacy of violence. Tombstone still reenacts the O.K. Corral shootout."

Her nose and tongue inhaled the unusual meld of salty, creamy and crunchy flavors from his offering. Then she shook her head and raised her fingers to indicate it was enough. "Arizona has had women governors and Sandra Day O'Connor as the first female Supreme Court Justice."

"Next month, I'm voting for the first female Senator here in thirty years."

"Becoming an Arizonan?"

"Sí. Corvettes and history are two of my hobbies."

In mock astonishment, she tilted her head. "I can't believe you finally disclosed something about yourself."

When the conversation lulled, the waiter checked about dessert. "Want to split some key lime pie?" Manolo asked.

Forks bumped as they shared the pastry and finished the bottle of wine. Her limbs and lips were loose from its liberating effects. For the first time, she initiated contact and touched his chin. "Fess up to anything else?"

Grin broadening, he taunted her. "What if I'm too chicken?"

"I don't believe it." She squeezed his hand. "I never met anyone more gregarious."

His expression became somber. "It's more deliberate than natural. My mother died of breast cancer when I was sixteen and I was incapacitated, useless to my father and sister. Had to get my act together, apply to college, and do something with my life."

"I'm sorry." She rubbed her bare arms to counter the whiff of cool air. "I forget how lucky I am to have loving, if overly doting, parents."

"We all experience loss." His hands clenched the white tablecloth, then relaxed. "It's what we do after that counts."

"Why hasn't someone snatched you up already?" With flutters in her stomach, she was shocked to say words she hadn't planned.

"Young lady, methinks you drank too much."

She almost opened her mouth to agree.

He stepped to her side and eased back her chair. "Or I might conclude that you're offering to correct my situation and take advantage of the casitas here."

Like a wave crashing on the shore, the words cascaded head to toe. She appreciated him providing a graceful way out and mimicked his lighthearted tone.

"Señor, if I didn't have to work tomorrow, I might have taken you up on that idea." She couldn't believe she was flirting back. First time for everything.

SIXTEEN

<u>June 15.</u>
My expelled friend John used to say we were all stupid because of marrying cousins.
Should speak for himself.

Without John, I don't keep up on news as much.
When we were road grading in front of our house today, someone sniggered that one of our leaders was charged with sexual assault on a minor. He's on a wanted poster.

SEVENTEEN

Her mind foggy after getting carried away with the food, drink, and conversation the night before, Maya returned to the health department early on Columbus Day morning. Manolo had kept the mood jovial on their way back to the hotel. The only indication of the evening's intensity was the light brush of his lips against hers as he hugged goodnight—probably too brief to count.

Drug-associated anthrax escaped from Maricopa County. Pima County phoned her about their first case, a forty-three-year-old homeless female who injected heroin under the skin of her left thigh a week earlier. A caseworker found her huddled beneath a palo verde tree near Tucson's Rillito River bike path, with extensive swelling and blistering of her thigh, lower abdomen, and genitals. Taken to surgery, prodigious amounts of affected tissue were removed. Her blood culture was positive for anthrax, and she was infected with HIV and hepatitis C. The hospital planned a skin graft.

The day's second patient was a thirty-year-old man from Glendale, a Phoenix suburb. An acquaintance injected him with heroin in his right buttock. When the area became swollen, red, and painful, extending to his genitals, a friend drove him to an urgent care clinic. Like the Tucson patient, he had surgical debridement and was intubated to treat respiratory compromise. Lab tests confirmed anthrax, hepatitis B and hepatitis C.

Late in the day, Flagstaff Medical Center called with an additional case. A sixty-two-year-old retired policeman had injected heroin into his left femoral artery. Still wracked with pain from a gunshot wound a decade earlier, it was his first hit in eight years. The injection caused a pseudoaneurysm, or bubble in the blood vessel, leading to compromised blood flow in his leg. Surgery was performed the previous day, and antibody titers were positive for anthrax. There were no other coinfections.

At five o'clock, Dr. Bingham stopped by Maya's cubicle. "With many of these patients having wound surgery, I'm concerned about clinical waste. Talk to CDC and draft a guideline by morning. Also let me know if they have any new, experimental treatments."

Maya searched European guidelines for incinerating or autoclaving instruments and wastes contaminated by blood or bodily fluids. Not finding sufficient detail, she called her Atlanta supervisor for specific language.

"Dr. Bingham's given you glowing reports," Dr. Jaworski said. "I appreciate your frequent email updates. This is one of the biggest public health issues in the country, so you're in the hot seat. We're evaluating how to deploy additional subject matter experts."

A high profile outbreak increased the pressure and Maya twisted in a tight self-hug. "I'd be happy to work with other SMEs. Are there new therapies we can recommend to health care providers?"

"In the Strategic National Stockpile, we have antitoxin, but there are conflicting results about its effectiveness. We sent it for a couple of your earlier cases, but may ramp it up."

Maya ran her tongue inside her front teeth. So many disparate infections, too many bases to cover. "Could it have worked for patients like Danny Koopee?"

"Some were diagnosed too late." The CDC manager's tone sounded defensive. "And we thought they were background soil-related. But now you have an unusual source. We can work with some hospitals to correlate toxin levels with clinical status to guide antitoxin use."

Dr. Jaworski promised to track down the exact language of European guidance before midnight. "As you know, the Bacterial

Special Pathogens Branch is in charge here. If they don't have anything, someone will contact our World Health Organization colleagues in Geneva."

Then Maya returned a missed call from Manolo. "I was tied up with Atlanta, sorry I couldn't pick up."

"Busy evening?"

She slumped in her chair, relieved the cell had a speaker because she had no energy to hold the phone. "Working all night on some guidelines."

"Can I bring something to eat?"

Her stomach growled. "Anything would be fine."

Thirty minutes later, she swung open the health department door. He was more casual than she'd ever seen him. Torn denim shorts, yellow t-shirt, and sleeveless, bronzed arms loaded down with sandwiches and sodas. "Do you have time to take a break and dine together?"

"Not really." She reached behind to rub sore muscles at the waistband of her gray skirt. "I should research and type while I eat."

"Before I go, would you like a brief back rub?"

Other than as a child after her surgery, she'd never experienced a massage from someone else. Her own fingers and the heating pad usually did the trick. But his previous touches had stimulated new excitement. She had to work with no distractions, and was conflicted by his offer.

"Make it quick."

"Yes, ma'am." He snapped a mock salute.

She perched sideways on the computer chair, leaning her right arm on it for balance. He pressed his fingers into her lower back. His strong hands made her so relaxed she started to collapse against him. Although he touched her through the blue cotton shirt, her skin began to tingle and warm. His fists kneaded her spine, fingers separating at her shoulders.

Her droopy eyelids popped wide open when his fingertips connected with bare flesh, circling around the back of her neck and the base of her skull beneath her loose hair. She was dizzy. Anxiety or arousal?

"Better take a hit of that coke." She leapt up, grasped the bottle, and screwed off the cap.

"No jokes about our drug problem. When you're done here, let me know."

She headed toward the front door, requiring him to follow. "I'll call a taxi. No reason for us both to be zombies."

He grabbed her arm, fingers wreathing her biceps through the thin fabric. "This is an isolated neighborhood and I'm not comfortable with that. Text me," he ordered.

. . .

Using Dr. Jaworski's emailed information, she completed the first draft of hospital waste guidance and turned off the computer. Her iPhone said 1:47 and she texted Manolo, too drained to disobey his earlier demand about contacting him for a ride.

He tapped at the glass door as she leaned sleepily against it. It had been hours since she ran out of caffeine.

"You look better than I feel." She shivered when stumbling out into the unexpectedly cool night air. "Did you know the name anthrax comes from the Greek word for coal, because of the black skin lesions?"

"And you're not functioning on all cylinders."

She collapsed in the car seat and he reached over to buckle her seat belt.

At the hotel, he continued to support her with one arm. The night clerk glanced at them and back to his paperwork as they entered the lobby.

"Sweetheart, that guy might think you're drunk," he whispered in her ear.

When they got to her room, she located the key card in her purse and he held the door open. "Want any more help?"

"I'm fine—can get by on three hours of sleep."

"Depending on when the driver comes, you might not get more than that."

He went to the clock next to the bed. "What time for your alarm?"

"Six."

"Your funeral. Might want to ask Siri for backup."

This time, his goodnight embrace seemed much longer. She started to drift off before he guided her to the bed, and heard him test the door after he exited.

Clothes were dumped on the chair and she reached for the iPhone charger to plug it in. But she forgot Siri when pulling the covers over her head.

. . .

"Call immediately for the best investment advice." The radio talk show blasted her awake, and she smacked it off. After reviving in the shower with hot, then cold water, she wolfed down a banana from the bureau and gulped a bottle of cranberry juice.

She was back to full function by arrival at the office. Dr. Bingham made final edits to the draft waste management guidelines before the Director released it to the medical facilities. Additional case reports from rural areas and cities flowed in. An information technology expert worked with Maya to transition her database into a secure intranet form for health workers to enter new ones.

With state lab staff working overtime on processing specimens, the total number of confirmed injection anthrax cases reached seventeen by noon. CDC flew a stockpile of antitoxin to Phoenix for use by health care providers when patients met the suspect case definition Maya developed. That number already exceeded fifty. She updated the Epi-X notification to other states, and some nearby ones reported a handful of cases by the end of the day.

Dr. Grinwold phoned just before sunset. "You promised to keep this corralled in Arizona. We got one confirmed and a couple suspects in Albuquerque."

"And that's *my* fault?" she snapped, headache reverberating between her ears like a jet plane.

He let her return to work.

. . .

The daily sequence of new infections, Dr. Grinwold's calls for updates, and Manolo's fast-food dinners continued. On October 18, more than a week since their disagreement over closing Holiday Home, Dave phoned from Albuquerque for an update.

Still stewing about his caving to political pressure, she jiggled her pen on the desk but didn't bring up the incident.

"You can't imagine how grateful I am to avoid this heroin problem," he drawled. "I'd never see my kids."

"You're right." She set the pen down. "I don't know how anyone manages a life with an outbreak this momentous."

"If there's anything I can do . . ." His voice trailed off before their quick goodbyes.

In the evenings, she wasn't the only one working overtime. Manolo guided treatment and investigation at the regional Indian hospitals.

Then CDC tasked her with managing the nationwide case count, which by October 19 ballooned to one hundred twenty-four confirmed cases, and three hundred more awaiting test results.

"Aiming to break Europe's record?" Dr. Jaworski tried to keep her energized in noon phone calls from Atlanta.

CDC ensured that other states were coordinated in their response. With Los Angeles and New York City leading the number of out-of-state cases, Lila Becker, her California counterpart, was detailed to work on the outbreak. And Dr. Faye Simpson provided psychological support when cornering Maya for a three-way consultation with a NYC Officer already at Mount Sinai Hospital.

The Drug Enforcement Administration and the FBI collected their own data to investigate the source of contaminated heroin. On October 21, a representative from Homeland Security flew in from Washington to meet with the Arizona health department. In the State Epidemiologist's office, Maya was introduced to the trim, middle-aged woman in the service dress blue uniform.

"This is Vanessa Wright," Dr. Bingham said. "Coincidentally, you're both veterinarians. You guys get around."

The officer's violet eyes narrowed as she shook Maya's hand. "Guess we're more versatile than just giving rabies shots. Pleased to meet you."

A dozen staff gathered around the rectangular conference table. With a rapid cadence, Dr. Wright reviewed the heroin fact sheet.

"When interviewing patients, keep up the good work of recording the drug's street name. For this outbreak, we heard about brown-colored heroin, referred to as Brown crystal, Brown Sugar, Mexican brown, Mud, or Mexican mud."

Maya examined names for mixtures of heroin with cold medicine, ecstasy, alprazolam, cocaine, and crack. At the bottom were slang phrases for heroin use. *Chasing the dragon.* Most people would run away from a dragon, but a lot of suffering ensued when an addict felt compelled to pursue one.

Pushing rimless glasses higher on her nose, Dr. Wright explained the connection between the opioid epidemic and heroin.

"Your health department has dealt with overdoses from opioids and other pain relievers like fentanyl. People receive a medical prescription but lose access and turn to heroin as a more affordable alternative. It changes them from a dependent person to a criminal, but they believe they have no choice. Eighty percent of new heroin users first developed their addiction with prescription opioids."

The next morning, Maya provided a statistical summary of the outbreak to the local team, with out-of-state staff on the videoconference call. Manolo and Vanessa Wright joined them in person. The conference room was jammed with more than seventy-five attendees, including the department's Director.

A microphone was fastened to the lapel of Maya's black blazer by the IT coordinator, recording the presentation for the department's website. She prolonged a drink of water as the audience stirred in anticipation. Their eyes pinned her to the podium like the Chinese moon moth in her high school museum display case.

Opening her mouth to describe the clinical patterns, nothing came out. With one more sip from the mug, her muted voice kicked into gear. She caught Manolo cupping a hand behind his ear, and slipped the microphone upward.

When she finished the vivid pictures of inflammation, putrescence, and necrosis, Dr. Bingham turned on room lights and mimed support staff to distribute a one-page statistical summary which had been emailed to the video conferees.

"You can see our analysis results to date," Maya continued with a shaky voice, grasping both sides of the podium. As the room rustled with minor murmurings like a rain shower through a grassy field, she looked for a signal to continue.

Dr. Bingham's brown eyes narrowed and she pulled out a chair in invitation to sit at the head table. After accepting the offer, Maya caught Manolo's nod of encouragement from the audience.

"The epi curve on the top of the page graphs two hundred nineteen confirmed cases nationwide by clinical onset date, with the largest number on October 16."

"Infections are lower. Does this mean the outbreak is over?" The health department's Director kicked off the questioning from the back of the room.

"For new cases," Maya answered, "we won't receive reports and confirmation until the end of the week, due to the time between symptoms, medical attention, and laboratory testing. However, this graph does indicate that exposures might be dropping off."

"Dr. Maguire, talk us through the measures of association you've calculated on the back of this page," Dr. Bingham instructed.

EIS training emphasized short, clear, and to the point messages, even for statistics. "At the top, confirmed injection anthrax cases are compared with injection drug users or IDUs hospitalized for other illnesses. Injection anthrax cases were 7.6 times more likely to reside in Arizona than other study areas. This was statistically significant, meaning we have confidence this is a true association. It confirms our theory that the outbreak source is here."

The Public Information Officer shouted from the doorway. "How do you explain cases in other states?"

Dr. Bingham, with a slight dip of her chin, signaled Maya to answer.

"Obtaining an accurate history is challenging from surrogates when cases are deceased or too ill to report. The data indicates cases in other areas are from people exposed here and then traveling elsewhere. The heroin also appears to be moving around."

Dr. Wright, seated to her left, grabbed the single table mic. "In the next data table, is there a pattern with brown heroin? Your conclusions will help us focus the investigation."

Maya reached for the mic but remembered the one fastened on her lapel. "The injection anthrax cases were 3.5 times more likely to report using brown heroin compared to other injection drug users in the study. This association was also significant at the .05 level like the association with Arizona residence. So there's only a five percent probability these results occurred by chance alone."

"And what's the explanation for those who report using other types of heroin?" Dr. Wright leaned to the mic and projected her voice.

"Cross-contamination of the product or misclassification. Cases could have been exposed to brown heroin, but bad information is recorded in the reports."

"Dr. Maguire, both of these disease odds ratios are high compared to other epi studies." The voice from the octopus speaker phone was Dr. Jaworski's.

"Exposures sometimes only increase risk a small amount." Maya reached deep for a forceful finish. "In this study, the high increased risk combined with the low probability of a false conclusion is evidence we have a strong association."

"If there are no more questions, let's wrap this up." Dr.

Bingham stood to indicate the end of the meeting. "Dr. Maguire has an additional summary next to the door with more detailed statistics summarizing age, gender, race and ethnicity, IDU status, and preexisting conditions."

The Public Information Officer waved her hand with the stack of papers.

"Questions can be directed to Dr. Maguire later today," Dr. Bingham continued. "Her analyses indicate exposures occurred from brown heroin in Arizona. The epi curve demonstrates a downward trend. Great news for potential patients, health care providers, and public health. Thanks to all who contributed data from other states."

As participants dispersed and Maya's trembling legs propelled her to a standing position, Dr. Bingham shook her hand. "Outstanding work. You hit it out of the park."

Dr. Wright also stood. "Your quick coordination of the nationwide analyses is game-changing. I'm consulting with law enforcement to focus the investigation. Getting a jump on this will save lives."

At the end of the line with her colleagues, Manolo was last to step to the front table and offer his hand. Like Dr. Wright, he was dressed in the PHS service dress blues.

"Congratulations, Dr. Maguire. You should be proud. Pretty challenging to make statistics understandable." His gracious compliment relaxed her enough to take a deep breath.

"It's a lot easier when the associations are this strong." She glanced around at her coworkers and stepped away.

After clicking on his cell phone calendar, he asked, "Do you know when you're headed back home?"

She gathered her notes from the table. "Dr. Grinwold wants me to manage the national database from New Mexico."

"Can I give you a ride to Sky Harbor?"

Like bubbles in a carbonated drink, her tissues effervesced. "I'd like that."

She returned calls and wrapped up immediate deadlines, then booked a flight home. He met her in the hotel lobby as she checked out, roseate rays slanting through the glass doors.

"I'm always coming or going during beautiful sunrises or sunsets," she said as they climbed into the Corvette.

His right hand rested on her sweatered shoulder and they savored the scene. "You're smart enough to appreciate nature's beauty and bounty. Seize the moment, I always say." After a quick squeeze, he started the engine.

At the airport, he walked her inside to check luggage and print her boarding pass. Short of the security lines, he swung her around to face him, holding both of her arms.

"Speaking of seizing the moment, I'd like us to get to first base in our personal relationship." He gave her a questioning smile.

Her eyelids dropped as her heart pounded. She had read him right, he was coming onto her. The crude phrasing was off-putting. What did first base include? But it was finally out in the open.

She opened her eyes to glimpse his wrinkled brow.

"I know it's crazy because we don't live in the same place," he said. Giving her another out, but what if she didn't want one?

"It would be nice if we didn't need anthrax as an excuse to see each other." She unclenched her shoulders, adjusting to this new phase of their relationship. "Did I ever say why I like your name?"

"No, you didn't." His face was open and eager for the story.

She focused on his smoky eyes. "A character on the TV series *High Chaparral* was named Manolo. The actor was Puerto Rican like you. One of Mom's treasured childhood souvenirs is a photo with his arm on her shoulder after a film session in Old Tucson."

He chortled and shook his head. "First Lin-Manuel Miranda, and now your mom's crush. I have two big stars to live up to."

"You don't need to compete with anyone," she whispered, leaning in to accept a real kiss.

EIGHTEEN

<u>June 21.</u>
Jacob and I work construction. I'm in charge of all the livestock. Mother sneaks out to the town library with me every now and then. Used computer for the first time.

Prophet is listed on FBI Most Wanted list. Our family is famous.

<u>July 4.</u>
New father found us after Mother and I snuck off this morning.
Beat me so hard I peed in my pants.
Got expelled from the church, my home, my family.

Dangled baby sister in my face.
You'll never see her again, he said.
He waved her in the air, I thought she'd get hurt.
Blue eyes, chubby pink hands grabbing for me, and brown sack dress hanging longer than her feet.

Mother didn't argue. Guess she loves her religion more than me.
Way to celebrate our country's birthday.

Jacob came after me. Brother, please take me with you. Crying. Only 10, a big baby. Knocked him down and ran as fast as I could. Can't condemn him to damnation.

<u>July 6.</u>
Slept in a field Tuesday night nailed by mosquitoes. Found abandoned shack. Don't know where to go or what to do. Find Father? But that was two years ago in Arizona.

<u>July 8.</u>
Scrounging for food but doing A.O.K. Know I can make it. Look older so can find work with cattle or construction. Can't leave Jacob, even if he will go to hell too. Going back for him asap.

<u>Aug 30.</u>
Road crew job, still hiding in shack. Safe to sneak back for Brother?

<u>Sep 2.</u>
Jacob came when I slipped in last night. He's brave. Mother caught us leaving and gave us a hug. Mothers shouldn't hug or kiss their children. Only one who should make a child feel valued is the Father or the Prophet. Right now, we don't have either.

Told Mother to come too. Still got 4 girls at home and new husband assigned. Second sister married this summer at 14, so one less. Even though Prophet wasn't around, he somehow assigned Sisters husband, 87 year old elder. At least he'll croak soon and Sister will be free. Until assigned to someone else.

<u>Sep 7.</u>
I bring in enough to rent a dump for us. Nobody asks for my papers. Road crew guy got fake ID for Jacob. Don't look like a Chili Choker alien so no problem. Got him in elementary school. First one in family for education.

I study on my own at the library when I have time. Would they let me into community college?

NINETEEN

Oleander red, foxglove purple, daffodil yellow—neon colors dancing through a sea of black. Skies and skin, Elephant Man faces, bloody stainless tables, grinning storyteller katsinas clutching dead babies.

Maya's legs locked into massive cramps, and she rolled out of bed to the cold, hard Saltillo tile floor. What the hell kind of dream was that?

She stretched both arms to grab the mattress and crawl up the side of the bed. Holding the footboard for stability, she paced out the throbbing contractions. Memories of beautiful flowers, sunrises, and sunsets alternated with gruesome deaths the last three months. She remembered with a start her vet school lecture on poisonous plants. Beauty masking death.

Her last day off from work was more than two weeks ago, but she was sleeping in her own bed for a few days, so why this nightmare?

She thought she was coping. Heroin-associated anthrax cases trickled in, with numbers declining as her epi curve had forecast. Outbreak slowly burned itself out, but one of every three patients was dead.

Yesterday the total case count blew past three hundred. Of the early cases included in her slide talks, two died after weeks of hospitalization and surgeries amputating more and more tissue— the teenage girl from Phoenix Children's Hospital and the Tucson homeless woman. These women had been alive and struggling with hidden demons, like Maya struggled with her own while condensing their lives to clinical and pathological data.

Her daily presentations were in dimmed rooms which amplified the shocking colors associated with destruction and death. She saw the mix of stoic and horrified faces in the audience. Her internal suffering couldn't compare with those whose stories she told.

The southwestern state laboratories and federal agencies worked overtime on anthrax. Heroin injected by the victims was no longer available for testing, but undercover cops confiscated any they could find on the street. If spores were isolated from the samples, genetic typing could help pinpoint the origin.

On the office computer, Maya checked for cases and stretched her legs, still sore from cramping and the tumble out of bed.

Erika's intensive efforts maintaining New Mexico's reportable diseases, including the state's heroin-associated anthrax, increased Maya's admiration for her colleague's diligence and dedication. She had no idea how someone juggled a two-career family and a young child. She could barely manage herself.

"Did you hear me?" Erika's demanding voice pierced her muddied musings. Maya's eyes jerked back from the high windows and her spine straightened. Vital to appear alert and engaged.

"Sorry, zoned out. Had one of my bad nightmares this morning."

"Not sure if this will help. We're taking Kyle trick or treating tomorrow. Hordes of screaming kids but you might enjoy it."

Energetic young life or devastating death. Not a hard choice.

"I should touch base with Manolo. We're trying to get together."

Erika grinned. "Invite him over. I'm dying to meet this *Hamilton* clone."

Maya's face lit up in alarm. "Don't you dare mention it. He gets reminded often enough."

"Maybe like Hamilton, he has a way with the ladies?"

"Can't say I know a lot about that." She opened up the east coast anthrax reports and focused on work to distract from her pattern of obsessive worrying.

At home when finished with her microwave dinner, she crawled into bed, a silk blanket with a large colorful crane draped around her body. She fretted about how to be bold and ask Manolo to visit. After tapping her phone, his charismatic face popped up on the videochat screen. Her heart rate rushed with anticipation.

"Maya, ¿qué tal?"

Reluctant to dampen the mood but determined to be more open about her feelings, she answered. "Had a bad night—not my typical truck nightmare. It was Dali anthrax mixed with impressionist skies and Milagro flowers."

"Lo siento, mi amor. ¿Cómo puedo ayudar?" On the screen, he was close enough to touch. His eyebrows were drawn together, a picture of concern. As usual, he was offering to help.

"Can you get away to Santa Fe? Dr. Grinwold approved me using comp days."

His magnetic smile brightened the melancholic night. "Me encantaría. ¿Cuándo?"

"Erika invited me—us—for Halloween." She broke eye contact. "Make it a long weekend?" There were several interpretations of the question but she decided not to clarify it.

Grinning, he cradled the phone and extricated a suitcase from the closet floor. "Moving to the 'meet the friends' zone?"

"Sí." She rocked back on the bed. "¿Por qué no?"

. . .

Although eager to reach the Sunport early, she watched the speed limit to avoid any State Police delays. After parking and noting his arrival gate, she glanced anxiously around the throng of passengers sweeping through the glass doors until spotting his dark hair and buoyant expression through the fog of other faces.

Natural hesitance in abeyance, she circled around a reuniting family and ran to his arms. "You're quite handsome today, Doctor."

He buried his face in her hair, then guided her into a leisurely, warm kiss.

"Only a bit more than a week, but feels way too long," he said.

"I agree." Her skin prickled as the crowds jostled them, and she broke the embrace.

He pointed to the baggage claim sign. "With this unpredictable fall weather, I checked a bag. Wasn't sure of your plans for me."

North of Albuquerque, she concentrated on her car's crawl up the thousand-foot rise of La Bajada Hill. She cowered in the far right lane as other vehicles rode her bumper and swerved around to the faster lanes. "My Prius struggles on this stretch. Your Corvette would take to it more."

"I'm escorted by a beautiful woman on a stunning day in the Land of Enchantment." He stretched his arm through the open window. "What more could a guy want?"

She gazed at the cloudless sky. "Erika says it can snow on Halloween, but I don't think we'll have any tonight. It's Indian Summer."

"I once tried to figure out that phrase."

"As only an amateur historian would." She refocused on the road ribbon. The area always generated visions of her car falling off backwards.

"An old novel said it represents a time when someone can recover the happiness of youth. The protagonist is jilted when young and doesn't find romance again until middle age."

"Nothing you'd know about," she said, hoping for a big reveal.

"Maybe."

By one o'clock, they pulled up to her apartment complex. She caught his slight frown as he glanced around the threadbare living room—window air conditioner, small table with two chairs, tiny TV on a microwave box, and a fraying couch.

"Santa Fe housing is expensive," she said. "This sleeper sofa isn't too bumpy." She looked away, wondering if he understood her intent.

Taking her hands, he turned her to face him. "What's important is this time with you."

They rode the bus to the Plaza, then ate burritos on one of the tree-shaded benches, shoulders and thighs touching. An exuberant toddler scrambled on the grass with two attentive young men rolling a ball. Traffic around the square lagged for jaywalking pedestrians.

He leaned back and put an arm around her shoulder. "I've never been here, so thanks for inviting me."

"In August, the Indian Market crowds were suffocating."

With a questioning expression, he gestured to the plain, concrete obelisk in the center.

"It's a monument to soldiers who fought 'savage' Indians," she said. "Someone gouged that word out."

"History versus political correctness, a long-standing battle."

"I think it's ugly and phallic." She blushed, still unused to expressing strong opinions. "They should replace it with a gazebo like in Albuquerque."

Shifting on the bench, she added, "On a more urgent issue, there's all these anthrax cases in different parts of Arizona in just a few months. Nothing before that."

He held her restless fingers. "We have known causes."

She vigorously shook her head. "We have explanations, but no real understanding. We need person, place and time," she ticked off on his forearm, "as we cite in epidemiology. Or 'who, what, when' as a news reporter would say. Our statistics confirmed contaminated Arizona brown heroin as the cause of the injection outbreak, but we still don't know how it happened."

"You should have been a detective." He traced stimulating circles in her palm.

Breaking the spell, she pulled him to his feet. "Well, they do call us medical detectives."

Tucking her arm around his waist, she guided him to the southwest corner of the Plaza for another Santa Fe tradition, ice cream at Baskin-Robbins. Back at the bench, he dipped into their shared banana split and scooped a spoonful for her. She followed his lead, offering the next bite to him.

"You're covered with whipped cream," he said with a smile.

"And who did that?"

He leaned over to lick her chin, nose, and lips. The toddler's ball bumped her feet and she bent away from Manolo, laughing. After she tossed the ball back, one of the men ran up.

"Thanks," he said. "Our son hasn't perfected his soccer kick yet."

Aware of the audience, she held Manolo's shoulders to keep him from coming in for another kiss. With a hurried swipe, she used her index finger to erase the cream from his lips. He grabbed her hand and put her finger in his mouth.

"Stop it," she admonished, dragging him to his feet. "Let me show you the Palace of the Governors, oldest continuously occupied public building in the country."

Holding hands, they explored the small rooms formed by thick adobe walls. She led him to the Segesser Hide paintings of Spanish colonial life. He tugged her over to the Pancho Villa clock stopped at 4:11 AM when hit by a bullet in the 1916 Columbus railway raid. They stood arm in arm at exhibits on New Mexico's atomic bomb legacy. Feeling sleepy in the dim rooms, they re-emerged to the front Portal lined with Native American artisans on chairs or blankets.

He stooped to pick up a pair of turquoise earrings. "Let me buy you something."

She demurred, fingering her small silver studs. "I never throw on much jewelry."

"Where are you from?" The regal Navajo artist wearing a striking turquoise and silver squash blossom necklace had assumed they were tourists. When learning Manolo worked for the IHS, the elder thanked him for the quality of care her husband received at Gallup Indian Medical Center before he died.

"I heard about the little girl with anthrax at the hospital. We appreciate your keeping it away from anyone else."

"We're lucky to have Dr. Maguire on the investigation," he replied, "but thanks for your vote of confidence."

"To keep your luck, the young lady should consider these bear claws."

Maya accepted the pair of beautiful silver earrings etched with black claw marks and embedded with a central turquoise stone. The artist gave her a small mirror to try them on.

"Bear claws are a good omen," he said while paying for his gift.

"I feel lucky already." She gave him a brief, self-conscious hug.

He tucked her hair behind her ears to display the jewelry more clearly. "Eres hermosa."

. . .

With low sun rays peeking around adobe homes, a tall, thin witch darkened the door opening, a man in a Superman cape looming behind.

"Double, double, toil and trouble," she cackled.

"Manolo, this is Erika and Rolf Anders."

Erika's sapphire eyes darted back to her husband before extending her hand. "We're happy you could join us."

Maya wasn't sure what their glances meant, but she hoped Manolo didn't notice.

"Is Kyle ready for trick-or-treating?" Maya asked as they entered.

"Better believe it," Rolf said with a faint German accent. "Where's Oggy?"

They peered around the spacious, two-story living room to search for the five-year-old. Giggles emerged from behind the couch before blue arms and a blue blob body crawled over it.

"This is Oggy, a famous cartoon cat," Erika explained to the confused couple.

"Meow." White gloves and tennis shoes, a lipsticked nose, and mascaraed whiskers completed the costume.

The Agua Fria neighborhood celebrated Halloween as seriously as Christmas. Real or fake farolito candles in tan paper bags lined rooftops and adobe walls. The nighttime weather was cool and a few families maintained luminaria bonfires in the street next to the sidewalks. Kids ran screaming from house to house for the candy treats. On their front porch, Erika left a help-yourself orange plastic pumpkin. Kyle's parents kept up with him while Maya and Manolo ambled behind.

"Your hand's cold. Mind if I warm it up?"

"Of course not." She wondered why he asked permission.

Instead of rubbing it with his hands, he brought it up to his face. He feathered hot breath over it, brushing his lips on each fingertip and her palm. Then he took the other one. She shivered, not from the cold.

He draped an arm around her shoulders. "Doing OK?"

"Muy bien, gracias."

"What do you think of all these rugrats?" His tone implied he was enjoying them.

"Entertaining when they're not mine." Her voice thickened. "I don't have anyone related to me biologically. So I'd like kids, someday."

He led her skipping to catch their hosts, visibly delighted by her answer. "I only have one sister, but an abundant extended family. Always assumed I'd have at least a couple."

She tilted her head, looking at him expectantly. "You're older, you could have started."

"Subject for another day." He picked up the pace and she hastened to keep up.

With a kindergartner on a school night, they were back to Erika's house by seven-thirty. Manolo and Rolf chatted about Meow Wolf, the interactive art attraction, while she joined Erika and Kyle after he changed to his Batman pajamas.

"Pick up your toys before bed." Erika stooped to help him.

"By the time I have a family, I'll need your advice. Don't even know how to change a diaper." Maya put Cowboy Woody on the shelf.

Erika laughed. "All parents say that, but we figure it out somehow. If we have a second one, you can practice."

Maya wrinkled her nose. "Can't be any worse than animal poop. By the way, what was the look you gave Rolf when meeting Manolo?"

"Just admiring your good taste."

"I agree." Maya decided to forgive her friend's teasing. "I think I'm besotted."

"Besotted?" Erika laughed heartily. Maya glanced at the door to make sure the men hadn't heard them.

"I have a crush." Her eyes danced. "Still don't know him well enough for anything more."

"Well, just keep going. Let nature take its course." Erika gave Kyle a kiss on the top of his head and turned down the adjustable light.

Back at Maya's apartment, apple pie and a chilled bottle of white wine tempted from her refrigerator interior. The lasagna before trick-or-treating was wearing off, but she was still on a Halloween candy sugar high. Manolo came up behind and nudged the door closed. "Flying always wipes me out. Mind if I turn in early?"

She pulled out sheets, blankets, and pillows and told him how to open the couch. Somehow, helping him make the bed would have been too intimate. Maybe he also thought things were moving too fast and wanted to wrap up the evening.

"What's planned for tomorrow?" he asked, lightly tracing the bare skin on her arm.

"Bandelier National Monument. I intended to go there before the injection anthrax."

"Sounds like a great idea."

His shutting down of the evening was countermanded by his long, passionate, goodnight kiss. No rushing for a plane or other staring eyes to interrupt. Their tongues danced before he stepped back a few inches.

"Hasta mañana, cariña."

. . .

His presence so close in the next room might have disturbed her sleep. Instead, it had the opposite effect. She had a rare night with no bad dreams. In the morning, he was in the hall with wet hair, dressed in a robe—much more bright and alert. She grinned as her finger muscles contracted in automatic typing of the term for a pet that was doing well. *Bright and alert.* It matched how she felt, too.

"Hope I didn't wake you," he said. "Rinsed off travel grime. I used your shampoo, but now my hair smells of hyacinth, or is it honeysuckle? Hibiscus?"

She smiled at his alliteration and let him pass into the living room.

They had an easygoing breakfast of cereal with strawberries before hitting the highway north toward Española. After crossing the Rio Grande River, the road began a circuitous climb flanked by taller trees. She anticipated Bandelier's entrance being crowded, but on a weekday, parking was available at the historic visitor's center.

"Glad I brought my hiking boots," he said. "Had a hunch you might want to walk sometime during our holiday."

The Main Loop Trail moved up in elevation along the sharp edge of a cliff wall with ancient alcoves carved into the volcanic tuff. The pit dwellings four hundred feet below on the canyon floor dated back eleven thousand years. He kept a tight arm around her when she felt unsteady looking down. In a few caves on the route, they spotted faded but colorful petroglyphs.

Down in the valley, the loop ended at a sign for the Alcove House. "We need to climb up over a hundred feet to reach it." She eyed the first of four long, wooden ladders. "As much as I love to walk, climbing is another matter."

"I got this, right behind you." His affirmative presence below her on each ladder rung gave her mental reinforcement. As she caught her breath at the top, they relaxed under the huge sandstone arch with expansive views of Frijoles Canyon. Sitting on a large flat rock, she countered dizziness by nestling back against his chest with legs and arms surrounding her.

"I can't believe that people eons ago lived up along this cliff wall," she said.

"It gave them protection from enemies." He showed her the brochure. "They could pull up the ladders rather than fight."

"More of a lover?" She leaned her head back to catch his expression, hoping he would take her comment as mild flirtation, nothing more.

"You got it," he laughed.

"Climate change and drought drove them out," she said. "The weather is still unstable with huge fires and floods here lately."

"A lot of people have to move due to climate change." He rocked her gently in a tight hug. "I wonder whether any humans will be alive to see our ruins."

At a small round kiva built into the cliff ledge, he cajoled her down a short ladder. Within close confines of the layered rock walls, she shivered.

He rubbed her arms with swift strokes. "What's wrong?"

"I just remembered. It's All Saints' Day, El Día de los Muertos."

"You can sense the ancestors' spirits in this place," he agreed.

Her head started to spin as she scrambled back up into the open air. She had enough high places and long views. "Want to have lunch in Española? I know a café recommended on Tripadvisor."

He laughed, running his fingers through the loose strands of her hair. "Is that your bible?"

"You know I'm a researcher. Just helps me do my due diligence." She separated from his embrace and headed toward the cliff edge.

Pausing near the top of the first ladder, she gasped at the vertical drop. "This was a mistake. Everything that goes up must come down, and gravity is not my friend."

"Turn around and face the rock wall," he advised her, "and keep your eyes glued to it straight in front. I'll go first and will stay close."

When reaching each flat area between ladders, he stroked her back until her breathing stabilized. Then they repeated the process, his head just below her, aligned with her feet.

"Just don't kick me," he reminded her halfway down as her legs trembled.

"Make sure my feet are in the right spot. No need to look any higher."

"Can't help it, eres guapa."

At the bottom, she circled his waist and spun with joy to celebrate their safe descent.

"Remind me to wait awhile before we do that again." She pressed her hand to her heart and tried to slow its rate.

As she navigated the steep, curvy drive back down to the Rio Grande Valley, a few aspen leaves flashed gold on the roadside amid the pines. At the tiny adobe restaurant, Manolo complimented the waiter's eagle tattoo when the bare arm slipped plates on the table.

The young Native American, left half of his head buzz cut, thanked him.

"My mother makes black Santa Clara Pueblo pottery, and this is based on one of her designs."

He rotated his forearm to show off the psychedelic pattern. "My own inspiration for the colors."

"Does it mean something special to you?" Manolo asked.

"Courage, wisdom, strength. The eagle is a leader among men."

Manolo shook his hand. "Good goals for all of us. Including women," he added as the waiter turned back to the kitchen.

"Speaking of high aspirations . . ." He scrunched next to her in the booth, left hand on her thigh, sharing fajita bites with his right. "What got you into vet med?"

"I had two cats, a small Lab-Beagle mix, and a parakeet." She returned the favor, placing a piece of soft sopapilla dripping honey between his lips. "My folks thought pets would distract me during the long periods of bed rest as my injuries healed. Along with the music lessons, they were a big help."

"When did you figure out that's the career you wanted?"

"Not until college."

Hours immersed in melodies and chords instead of school

books—frivolous, timid, unstable. Nothing like her mother, who was always in control.

As she gazed through frilly lace curtains to the ruddy hills beyond the parking lot, his hand opened up to cup her hip and she flinched. Her flesh yearned for his touch, but there were brief moments when she was repelled. His personal panda. Was he enchanted with the exotic Asian girl myth?

Only once before had someone been so intimate. Her first college party with too many tasty drinks. She pushed aside the remembered sensation. Not the time to divulge details.

"I was sixteen, living in a CU Boulder dorm over Mom's objection. First time alone since my childhood hospitalization, and it was a reality shock. I had no piano, and my overloaded hamster brain strained to keep up with the college courses."

Pounding narco beats reverberated through the open window as a black lightning-streaked lowrider bounced on by. That was confidence. Look at me, the souped up car shouted. Her legs still quivered from scaling Bandelier cliffs like Native Americans a thousand years earlier. But she had fought the fear, if climbing four ladders counted.

Tugging his hand out from under the table, she passed over the plasticized dessert menu to change his focus. "Still hungry?"

Her fingers twirled the lace curtain edge. "I was frantic about which direction to take. My hyper-achieving mom didn't have much advice. Probably afraid to fight about it."

He set the menu aside. "When I was a kid, I didn't play doctor, except for one thwarted attempt with MaryAnn Williams."

Was that snarky comment intended to put her at ease?

Her mind meandered back to the mysterious kiva carved out of the volcanic tuff more than a hundred feet above Frijoles Creek. Everything couldn't be explained by science.

"During winter break in freshman year, we were eating lunch while cross-country skiing near Vail Pass. Dad told me I was born at the end of Aquarius—air sign, intellectual and curious. On the cusp of Pisces—water sign, intuitive and emotional. I would choose something requiring life-long learning, but a career that resonated in my heart."

"What did your formidable mom say?"

"She blew up about his use of astrology. When I returned to school, the counselors suggested medicine. I'm not exactly a people person, so I picked pre-vet."

Moving his hand to her chin, he turned her to look deep in his eyes. "Wise choice, you're all those things your dad said."

She pivoted away and scrubbed sticky fingers with the red cotton napkin. "I don't feel particularly smart. I'm still having palpitations about all this anthrax."

With a smile of sympathy, he caressed her arm. "Water sign?"

Digits still tacky, she winced. "Day of the Dead."

TWENTY

<u>Nov 8, 2006.</u>
Mother has a new fourth husband assigned by our Prophet.
How does he make that happen, even though he's locked up?

Convicted of rape and sentenced 10 years to life.
I know what that means now.

TWENTY-ONE

As they approached the Santuario de Chimayó, New Mexico's most famous church, Maya's iPhone rang and she swerved her Prius to a dirt shoulder.

"Remember the UU Minister in August?" the Pima County epidemiologist asked. "Now her daughter's hospitalized and receiving antitoxin for cutaneous anthrax on her hands."

Maya set the phone on the dash. "Two months later, how could that happen?" She remembered Reverend Tompkins, raising a child alone and trying to prevent other kids from dying of thirst in the desert.

"You don't need to come down." Janey Johnson sounded reassuring. "We talked to Dr. Schwartz and will follow his USDA protocol for soil sampling. We're also checking the Reverend's gear for anthrax spores."

"Secondary case," Manolo said after the call. "Common in other diseases, but not anthrax."

"Does Arizona take pride in being first for everything on this disease?" Maya shook her head and massaged her fingers in sympathy for young Cecilia. "Reverend Sophia recovered. There's no way for a mother to transmit anthrax to her daughter."

. . .

She heard about the healing power of Santuario soil and needed it for the bad news from Tucson. They stepped through the hand-rounded adobe arch and walked in silence down flagstone steps to the central nave. Then they entered el pocito, the little well, and Manolo put a donation in the box in exchange for the plastic bag.

As he scooped up a small amount of the sacred soil from the ground, she gave him a wan smile in appreciation of his effort to help her chronic pain. But outside, whipping winds and charcoal clouds were eerie, and she could only think of nesting back home.

They finished leftover lasagna and a bottle of Cabernet Sauvignon at her apartment while the sun slipped below the horizon. After cleaning up, they cuddled on the couch and he held her hands. Alcohol countering inhibitions, she cast the die on diving into the unknowns between them. The light in the living room was dim with only one lamp—intended to be romantic but instead El Día de los Muertos moody.

"I'm missing something about anthrax." Her tone was fierce as she twisted away. "And something about you."

"What do you mean?" He shifted to face her.

"Our first dinner in Phoenix, you said you'd share more the next time. At the Milagro restaurant, you told me about your mother but not much more. At Sky Harbor when you asked about making our relationship personal, I thought it meant getting to know each other."

"We're doing that here in Santa Fe," he said with a frown.

"Last night, you started a discussion about kids, but changed the subject. Today, all we talked about was me."

As he slumped, his fingers traced the pattern in the afghan throw. "What do you want to know?"

"You might have focused on school and work like me, instead of personal relationships." Her speech was rapid and slurred as she pushed to expel her gremlins. "But you're much more outgoing, so I'm guessing you're not celibate."

Before he could answer, she had a horrible thought. "You're married."

There was a notable pause before he answered, "No."

She grimaced and her tone was higher. "I *know* I'm immature. I haven't dated and I'm twenty-five. You're thirty-two and I don't believe you waited for me to come along."

Drawing back further, he looked as if she'd slapped him. He rubbed closed eyes and muttered words so indistinct, she almost didn't understand them. "You're right, I was married. I'm divorced."

Her head swam. She was falling into the basement, if she had one. "Okay, how long?"

"How long what?" came the staccato response.

"You're driving me nuts," she shouted, leaping up. "How long for both, the marriage and the divorce?"

With force, he scrubbed his forehead, then fingers scraped back through his hair.

"I said I was distraught after Mom died. Threw myself into school and that was enough. Med school was way more challenging. I yearned for personal support, and Angela was there."

She turned back to stand like a stone statue. "Angela," she parroted.

"We met at a party. She was in med school, too, from a politically connected D.C. family. I needed a rock, and she provided it. When you say you're immature, I was worse. Never should have married at twenty-four."

Like a puppy caught shredding the upholstery, he sank into the couch, sodden eyes begging for understanding. She poured another glass of wine, took a long sip, and sat down next to him, taking his hands.

"Talk to me, I won't bite," she said in a quieter tone.

"There were issues. We discussed the future, but couldn't agree. I had my commitment to the Public Health Service. She had more flexibility but insisted we stay in Washington. As she developed a high stakes cardiac transplant surgery career, she wanted me to move up the military medical ranks. We'd be a wealthy power couple. It was apparent she didn't want children, ever."

Her body went completely still. "I can't even—"

His words stuttered out. "She supported me emotionally and financially all those years . . . just couldn't wrap my head around the life she planned. I'm grateful and respect the outstanding career woman she's become . . . helping a lot of people."

"What happened, exactly?"

"I requested an end to the marriage." His jaw muscles tensed as he gritted his teeth. "She was outraged, didn't believe me, and refused. I took the position with Indian Health Service and left."

She fiddled with her earlobe. "You've been in Phoenix a year?"

"Yes, and she obstructed the divorce process, but now it's final."

Despite her spinning head from wine and the surprising story, she added things up. "You were married for, what, about eight years?"

"But I've lived alone for a year. The marriage essentially ended when I left."

"Essentially?" She rose again, hugging a couch pillow to her chest. "Did I imagine you were flirting on our anthrax investigations this summer?"

He grabbed her shoulders and turned her around. Their eyes locked and she took in his pleading smile. "You're right, I was attracted to you at the hospital doorstep when we met." He caressed her cheek.

Her ribs tightened as she thrust his hand down. "And when was your divorce final?"

"A few days ago."

She slammed the pillow to his chest and broke away.

"You start a relationship with me, and *then* you get divorced."

Recoiled in a kitchen chair, she lifted her legs up within the tight embrace of her own arms and tugged the loose skirt of her caftan down to her ankles. Like a ping pong ball, she imagined a heavy spin through the darkened window.

"I didn't plan this," he said in a strained voice. "I met you when I met you."

He poured himself another full glass of wine and ran his finger around the rim before downing it in one gulp. When he turned back, he had tears in his eyes.

"I'm not trying to replace Angela. I told you I'm a deliberately optimistic person, and strong, in a good place. You are you, with no relation to her."

He stopped talking, wrapped his forearms around his neck, and leaned forward, as if he couldn't stand. "I'm starting to fall in love with you and can't help the timing."

Love? He must be kidding. She glared out the window. Tree branches lashed the window panes like skeletal fingers.

"All those times together since early August, there wasn't any point where you could say something?"

"I was a coward." He stood straighter and attempted to recapture her focus. "I fell for you hard and fast but couldn't figure out the right time to bring it up. We started out more professional than personal and I sensed that's how you wanted it."

With a strangled laugh, she gave herself up to the pull of haunting darkness. Was it the wine, or the stormy night?

"I didn't know *what* I wanted, but you're right, I wanted it slow."

He approached her chair, reaching to stroke her hair. "It's just paperwork, and all finished."

She leapt up, shoving him aside. "I realize this doesn't make me a twenty-first century woman, but I'm not comfortable with how this went down. You started things with me when you weren't done with your marriage."

Shaking his head in denial, he grabbed her arm again. "I was separated. I *was* done with it."

"You deceived me." With her right hand, she massaged her chest while she rubbed the base of her skull with the left.

The sad puppy transformed into a pitbull. "I'm not the only one holding back important information. You responded to me when I touched you. I didn't imagine it. Just how inexperienced are you?"

Her limbs quaked like wind-lashed vines, but his strong grip kept her from collapsing. No success in pushing him away. "I don't have a clue how to deal with this, and I'm too drunk to answer your questions. But you can't stay here."

He lowered her to the chair and pulled out his cell phone. "I'll change my flight."

Nerve-racking silence engulfed the room until bright lights of a cab bounced through the window.

"Maya, I'm sorry."

The door made a final, muffled click. She tried to convince herself she didn't care enough to be really upset, until tears welled up in her eyes and she crawled into bed. When she came to New Mexico, the sole focus was becoming a competent contributor to public health. Saving lives, making the world a better place. She should have stuck to that plan, been more in control, and not allow this attraction to happen.

Pressing her head into the pillow, she felt the bear claw earrings and yanked them off to drop in the end table drawer. Magic dirt from Chimayó mounded the tabletop. Where was the healing power now? She tossed the bag into the trash can and lay awake most of the night, trying to hush her brain and quell her churning body.

· · ·

In the morning, she poured milk over shredded wheat and pretended nothing had changed. Her stomach pinched like it had been forced to digest food from a room temperature buffet. Probably stress or a hangover, not coming down with something.

Catching up at work was the right thing to do. Using limited vacation hours made no sense after he left. Glancing at the clock, she realized with a start they were scheduled to join Stephanie for breakfast. She texted to cancel but Stephanie called back.

"What's going on? You wanted me to meet Manolo."

Maya answered by rote in a monotone. "We broke up. Guess you could call it that. We weren't ever together, but yeah."

"I'm stopping over." Stephanie's voice was high-pitched, spilling over with concern.

"Don't bother, I'm coming into the office." But the call disconnected before she finished warning off her friend.

Twenty minutes later, Stephanie and Erika were at her front door as Maya grabbed her purse, ready to head out.

"I won't apologize for butting in," Erika said. "What happened? I thought you guys had something special the other night."

Stephanie led Maya to the couch, then she and Erika sat on either side.

"Spill the beans," Erika said in her blunt manner.

"He told me he was married." At her friends' expressions, she swiftly clarified. "*Was*, not is. His divorce was final a few days ago."

"So that's why he's thirty-two and still available." Stephanie seemed like she was attempting a joke.

"He's divorced, what's the problem?" Erika pressed on.

"He was married for eight years, most of his adult life. She put him through med school. She's a cardiac surgeon, no less."

"Rolf's my second husband. I married young, broke up, moved to Santa Fe and met him here. Divorce isn't the end of the world these days."

Maya felt a lump forming in her throat. "I'm not comfortable as his rebound. And he was making love to me—"

She spotted Erika's eyebrows arching toward her hairline. "No, not that yet. Sweet and sexy, he seduced me while still married. He said it was a technicality, but I knew nothing about it. Makes me question what else I don't know."

Erika grabbed a glass of juice from the refrigerator. Turning back, she was direct. "Love doesn't come with a plan. You wanted to go slow, so do it. Don't throw the baby out with the bathwater."

The cliché provided a painful reminder that Maya had imagined mini Lin-Manuels running around one day. They were just on different trajectories and timelines. Her focus needed to be on work. Fantasy clobbered by reality.

She gave them hugs and pushed them toward the front door. "I appreciate your checking on me. It's not like anything happened between us. Not much to lose." As she said it, she knew that wasn't quite true. They hadn't been intimate physically, but both of their emotions had jumped the gate.

Stephanie offered to give her a ride to work.

"I've decided to decompress." She hugged them again after they stepped out to the parking lot. "See you Monday."

She grabbed an afghan, snuggled into the couch, and turned on the TV. What kind of old movie would be an effective distraction for alcohol withdrawal and a sort-of-broken heart?

. . .

Her first Santa Fe snowstorm started Friday night and she was relieved Manolo didn't get stuck at her home. A binge weekend with *Breaking Bad* erased any remaining romantic yearnings.

November 5 dawned gray and gloomy, leaving her chilled when the office phone rang at nine.

"Hey, long time no talk." Dave's taciturn drawl sounded wary, even though they had broken the ice during the heroin outbreak. "They're dragging me into something at the Mexican border again. I could use your help."

Her pulse increased. Between her inebriated fight with Manolo and getting crosswise with Dave over the holiday-themed petting zoo, nothing was working out. But for this request, there were no personal complications. She grabbed her pen and pad to take notes.

"I'll see what's feasible."

Based on Dave's expertise with anthrax, the Arizona Game and Fish Department had contacted USDA earlier in the morning. The Cabeza Prieta National Wildlife Refuge was further west along the border than the area they investigated around Labor Day.

"Endangered animals this time. The refuge has an important captive breeding program for a subspecies of Sonoran pronghorns."

Border refuges had been unlucky for their team, with the reprimand on cache sampling. She dreaded being drawn back there again.

"What happened?" She prayed it was just animals and not people.

"Several dead antelope last week. They hate to lose any with only a hundred-fifty remaining on this side of the border. Got initial lab results for anthrax on one of them."

"Are you doing animal and soil surveillance again?"

"Gets worse." He cleared his throat. "There was an invitation-only raw meat feast in Ajo last week. Guys on the paleo diet are into it. All legally hunted animals—deer, rabbits, captive buffalo. But the preliminary anthrax results got out, and some participants admitted there was pronghorn."

She blanked, unable to recall all the particular wrinkles for ingestion and anthrax. "Do you want my help with that part of it?"

"I know you need approval. Fortunately, I hear your two State Epidemiologists are good buddies."

After he hung up, she stopped by Erika's office to verify she could coordinate the lower rate of injection anthrax on her own if Maya went to Arizona.

The statuesque blonde swiveled away from her computer screen. "I've been thinking about your situation." She offered Maya the guest chair.

"I didn't criticize Manolo on Friday, but his withholding information has been gnawing at me. Dating a colleague complicates things. I talked about it with Rolf. We think you're getting a raw deal."

Rolf dissecting her love life—Maya writhed in her seat.

Erika's expression turned sour. "I've got a workplace complaint on file with Human Resources. A guy over in Chronic Diseases harassed me. Dr. Grinwold's not his boss and can't do anything. Dude's supposed to stay away from me, but we're not a huge department and I still see him occasionally."

Maya leaned forward. "That's awful. I remember you said you wanted to leave."

"This guy's just one of many dirtbags. I don't have a great

opinion about men out here in the macho west. Lucky for me, Rolf's the rare exception."

"I can't imagine this looming over you at work every day."

"You know I don't have a problem with divorce." At Erika's reminder of their conversation in her apartment, Maya sat back, realizing the focus had returned to her.

Erika tossed her hair, stern blue gaze nailing Maya. "Manolo's been stringing you along. When would you hear about this huge chunk of his life? After you'd slept with him?"

Maya's chin quivered. "You're verbalizing some of the worries I've been pushing aside."

"Manolo won't be involved in your trip and Dave's not a problem?"

"Yes to both. Dave's in love with his wife and kids. And he's respectful and collaborative." She rubbed the bridge of her nose, trying to reassure herself. "Although we've had a few differences of opinion."

Erika patted her on the shoulder. "You're young, hold out for one of the good guys."

. . .

Despite driving snow and poor visibility in Albuquerque, the flight for Tucson got off the ground. Even with cooler November temperatures, the Arizona desert still bloomed with purple mounds of Texas ranger blossoms and the slender waving green stalks of the orange Bird of Paradise.

"Game and Fish will probably take us around." Dave booked a high clearance rental SUV. "But this is rough country, so I want to be prepared."

As he pulled out on the highway, she yanked her cap down and slipped on her sunglasses to avoid the headache-inducing Arizona sun. Finally alone without a public audience, it was time to address the elephant in the room.

"Can we clear the air about Holiday Home?" she asked.

His fingers tightened on the steering wheel. "We disagreed about when to close them, but they're shut down now."

"You were more aggressive about control with the Koopees."

The stubborn tone continued. "Holiday Home had more to lose financially."

Prolong the argument? "I don't think we should compromise our judgment based on political pressure."

He glanced over, still implacable. "Why can't people go to their representatives if they need something? And my work was under more scrutiny after our cache crisis. Wouldn't help if I got fired for disobeying a direct order."

Reviewing his point, she vacillated on how to respond.

"We advocate for what we think is right," he said. "Then we acknowledge that others can have the final say. Hard for me to accept, but we work in a bureaucracy."

"Play the game to score points?" She pretended to shoot a basketball toward the windshield.

He gave her a faint smile. "You're figuring it out."

She didn't agree but her respect for his experience prompted letting Holiday Home go. "Does it bother you the only place in the country with human anthrax is Arizona? Except for the heroin cases in other states, but they're related to drugs here."

"Ever hear of the Texas Triangle of Death? Those are the counties with the most confirmed animal anthrax cases. My home area." He drummed his fingers on the door jam in time with the latest Luke Combs' release *She Got the Best of Me.*

"Studies demonstrate changes in distribution for many diseases with weirding weather," he said. "Some Texas ranches lost more than half of their captive deer herds to anthrax. We accept the risk and use sensible management practices."

Beneath the strain of the seat belt, she swiveled to face him. "Like what?"

"If deer and livestock become too numerous, they graze close to the ground, disturbing the soil. We raise the level of feeders or put material under them. Vaccine controls the risk in cattle, but we don't have one for deer or antelope."

"So you're not freaked out."

He slouched against the SUV door jamb, seat pulled far back to accommodate his long legs. "You're right, it's strange, especially the heroin. Who knows what the Mexican cartels are up to?"

"I can't shake a bad feeling about this." She turned away and traced the dust on the passenger window with her fingers. "Not very scientific, but maybe epi hunches are an unconscious processing of disease patterns."

"Rooting for you to be wrong," he said. "You're just a worrywart."

. . .

They stopped at the Ajo refuge headquarters where a state Game and Fish officer helped transfer sampling equipment into the covered bed of the government truck. Maya's energy level was low despite the cooler air in the shadow of the building behind the lowering sun. "Can we wait until tomorrow?"

The twenty-something officer rocked to his toes, meeting her at eye level. "No problema, señorita. We'll locate the spots where we found the dead pronghorns by dark."

Before they all jammed into the front seat, he had them sign a waiver acknowledging they could run into unexploded military ordnance and dangerous drug dealers.

Two pronghorn fatalities were near the Camino del Diablo close to the Mexican border, and their guide hadn't found the sites when the sun dipped behind low hills. "Thought we marked 'em better than this," he said with an apologetic glance past Maya to Dave.

The road soon became a tunnel of darkness lit only by bouncing headlights as the vehicle heaved like a roller coaster over rocks and ruts. A road sign sprang into view. "Illegal entry and drug smuggling activities are common within the refuge. Do not travel alone or approach suspicious people or activities."

When the officer increased his speed, her stomach quivered with motion sickness at the jerky shifts of direction. After one walloping leap of the vehicle into the air off a rocky ledge, they painfully whacked the cab roof despite their seat belts. She grabbed Dave's arm to keep from bouncing again when the truck landed with a loud bang on a high- centered boulder. The engine and all the lights promptly died.

"Fuck." The officer whacked the steering wheel.

Dave snatched his phone from the bag on the floor. "Should I call someone?"

"Cell phones don't work here," came the truculent response.

"What can we do now?" She chose a calm tone to counteract the rush hour traffic of blood at high speed through every artery and vein.

"I wouldn't recommend getting out of the truck. Rattlers are thick as your arm and long as your body."

She unbuckled her seat belt and shifted closer to Dave. Was the state warden exaggerating just a bit for effect?

Swiveling his head to look directly at her, the officer said, "And you won't be comfortable with a leg full of cactus spines."

"'Everything in the desert either bites, stabs, sticks, stings or stinks,'" Dave replied in a monotone. The quote was familiar. Her dad was a big fan of Edward Abbey, deceased environmental gadfly. Perhaps Dave wasn't one hundred percent the conservative rancher he made out to be.

"There's emergency beacons with water stashes." Their guide unbuckled his own seat belt and unlocked his door. "Going to grab a flashlight and find one. That will orient me with my map to our position. Plus, we'll have more water if we run out of what's stored in the back. You two drink a lot?"

This guy was getting more and more annoying. Crowded on the front bench seat, their bodies emanated musty sweat, and the air was stale. With the truck dead, the electronic mechanism to roll down the windows wasn't working. They could open the truck doors, but that might invite wayward bats—or worse—to pass through.

The officer for the first time also appeared apprehensive as he prepared to leave. "Don't worry, I'll be back soon."

He hadn't returned in the last unnervingly quiet and inky black twenty minutes. They popped the doors to reduce the ripe aroma. Like a runaway train bearing down on them tied to the tracks, lights and a deafening engine roar flooded the vehicle compartment. Were they about to be run over by a drug gang?

TWENTY-TWO

<u>Dec 25.</u>
Tried to sneak into ranch for Christmas,
but Mother only wants to see Jacob.

She doesn't like my smoking and drinking. What the fuck am I
supposed to do?

I think I'm doing pretty good. Knew nothing about the world.
Here outside, people will manipulate you, cheat you.
Get kicked out from home, burn in hell for all eternity.

TWENTY-THREE

"Dave, do you have any firepower?" As the rotating sound of helicopter blades became clear, she scrunched her thin frame lower on the truck bench seat.

"Nope, but I can use anything the warden might have." Hunched down, he explored underneath. Pulling out a pack of cigarettes, he shakily shook one out and put it between his lips. "What I'd give for a lighter or match right now, 'cept I recently gave 'em up."

Exploring the glove box and passenger door panel, he asked, "Can you feel anything on the driver's side?"

She stretched from her middle seat under the steering wheel, shaking off dirty napkins and candy wrappers sticking to her fingers. "Nothing useful here, unless we can gross them to death."

Glaring lights shafting through the cab hampered their vision, but she noted the rifle hanging behind them over the rear window.

"Dave, I'm really not willing to lose my life to coyotes, and I'm not talking about the animal kind." She pointed to the weapon.

He started to reach up for it, then hesitated. "They'll have more of those than me. Been accused of being reckless, but not totally crazy."

The whirring noise above grew louder. "Coyotes smuggling people or drugs wouldn't want to be this visible," he shouted. "Probably La Migra. Safer to be without a weapon in my hand when they get here."

More lights flooded the compartment from multiple angles.

"Out the doors, hands on your head!" The disembodied order was barked behind them in English. Agents with guns drawn surrounded the vehicle on both sides—Maya could narrowly make out the dark green Border Patrol uniforms.

She crawled out the driver's side door while keeping hands visible above her head, spotting Dave on the other side. An agent grabbed her bare arms and roughly bent her over the hood. Pulling her hands behind, he locked cuffs around her wrists.

"You're in a state Game and Fish truck on federal land but not in their uniform," he yelled in her ear. "Who the hell are you and what are you doing here?"

When a second agent waved he had Dave under control, the helicopter backed off and landed a few hundred yards away. Once the aircraft engine was cut, the noise level diminished to the idling motors of three border patrol vehicles.

"We're feds, too." She twisted her head, trying to placate the beefy officer leaning on her from behind. "CDC and USDA."

"What?" the confused voice bellowed. "Where's Game and Fish?"

Before she could answer, their adventurous driver returned, escorted by two CBP officers. They allowed him to pull out his identification and vouch for his guests.

After their IDs were also checked, the cuffs were removed. The Border Patrol was incredulous that the three of them were exploring Camino Del Diablo at night for soil sampling, especially when the pronghorn carcasses were no longer there.

One of them crawled under the truck and the verdict was in. The vehicle was going nowhere.

As CBP agents relaxed and chewed out the state officer, Maya climbed back into the front seat, fuming. The trip *was* a bad idea—not smart to be deferential about heading out so late in the day.

Dave retrieved his equipment and CBP provided a jeep ride to their rental vehicle in the parking lot. At ten o'clock, disgruntled, dusty, and famished, they spotted an open aging Ajo café.

Turning off the SUV, he appeared sheepish about another border debacle. "Eat first, then find a place to stay?"

She nodded in weary agreement. The warm ham and cheese takeout sandwich filled her belly but made her sleepy. The nearby La Siesta motel provided what they both needed.

. . .

The next morning, a sturdy middle-aged Game and Fish officer met them at the headquarters with a new state jeep.

"Sarah Vaughn," she said as she offered her hand. "Sorry about my newbie's recklessness."

"My fumble, too." Dave looked over at Maya. "Eager to go out there."

As they renewed their search, the sere landscape burned with blazing morning light and was no less intimidating than the night before. Sarah slowed to park on a rutted pullout and soon had binoculars on a distant pronghorn. When she passed over the binocs, Maya spotted the tan animal, black and white bands across the neck, belly and rump. The black cheek patches and black horns indicated a male.

"What a beauty," Maya said as Dave did his own scoping.

Sarah turned west on Charlie Bell Road for a more accessible area where a dead antelope had been found. "Locals say Edward Abbey is buried somewhere here. You guys know who he is?"

Maya smiled. "We both grew up here in the Southwest."

"Hope I'm sampling anthrax and not ecoterrorist ashes," Dave muttered from the back.

She turned in her seat to verify he was joking. "He was an author. It wasn't his fault he inspired ecoactivists."

"Caused some disruption himself," he said. "Pulled up survey stakes in Arches National Monument."

When they stopped again, he collected soil in the area Sarah indicated. Maya admired the geometric pictographs painted on the volcanic rocks. Animal shapes were recognizable, but it was strange how the humanoid figures looked like ancient aliens. She took careful steps around the green-brown cholla jumping cactus and its long-barbed spines.

Sampling was complete on Charlie Bell and Dave asked to inspect the three carcasses in the headquarters walk-in freezer, before revisiting last night's Devil road.

"We necropsy all dead pronghorns," Sarah explained. "In hindsight, it wasn't safe to open up an antelope with anthrax, but we didn't know it was an issue. We've done extensive disinfecting."

The transparent, sealed frozen bags displayed hemorrhagic organs like those Maya had seen in August at Danny's autopsy. Lots of anthrax events since then. Too coincidental to be unconnected?

For the afternoon, they made a decision to divide and conquer. Dave went back out to Camino del Diablo with Officer Vaughn to find the sites they hadn't reached the night before. Maya took the rental vehicle to start on the raw meat party interviews.

Her fingers tapped the steering wheel as she drove out alone and vulnerable for the first time on any disease investigation. Should she try to call Dave and let him know each address where she was headed, in case anything happened and she didn't return? But it was ridiculous—he wouldn't feel the need to do that during his own field work, and his cell phone service might be sketchy.

She located the party host in the Ajo taxidermy shop behind his small adobe home. Wiry with disheveled, gray-flecked hair, he wore a long-sleeved black shirt, blue jeans, and a mottled tan apron stained by bodily fluids. As he processed a deer, blood and water drained to a hole in the concrete floor.

"Mr. Kimball, I'm Dr. Maya Maguire, a veterinarian with the Centers for Disease Control and Prevention." She decided not to initiate a shake of his bloody hand, and he didn't offer it. "I'm not law enforcement and don't want to get anyone in trouble. I have some questions about your raw meat party last week."

"Yeah, we had it here."

Her eyebrows raised as she glanced around the filthy building.

The taxidermist looked offended by her expression. "I cleaned it up, there were folding tables. We had local game animals. After hearing about the antelope dying from anthrax, one guy admitted he brought some."

He started skinning the deer again with his long knife. "Not gonna tell you who did it."

Trying to project a relaxed posture, she shifted her weight. As a civilian working in the field, she was allowed to dress in jeans. If Commissioned Corps like Manolo and some EIS Officers, she'd be in a PHS uniform. Counterproductive in this environment.

"I'm concerned about those who ate here. If eating raw or undercooked meat from an infected animal, you can swallow the spores."

How much more federal grilling would he accept? "Spores can cause bleeding and other problems in your throat, esophagus, stomach and intestines within a couple of days up to a week. If not treated, more than half of those infected will die."

"You're shittin' me." He amplified the force and speed of his slashes.

"Did you hear anything about the animal? Was it a healthy one he shot or a fresh carcass he found? Where was it processed?"

"Don't know nothin' 'bout that."

As he hacked at the deer, his face appeared uneasy. "They make it impossible to get a permit and hunt one. So he took it. Don't matter to me where it came from."

"Today is the sixth. When was the party?"

"Halloween." The answer was a low, barely audible animal grunt.

"Okay, we're a week out. I need to reach everyone and verify you're healthy with no compatible clinical signs."

He stabbed the tip of the knife into the wooden bench. "The names and phone numbers won't tell you who did it."

Her heart raced. Maybe he was going to cooperate, if she could just encourage him. "My interviews are confidential. I won't report who's involved."

CDC lawyers struggled over these issues. Sometimes court orders and Freedom of Information requests forced release of more than they wanted to provide. But it was rare. They protected identifying data even for the owners of infected animals. That gave their attorneys stomach pains. Her primary job was epidemiology, requiring analysis of patterns, not public identification of individuals.

Trying to establish some level of trust and reciprocity, she ran through the list of gastrointestinal anthrax signs and symptoms. He didn't report fever or chills, headache, swelling of his neck or glands, sore throat, painful swallowing, or hoarseness. No nausea, stomach pains, abdominal tenderness, vomiting, or diarrhea.

"As a vet, I can't give you a checkup."

Awkward thing to say, and she ducked her eyes, slipping the small notebook into her pocket and pulling out her CDC business card. "But it sounds good for you. If anything changes, seek medical attention and mention anthrax as a rule-out. Here's my contact info if you have any questions."

She set the card on a chair and decided to ramp up her charm. The guy and his aggressive hacking made her nervous. Nobody knew where she was. Did the ends justify the means of pretending more friendliness than she felt? Making direct eye contact, she forced a broad smile. "Any chance you could give me the list now?"

He picked up the knife and removed the lungs from the chest cavity. She waited, recognizing his need to feel in charge of the decision. Finally, he dropped the blade to the bench and let the carcass fall to the floor. From a rusted metal desk in the corner, he plucked a torn yellow page stained with blood.

"Tell 'em I'm vouching for you." For the first time, he smiled back.

Deciding to take advantage of his interest, she touched his hand. "A lot of vets hate gloves because we lose tactile control, but wearing them can keep you safe. I don't want anything bad to happen to you."

After hopping back into the driver's seat of her vehicle, she took deep breaths and scrubbed her hands with sanitizer. She pathologically avoided all conflict, but within a few days she had fought with Manolo, confronted Dave on caving to authority, and played the flirtatious female to an unsettling man hacking apart an animal. What was anthrax doing to her?

For the rest of the day, she worked down the list. There were no women. This was their version of a knitting circle or the big boys' night out on the little kids' holiday, involving a banker, bodybuilder, sheriff's deputy, hunting guide, rancher, and cook.

The deputy was a challenge. He glowered from his antique chair, clearly unhappy at being questioned. Perched on the edge of his desk, she double downed on her earlier flirtation success, and asked about his interesting cases.

Everyone respected their party host and was cooperative, also healthy. Some reported other medical issues, but nothing pointed to gastrointestinal anthrax. Locating the rancher required a trip out of town, but the four-wheel-drive worked fine, and she completed the interview by five o'clock.

· · ·

From a distance, she spotted Dave lounging against the refuge headquarters, one booted foot up against the adobe wall, rumpled cowboy hat pulled down over his eyes, and drinking something from a Styrofoam cup. Doing his carefree, Sam Shepard impression again. The actor was on her mind, having died just a year earlier, and living so many years in the Southwest. He'd been a playwright and director, too. How many more sides of Dave didn't she know about? Both men in her life were too enigmatic.

"Productive day?" she asked as he hopped into the passenger side.

At the same café near the motel, they ordered Negra Modelos followed by dinner, and he filled her in.

"The Game and Fish supervisor was confident we located the sites for all three dead antelope, the one on Charlie Bell and the two we tried to find last night." He snickered. "Overheard her chewing out our cocky guide. He looked pretty pussywhipped."

Shocked at his vulgar phrase, she raked fingers through her hair. "I'm sure you were never that young and arrogant." Her words sliced the heated air.

"I'm not much older." He twirled a fork through his pasta. "And arrogant? You tell me."

She ignored his provocative probe. "I completed interviews with the host and five men who attended the party." She'd been slumped over in exhaustion but straightened up her posture.

He gave her an admiring smile. "Must've been difficult getting them to talk about an event with illegal food."

"Alonzo Ortiz is the hunting guide I haven't located." She drooped back down against the clammy plastic bench seat. "Assuming he brought the pronghorn, you wouldn't think he'd risk his permit and a fifty thousand dollar fine."

"Endangered species act doesn't allow any hunting. They'd get more local support if a few could be taken." He tipped the bottle for another swig.

She followed his example and the heady hops spread a slow burn all the way to the tips of her toes. "I'm bothered by the missing guide. My favorite epi rule of thumb—look for outliers. He could be out of town because he's sick with anthrax."

"Or on a hunt."

The older waitress plopped the check in front of him, and they stopped by the ancient cash register to pay the bill.

Maya completed phone calls from the motel, then knocked on Dave's adjoining door. He yelled, "It's open," and she entered to find him reclining against the metal headboard, boots on the bedspread. He gestured to the chair and turned his cell screen toward her.

"Hey, kids, say hi to Maya." The two young girls kicked at each other from bunk beds.

"Sorry to steal your dad away for work, but we'll bring him home soon. I can't wait to visit. Will you show me BioPark Zoo?"

The girls' faces lit up and they clapped, before he took the phone back. After saying goodnight to his daughters, his voice lowered as he whispered, "Melia, love ya."

Maya blushed at her intrusion.

"Emilia wants us out of here." He set down the cell. "Did you hear about the LDS mothers and children massacred in Mexico? Used to know some of them."

Her terror when stuck in the state Game and Fish truck flooded back. "What happened?"

Shifting closer on the bed to Maya's chair, he spoke in an apprehensive tone.

"Cars were ambushed as they headed here to Arizona. One car burned with babies in car seats."

Her mouth dropped open and her eyes filled with tears. "That's barbaric. Do they know why?"

"No one knows for sure, but the town's been threatened by drug cartels. Rival gangs disputing territorial control."

"Drugs have a monstrous toll—addiction, overdoses, violence, and anthrax." She shook her head and oriented on the reason she knocked on his door.

"The missing hunting guide's at the UA med center with symptoms of g.i. anthrax."

He glanced at his watch. "We can head back to Tucson early tomorrow. I got samples of soil, antelope organs, and hair."

They agreed to meet for an early breakfast and she sent an alert to her supervisors.

A wash of conflicting feelings flooded over her as she tossed and turned between the rough yellowed sheets. Adrenaline and fear from last night's abortive desert excursion and news of the attack on Mormon families. Exhilaration with some quick success investigating the raw meat party. And regret about her unsettled relationship with Manolo. Had she been too precipitous in rejecting his interest? Was she passing up a chance at a loving family like Dave's?

In Tucson Wednesday morning, TV cameras crowded the hospital while newscasters dramatized the horrifying executions of the Mormon families.

"Sorry for the craziness today," the haggard young intern said. "We got the injured kids from the cartel attack."

The hunting guide had onset of fever, vomiting and bloody diarrhea while shopping on November 5. After developing septic shock, he was moved to the ICU with serology and blood culture pending. Maya glanced in to see him—unconscious, pale, hooked to IVs—before she searched for his wife in the cafeteria.

A Hispanic woman in her thirties with tears streaming down her face sat alone with a coffee cup on the table.

"Mrs. Ortiz?"

The woman tilted her head up with glassy eyes.

"I'm Dr. Maguire, working with the state health department." She selected her state connection, not federal. Feds weren't always respected in the West, especially if her husband was in violation of the Endangered Species Act. "May I sit for a minute?"

Manicured fingers with a ruby ring tapped the adjacent chair, and Maya joined her.

"We're concerned about an event your husband attended on Halloween. He and his friends ate raw meat. That can be risky for infection." Based on the blank look, Maya wasn't certain she understood.

"Do you know what kind of meat he brought to the party?"

Cherry-red lips eked out a word. "Pronghorn."

Maya's heart raced with confirmation of where the antelope came from. No one else at the feast had implicated him.

"Did he say whether he hunted or found the animal? Do you know who ate any?"

The teased and sprayed hair remained in place as the woman shuddered and mumbled an answer. "Both of us—still have some left."

Maya buzzed with mixed emotions. The pronghorn meat was

available, but at least two people, and probably more, were exposed to it. "County health can pick it up for testing. If you feel sick in any way, let your doctor know about the situation with your husband."

With the woman's continued blank stare, Maya squeezed her hand. "It'll be okay. We're on top of it."

She found Dave in the ICU waiting room and they located a vacant corridor. After updating Janey about the guide and availability of suspect meat for testing, she called Dr. Bingham to review options. Dave had completed his work and was headed home, but Maya was uncertain.

"With the g.i. anthrax incubation period up to a week, I'd like to stick around a couple more days."

"I appreciate your offer."

"Could you talk to Dr. Grinwold about me staying? You'll have more luck than me."

The brusque voice of the State Epidemiologist became warm. "No problem. I can make it up to him."

Maya glanced at Dave when they hung up. "Do you think they have something going on?"

He laughed. "Wouldn't be the first workplace romance, even across borders. Older folks have urges, too."

She flushed at his joke and they headed to the rental vehicle. He located street parking in Tucson's revitalized downtown, and they stepped into the lobby of the historic Hotel Congress. Proud of her family's Tucson heritage, she played tourist guide.

"A fire here in the 1930s led to the arrest of the Dillinger gang, so they have an annual Dillinger Days to celebrate the capture of Public Enemy Number One."

He held the door as they strolled into the casual, western-themed restaurant. "I think Arizona wants to out-cowboy Texas."

When he had consumed his first rapid bites of the chile, he continued. "So what's happening with the friendly IHS doctor?"

She swallowed several ounces of milkshake to counteract the chile's heat, and considered her next words. "What do you mean?"

"Got the idea you might like each other. The M&Ms—Maya Maguire and Manolo Miranda." He grinned.

She twirled her hair between her fingers and looked down at her food. "He came to Santa Fe for a visit. Turns out he's been married for the last eight years."

His spoon dropped with a loud clunk to the plate under the bowl. "Never got that vibe."

"He got divorced—*after* he asked me for a personal relationship."

Dave picked up the utensil and dipped it into his chile. "O-k-a-a-a-y. I'm guessing you weren't happy to hear it?"

"He was hiding it."

With an abrupt snort, he set down the spoon again and stuck out his left hand. "'Hi, I'm Dr. Miranda, see this white spot around my finger? Not quite done with a wedding ring I've had for a decade.'"

Her skin darkened with his mockery. "We spent time alone in Phoenix during the heroin investigation. Had dinner, got to know each other better. He never mentioned being married."

"Probably afraid of your reaction. Who's the ex-wife?"

"Transplant surgeon in D.C."

The faint wrinkles above his eyebrows deepened. "He's attracted to accomplished women. Isn't that something you appreciate about him?"

She took a bite of corn muffin, then retorted sharply. "I don't want to be compared. His life has been a different world than mine."

Tilting his head, he appeared to acknowledge her observation. "You've got an age gap, seven years or so?"

Appetite lost, she moved the bowl aside.

"What kind of history would make you happier? Tomcatting around like his look-a-like Broadway character? If he didn't get married, he would have had several relationships by now. Would that have been easier to take?"

"When you put it that way—"

"I wasn't roped in 'til my last year of vet school. Met Emilia at a San Antonio Riverwalk restaurant where she was a cook, only eighteen-years-old. She was immersed in the Catholic teachings of waiting until marriage. I was past twenty before I got confident with women, but had a ton of activity before her."

A peacock fanning his plume, calloused fingers tousled his hair as his body inflated into a manspread. "Don't think it was easy for her to accept, but I was worth it."

Was all that true, or was he exaggerating to make a point? She guessed he was teasing her out of an unhealthy fixation on Manolo's history. But with her silence, he continued. "Where are you at with him now?"

"Nowhere. I sent him home early from Santa Fe. We haven't talked since."

"You're being too hard on him. We all have different histories and perceptions to resolve in a marriage. You need to decide if he's worth the effort."

Waving at the waitress for the check, she cut off the discussion. "I'll take it under advisement."

TWENTY-FOUR

<u>Feb 24, 2007.</u>
Fuckin govment raided ranch today, ripped away hundreds of kids to "protect them".
All my siblings, biologic and otherwise.

SWAT teams, snipers, helicopters.
Figured something was up with all them pigs running around.

Not enough men left.
Prophet kicked em all out to keep women for himself.
Should have had more balls and another Waco.

<u>March 7.</u>
Put kids in concentration camps.
Tejas complains that lots of our girls have kids or are pregnant.
Duh!

Mother gets ants in her pants and fights.
Fuckin unbelievable, court agrees. Kids can go home.

TWENTY-FIVE

Within an hour, the hunting guide was dead and another of the raw meat party attendees had come into the hospital. The call came as Maya drove the Benson Highway back into town after dropping Dave at the airport, and she pulled over to one of the ubiquitous gas stations. Leaning over the steering wheel, head in her hands, she pictured the man she had seen in the hospital and imagined his wife's pain. Public health was easier when cases were just numbers, not individuals she met.

Alonzo's autopsy was underway when she returned, but she skipped it. More images of bloody organs and pus-filled bodily cavities didn't need to imprint her brain.

She was directed to the hospital room for the banker, who gave her a slight wave, unable to speak with a bulging swelling underneath his chin, covered with a white gauze bandage.

The nurse indicated that his fever, sore throat, problems swallowing, and hoarseness began the previous day. When his neck ballooned earlier in the morning, an employee drove him to the hospital. They tapped the lymph node under his jaw and did a smear of his left tonsil, which found bacilli looking like anthrax. An IV delivered fluids and penicillin.

Maya thanked the nurse for the update and turned to the patient. "Mr. Wilson, you didn't take antelope meat home, did you?"

He shook his head. Ignoring the medical personnel rushing by, she collapsed on a chair in the hall. Gastrointestinal and now oropharyngeal anthrax from an endangered animal? But she shouldn't jump to conclusions. Neither case was confirmed.

Why were people dying from all these different types of anthrax? Inhalation for Danny from the sheep in Keams Canyon, cutaneous for Rickie from the Flagstaff petting zoo, and hundreds of people she didn't know from heroin injections.

She moved to a quieter corridor and called the state health department. "What's the deal with these lab delays? Don't they know people are dying?"

Dr. Bingham responded in a cool voice. "As you know, we have plenty of cooks in the kitchen. But agencies need to be careful. They're spooked about safety with all the specimen shipments and testing. USAMRIID was shut down after a failed inspection, and they were the hero Army lab in the *Hot Zone* book about Ebolavirus in Virginia monkeys. CDC itself, in 2014, sent live anthrax bacteria to facilities without safety equipment to handle them."

Anthrax and yelling at the boss—both triggers for skipped heartbeats. "Who can we trust if they can't process the workload?"

"They have to be cautious," Dr. Bingham answered. "There's been at least seven hundred incidents of the loss or release of select agents and toxins."

Maya glanced around the corridor, verifying it was still empty. "Did they ever find anthrax in the heroin?"

"Not announced yet, but it matches Texas cattle, so no evidence of an imported drug issue. Apparently it's natural contamination as drugs move around the Southwest."

Maya allowed herself a deep sigh of relief. "Dave tells me I'm a worrywart."

Dr. Bingham's voice was soothing. "Things are more alarming when you're not acclimated to them. Human nature—we fear the strange and unknown. Anthrax is neither of those things to Dr. Schwartz and the USDA."

Brushing down her wrinkled skirt, Maya prepared to go back into the fray. "Thanks for talking me off a cliff."

"I appreciate your improvements to keep me in the loop and recognize our bureaucratic limitations."

The pathologist caught her in the hall and showed her Alonzo's report. Thick, yellow abdominal fluid and swelling in lymph nodes and bowel, with multiple specimens sent for testing. Next, she verified with Pima County that the antelope samples were on the way to a Food Emergency Response Network lab.

"Food can be a terrorism target," Janey said on the phone. "Japan and South Africa both laced chocolate with anthrax to poison people. And an Oregon fringe religious group sprinkled restaurant salad bars with *Salmonella*."

Maya tried to follow Dr. Bingham's example and put a positive spin on the developments. "There's no evidence someone deliberately contaminated the raw meat party."

Janey's warnings about mass terrorism attacks with food boggled her brain. Her back muscles locked up and she leaned on the wall to keep from collapsing. After calling her grandmother to verify a bed for another night, she waddled out to her rental SUV.

In the senior apartment, she dug out her heating pad and plugged it in as she settled on the sofa. The sable Persian gave Maya a sprightly meow of hello, then smushed into her side, sharing the warmth.

Her grandmother handed her a cup of hot chamomile. "Back acting up again, sweetheart?"

"You wouldn't believe the night we had at Cabeza Prieta. We broke down in the desert—rescued by border agents with guns drawn."

The tiny woman's face creased with anguish. "I thought your job was crunching numbers at a computer. Are you sure it's safe?"

"Yes, Grandma, we work as a team. We weren't in any real danger. Remember Dave from the USDA?" She left out the raw meat investigation, driving and doing interviews alone.

"Your folks talked about him sharing pancakes in Flagstaff. He's got kids, right? Sounds like a nice boy. Too bad he's not single."

Maya shook her head in exasperation. "Are you trying to fix me up?"

"Well, dear, you do work hard." Her grandmother's voice was reedy but strident. "I taught school while raising your mom, even when most women didn't do that. You can have your job and a personal life, too."

"I'm thinking about it. During our first border trip, I mentioned working with the Indian Health Service." She realized Manolo didn't know her family, unlike Dave.

"Here's a picture." She opened an iPhone selfie taken at the Alcove House cliff dwelling in Bandelier.

"Definitely a keeper, dear. If I was sixty years younger . . ."

"Grandma, better not flirt with my b—" Catching herself, she didn't add anything else about their current situation. She never had a boyfriend, and Manolo didn't qualify now. Her Catholic grandmother was liberated in some ways about working women, but she and her daughter had each been married just once.

·   ·   ·

She hurried to the University hospital early the next morning. With her unpredictable schedule, she didn't commit to staying in Tucson another night. The lab worker met her with anthrax confirmation on both Alonzo and the banker, and she phoned the county.

"I was going to call you," Janey said. "Mrs. Ortiz drove back to Ajo last night for her husband's funeral arrangements. This morning she started throwing up blood and her temp is 105°. A neighbor is speeding here with her."

Maya decided to wait at the hospital until Mrs. Ortiz arrived, but Dr. Bingham called a few moments later.

"I'll organize the antelope follow-up with the county, but I need you in Buckeye. Migrant farmworkers at a dairy have bloody diarrhea and fever. They're at various Phoenix hospitals with preliminary diagnosis of *Salmonella* or *Shigella*, but those microbes were ruled out with stool samples. There was one hit on anthrax antibodies, perhaps past infection in Mexico."

Dr. Bingham sounded frazzled. "There's another major problem. The Border Patrol filed a complaint about your night excursion."

"Game and Fish drove us. I texted you just before we started out, and didn't go behind anyone's back."

"I realize that. You kept us in the loop." The older woman sighed. "They're upset at resources for your rescue. Don't worry, just follow state Ag's lead on the dairy."

Maya forced the latest censure aside, found the dairy address, and called Dr. Ben Smith, who agreed to meet her at noon. Then she headed north on I-10.

At Marana, the skies let loose with sheets of pounding rain. When visibility reduced to zero, she swerved off to park under a highway overpass. The radio issued an emergency warning. Remnants of a late season tropical storm threatened roadways. The weather reflected her mood. She didn't know how much more anthrax she could take. How many mistakes until she lost her job?

Brakes from another car screeched as it slid in behind hers, so she slipped out her passenger door and paced. If someone skidded out of the storm and slammed her vehicle, she was safer next to the concrete support pillar.

The cool air was refreshing. She recalled sense memories of damp pine needles in Flagstaff and wet fall leaves in New York, but no smell was more soothing than the desert after a rainstorm. Within thirty minutes, the deluge moved on, and she resolved to keep going, one step at a time.

. . .

Buckeye, fastest growing city in the country, didn't jog childhood memories. Multiple master planned communities were interspersed with dusty desert and cacti. How much longer could agriculture continue as development exploded?

The northeast dairies on weekend trips during graduate training were small, green, and bucolic. Nothing like this one. Acres of soil grew animal feed, punctuated by huge gleaming metal silos and a waste lagoon the size of a small lake, covered with a blue tarp.

Two months since they worked together at the first refuge, and a spacious smile creased Ben's face. At the entrance of the main office building, the dairy's hulking manager appeared, cautious but eager to show them the huge property.

"Most people don't realize Arizona has the largest dairies in the country," he bragged, looking up at Ben. "We have a modern mechanized operation, milking about seven thousand Holsteins. Each wears a pedometer so we can track all the steps and maximize their care. We also reduce energy usage with a methane digester to create our own electricity."

At the end of the quick half-hour tour, Ben thanked the manager and pulled Maya aside. "There's no obvious issues and you don't have lab confirmation on those workers yet. I can review animal health while you scope out the personnel files."

She re-entered the office crowded with file cabinets, book shelves, and supplies piled on the floor. The manager's wife logged into the computer and rotated the monitor. Dairy records included twenty-four employees, but the portly blonde was vague on how many were on contract, including migrant workers.

Maya had a list of twelve hospitalized dairy staff, but recognized only four of their names on the company database. "Is your work force stable, or has there been recent turnover?"

"It varies," the middle-aged woman admitted.

With confidential information about the sick workers, Maya didn't say who was ill. Instead, she asked for a copy of the employee list and contact data, so someone from Maricopa County or state health could track the group.

"Have any of these staff members taken time off work for illness in the past couple of weeks?"

"Someone gets a cold and isn't feeling well, that kind of thing. We hire young, healthy people, so not much of a problem." The woman admitted the dairy didn't provide insurance, so employees had an incentive to keep working when ill.

"Can you point out any specific individuals who aren't here because they're sick?"

Two names on the screen matched Maya's list. The wife said, "These two didn't show up today and didn't call. Don't know what's going on."

With as much information as she could retrieve on the first visit, Maya thanked the office manager for her assistance. She texted Ben, who was in the same boat.

"I'm limited until we confirm a reportable disease in people or animals," he said when they met at their vehicles. "One of my staff will come out again tomorrow and look for any red flags."

She drove the thirty miles back into Phoenix and parked at the state health office, a month since she began working there on the injection anthrax cases. Too much was going on and everything ran together in her brain. Was she making any impact? Anthrax seemed to subside, then change whenever she started to investigate it.

Dr. Bingham took the list of dairy employees and assigned them for follow-up. "Stop back tomorrow morning," she requested.

. . .

Having lived at the hotel for two weeks in October, she developed some fondness for its bland, boxy frontage. The free Raisin Bran at the breakfast bar was tolerable.

After grabbing a chocolate chip cookie from the front desk, she tucked her legs on the one comfortable chair in her room. She entered the passcode into her iPhone, hesitating with her finger over Manolo's name before hitting the number. She tried to slow her respiratory rate.

"Maya?" His voice sounded fantastic, and confused.

With a tight throat, she forced herself to keep going. "I'm in town for another weird anthrax thing. Can we get together and I'll tell you about it? Well, not only that. I want to see you again."

"I'd love to see you, too. My sister is visiting and she flies home tomorrow. Can I introduce you?"

That was more than she was prepared to handle. What could she say to his sister?

His voice interrupted the silence. "Based on past experience, I bet you have no plans for your next meal."

Despite their estrangement, he did know her patterns. "Bingo."

"Ramona cooked up a batch of Sancocho, Puerto Rican beef stew. Plenty for the three of us."

Within a half-hour, she parallel parked in front of the red brick complex where he waited on the porch outside the door. Getting out of the car, she noted the meditative expression on his appealing face as his feet shifted up and down the step. He couldn't be more nervous than she was.

Skipping their customary hug, he touched one arm. "You look spectacular."

"You should have smelled me before my shower." She teased her damp hair, hoping it would dry quickly. "Spent the afternoon at a Buckeye dairy. I forgot about the glorious, pungent smell of Holsteins and manure."

"Come into my humble abode." He gestured for her to enter in front of him. "Not a huge place, but better than yours."

A woman draped in a billowy art print dress rose from the chair. Long black hair draped her shoulders and a smile resembling her brother's flickered as she shook Maya's hand. "Glad my visit from New York coincided with your trip from New Mexico."

He glanced between the women. "I'm picking up wine for dinner. Leave you two alone?"

"Don't go out on my account." Maya was determined to avoid alcohol and loose lips. He went out anyway. Maybe he needed a drink to deal with her.

"Mano told me about your anthrax investigations." Ramona broke the awkward silence. "We saw articles in the press. You must be exhausted."

"It's challenging to keep up." Maya joined his sister at the round kitchen table.

"How did you like NYC when you went to school there?"

The two years seemed like a lifetime ago. "There was always something exciting to do or see. It was nice to be anonymous for once, instead of feeling like the only Chinese person in Arizona or Colorado."

Ramona nodded. "The city's diversity is a big advantage. Some move to the burbs when they have kids but we're happy to be out of our cars, experiencing the City in all its glory and its terrors."

Empathetic and vivacious—the long face reminded Maya of Manolo. She plunged in. "You must have known his wife."

"She was something else." Fingers toyed with a napkin.

"Is that good or bad?"

"Force of nature. She swallowed Mano up in her world, and he lost himself for a long time. But he's comfortable out here. He loves the work." Ramona broke eye contact and crossed her arms. "He had been overjoyed to meet you."

Maya was a squirrel on the yellow line, unclear where to turn before getting slammed. Breaking her paralysis, she refilled her water glass from the sink, then turned to sit down. "We both messed up."

Ramona shrugged. "Recognizing it is the first step to fixing it. You're here tonight."

"It's hard for me to understand how I could compete with his wife." Maya spread her hands on the table. "All that history, all that accomplishment."

"Hermana, you don't need to compete, you shouldn't compete." Ramona got up to increase the air conditioning at the wall switch and rejoined Maya.

"Mano has no interest in comparisons. He's moved on. Of course he won't forget his previous life but those lessons informed what he wants and needs. He's confident now in his future direction, except for what role you want to play in it."

When he returned with the Merlot, Maya was grateful for a

switch to less personal discussion. As they sipped the stew, she shared her latest adventures. She pushed the CBP complaint out of her mind and made the border incident a Will Ferrell comedy.

But Manolo was troubled. "You and Dave should be more careful. Like you, I'm worried about all the anthrax in different parts of Arizona and nowhere else."

Maya mentioned the dairy workers while Manolo refrigerated the half-empty bottle of wine.

"It's more of a migrant-dominated industry," he said. "There shouldn't be many Native Americans at risk, but I'll review any unusual g.i. syndromes within the IHS. Our electronic records system has problems, but I can still check and make calls."

"With an early flight tomorrow, I'm going to turn in." Ramona headed for the hall. "Maya, I hope to see you again."

Silence descended like in a tomb. Avoiding his eyes, Maya finally interrupted it. "Your sister was very kind."

"A year older, the more mature and wiser one."

"I should get going, too." She stood and picked up her purse.

While following her to the front door, he looked like he was struggling with a decision. "How long will you be in Phoenix?"

"As usual, I have no idea."

He grabbed for her hips before she could reach the doorknob.

"Can we start over?" His hands increased their pressure as his voice hurtled on. "I was a hundred percent wrong to hold off telling you about my marriage until the divorce was final. Between my mother's death and Angela, I learned to shut down my feelings and keep important things close to the vest. I swear to share everything, no holding back."

Her heart raced. "This is all new to me. My job is my priority."

He wrapped one arm around her shoulders and stroked her forehead with the lightest touch of his fingers.

"Why can't we have it both ways?" he asked, keeping their eyes locked.

"What does that mean?"

"I want to be with you, under any circumstances. And you need time to find out if you can love me the way I'm already loving you. We can figure out how to make a long-distance relationship and our careers work when we put all this anthrax behind us."

Unable to maintain his intense gaze, she ducked her head to his shoulder. "Sounds good."

"We'll take it slow." He massaged her neck with one hand while the other arm held her tight. "We have all the time in the world."

TWENTY-SIX

<u>July 19.</u>
Jacob and I snuck in to say goodbye before family caravanned back to Arizona. Our little sisters sobbed and clung to our legs. Mother said "Jacob, you're 12. Don't listen to your brother. Come home with us."

Scrambling through the brush out of the compound,
Jacob knocked me to the ground.

"A red laser lit up the back of your shirt," he whispered.
Might have been on a gun, the security force uses AR-15s.

We crawled to a ditch and waited in the cool damp until the coast was clear.

Mother blames me for helping him escape. I hope she didn't snitch on us.

But Jacob knows he's got it good. Once you taste freedom, you can't go back.

Now she has no sons. She can make more.

TWENTY-SEVEN

After twenty-four hours of anthrax-associated fever, delirium and bloody vomitus, the game guide's wife clung to life at the university's medical center. She didn't appear to remember her deceased husband or the raw meat Halloween party. At six-thirty on November 9, Maya received an update from Janey on the wife, the banker, and the surprise death of the sheriff's deputy.

Bragging to the end about his ability to handle anything, he'd been admitted to TMC with bloody diarrhea, hypovolemic shock, and an abdomen distended with fluid. Penicillin and IV fluids failed. Like the others, he received anthrax antitoxin stored at the hospitals since the October peak of heroin-associated cases.

By seven-thirty, Maya had showered, inhaled rubbery scrambled eggs at the hotel continental breakfast, and driven to the health office. With the raw meat outbreak expanding, her instincts were to leap back in, but Dr. Bingham ordered her to focus on the dairy. Of the dozen suspect dairy workers on Maya's list, the bacteria had been cultured from two. Another three had detectable antibodies.

When anthrax was confirmed in agricultural employees, Ben Smith requested that Dr. Vanessa Wright fly back from Washington. The Homeland Security veterinarian had come out to Arizona in October to investigate the anthrax-associated heroin cases as a possible bioterrorism event. She had expertise on consumable products as potential BT sources because of her prior work at the Food and Drug Administration.

Everyone wanted to make sure the milk supply was safe. The Buckeye dairy employing the anthrax-infected workers contributed to the more than one million gallons processed daily at the regional cooperative. The agencies held off on public announcement while their investigation got underway, but knew they couldn't wait long with patients and health care providers knowing the results.

Chasing down information on the sick employees filled up Maya's day. The electronic records database was used to find cases of bloody diarrhea hospitalized in the past week. As a non-specific approach, it swept in people ill with more common gastrointestinal bacteria. Once lab results came in for the other diseases, patients were removed from the suspect list. It was a starting point. Like the heroin-associated cases the previous month, state and federal labs worked overtime.

At the dairy where all the cases had worked, Ben coordinated Ag staff, confirming infection control processes during milking. They swabbed equipment, took samples of milk and cattle feed, and blood samples from all the cows for antibody testing. With Maya tied up on the human cases, Dave Schwartz drove into Arizona from his Albuquerque office and assisted at the dairy.

After Maya picked up Vanessa from Sky Harbor, they walked two blocks from the health parking lot to the agriculture department. At the front of the red-tiled, historic building facing Wesley Bolin Memorial Plaza and its World War II artifacts, Maya paused.

"These remnants from the USS Arizona downed by the Japanese in Pearl Harbor remind me that big external threats can still surprise us. Glad you could fly in to help us sort through this one."

The four veterinarians gathered in a small conference room. Until news about anthrax in dairy workers was released, they met in an area away from others to ensure confidentiality. Maya initially watched and listened, trying to learn from colleagues who had experience timing investigatory steps with information release.

During the evidence review, Ben called in his secretary to bring sandwiches from the vending machine. Maya stood at the window looking out to the Plaza. "When you tell people you're a vet, how often are you asked, 'Where do you practice?'"

Vanessa joined her for a moment taking in the view. "With my uniform looking like Navy, the most frequent question is, 'Are there military dogs on ships?'"

Maya caught Ben's narrowed eyes and tight lips.

"We need to get this one right," he said. "My decisions about this dairy and the others can result in a multimillion dollar impact. The state vet is not a popular position out here where no one wants government regulation."

As sandwiches were delivered, Vanessa summarized the situation. "Although Arizona has dealt with anthrax for several months, this is the first time it hit the agriculture industry. Dave had those Hopi sheep, but that was Native American jurisdiction. The moose and reindeer at the animal attraction were USDA Animal Care, and the endangered antelope were a special state/federal wildlife program."

"I'm betting these dairy workers are like the other recent human cases." Dave, as the federal vet responsible for cattle diseases in the region, appeared relaxed and bit into an egg salad sandwich on white bread. "They got it from contaminated soil, so the milk supply itself might not be affected."

"If employees can inhale it from dirt, cows can too," Maya said.

Ben paced, thumbs hooked in his pockets. "We have a much bigger issue if the milk has anthrax. Pasteurization is important, but not a hundred percent effective at killing all the spores, depending on the level of contamination."

Turning toward him, Maya arched her neck as he towered above. "Pasteurization has become a bad word. A lot of people are on the raw milk bandwagon, which is an infection risk."

"Ben, there's no current evidence of a milk problem." Vanessa gestured to the empty chair, inviting him to sit back down. "But we have to consider an intentional threat. I agree that naturally contaminated soil may be the culprit, but want to make sure we don't have a human one."

With Vanessa's thoroughness, Maya felt emboldened to share her worries. "From a time and space problem, it bothers me that we keep having these discrete, isolated incidents with different types of anthrax." She tapped her pen on the table with force. "First inhalation, then cutaneous, followed by injection, and now gastrointestinal. None of them last long. One's over and another starts."

"It's odd that spores in the heroin match those Dave has in the Texas anthrax triangle." Vanessa slapped his weathered hand. "You're not the cause of all this, are you? Trying to keep busy and useful? Need to justify the budget for your position?"

"That's all we do, feed at the government trough." He tilted the chair back, fingers laced behind his neck. Slight smile, tight muscles, like a panther ready to pounce.

"We hear that about climate change too." Maya tried to break the tension. "We're all spouting fake news to get ourselves more money."

"If Maya's point about the limited, short-term pattern is true, this will burn itself out soon," Vanessa said. "And I can stay home in the peace and quiet of D.C."

Ben patted Vanessa on the shoulder and took a distracted bite of his sandwich. But Maya's hamster-wheel brain kept turning. "I'm not blaming Dave, but the anthrax letter attacks in 2001 were an inside job by a government employee. All these different types of anthrax in a short time and one state—I don't think this can be due to chance."

"Not saying this is chance, either." Dave kicked the table leg, spilling soda from the plastic cups. "We have lots of Texas animal cases this year. Older vets say it's the worst in their careers. Changing climate, expanding population, and humans moving livestock into new environments."

"You sound more like an environmentalist than a west Texas rancher." Vanessa continued to tease him. "Which president are you working for?"

Releasing an audible groan, he pivoted away in his seat.

"We need to complete our initial investigation and work out an interagency public announcement." Ben redirected the discussion to the dairy. "Despite large numbers of anthrax cases with heroin, the public didn't feel it affected them directly. Any possibility of a milk problem will ratchet up hysteria."

"I worked on the 2001 Amerithrax investigation Maya mentioned." Vanessa's change in tone reflected Ben's sober summary. "Arizona's anthrax doesn't have much in common with that terrifying event, but these heroin cases triggered FBI consideration of an intentional source. That includes government employees with access to the bacteria and knowledge of how to deploy it."

Dave uncurled his long limbs from the metal folding chair, got up for another cup of coffee, and remained vertical.

Vanessa rose to stand next to him. "All kidding aside, with your expertise and lab connections for soil testing, someone's going to ask questions. The FBI's under a lot of public and congressional scrutiny. Who knows how they'll respond? You could get crosswise with them, like you did with the refuges and the Border Patrol."

He stormed out of the meeting. Maya looked at Vanessa with astonishment. Surely her Homeland Security colleague was over-reacting? She trusted Dave implicitly, but was also certain they were missing something important.

. . .

Arizona agriculture, the milk-drinking public, and Dave's reputation dodged a bullet when the newest anthrax outbreak burned itself out within a week. Maya assisted with the herd's serologic sampling in addition to managing the human case database.

Despite extensive testing, only twenty-one cows were antibody positive. Pasteurized milk was negative for anthrax, but spores were found in the dairy's bulk milk tanks and on some surfaces in the milking parlor. Ben ordered the tanks disinfected, and recommended a cattle vaccination program to the facility's contract veterinarian.

Ten dairy workers responded to the antitoxin and recovered. Two others were released with other diagnoses. The official report concluded workers were exposed on the job through soil and spores at their workplace. No contamination was found at other dairies in the region.

One downed cow necropsied at the dairy before the investigation had an enlarged spleen. "Disposed of and nothing left for testing," Ben told the vet team as they assembled for the press conference. "Our current regulations kept it out of the meat supply. Another name for anthrax is 'splenic fever,' so that's probably what it was."

Dr. Wright stayed in Phoenix long enough to join the November 13 press event. She assured the public there was no evidence of any deliberate contamination and the commercial milk supply was safe. Dr. Bingham represented the health department and Maya sat in the audience to support those at the podium.

The press event also released information about additional human anthrax deaths. After purchasing raw milk from one of the migrant workers, an eighty-six-year-old prostate cancer patient developed bloody vomiting and diarrhea. He was diagnosed with gastrointestinal anthrax and died two days later.

Two deaths from the antelope were reported, the sheriff's deputy and hunting guide's wife. Maya didn't know either of them well, but their alive and healthy visages danced in front of her eyes. She had warned them about anthrax risk from eating the antelope, and a week later they were dead.

Immigration and Customs Enforcement swept in and detained nineteen undocumented Buckeye dairy workers, even though the investigative team hadn't provided their names.

Maya understood that she didn't bear responsibility for the bad outcomes, but a feeling that her inadequacies might contribute to any of them disturbed her sleep. She coped by working almost 24/7. No time for communicating with Manolo. If they couldn't pull it off in the same town, how would they handle a long-distance relationship?

Curled like an armadillo over the keyboard, she slowly unwound and phoned Manolo. "We're almost done with the dairy and Dr. Bingham said I can take Friday off. Could we get together?"

"What would you like to do, querida?"

She never tired of hearing his warm, lyrical accent. "I'm thinking of visiting my family in Flag. But I don't want to put expectations on you, and we don't need to spend the whole time there. We could run up to the Grand Canyon."

He picked her up from the hotel Friday morning, dressed in a navy blue suit and dark tie dotted with tiny yellow stars. Trying to impress her astronomer mom? Maya leaned into the long embrace without hesitation.

"Different weather than our last drive north in early August." She fingered the fabric of his lightweight jacket. "I hope you brought warmer clothes."

He nuzzled her ear. "Boy Scouts are always prepared."

"I didn't know you were a scout." She stepped away and climbed into the passenger seat of the sports car.

He got in and they headed north. "I was an Eagle Scout. The discipline was one thing that kept me going after my mother died."

"Does it bother you that scouts have suffered sexual abuse by a few of their leaders?" She swallowed hard, hoping they were back to being open with each other.

"Come on now," he responded with mild irritation. "They're not the only organization with that problem."

"Sorry, I don't mean to cast aspersions. My grandma is angry Tucson was a dumping ground for abusive priests. Perhaps the church thought Hispanics were so strong in their beliefs they'd accept the dregs. Communities of color seem to bear the brunt of bad things in life."

He nodded. "If people are undocumented, they're not going to make waves."

As they continued north on I-17 to a higher elevation, Maya noticed changes from their trip to investigate Danny's death. In

August, there was inherent tension from anthrax, attraction, and unfamiliarity. Now off the clock, they'd committed to finding out where their new closeness would take them.

She relaxed into easy intimacy. Anxieties about being inexperienced and inadequate faded. Their compatible perspectives were comforting, although she didn't require a shared belief system. Respect was more important. She and Dave were friends despite his more conservative background.

At her parents' Flagstaff apartment, her mother greeted them in a floral print dress and her hair piled high with a silver and turquoise Navajo barrette. Flaming red hair on someone seventy-years-old was an indication to Maya that her mother didn't accept the aging process.

"Dr. Miranda, we appreciate your bringing our daughter home. She never gets a break." Barbara Robinson shook Manolo's hand. "Tom's at the gym but he'll be home soon."

Her mom invited them to sit down for chimichangas. "You should have let Maya stop in during your first drive up here. That nice New Mexico vet came by with her."

Unbelievable, comparing Manolo with Dave. Was she testing him? But he didn't flinch. With an extended family, he might be tolerant of a few challenging relatives.

"Glad you're having me now. Maya told me about your career at Lowell Observatory. Any chance you can give us a tour?"

They didn't discuss specific plans for the day, so his question was unexpected. He must know the way to a potential mother-in-law's heart. Not a thought to dwell on, way too early.

"Of course, how delightful of you to ask." Her mom beamed with pride. "I still volunteer there, so I can do a backstage tour."

Her dad appeared more circumspect when he joined them as they finished lunch. Polite, but quiet, his eyes assessed Manolo.

The last time Maya had been on Mars Hill Road, she and Dave were investigating little Rickie Sanchez who died of cutaneous anthrax from moose slobber.

"Remember when you shut that place down?" her mom exclaimed as they drove past Holiday Home.

"I didn't shut it down, and it's reopened." The child's bloated face tormented her, but she was determined to put anthrax aside for the next couple of days.

As they got higher into the foothills, the view of the San Francisco Peaks was mesmerizing. Painted with a light snowfall from Veterans Day, the high peaks split the brilliant blue sky at the top and puddled down into the softer, blue-green ponderosa pines of the hills and town. Starting from the hundred-year-old Rotunda Museum, her mom led them on short walks to the Clark and Pluto Discovery telescopes.

"Percival Lowell began his search for Pluto here in 1905. After this telescope was completed in 1929, Clyde Tombaugh repeatedly photographed the sky to look for motion against the more distant stars. On February 18, 1930, he found Pluto. I think Maya has that same dogged perseverance and will make noteworthy discoveries."

Sensing a flush on her face, Maya changed the subject. "Mom, what did you think when they demoted Pluto?"

"Makes no sense to me, just semantics," her mom answered with an angry flounce.

Manolo reminded Maya of a teenage Boy Scout working on an astronomy badge as he monopolized the telescope to see solar flares, peppering her mom with questions.

A barbeque restaurant three miles away beckoned. Maya's dad shared his emergency preparedness experiences including infrastructure mapping at the Denver Federal Center and Manolo had entertaining stories about NYC and distant Puerto Rican relatives.

At the end of dinner, her mom offered to take them to the Observatory for night telescope viewing. Maya demurred, mentioning an early start for the Grand Canyon. Her dad put bedding on the living room couch for Manolo. When Maya brushed her teeth, her mom came in to talk alone.

"I don't want to hear you two getting together tonight." Before Maya could open her mouth with a sharp reply, her mom said goodnight and left.

. . .

By midmorning, they parked at the Grand Canyon visitor center. On a November Saturday, crowds were light. At Mather Point, the view of the multicolored canyon was memorable, but they couldn't wait to find a more private spot.

After the blue loop shuttle bus through the developed area, they changed to the red loop, hopping off early at Mohave Point with its unobstructed views to the west, north, and east. Holding hands, each took in the magnificent view.

"A huge pink and red layer cake, with white snow frosting." She pointed to the North Rim cliffs in the distance beyond the narrow strip of brown Colorado River several thousand feet below. She noted dark green scrub and pines on top, bright red sandstone and limestone layers underneath, then the wide shelf of loose, tan soil dappled light green with smaller bushes.

He shaded his eyes. "I like puffy white clouds painting shadows on the canyon walls. Did you come here often growing up in Flag?"

Smiling, she nodded. "It's so different depending on the time of day, weather, and season."

"River's been carving this canyon for five million years."

She put her fingers on his lips. "No science on this trip. I just want to revel in the beauty."

They found a picnic table to enjoy the chicken salad sandwiches her mom had packed. "I see you have a lot in common with your folks," he said between bites of the multigrain bread.

"Most people don't make that observation about adoptees." She laughed, poking at his arm.

He grabbed her hand and held it. "You have your mom's extreme passion for work. From your dad, I think you got his instinct for planning and always being prepared. And your shy smile."

"You mean I'm not bold and brassy like Mom?" She withdrew her hand in pretend indignation.

"No, but that's fine. She's entertaining."

"One way to put it," she countered. Her gaze drifted over again to the dominating view. "You see the middle shelf with the trees? I went on a ninth grade school camping trip to that area."

"Getting down that far must be easier than coming back up."

"With my back and leg injuries, I can't carry much, but we only had lightweight sleeping bags. Hiking was challenging because I had new stiff boots rubbing my feet raw." She reached down in memory toward her sneakers. "I took them off and hiked barefoot."

"You *are* tough. That didn't hurt your feet?"

"Not as much as hard leather rubbing against soft spots. But the funniest thing about the trip was the overnight campout."

He stretched an arm around her shoulders, pulling her close. "Do tell."

"Our guide picked out a flat, grassy area to set up camp. It was early September and warm, so no tents. I'm a tiny bit claustrophobic, so I was on the outside."

"Starting to sound spooky." He slipped her loose hair back, stroking her ears in the process.

"In the pitch-black night, something nuzzled at my face and I heard noise from shifting rocks. I hollered over to one of the school counselors, who said it was mice and I should zip up my bag and go back to sleep."

He kissed her cheek in imitation of the story. "Were they right?"

Her skin tingled where his lips touched. "I tried to follow instructions, but was too freaked out. I called out to him again. 'Too big and loud for mice.' He waved a flashlight. In the shadows next to my sleeping bag was a herd of restless wild burros."

"You were in their bed?"

"We all were, but the counselor refused to wake everyone to find another spot. I moved my bag right in the middle of the group. To heck with claustrophobia, I slept much better."

His fingers stroked the back of her hands. "You mentioned a Chaco hike your first weekend in New Mexico. I always wanted to visit—Native American history, spirituality, even ghosts. Could we camp there soon?"

"Sure," she said slowly.

"Don't worry, I have two sleeping bags and a tent."

She paused and glanced away. "Mom said last night she didn't want us sleeping together."

"Maybe she meant at her apartment?"

"Don't think so. As a strict Irish Catholic, her sex ed discussions were limited to 'Wait until marriage.'"

"Not very twenty-first century. I hope you don't agree with her." His laugh was quick, but tentative.

Maya pulled away and hurried to the railing. He was throwing back her Santa Fe admission of not being experienced and modern.

He moved to her side. "Sorry, forgot that's a sensitive issue." He cupped her chin and turned her face, looking into her eyes. "At your apartment, we were both too angry and intoxicated to clarify our levels of experience."

She stooped to pick up a golden Gambel oak leaf. "I already told you. I never dated. That means no sex, too."

"Dating and sex aren't always linked, but for you they clearly are. Me too, I've only been with Angela."

She dropped the leaf and gripped the metal bar protecting her from falling over the cliff. She needed to confess why she gave him mixed signals. "I haven't had consensual sex. But once, it wasn't."

His fingers crept toward hers on the railing, then stopped. "Can you talk about it?"

"I never told anyone, not even my family." She turned her head to take in his reaction. Would he be repulsed like she was sometimes?

"During lunch in Española, I mentioned my freshman year at CU was rough. My parents rarely had alcohol in the house, and my body wasn't adjusted to it. The first week of college, there was a party in a boy's room. I loved the taste of whisky sours and drank too many. When I woke up at two o'clock in his bed, he was on top of me. We were both naked."

As she began to sway, he guided her back to the picnic area.

"You're not obligated to go into this, if it's too difficult."

"Nothing happened. The college health center confirmed it. He was too drunk and I got lucky. But I have wisps of memory—cold digits on my breasts, his skin next to mine. Sometimes any touch, even yours, makes me scared."

"It's understandable you'd be cautious. We can take our time."

She leaned on his shoulder, grateful it was out in the open.

"Is being married important?" he asked. "Or are you worried sex might be difficult or painful because of your truck-bike accident?"

She felt her skin turn red again, not from the warm afternoon sun. "Mom and I rarely agree about things, including a requirement for marriage." Then she added, "My bionic bones shouldn't be a problem, but I can check with my doctor."

He pulled her closer. "We're in no rush and I never want to pressure you. But I love to touch and hold you. I hope we can move ahead when you're ready."

While he feathered kisses over her closed eyes and mouth, his fingers crept up under her shirt to trace the bare skin of her back. Warm breath and slow sighs relaxed her into a secure but sensitive torpor. Giving into the moment, not something she was hardwired for.

At the sound of the bus, she pushed away but he retained her hand. From his calm expression, she concluded he wasn't upset.

"Let's hold this until later when we're alone," he said. "Should we catch the shuttle and see more of this striking scenery?"

TWENTY-EIGHT

<u>July 30, 2008.</u>
Jacob and I both focus on getting ahead, learning new stuff.
Try not to think about never seeing family again.
He misses them more than me and hates being a traitor.

Just found out Court overturns Prophet conviction.
Hah! He's got nine lives.

<u>Aug 9.</u>
Prophet guilty of more sex assault. Life plus 15 years.

What the hell does that mean?
They'll keep his dead body in the jail?

FOMITES

Bacteria are hardy microbes. Some even survive on objects—fomites. Leap from nature to human creations.

Despite what they think, humans aren't the conquering hero. Microscopic life persists, thrives, adapts. Zillion years of survival. Nature wins all.

But if humans want to be stupid, or evil, that's fine too.

TWENTY-NINE

Riding the shuttle and jumping off at all nine viewpoints provided them a joyful afternoon, one of the first that was anthrax-free. Manolo's promise about getting more physical when they were alone niggled in the back of Maya's brain. As the sun dipped to the west, she recalled warning her parents they might be late getting back to Flag. She'd never be intimate with Manolo at their place, but wouldn't welcome another reminder from her mom.

During a lighthearted argument over the viewpoint to stake out for sunset, both of their cell phones rang. They stepped apart to take the calls, moving back together when done.

His call had been from the Director of the Phoenix Indian Medical Center and hers from the Arizona State Epidemiologist. About forty miles northeast of Phoenix, the 37th Anniversary Orme Dam Victory Days Intertribal Pow Wow started on Friday and was scheduled to finish Sunday evening.

The Fort McDowell Yavapai Nation celebrated the tribe's 1981 defeat of the dam at the junction of the Verde and Salt rivers, which would have flooded most of their reservation. The Pow Wow was a popular event with an All-Indian Rodeo, parade, and cultural performances.

Some Friday Pow Wow attendees started showing up at IHS and Phoenix urgent cares with the characteristic lesions of cutaneous anthrax. But a few additional patients had similar lesions who had not attended the event.

Exceeding the speed limit, Manolo got them to Phoenix in three hours despite the brief stop in Flag to pick up their suitcases. Maya avoided another disagreement and panic attack by locking her eyes on the cell phone, a deliberate diversion from the scenery and lights rushing by at high speed. He parked in front of the state health department by eight-thirty and she texted Dr. Bingham.

"First time at the Grand Canyon. It was awesome, including meeting your family." He reached over for a quick kiss.

"At least I'm not to blame for cutting our plans short this time," she said.

"We can never predict anything with these insane anthrax outbreaks, but I'm flying home to NYC in a few days for Thanksgiving. If we wrap this one up soon, I would love to introduce you to more of mi familia."

Through the glass entrance, she spotted Dr. Bingham and swung open the car door. "Doesn't sound practical at this late date."

He frowned but waved goodbye before he sped away.

Dr. Bingham rushed her into the building and down the hall. "IHS has the Native American cases. Here's a list of five non-Native patients to interview for possible exposures while waiting for lab confirmation."

Next to Dr. Bingham's desk, Maya perched on the guest chair. "When we had the cutaneous cases from the Flag petting zoo, I researched unusual potential exposures. Bone meal fertilizer can get contaminated by using the bones of infected animals. Also, skin cream from Iran is called Venetian Ceruse or Spirits of Saturn. It's made from sheep spinal cord. In the low-tech manufacturing process, the cream gets spores from infected animals or soil."

"Spirits of Satan?" Dr. Bingham asked, fussing with her short graying hair.

"No, Saturn." They laughed, punch drunk after the long day.

"In Italy, someone got cutaneous anthrax on his arm from the bites of blood-sucking gadflies," Maya said. "Flies picked up spores from infected sheep. Other species like blowflies are implicated."

She continued voicing her mental list. "Contaminated wool or yarn—woolsorters' disease. Animal hair shaving brushes. And animal hide drums. Are there drums at this Pow Wow?"

"Of course," Dr. Bingham smiled. "And anyone can attend, even a Chinese American vet." As she stood to leave, she gave final orders.

"Develop your questionnaire tonight and let me see it by seven tomorrow. If you get any Pow Wow hits when you start your interviews, head on out there. I assume Dr. Miranda or someone from IHS will be there, too."

Maya worked until midnight, emailed the draft to Dr. Bingham, and called a cab for the hotel, assuming Manolo was busy with his own cases.

. . .

Sunday morning, she worked through her patient list using the approved questionnaire. Three were Anglo senior citizens whom she reached at their hospital rooms. The medical facilities were aggressive with antitoxin use and all three felt well enough to answer questions on the phone.

The skin lesions were limited to their hands and arms. For potential exposures, one woman did yarn projects with alpaca wool. The second mentioned using an imported anti-aging cream, but couldn't remember its name or where it was from. None reported any fly or other type of insect bites.

But they all participated in a November 14 drum circle sponsored by a senior citizens group at a Scottsdale church. The seniors described the drums, provided by the event leader, as colorful, tactile, and imported. They were held on the ground between the knees and pounded with the hands.

The spouse of the male patient was able to look up a name and email address for the leader. Maya sent a note and asked him to phone her as soon as possible. Ruth, another epidemiologist sharing Sunday phone duty, agreed to find other ways to locate him.

With the initial information, Maya called Dr. Bingham who was working from home. "I looked up drum-associated anthrax cases. First was Florida, 1974, from a Haitian goat hide drum. In 2006, there was inhalation anthrax in Scotland from a West African drum. Another 2006 inhalation case in NYC had similar exposure. The next year, a Connecticut father and his son developed cutaneous anthrax when the father made djembe drums using goat hides from Guinea. And there was a 2009 New Hampshire gastrointestinal case from a community center drumming circle."

"Make sure to ask Ruth to check the hospitals for any suspicious g.i. or inhalation cases," Dr. Bingham said. "Although those syndromes are often more serious, the clinical signs are less specific and the clinicians might not recognize them as anthrax-associated."

"Will do. She's helping me reach the event leader."

"Nothing related to the Pow Wow?"

"No, but two more patients to locate. I'll keep you updated."

An elderly patient was hospitalized for treatment in a hyperbaric oxygen chamber. With congestive heart failure, he'd been treated several times before for skin wounds that wouldn't heal.

The hospital was in Goodyear between Buckeye and Phoenix, so anthrax was higher on the list of differential diagnoses due to press about the nearby dairy. The senior's CHF was well-managed, and he had no discomfort from the red and purple erosion on his thumb. But they kept him overnight as a precaution due to his previous history. After sharing all the information, the nurse put his wife on the phone with Maya.

"Dr. Maguire, what do you need to know about Bernie?" Her voice reminded Maya of a Rocky Mountain pika.

"Are you aware of his anthrax test?"

"Bernie didn't get raw milk from the dairy."

Maya settled back in her chair. At least that outbreak might be over. "We're checking into a few people who participated in a community drumming event on Thursday at a church."

"He drummed at the Orme Dam Pow Wow on Friday. He's a

lawyer and gave some advice to the tribe when they fought the dam. His friend let him try out the drums before the Grand Entry."

Drums, but not the senior group. "Can you tell me about that friend, Mrs. Young?" Then Maya called Manolo.

"Maya, ¿qué pasa?"

She shifted in her computer chair, glancing around to see if Ruth was nearby to notice her blushing. And wondered whether his low, kind voice would always stimulate this warm rush. "Where are you?"

"Pow Wow," he said. "Yavapai suspect cases."

"Me, too. Well, an Anglo case but Pow Wow connection. Can I join you?"

"Sí claro, amor. It's at the Fort McDowell Rodeo grounds. Let me know when you're here."

With no workday commuter traffic, the trip took less than forty-five minutes heading east through Phoenix. The landscape became stark as she drove through the Salt River Pima-Maricopa Indian Community.

She remembered summer tubing down the Salt River as a child. The area was more verdant in her memories, but it was mid-November, not August, and there had been repeated droughts since then.

When crossing over the banks of the Verde, a riparian valley replaced the desert landscape. On the other side, the road rose up past a more barren island mesa before she reached the parking lot.

She couldn't tell whether anthrax rumors had reached the anniversary event attendants. The crowd was huge and jovial, with license plates from neighboring states. After texting Manolo, she waited by the entrance. The Sunday Grand Entry was scheduled for one o'clock.

Adorned in the back by huge feathers, the men's ceremonial outfits were long and beaded. Some chanting and drumming had started. To the side, teenage girls rehearsed. Horizontal rows of ribbon stripes embellished the bottom of colorful dresses and capes.

The dramatic costumes reminded her of an old family photo framed on the living room wall. Zuni Shalako white and black striped mud-head clowns pointed yucca whips toward transgressors in the crowds lining the road. Her parents had taken the picture before the magical nighttime ceremony was closed to outsiders.

Even more vivid than the photo, the current day's cloudless blue skies provided a spectacular backdrop to the bold red, blue, and yellow colors swirling around her. With a sudden pivot to take in more of the vibrant scene, Maya slammed into a cowboy about Dave's height. But thinner, blond, and piercing pale blue eyes. A cigarette slipped from his lips to the dirt, followed by a mottled leather bag from his shoulder.

"Sir, it's my fault, I wasn't looking, are you all right?" She bent to grab his bag, but he snatched it up and twisted away into the crowd.

There was a familiar, warm touch on her shoulder.

"Manolo." Her smile was as wide as the horizon, shyness dissipated into the clear air. "I'm amazed you could find me."

"You stand out to me anywhere."

"My suspect patient has a Yavapai friend who let him try out a drum on Friday. No idea how to find him."

"Two of my patients participated in the Friday ceremony." He directed her to the side around the main group of dancers. "If I can locate the Tribal Council Secretary, she can help."

They skirted the ceremony and onlookers for an hour before he spotted the young woman. In between assisting with the schedule, she located the Yavapai contacts for their cases. Drums were in use for three days and no one there had skin lesions, but Manolo rubbed sterile swabs in crevices for stray bacilli. Without confirmation of human patients, they had no justification for confiscating drums or closing the event. He left business cards in case they developed a fever or skin changes.

Having accomplished all they could, Maya let go of her hyperfocus and relaxed into the multisensory celebration. They were minor pebbles in the sea of movement, and no one paid them attention even with Manolo in uniform. But Maya's spidey sense was triggered. Why did she feel under scrutiny? She brushed it aside. Her scientific training didn't allow for premonitions, even though her family's Catholic faith recognized realities beyond the reach of human perceptions.

Back at Manolo's Corvette, they drained the final drops from their water bottles. "Four hours, and not much to show except these swabs," he said.

"Three people with potential exposures are aware of the symptoms." She put a positive spin on the overstimulated afternoon.

"Spores could be anywhere. All these drums, all this dirt."

"Dave said that's anthrax, hit or miss, never in plain sight."

"The Secretary will talk to the Council President if we confirm cases," Manolo said, "and get everyone on heightened alert."

He took her hands. "Hungry? Want to grab anything here?"

Her natural caution worked overtime. "I'm nervous to eat here, and I'm protected. Do you ever regret not getting vaccinated?"

"I don't know any physician who's done that. I'm at no more risk than anyone else here. We're both overloaded with paranoia." He brushed the dust off her cheeks.

Shy about public contact with Manolo in uniform, she pulled away and turned to her vehicle.

"I should check in with Dr. Bingham. We're waiting to hear about another drumming event."

He gave her a quick embrace. "We've got to get our weekends for ourselves."

"In your dreams, señor." She climbed into her rental SUV.

Leaning in through her driver's side window, he touched his lips to hers. "You're always in my dreams, señorita."

When she checked her email from the health department cubicle, the leader of the Scottsdale drumming event had responded, and she gave him a call. He confirmed their organization provided drums imported from Jerusalem and Africa for the monthly church events.

"The djembe drums from Guinea are beautiful. Some

participants are retired Jews from New York, and they enjoy having drums from Israel," he said.

"Those countries had anthrax and drum contamination in the past. Please email a list of participants. Notifying people of their potential exposure can make a critical difference in early diagnosis and successful treatment."

"I can find names of those who registered, but others just show up."

"Thanks, we'll do the best we can with the information you provide. If necessary, we'll make a public announcement for those attending your event to contact us."

Maya felt guilty about the implied threat, but realized its effectiveness in motivating cooperation because businesses preferred to keep outbreaks quiet. As she looked for Ruth to check on case ascertainment progress, she spotted Dr. Bingham in her office and poked her head in.

"Don't know how we would connect drums from Israel and Africa to a Native American event." Maya pushed stray strands of hair behind her ears. She had stopped in the restroom to run a cool paper towel over her face, but sweat and dirt still clung to her skin.

Staying for follow-up, she called the lab at seven and received confirmation on one of the Scottsdale church cases. Manolo texted that a Pow Wow hospitalized case was confirmed, too. They notified their bosses and put together notes for the public information officers.

Maya left the drum circle leader a phone message and a stronger request for the attendee list, without revealing the test result. She didn't want him sharing information before the press release. An unfortunate delay in alerting the community and church members, but she was starting to learn the pecking order and protocols.

Manolo called to see if she wanted dinner at his place. "I don't want our weekend to be over. Shit's going to hit the fan tomorrow, and I could use quiet time with you tonight."

"Can't pass up a home-cooked meal."

When she arrived at his apartment, he opened the door with gleaming, wet hair, looking refreshed. She was even more self-conscious about her dusty skin and clothes.

"Hate the thought of tracking all this into your home."

"Why don't you jump in the shower while I finish heating things up? We're similar in height. You're welcome to grab a shirt and pants from my dresser so you won't need to put your dirty clothes on again."

She shed her grimy garments and luxuriated under the rain showerhead spray. When stepping out to the bath mat soaking wet, she regretted not picking out new clothes first. She swaddled in one of his thick, powder blue towels and poked her head out the door, then scurried into his bedroom.

His Public Health Service uniforms hung in the closet. From a wooden dresser, she grabbed a soft, long-sleeved baseball jersey and a pair of jeans. No clean bra or underwear, but she could do without.

Wafting smells of tomato sauce lured her out into the hall where she noticed for the first time the black and white southwestern landscapes framed on the walls. Presented with the kitchen domestic scene of Manolo stirring spaghetti, she wrapped her arms around his waist from behind.

"I love those photos."

"They're mine. I develop them at a nearby art center."

Impressed at his skill, she pointed to the first one closest to the kitchen. "That reminds me of Ansel Adams's *Moonrise*."

"You give me too much credit with the comparison, querida. Let's eat."

He stepped away from her embrace and brought the food to the table. After the quick meal, she started for the bathroom to retrieve her clothing. Fingers brushing the soft cotton of his shirt, she wondered if she should change back to her own.

"Cariña, keep the clothes. They fit you nicely." He gathered the dirty ones into a plastic bag and walked her outside.

"I'm flying to NYC early tomorrow. Think again about whether you can join me sometime this week."

She couldn't answer. Too much was happening, and it would be one more step toward entwining their lives. "I'll see how it goes."

While enveloping her in a long embrace, he buried his face in her clean hair. "I'll be ecstatic when we don't need to say goodbye."

His brief remark swirled nonstop around her brain as she drove to the hotel and nestled into bed.

THIRTY

<u>April 2, 2009.</u>
New Prophet says world will end soon and we're to prepare.
Jacob said if the world's ending, he's not going to school.
What a pisser. Wants to have fun with me.

We moved south to Uvalde.
Smugglers, desperadoes, my kind of place.
Even Pat Garrett hid out there after killing Billy the Kid.

THIRTY-ONE

When they met in her office on Monday, November 19, Dr. Bingham hit the speakerphone button and Dr. Grinwold's voice blasted through.

"Can't remember what Dr. Maguire looks like. Irish, right? I seem to recall two weeks ago she headed to Arizona for antelope, and then it's a dairy and drums. We do have other public health problems in New Mexico."

Dr. Bingham grimaced and mouthed *S-o-r-r-y.*

"Fred, you're more than generous. I'll send her home today."

The Yavapai-Apache Nation, Indian Health Service, and Arizona Department of Health Services issued coordinated press releases about confirmed cutaneous anthrax cases in six drummers at two different events. Maya's initial investigation found no commonalities between the monthly senior-sponsored community drumming using imported Middle Eastern and African drums and the Pow Wow using Native-made drums.

As she packed up her laptop and notes before heading to Tucson for the rental car return, Dr. Bingham stopped by her cubicle. "One new wrinkle—we've got an infected pregnant woman with complications."

Maya froze. "What's the exposure?"

"This new case brought her elderly mother to the senior drumming event last Wednesday. Over the weekend, she got a weeping open lesion on her neck, and aspirated her stomach contents because of decreased gastrointestinal motility. They had trouble intubating her due to neck swelling. At thirty-nine, she's a geriatric pregnancy, so at higher risk. They've got her in the ICU with monitoring to make sure she doesn't deliver early."

Maya sank into the chair. "We've had no fatalities with drums, and events are over."

"You don't need to stay here. Everyone is on heightened alert for skin lesions and systemic g.i. or respiratory signs. The system is working. That's why we detected her."

"I suppose you're right," Maya said. "I checked this morning and the environmental collection at both sites is done. Drumhead swabs, surface wipe samples, and random soil collection at the Pow Wow grounds. The church won't use that room until testing clears it."

During the drive to Tucson, she wracked her brain. Anthrax from two different drumming events couldn't be coincidental. Her short trip to Flagstaff and the Grand Canyon with Manolo had been stimulating yet relaxing. But whenever she tried to have a personal life, anthrax hit again in another weird way, like the disease was a living entity insisting on her full attention or it would kill lots more.

After going through security at Tucson International Airport, she called Manolo while waiting for the Albuquerque flight.

He answered from LaGuardia airport in New York City. "You're too far away."

Like a startled porcupine, she slapped back. "You said we could manage a long-distance relationship."

"Mi amor, not criticizing, just missing you."

Unhealthy to focus exclusively on the job, but she couldn't let go. "I hate heading back to New Mexico without understanding what happened."

"Imported drums are recognized as an anthrax risk from previous cases," he said. "And the Yavapai drums could be background soil contamination again."

"At the same time? We assumed the Yavapai drummers brought

their own drums. But could there be a common source with the senior event—borrowing some drums, or transport?"

"IHS is looking into it," he assured her.

"I'm still bothered by our meeting with the Homeland Security vet a week and a half ago, when she was out here for the dairy cases. She specifically warned Dave about FBI surveillance of government employees with anthrax expertise. It didn't help when I reminded everyone that a rogue federal scientist perpetrated the 2001 Amerithrax attack."

"From what I hear, Dr. Ivins was unstable even though married with kids," he said, "and he worked with the bacteria. Most of the time, Dave's a pretty even-tempered guy, and he doesn't work in a lab."

She never met Dave's wife, just overheard them talking on the phone and saw his girls during the videochat. But she knew he was an honest, down-to-earth Texas rancher and dedicated USDA vet.

"Your work schedule has been a nightmare," Manolo said. "I realize the timing is lousy, but if your boss will let you travel, catch a flight tomorrow to join me."

They said goodbye, then she splashed cold water on her bare skin and patted a wet tissue over her puffy, sleep-deprived eyes. With a black barrette from her purse, she formed her hair into a neat ponytail.

Manolo's silver and turquoise bear claw earrings glowed under the fluorescent airport bathroom lights. One of the drummers had admired the jeweler's artistry and said that bear claws were worn by those seeking leadership. If she looked like she had her act together, maybe she could do it. Fake it until you make it.

· · ·

She gave Dave a call from Albuquerque. With dairy sampling completed, he went home, so they didn't touch base when she went to Flagstaff and the Grand Canyon.

"It was stupid of me to bring up the anthrax letters while

Vanessa kidded you about being a suspect," she said after hopping into his pickup truck at the Sunport.

"She did kind of run with it, didn't she?"

"Sounds like her experience on the Amerithrax team colors her viewpoint."

Shielding the left side of his face from the glare, he drove north on the freeway. "Normally I wouldn't worry about it, but we both got in trouble already, more than once."

"What is it about us and wildlife refuges? I thought my CDC job was over before it started."

"Things are so unpredictable in the current administration. I'm concerned about my family's welfare. Beyond any threat of losing a salary, the process of being under suspicion would devastate Emilia. Please don't mention anything during dinner."

"Of course, I owe you for taking the brunt of the criticism."

"Never told her about La Migra at Cabeza Prieta." He massaged his temples and pulled on sunglasses as they turned west into the setting sun. "She worries about my time out in the field. People are gun crazy these days, especially with border issues. The funeral footage for the moms and kids killed by the drug cartel was devastating. We discussed driving down for the memorials, but I was tied up in Arizona and it was too hazardous."

His nine-acre Bernalillo ranch near the Rio Grande Bosque was beautiful despite late fall weather shutting down the growing season. The towering Sandia Mountains were glowing coral battlements in the eastern sky. In the valley, cottonwoods, coyote willows, and New Mexico olives provided a tranquil green-brown canopy, even with most of the leaves already on the ground. Two small pinto ponies danced in the fenced back acres to the gentle clucking of chickens and cooing of doves.

"What a peaceful place. I can see why you're always eager to get home," she said as they walked to an entrance off the back porch.

"Peaceful until you hear the kids screaming over who won the race to the barn."

Emilia, almost as tall as Dave's six feet, opened the blue-painted door to welcome them. His daughters squirmed at the kitchen table, a friendly black Lab resting in the corner.

As Maya knelt down, Emilia bent over to introduce him, long dark braids falling over her shoulders. "This is Bo, our fierce guard dog. Girls, when you finish your tacos, take Bo and put the horses in the stalls."

Their daughters ate quickly and Emilia excused them to their chores as she cleared the table.

"Dave says you're seeing an Indian Health Services doctor?"

"I owe your husband for that. We hit a rough spot, but Dave had much to recommend about wedded bliss, so we're giving it another try."

Emilia beamed. "Mi esposo, you surprise me."

He looked awkward when taking his wife's hand. "Figured Maya could benefit from my school of hard knocks."

After Maya checked the shuttle schedule, he drove her to the Sunport. She caught glimpses of his rugged visage in the flashes of freeway lights. Dr. Bruce Ivins had been a microbiologist with anthrax-related patents. He worked in a lab with access to the bacteria and knowledge to create pure, concentrated spores. Authorities concluded he was obsessed at getting more funding for his anthrax research and vaccine. Her veterinary friend and colleague had nothing in common with Ivins and no motivation for spreading anthrax.

"Thanks for sharing a quick slice of normal life," she said as they approached the terminal. "All these cases are overwhelming me. When I was in Tucson, I heard Reverend Tompkins' daughter is still recovering from her unknown exposure."

He gave her a side hug after she mentioned Manolo's invitation to NYC, and encouraged her to go.

"Keep in touch, Maya, even if we've put anthrax behind us."

. . .

She stopped by the Runnels Building at seven o'clock Tuesday morning, hoping to broach in person with Dr. Grinwold taking the rest of Thanksgiving week off, but with little expectation her request would be granted.

All hopes were dashed when Dr. Bingham called with two more cutaneous anthrax cases from Arizona drumming events, including the Yavapai man who shared his drum with the attorney.

"We also have our first drum-associated deaths. Not one of the elderly folks—it was the pregnant woman."

Maya closed her office door. "And the baby?"

"He only lived a couple hours. Pre-term, thirty-one weeks. We fast-tracked autopsies and they're finding bacilli in maternal and infant tissues including amniotic fluid."

Doubling over, it felt like someone punched her in the stomach. She thought the fallout from the drums was over. Too many surprises and not enough bandwidth to handle all of them. Dr. Jaworski's call from Atlanta came on her cell as she lowered the office phone.

"Take the lead on the *Morbidity and Mortality Weekly Report* for drums. You also need to work on a presentation for the late April EIS Conference. I'll need your draft by the first of the year."

Maya propped the iPhone on the desk and dropped into the office chair, both hands over her eyes.

"Are you still there, Maya? Arizona reported the pregnancy-associated deaths this morning. Dr. Bingham appreciates all your work in her state."

"Not sure I prevented any cases. I have no experience in scientific writing for publication and I'm terrible at presentations." She rested her head and torso on the desk as the overwhelming expectations of competence swirled through her brain and down through all her blood vessels and nerves.

"I don't know why you're so down on yourself. As a brand new EIS Officer, you've done amazing. We would send someone out if you were messing up. Fred is proud of New Mexico's publication record. He'll guide you."

Before hanging up, Maya promised to talk with him. Presenting anthrax in front of her EIS peers and new officers seeking assignments—how could she find time to prepare? She was too busy fighting forest fires to document the damage. Should she take propranolol like some other officers to slow her heart rate?

After finding Dr. Grinwold in his office, she shared the two phone calls. Rather than being angry by new CDC requests for a presentation and lead role in drafting a MMWR article, he rounded the desk and sat on the front edge, energized and gracious.

"Don't get upset. We'll take these one at a time. I'll help you make a plan and timeline for completion, working back from your due dates."

She marshalled her confidence and broached the subject of days off. "I know you wanted me back, but could it wait until Monday? I'm at my limit, and thinking of heading to NYC later today to spend the holiday with Dr. Simpson and my Columbia colleagues."

Was it dishonest not to mention Manolo? She tried to get a read on Dr. Grinwold's answer by studying his face and body language. Hopefully the allusion to the veterinary epidemiologist and EIS alum at the NYC health department would help.

"Flying across country won't make you well-rested," he cautioned.

She kept any pleading or whine out of her voice. "Anthrax has been nonstop for almost four months. I need a mental break as much as a physical one, so I can come back re-energized to do what you need."

He rested hands on his wide midsection. "If it gets you ready to hit the ground at eight AM Monday to finalize a schedule for the MMWR and slides, take the days. Been a long time since I've been to NYC. Say hello to Faye for me."

Her heart leapt and she grinned, unable to believe he had approved the vacation days. "I really appreciate it. I'll take my notes on the plane and start a draft."

Online, she found one of the few remaining tickets and arrived at the Sunport by ten-thirty. Her journey had two legs with a brief break in Atlanta. Not having direct flights lengthened the trip but shortened the time trapped in a sardine can.

The aisle seat was a welcome sight. She stretched her muscles that didn't tolerate long times of immobility, and went through her purse to find the small black oximeter. If claustrophobia and panic increased her respiratory rate, she could quietly slip it on and verify that she was still getting enough oxygen.

. . .

She exited the secure area at LaGuardia, and Manolo greeted her with a sensuous kiss despite the crowds. At baggage claim, he asked, "More construction than you remember? They're working hard to improve the infrastructure."

"When my parents went to China in '93 for my adoption, the Beijing airport had unisex pit toilets. Smelly urine- and feces-encrusted holes, no privacy. Can you believe they made that long, challenging trip for me?"

"It looked better on TV during the Olympics."

"You're right, when we went back twelve years later, everything was modern. Even traffic signals."

Millions of lights and grinding brakes bombarded her senses as they took the bus and subway to arrive at his sister's walk-up apartment in Little Italy just west of the Bronx Zoo.

"I'm in my father's studio while he's off to Florida for a Road Scholar painting class. You can barely turn around in it. Can you stay with my sister? She works part-time as a graphic artist, but she's home now."

"Artistic skills must run in the family." Ramona had been kind on Maya's first visit to Manolo's home, despite the breakup. On the second visit with the remarkable black and white landscape photos in the hall, Maya got her first glimpse into his life outside work.

Ramona welcomed her with a brief hug and Manolo introduced his three-year old nephew. "Maya, meet Señor Johnny Miranda-

Harun." The child zooming firetrucks on the living room wood floor didn't look up.

"Good to see you here," Ramona said. "Hope you don't mind sleeping on our futon couch. Johnny's headed to bed soon and won't be doing this at three in the morning."

Wearing a dark woolen coat over a brown suit, a slim man with obsidian skin and yellow-rimmed glasses pushed open the front door with two large pizzas. Ramona jumped up to take the boxes out of his arms.

"This is my husband, Abdi Harun."

With Manolo's strong Puerto Rican culture, Maya didn't anticipate a biracial family. Maybe there was room for Chinese, too. She whisked aside the ridiculous thought. They'd only been dating for two weeks after putting his previous marriage behind. She had a loving family. Why did this one with a young child tug on her heart?

Slaloming toy trucks amused Johnny while the grownups talked and drank beer. Abdi apologized for his workload during the visit. As an attorney with the Natural Resources Defense Council, he was slammed with lawsuits related to environmental justice.

"Let's all do the parade on Thursday," he suggested.

"We heard about your anthrax work," Ramona said. "I worry about both of you."

Manolo broke down the pizza boxes. "It's not contagious."

"But you're right where everybody's getting it."

"Maya was vaccinated for her field and animal work. Anthrax isn't easy to catch from people."

"Sorry, terrorists are on my brain from living here through 9/11," Ramona said. "I think we all changed that day. Last year there were three incidents. First a white supremacist stabbed an African American man to death, then an Islamic terrorist slammed his pickup into pedestrians and cyclists on the West Side Highway, and a suicide bomber tried to detonate himself in the Port Authority."

"Mom phoned me to drop out of Columbia after every one of those."

"Sometimes we wonder about living in a target city," Abdi said. "But this is paradise compared to growing up in Somalia."

"When did you come here?" Maya asked, always eager to hear other immigration stories.

"NYU, that's where we met." He reached for his wife's hand.

Maya piled her empty plate on top of Manolo's. "Speaking of bioterrorism, a vet from Homeland Security said they always consider it when something unusual is going on. She came to Phoenix twice when we had the heroin-associated anthrax and the dairy workers."

"Our anthrax is a flare-up from contaminated soil," Manolo interjected. "Maya's USDA associate said they're having an outbreak of animal cases this year in west Texas, right?"

She nodded, but was dissatisfied with the background level explanation. The media and public were understandably alarmed even though the case count was small outside of the heroin addicts. Arizona was the only state with human cases except for the injection ones. That made it a big deal. But in most of the Arizona incidents, the infection rate was minimal despite huge personal, medical, and public health impacts. And nothing connected up.

"The FBI has been assessing the Arizona situation. They're even looking at government scientists like the presumed culprit with the anthrax letters." She thought back to her worries about Dave.

"You're everywhere trying to control it. That could make you targets, too," Ramona said.

"Targets of the bad guy or the FBI? No one has talked to me about bioterrorism. How about you, Maya?"

"Maybe there's been confidential discussions with our bosses."

Manolo and Maya washed up the dinner dishes. "The parade balloons are inflated at three tomorrow afternoon," he said. "Too much for Johnny, but we could bring him to the zoo in the morning."

Ramona joined them from the dining room. "I'll never pass up a free babysitter. I do graphic design work for Abdi at NRDC." She shouted back to her husband. "What do you think, honey, could we arrange a morning work date at your office?"

At the Bronx Zoo Wednesday morning, Maya cuddled the three-year-old as the gorilla movie finished and the exhibit wall moved away to expose the huge landscaped enclosure. The giant animals looked just like them, waiting and watching for a chance to connect through the massive clear panels.

She loved Johnny's short arms around her neck and his head nestled against hers. As the restless toddler wriggled, she felt a twinge of back pain and reluctantly switched him to Manolo. Before bringing him home, they stopped for chicken nuggets and he gave her a strawberry ice cream-flavored kiss.

In the afternoon, they joined thousands crowding streets around the American Museum of Natural History to watch the giant-sized helium balloons come to life.

"Which one's your favorite?" he asked, arm draped across her shoulders.

She stretched her arm around his waist. "Kung Fu Panda. He's modest and loves his adoptive goose father like I love mine."

"Mine's Snoopy. I always liked the Charlie Brown story. Sometimes you're like Lucy snatching away my football just when I want to place a kick."

His grin didn't tell her everything she wanted to know. "Dr. Miranda, are you saying I keep you off-center?"

He kissed her cheek. "Only enough to keep me interested."

. . .

Thanksgiving dawned cold, dry, and windy, more like January. The family relaxed on the west side of Central Park to rejoice in the parade. Johnny gyrated in restless abandon to the band performances between animal and cartoon balloons gliding overhead. Maya danced with him to the music of a high school group from Tucson, and Johnny squealed when Olaf's huge carrot nose came close.

"We watched *Frozen* again this week," Ramona said.

Following a low-key Thanksgiving dinner with Ramona's family, Maya headed out on Friday to Long Island City for a visit with her old mentor, the Public Health Veterinarian who kept threatening retirement. Dr. Faye Simpson enveloped her in a hearty hug.

"Kid, haven't talked to you in ages. You know we New Yorkers like to be the center of the universe. But here you are heading up the biggest anthrax investigation since 2001."

The noisy sirens disturbed Maya and she was relieved not to work in that environment anymore. "You know these responses are a team effort, but it's kept me going nonstop."

"Many EIS Officers get a lot of responsibility and intense pressure right out of the gate," Faye said. "These days will be among the most rewarding of your life. Plus, now you're part of the club. Do well and you'll have a bidding war to hire you when your two years are up."

"Too far in the future for me—just need to make it through all this."

"You're selling yourself short, Maya." Faye took the familiar posture leaning back on the chair with her feet on the desk. "Where are you staying?"

"With the sister of my IHS colleague. We're dating. Well, we had a breakup when he was late to tell me about a recent divorce. But we've worked it out. Nothing's forced or rushed. It's a great change of pace from the high pressures of work."

"I'm happy for you, kid. Never married, but had my fun along the way. You deserve something in your life besides the job."

Maya spent the rest of the day in Manhattan, visiting friends among the Columbia faculty and public health students still working on their degrees. When she returned to Ramona and Abdi's brownstone, Manolo kissed her hello and handed her an envelope.

"Some tickets for a Broadway matinee tomorrow," he said with a hesitant smile.

After ripping open the envelope, she squealed when she saw *Hamilton*. She twirled him around, dancing in delight. "You know my obsession. They're so much in demand, how did you make it happen?"

"Let's just say I know somebody who knows somebody." He kept her at arms' length, clearly taken back by her atypical uninhibited joy.

She pulled him close, wrapping her arms around his back and reaching up to stroke his hair. "Not sure what I did to deserve this, but you make me very happy."

The next day, dressed in a flowing, black silk gown she had rolled into a corner of her suitcase for any dressy events, she twisted in her chair to take in the beautiful, historic Richard Rodgers theatre. For almost three hours, the multisensory spectacle of singing, dancing, and throbbing orchestra washed over her like a wave. Having memorized the lyrics from the cast album, she was tempted to sing along, but was too busy gripping Manolo's hand and darting her eyes around all the activity in every corner of the stage.

Early shadows of sunset darkened the streets as they burst from the theatre with crowds of exuberant patrons. "Everything you hoped for?" he asked.

"Are you kidding? Best show of my life."

He held her tight as they worked through the mashing mob. "Do you need time to recover, or would you like to extend the evening?"

"What did you have in mind?" She put her arms around his neck and kissed his ear.

"We're invited to a party in my dad's neighborhood. Buffet dinner, nothing formal, no end of wine and lively conversation. Up for it?"

"Your wish is my command." She seized his hand as he led them to the subway.

Having grown up with a sedate family and friends, she relished the unfamiliar, rapid banter and infectious laughter spilling out of different rooms in the cluttered Bronx brownstone. She met his childhood friends and ducked anthrax talk.

Sunday morning, after clearing security at LaGuardia, they hurried to her gate since she had the earlier flight. Before she joined the boarding line, he held her tight.

"This was a quick trip, and I'm glad I was able to show you

where I'm from. Hope we can squeeze in more times without work demands."

"I'd like that, too." She sighed, reluctant to let go.

"I'm relieved my clone doesn't star in *Hamilton* anymore. He's definitely more attractive and talented, and I wouldn't want the competition."

"Manolo, he's married with kids."

"That doesn't stop women from falling in love with him."

"Nothing to worry about, there's no one else in my heart." For the first time, she initiated their long, tender kiss goodbye, before slowly pulling away.

THIRTY-TWO

<u>Jan 9, 2015.</u>
Had a few years of good jobs 'cause Uvalde LDS guy took pity on us.
He managed family ranch and needed someone to spell him.
But jobs dried up so we're headed to Utah.

Jacob got GED and applied to Dixie State University in St. George. Shithead egghead. Kinda proud of him.

We talked about finding normal life but never talked to girls.
They recognize wounded animals and shy away from us. Assholes.

<u>April 16.</u>
Accounting. Fucking accounting.
Next fall, Jacob was going to learn about counting money.
Until the jerkoff grabbed for my wrench on the fast-food restaurant roof repair.

Both of us ended up at Dixie Regional Med Center with head injuries.

I just got out, worse for wear.
He didn't make it.

THIRTY-THREE

The first anthrax threat letter was postmarked in Yuma, Arizona on December 3 and delivered to the Senator-elect's Phoenix office two days later, where decorations celebrating her election still hung from the ceiling.

"Get to the airport tomorrow for the earliest flight," Dr. Bingham commanded Maya by phone. "Be prepared to participate in a press conference."

Maya tried everything to sleep—warm milk, down comforter, lowering the room temperature. But nothing worked. She was right. Arizona anthrax didn't just pop up. A human hand was revealed. Each time she started to drift off, Dr. Bingham's words echoed in her ears and she shivered. Her increased heart and breathing rate woke up her brain, and she had to begin her relaxation processes all over again.

Dr. Bingham updated her on the details when she arrived at the Arizona health department. A secretary in the Senator-elect's office had opened the padded 8.5" x 12" tan envelope. Inside was a yellow-lined sheet of paper with a letter in handwritten, hard-to-read cursive.

Voters elected the first female Senator in Arizona and the second openly LGBT person in the Senate nationally.
Changing God and earth's natural order = anthrax.
For this cause God gave them up unto vile affections; for even

their women did change the natural use into that which is against nature; And likewise also the men, leaving the natural use of the woman, burned in their lust one toward another.
[1 Romans 1:26-27. King James, The New Testament.]

Enclosed was a separate, sealed 6" x 10" padded envelope that was full and squishy to the secretary's touch. She noticed the seal was slightly loose and there was dust coating the inside of the bigger mailing envelope. She set both envelopes and the letter down on the desk and called her boss, who contacted the Phoenix Police Department.

The Postal Service protocol was followed. After advising the secretary to wash her hands with soap and water, the police officer instructed her to shower as soon as possible and isolate her clothes in a sealed plastic bag. The supervisor developed a list of individuals who handled the envelope, along with their contact information.

Before touching the materials, the officer took photos. Following the Arizona Suspicious Substance Protocol, she put on gloves, double bagged each item separately, and placed them in a sealed container for transport to the Public Health Laboratory. The FBI and Dr. Bingham were notified.

The material in the inner envelope was unlike the white powders from sugar, flour, or starch used in fake threats or accidental contamination of the mail. It appeared to be dirt with particles in various sizes of an indeterminate brown color. Based on the type of material, the lab was waffling on whether testing was required or feasible. But Dr. Bingham reminded them that with the recent anthrax cases, testing would be necessary for any threat letters.

Despite the clear anthrax warning in the text of the letter, no spores were found. The agencies concluded it was a fake threat and the work of a copycat hoping to inspire terror with heightened public attention from the recent anthrax cases. Maya didn't feel similarly reassured. The agencies decided not to publicize the incident but retained the evidence.

A second similar envelope postmarked December 4 at Nogales arrived December 6 at the Guadalupe offices of the Pascua Yaqui tribe. Not having been alerted about the first envelope, a mail clerk opened it.

Our services promote healing, personal growth, and healthy living for the individual, the family and the community. [Pascua Yaqui Behavioral Health Centered Spirit Program]
What about me? Try this for healthy living—anthrax.
I pledge allegiance to the Flag of the United States of America, and to the Republic for which it stands, one Nation under God, indivisible, with liberty and justice for all.

Protocols were implemented similar to the Senator's letter. Samples didn't arrive at the lab until five o'clock. Working late, they concluded at ten that the desert soil sample had *B. anthracis* bacilli.

A third letter postmarked December 5 in Prescott was delivered on December 7 to the Phoenix office of the Arizona Coalition for Migrant Rights.

An electorate that is fearful of Arizona's changing demographics and an organized and well-funded anti-immigrant leadership has contributed to putting Arizona at the cutting edge of anti-immigrant rhetoric and legislation. [Arizona Coalition for Migrant Rights, website]
No joke. Neither is this—anthrax.
He informed me of great judgments which were coming upon the earth, with great desolations by famine, sword, and pestilence; and that these grievous judgments would come on the earth in this generation.
[Testimony of the Prophet Joseph Smith, The Book of Mormon.]

The confirmatory lab tests from the third letter came in just before the late afternoon press conference and the team adjusted their remarks. Raul Gomez, the FBI's Special Agent in Charge for the Phoenix Field Office, anchored a table in the meeting room of the massive glass-boxed Phoenix Convention Center.

Maya straightened the collar of her red blazer and looked away from the packed hall's probing eyes. Why did it feel like they were fixated on her? She was the youngest and least experienced professional on the stage. Could everyone see that?

She refocused on her colleagues at the table. With the second letter addressed to a Native American group, Manolo sat next to her for the Indian Health Service. He seemed to pick up on the import of her shifting posture and clasped her hand before she pulled it away.

Dave was next for USDA. Vanessa Wright, who had flown overnight from Washington to represent Homeland Security, huddled with Gomez. On the other end were state agency reps, Nancy Bingham for health, Ben Smith for agriculture, and Sarah Vaughn for Game and Fish.

"Beginning December 5, three offices received anthrax threat letters." Agent Gomez clicked on the laptop and projected a photo of three outside envelopes with addresses.

"Inside these outer envelopes were threat letters and smaller, sealed envelopes with soil, perhaps to avoid detection." The second slide showed the soil packages. "The health lab got a positive test on the soil from the Yaqui letter last night, with a second positive today from the letter to the migrant rights group. Soil from the Senator-elect's letter was negative but will be retested."

Camera clicks and the audible shock from newspeople and others in attendance distracted Maya. She knew the time was coming for her prepared remarks and was praying she didn't black out. At the end of the table, she could slip out if necessary. But she was sitting down, a glass of water nearby, and Manolo next to her. Those were her coping mechanisms. The front of the table was hidden by a long white curtain, and he held her fingers under it.

"We have not determined with certainty why these offices were targeted. The two organizations provide support to Native

Americans and migrants. The threat letters should provide us a clue." Gomez displayed all three letters side by side.

"If you have trouble reading this handwriting, information packets are located in the back of the room. A website quotation is at the top of each letter, followed by a statement apparently written by the perpetrator, and a reference at the bottom that may have provided inspiration. The attributions at the bottom are from the King James version of the New Testament, the Pledge of Allegiance, and the Book of Mormon."

Agent Gomez concluded. "Before I turn this over to Dr. Wright of Homeland Security, anyone receiving envelopes like these should call your local Police or the FBI. Do not open them. Dr. Wright?"

"Thank you. We are treating this as a presumptive hate crime, and threatening government officials is a felony. We have no connection to other anthrax infections over the past months. Someone may be piggybacking on public concern about anthrax from naturally occurring periodic acceleration of anthrax in the soil. But the federal agencies are offering full support to Arizona as the investigation continues. Next we have the state health department."

Dr. Wright passed the microphone down to Dr. Bingham.

"We are monitoring employees who opened the letters, and offices are identifying others who handled the envelopes before they were opened. The Postal Service is assessing mail routes and will determine if anyone was exposed. Environmental testing has started in the organizations and mail facilities. Dr. Maguire?"

Maya gulped a deep breath. "As a CDC representative, I investigated all anthrax cases since August. We have no cases from the letters and anthrax-contaminated soil is *not* an effective route of exposure in the mail compared to the 2001 anthrax letters with a purified powder. However, we urge Arizonans to be alert for signs of anthrax and to contact medical providers with concerns. Handouts will be provided after this press conference and information is available on state health and CDC websites. Dr. Miranda?"

Brushing her fingers as he took the microphone, his lips turned up in a slight smile. Then he faced the audience. "Representing the Indian Health Service, we are prepared to respond to any anthrax infections among members of tribal nations. One letter was sent to a Pascua Yaqui health program office in Guadalupe, Phoenix metro area. There's no evidence of anyone exposed to the soil in that letter. We coordinated with federal agencies and the state on previous Native American infections, and will continue to do so."

Agent Gomez took back the microphone. "That concludes our current findings. The Senator-elect will issue a separate statement. Agencies involved in these incidents are available for questions."

The press had their usual who, what, and when questions, wanting to pin down when the letters were received and how they were detected. They also pressed the presenters for predictions and interpretations. Maya was dissatisfied. She attended press conferences for the previous incidents, but didn't participate. The statements were short, with less room for misinterpretation. And they were always positive. An agency's primary mission in this type of press announcement was reassurance. We're dealing with it, you're okay. But she didn't feel okay. She was scared.

When she thought they were finished, a reporter from the Arizona Republic raised his hand. "Dr. Maguire, CDC is considered the preeminent public health organization in the world. Why aren't you more on top of this microbial mess?"

The TV cameras swung to catch her reaction. She flinched and began to say, "I, um . . ."

Dr. Bingham jumped in. "Barry, you should know that CDC is here at state invitation. Dr. Maguire is in a supportive function, except when diseases cross state lines. Given the legal implications, the FBI is in charge. The public health procedures established after the mail attacks in 2001 are working well. We've had no human cases from these letters."

Agent Gomez stood up, and the others on the podium followed his lead. Dr. Bingham strolled over to Maya.

"Sorry to cut you off, but that question was over your head. Get a few more years of experience with these press conferences and you'll do fine."

Ashamed she hadn't been ready with a politically expedient response, Maya responded with a weak smile. "No problem, I appreciate the save."

With the crowd dispersed, Manolo caught her alone. He gave her a hurried hug. "First one? You did great."

"I'm not so sure about that, the question threw me. But for my statement, I followed your Boy Scout motto of 'be prepared.'"

"Do you think you'll stick around?" he asked.

She rotated her shoulders, trying to relax. "I think so. These letters were one each day. We don't know if there will be more, but it's good no one's showing clinical signs. Dr. Bingham said there was loose powder in the first note to the Senator where the soil was negative. I don't think we're out of the woods."

"Would you like to stay in my second bedroom?"

Too much to manage—still overwhelmed with anthrax. "I should stick to my home away from home this time."

He responded in a halting voice. "But we'll get together as much as possible?"

"Por supuesto, as you would say." She lifted her chin and tightened her shoulder blades with an intrepid air.

. . .

On December 11, Maya presented her summary to Dr. Bingham, including a fourth letter delivered to the Tucson office of the National Association for Hispanic Elderly on December 8. A senior volunteer opened the mail after coming in to work on a grant proposal.

Tucson was a different media market than Phoenix, and there was a strong intercity rivalry. Sometimes those in southern Arizona didn't pay close attention to Phoenix news, even related to their politicians.

The volunteer ripped open the inner soil packet before she turned over the yellow page and read the letter. In shock, she dropped the packet, spilling soil over clothes, skin, and furniture. She called the Tucson Police Department. Janey Johnson supervised collection of specimens and the environmental cleanup for Pima County.

Three more letters were intercepted before delivery based on similar appearance and handwriting, although the final two were in umber envelopes and had been placed into New Mexico mailboxes for Arizona targets. It appeared the letters had been mailed one each day, on the third to the ninth, from seven different cities.

Only one letter went to a politician. The others were addressed to the Native American health center, three groups supporting Hispanics or migrant rights, the Arizona Republic newspaper, and the Arizona National Organization for Women.

"These references at the bottom of each one, where are they from?" Dr. Bingham asked.

Maya reviewed her notes. "Three from the Bible, King James version, with two from Exodus related to the ten plagues of Egypt. Three from the Book of Mormon, and one with the Pledge of Allegiance."

"Which plagues?"

"The first related to blood and the sixth related to boils."

Dr. Bingham massaged a wrinkled hand through short thick hair to her scalp.

"Guess they're familiar with anthrax. By the way, the lab finally got it from the Senator's letter, but not the last one. Challenging with a mixed substance like dirt."

"Dave found the same thing with the earlier incidents when he collected soil for the Texas lab." Maya glanced down at her cell phone. "Can I step out? Janey in Pima County tried to call me."

"No problem. Agent Gomez from the FBI is stopping by later today. Based on the three Book of Mormon references, I assume they're looking at someone associated with the Latter-Day Saints."

Leaning against the wall outside Dr. Bingham's office, Maya hit Janey's number on her screen.

"Hi, Maya. Good news and bad news."

"Good first?"

"The Reverend's daughter is doing better, but she needed plastic surgery to replace debrided skin on her fingers. May have some limited dexterity. Still don't know how she got it."

"Her mom must be devastated jeopardizing her daughter's health by trying to help others." Anthrax wasn't prolonged in an outbreak like other diseases, spreading person to person. But it still had long-ranging effects by lingering, hiding, in the soil.

"Now the bad news," Janey said. "The volunteer at the Association for Hispanic Elderly who opened their letter has bug bites on her hands. This time of year, less likely to be bugs. She's at TMC and they're testing. May start antitoxin."

Maya wheeled in frustration. She glanced into Dr. Bingham's office but didn't see her. "I'll check with the lab. None of the other inner envelopes were opened. We could get lucky, and she's our only case."

After updating her spreadsheets and draft reports, the bottom corner of her computer screen said 7:09 PM. She leaned against the cubicle wall, then crawled her fingers up the barrier as far as she could reach. It was blissful to counteract the hours of cramped hunching over the keyboard. Maybe she would finish early for once. She remembered the FBI briefing and strolled down the hall to check in.

"Dr. Bingham, I'm heading to the hotel. Just called the lab and they finished the antibody specimen for the Tucson lady who opened the envelope. Her titer is low positive, so maybe our first case, unless she was exposed somewhere else, another time."

"Lab probably reported it to FBI, but I'll verify. With no more letters, I hoped we were done with public health risk."

"Me, too." Maya rubbed her neck and tried to take in a deep abdominal breath of relief. "That would be amazing if it's wrapped up quickly like our other anthrax incidents. But this was deliberate, and the others weren't. At least, we didn't think so."

"It may be over for new cases, but not the criminal investigation. FBI agents are still in the conference room, and they want to talk to you. You're a person of interest."

. . .

Maya recognized Agent Gomez from the shared podium announcing the anthrax letters. For the first time she had his unblinking dark gaze totally focused on her. She flashed to movie star Andy Garcia as obsessed Agent Raymond Avila in the movie *Internal Affairs*. With his black hair in a widow's peak and his nervous, shifting energy, he perched tensely on the chair.

More controlled, the thirty-something female agent with a short brown bob and bangs looked like Avila's partner. When Maya's nightmares woke her up and she couldn't fall back sleep, she sometimes binged on old movies. This one haunted her, not only for the amoral bad cop played by Richard Gere, but Agent Avila's willingness to go to any lengths to solve his cases.

Maya had nothing in common with the Richard Gere antagonist masquerading as a good guy using misdirection to escape detection. So why did Gomez's hairline make her brain circle around that old fictional cat-and-mouse confrontation?

His next words didn't help dispel the morbid movie memories.

"Dr. Maguire, this is Agent Laura O'Brien. We believe the Arizona anthrax incidents are all connected by deliberate distribution of anthrax-contaminated soil from West Texas. You and Dr. Schwartz overlap with them, and we need to confirm you didn't have a role in causing them."

Maya melted under the table. At least figuratively. Her mind puddled on the floor, but her body was frozen to the cold metal chair. Temporarily blinded by fear, she stayed silent.

"We acknowledge you were at each scene to investigate it. We're not aware either of you have a motive, but firefighters are known to set fires just to become heroes who put them out."

He paused to push a wad of papers to her. "Here's search

warrants for your hotel, apartment, offices here and in Santa Fe, and your vehicles. We'll be looking for anthrax. If we find nothing, we'll apologize for the inconvenience and let you get back to work."

She opened her eyes. Although fond of thirty-something, Hispanic male faces, this Andy Garcia clone wasn't one of them.

The female agent was gentler. "Dr. Maguire, are you okay?"

Even if it was untrue, Maya nodded, always trying to be cooperative.

"Dr. Maguire," O'Brien said. "I need to take you to Dr. Bingham's office while Agent Gomez and our team start on your cubicle. I also need your purse, keys, and phone."

Somehow she stood and followed the female agent down the hall. At the State Epidemiologist's office, Dr. Bingham took the arm of her zombied trainee and helped her to the chair, then asked a staff member to pick up fast food.

O'Brien dug a yellow pad out of her leather case, apologizing as she required Maya to write out words from the anthrax letters. The task brought her back into conscious functioning. Wouldn't she change her handwriting if she was really guilty?

After they ate, Dr. Bingham asked about next steps. The agent put them off until Gomez returned.

"We've completed our initial work here," he said. "You'll travel with us on a flight to Albuquerque tomorrow morning. We're retaining your belongings, and you can't go back to the hotel because our team is still there."

"She can stay with me," Dr. Bingham said.

Agent O'Brien followed behind them and parked across from the suburban single-story ranch home.

"I'll put out p.j.'s, a toothbrush, and a towel in the bathroom. Maya, I'm devastated by this. You two can't be top of their list. They're going through the motions to rule out low-hanging fruit. It will be straightened out soon."

The food at her boss's office had re-energized Maya's brain from its stuporific state.

"They mentioned Dave. I need to reach him."

"I was told you shouldn't place calls. They're in New Mexico and it's too late to warn him."

"Manolo?"

"Better not. Don't want to drag him into this."

She took cover under the cool, cotton sheets and warm futon, not bothering to shower. Was this just a film noir movie?

THIRTY-FOUR

<u>July 4, 2018.</u> Big anniversary, might as well start writing again. 13 fuckin years since banished. Lucky 13. No family, not after Jacob died. Not my fault, but they wouldn't see it that way. I encouraged him to leave, got him the job. Should've given him the wrench when he asked for it.

Hid out after that with Pat Garrett back in Uvalde. Used to be smarter. Flying off the roof and landing on my head didn't help. Still have Mother's Moroni journal, so guess I can write. Not totally useless in the smarts department.

Never did construction again. Not getting any higher than back of a horse. And never want to see another fuckin tool. Back to Texas ranching like a duck to dirty shit-hole wetland.

Nothing to lose pushing livestock around. All they can do is run over and kill me, like Jacob used to be scared of.

Speaking of killing me, Uvalde is fucking anthrax capital of the world! One of those weird African diseases, right? Hundred cases just in one damned county. Ranches vaccinate their cowboys for shit job of burying and burning all the dead animals. Got to be a specialist. Nobody else wanted to do it and I had an in, working for a LDS vet who sold his soul to the feds.

What gave Texas Triangle magic anthrax touch? Maybe it was our Palace and angel Moroni. Started collecting souvenirs. Kept dirt from every place with anthrax. Little or big memories, depending on my mood. Spores can get you after 40 years, gift that keeps on giving.

Fucking ragheads changing the world. Why not me too? Last time anybody used anthrax, he had more degrees than you could count. We're not lost boys. God and earth's natural order. Gonna try and make it right again.

July 18. Making big change. Driving back to God's country. Stopped off in Hopi Land, peaceful place to figure out my plans. They're always fighting with fuckin Navajos about who owns what. But we can't have a tiny piece of the Four Corners?

Keams Canyon, hip Hopi kid at sunset singing to sheep, fuckin Michael Jackson's Thriller. Jackson's a fuckin fag, molesting kids like Prophet. Bible forbids men's and women's vile affections, but Prophet and Jackson didn't read that part.

Something Arizona can brag about, having a bisexual slut running for the Senate. Pickup loaded with prime anthrax dirt. Can I dump Texas values into Arizona?

July 26. Watching clueless kid while working things out. He could be my experiment?

Doesn't do much except write songs, chant, sleep, and eat. So confident. Nice voice. Dances around the campfire. Bet he doesn't have trouble with girls.

Used to think I might have a shot at learning how to talk to them, before the accident. If I was poison before, they're definitely wary of me now. Slow talker, sound retarded. Nothing super obvious but enough to put people off.

Kid's Father trades places with him Sat. morning and again Sunday night. Wonder what he does with time away from the dumb animals. Stud at parties.

Sleeps like the dead under God's heaven at night. I spent last week giving him a Thriller. Spread dirt where he had his flock in the early morning hours. I'm vaccinated, not brain dead. I wore protection. No shittin me.

Woke up this morning, one of the sheep was dead. My anthrax? Kid must have been bored and decided to cut it open to see what was going on. Stupid.

July 29. His Father didn't show up yesterday. Wonder what happened? But fine with me.

Two more downed sheep and got to see the kid collapse. "Masauwu?"

Looked it up after back in cell range. Lord of the Dead. Warned the Hopis about dangers of the world. Did the kid know?

Had to hide in cave til storm passed. Then Father took kid away on a horse. Wondered if he'd show up before kid drowned. Should have been on time and kid'd be okay. Fucking restaurant roof, fucking hospital, took Jacob. Now nature is evening the score.

Aug. 7. Cell phone to check news, nothing on the kid. What the fuck's going on? If it was anthrax, wouldn't they want to freak out the world? No problema, plenty of time to collect more magic dust.

<u>Aug. 14.</u> Wow! Triple play! Kid, sheep, soil! Who knew I was so good? Press said he was oldest kid. "Thus saith the LORD, About midnight will I go out into the midst of Egypt; And all the firstborn in the land of Egypt shall die, from the firstborn of Pharaoh that sitteth upon his throne, even unto the firstborn of the maidservant that is behind the mill; and all the firstborn of beasts." Death of firstborn, Plague of Egypt #10. Ex. 11:4-6.

<u>Aug. 15.</u> These liberals have no respect for God's teachings and the natural order. UU's are the worst. Trying to help illegal hordes take over our country. Damned Mexicans think they can take back the southwest.

"LESS GOVERNMENT—MORE RESPONSIBILITY AND WITH GOD'S HELP—A BETTER WORLD." John Birch Society tells it like it is.

Got no love for PIGS when they're telling us what to do with our families. But if they keep the caravans from invading, we should support them, not help the invaders. There's nothing I can't do for my country.

<u>Aug. 16.</u> Followed minister from church to border. Fuckin interfering with nature. Poor immigrants need not apply. Words on Statue of Liberty: "Give me your tired and your poor who can stand alone on their own two feet." As long as they pledge allegiance to our country, not the fuckin places they came from.

<u>Aug. 22.</u> Went out to Brown Canyon again. Spread my special soil in area where she dug in water bottles. People not grazers so harder to get them exposed. Her digging will help.

LDS recruits immigrants. Why dilute our White race? Smarter to be more pure, closer to God.

<u>Aug. 23.</u> Pay dirt! Minister came again. Weather variable, some rains today, not too much to wash away my handiwork. She dug around to make sure bottles are partly covered with dirt. She looked at junk, sank into the soil to pick up baby's rattle. Pressed it to her face, kissed it, and prayed. Hallelujah.

<u>Aug. 24.</u> Who's the native fucker gathering grasses? Reaching down, feeling them from the base, picking just the right bundles, pulling up from the roots, not breaking them off. Standing back up, shaking the soil off the roots. Collateral damage.

<u>Aug. 25.</u> Small woman with long, dark braids and two kids snuck through. Same age as me and Jacob when I was banished. Did they get expelled from somewhere?

She and the kids lie down and rest under the sycamores. At least cooler in the dark of night. No one put everything out as handout for me. I made it on my own.

<u>Aug. 26.</u> La migra was busy. Looking for family coming through last night? Back to Tucson. Got there in time for minister's sermon. Not at church in long time.

"We are a welcoming congregation. If there are any guests here for the first or second time, please raise your hand so we can welcome you." Why not? What's so suspicious about a 6' blond, blue-eyed, skinny 29-year-old? Old lady next to me shakes my hand. I pretend she's Mother and smile sweet.

Minister talks about how we're all part of the interdependent web and we should respond to challenges with open hearts, open minds, open hands. Then she falls off the podium. Everyone rushes forward and I just watch.

<u>Sep. 3.</u> Labor Day, should honor Jacob's death from laboring. Stopped by cemetery. No trees, dead park for dead people. Thought about whether to find Mother or sisters, but they wouldn't recognize me. Maybe they would, but pretend not to. That'd be worse.

<u>Sep. 10.</u> Got both of them! Minister and blanket-ass artist. But they're not dead. And nothing about the illegal family sneaking in. Not up to Dylann Roof on the body count, but patience is its own reward. I'm enjoying my freedom and he's not.

<u>Sep. 11.</u> Honoring all who died by those fucking Towelheads taking down the Towers. And the Pentagon. And the Pennsylvania plane.

Wildlife refuge worked last time, so try again. Nobody knows bison real susceptible, whole bunch dead in Canada farm. Raymond Bison Conservation Herd east of Flag preserves rare bison genetics. Why the fuck is that important?

Prophet Joseph Smith knew what he was talking about. "He informed me of great judgments which were coming upon the earth, with great desolations by famine, sword, and pestilence; and that these grievous judgments would come on the earth in this generation." 200 years since he wrote that. Fulfillment has been a long time coming.

<u>Sep. 19.</u> Nobody else knows all the animals who can get anthrax besides me. Who the fuck would think of reindeer? And moose? Fucking petting zoo? Holiday Home. I say God's Gift. Easy access to pens through forest. Don't climb over, just toss soil through chain link with shovel. Riskier than remote refuge, but no cameras.

No bison or people knocked off at refuge east of here. Not enough people visiting. This will be much better.

Sep. 26. Last day at Holiday Home. Spending a week or so in each area of the state works out. No luck here yet. Need to move on to avoid detection. Everytime I turn around, someone shows up, investigating.

Running out of cash. Hate cities and Mexican drug cartel but know a lot of guys. No shame in heroin, cheaper than opioids when you run out. Only thing got me through after my fall and Jacob. Good-looking faithful guy shouldn't have any pain, right? Maybe head back to Albuquerque. Find some Breaking Bad Anglo guys.

Sep. 28. Got hooked up with right guys. Brown crystal perfect for mixing dirt. Hundreds sick from contaminated heroin overseas, why not here? They're reassured by Mormon missionary dealing. Don't attract suspicion on the street. Invited into all those white, happy homes just getting by like me. Besides, just giving them what they're asking for. If you can't control your freakin habit, it's on you.

As the Book of Mormon says, "if my people shall sow filthiness they shall reap the chaff thereof in the whirlwind; and the effect thereof is poison."

Oct. 11. Another dead kid. What parent lets their kid kiss a moose? Reap what you sow. Fucking Flagstaff North Pole Disneyland is out of business. Prophet said Walt Disney and Care Bears and all the little creatures are lies. No fucking joke.

Uvalde vet worked on this for the feds. It's a small world after all. It's a small world after all.

Nobody sick yet from heroin. Not doing it right. What am I, a fucking scientist? Nobody's ever done this before. If it was easy, it would've been done already.

Oct. 14. Just 3 cases, 1 dead. Slow start, but ok. At least it's working. Dead guy a fucking undocumented Honduran. What did I tell you?

Oct. 22. 219 fucking cases! Coast to coast! Maybe I should quit when I'm ahead.

Fucking Homeland Security and FBI at press conference. Dr. Maya Maguire did all these fancy numbers trying to figure out my pattern. Know what the slant-eye looks like from newspaper photo, but wasn't on TV.

I'm the biggest thing that ever happened for anthrax. I know, been researching it like crazy at libraries and cell phone. Hundreds dead from lab leak at Sverdlovsk. Same for injection in Europe.

I'll never achieve Zimbabwe '79 -'80. Over 10,000 mostly in tribal trust lands, not the white-owned farming areas. Maybe blowflies or horseflies. Or someone beat me to a way to contaminate the land and everything in it.

They're calling my work 'climate change' and 'background soil contamination,' just like they did in Zimbabwe, at first. Longer I stay under the radar the better.

Oct. 23. Wrap up a few loose ends. They're not arresting Minister for helping the wetbacks. And she's not stopping. BIG MISTAKE! Quick trip to Tucson. Sparkly dust in the backyard will cure her.

Wildlife again. Safer. Remote. Plus the border, my least favorite place. Didn't work with the bison. How about antelope? Fucking endangered species. I'm endangered and nobody cares.

Fuckin Lost Boys, they call us. Kicked out of the only life we ever knew because the numbers didn't add up. If there's plural marriages, elders get multiple wives, and there's extra boys. We're not valuable. We're competition.

Survival of the fittest. None of this coddling like with the fuckin buffalo and pronghorn.

My Father, my first Father, used to choke me sometimes. It was his way of showing he loved me so much. He wanted me to live forever in heaven.

Oct. 24. Fucking border patrol worse than other refuge. Fuck, you only live once!

Gonna try everything before I go. Pulled over, asked what I was doing. Dirt in the back, not illegal immigrants, they let me go. Spread my gold dust several places. Tried to find spot where that Activist Ed Abbey was buried. I should like him, he talked about blowing things up.

Oct. 28. 3 antelope down, ready to spread more seed. Raw Halloween feast, good old boys like me. Want to make my contribution. Lots of money from Heroina, hired hunting guide. Fucking Potato, best in area. Helped me bag a pronghorn from area where I was working.

Beautiful tawny body in my crosshairs. Chose one looking draggy, hoping he was sick. Gave guy whole carcass as a tip. Told him hunting just for the sport. Love thinking of those dudes slopping down spores.

<u>Oct. 29.</u> No more beasts for the Lord's dominion. Food and drink are life. I am blood and death.

Why not milk next? Nature's perfect food. Milk is not just for kids. Milk does a body good.

Braceros sneak across border and head up to the dairies. They appreciate hiring a white guy. More reliable, won't be ditching work to run home to see family on the other side.

Hard getting alone to spread my special ingredient, but work it out. First one on the job in the morning. Last one at night.

<u>Nov. 6.</u> Cartels execute Mormon Mothers and babies across border. Remember meeting one, beautiful blonde hair like Mother. Innocent independent families, peaceful pecan farmers in Mexico for decades. Not hurting anyone, just driving. Can't write today, in whirlpool going down.

FUCKING PAYBACK at the dairies where most of the workers are from there.

<u>Nov. 8.</u> Press said I got the Potato, dying with bloody diarrhea. And someone else at the dinner sick. Socialist Spies at dairy. Need to get the hell out of here. Too close, always on my fuckin tail.

<u>Nov. 12.</u> I'm Anthrax King! What's left? Getting harder to invent and not get caught.

Internet lays it all out for me. Animal hides. Drums. This will be fun. Hired by a trucking company today. Nobody wants to work the Veterans Day Holiday. Everybody's lazy. Two drum events this week, I'm working both of them.

<u>Nov. 13.</u> 10 dairy workers with bloody shits, dead cancer patient, sheriff's deputy, and Potato's wife (sorry not sorry). Some cows and milk. Not bad for a week's work.

<u>Nov. 14.</u> Retired Persons had me pick up the African and Jew drums from the business that runs the event. Worked good all week, delivery company lets me do it alone. Rubbed my sweet stuff deep in animal hides and grooves and crevices on the sides. Wore protection and vaccine holding up.

Fun seeing the spinsters and toothless old guys rush to grab their favorites. Wondering which one I'll nail. I know the Prophet said to respect the elders. But they didn't earn my respect when they kept taking my Mother and Sisters.

<u>Nov. 16.</u> Picked up Apache drums. Few might bring their own, but I'll have access to some. Might even be some spores in the truck from last night, could nail the next driver.

<u>Nov. 18.</u> At Pow Wow waiting to transport drums back. Chinese broad almost knocks me to my knees then got friendly with beaner in uniform. BLASPHEMY—she almost touched Moroni. Checked to make sure I have everything—their pictures are in my newspaper clippings.

They don't see me. How stupid are they if they don't see my genius? Hard to know what the fuckin feds are doing, so I trailed them for a few hours. Not a hard job traipsing after hot Asian girl. Well, maybe a bit of hardness involved.

Can't stand being around these prairie niggers. All these rights, their own health care centers, won't acknowledge state authority. What makes them more entitled than us?

<u>Nov. 19.</u> Six people with Egyptian Plague #6 Boils. Ex. 9:8-9. "And the LORD said unto Moses and unto Aaron, Take to you handfuls of ashes of the furnace, and let Moses sprinkle it toward the heaven in the sight of Pharaoh. And it shall become small dust in all the land of Egypt, and shall be a boil breaking forth with blains upon man."

<u>Nov. 20.</u> Mother and baby, not my targets. But from New Jersey—probably fuckin kikes.

Running out of ways to get this spread around. Don't have Ivins fancy degrees or equipment.

But why not send my stuff in the mail? They might not even test it, looking just like dirt. Not as powerful as the pure white stuff like he had. Nothing ventured, nothing gained! Big decision, lots of planning. They'll finally know I'm here.

<u>Dec. 3.</u> Senator Slut gets the first one. She's a reason I got started. Fucking Dems trying to steal the country back from our President. If I was still in the family, I couldn't have voted for him. We're supposed to believe Prophet is our President.

Probably some low-level peon who opens it. Brought letter up to the counter in Yuma. Have to know the postage. Others should be same. Joked with the attendant about sending a gift to my representative. Bit dangerous because they might wonder what's in the package.

Those politicians are paranoid. They SHOULD be. Jared Lee Loughner got Gabby Giffords in 2011 and 18 others. Ever since Tombstone, everyone in Arizona should know they could be a target. But Jared took the easy way. They'll all respect me when they see what I pulled off. Most inventive crime in history.

<u>Dec. 4.</u> Letter #2 sent from Nogales to Yaqui health group. "Personal growth!" Their website motto.

Give me a break. Where are all the social services for the lost boys? And the girls still stuck there behind the walls? Sure, some agencies pretend to help some of us. But we're not taught to think about this life, just the next one.

We're fucked up when we leave. Doin' drugs real hard and other stupid shit 'cause we don't care anymore. My family's out there and I'm here, so what the hell am I supposed to do.

Joseph Smith was about my age when he wrote The Book of Mormon. Started everything. If he can do big things so young, so can I.

<u>Dec. 5.</u> Postmarked from Prescott to Arizona Coalition for Migrant Rights. What don't you understand, fucktards? They're not citizens, they have no fucking rights.

Not taking more chances, using post office drop boxes now instead of the counters. Too many cameras, nosy clerks.

<u>Dec. 6.</u> Post box at Glendale, to National Association for Hispanic Elderly in Tucson. We don't need more old people screwing things up, always telling us what to do.

Except the President, he's at least trying. Understands about us all needing opportunities to get rich like him, have pretty young wives. But he didn't have the Prophet saying we burn in hell if we talk to a girl. Or kicking us out so we can't compete for them.

<u>Dec. 7.</u> #5 in Phoenix postal box to the fucking Arizona Republic. Writing articles for years about Martin Luther King and how

fucked up we were to cancel his holiday. FAKE NEWS! The dude was a whoremonger.

Great timing, downtown to mail the letter, and sauntered into press conference. Didn't ask for press credentials or nothing.

THEY FINALLY KNOW ABOUT ME! Now I'll get some credit. FBI, Homeland Security, whole shit.

Putting faces to names in the papers. Wow! Dave Schwartz, guy who hired me to help in Uvalde. Other Ag guy for state is Ben Smith. What did Prophet say about Negroes and devil's spawn?

Manolo Miranda, the fucking Puerto Rican spic I trailed at the Pow Wow. Trying to save all the Indians. Why should he care, he's not one of them. Maya Maguire? She's even more of a looker, all dressed up pretty for the cameras. Glancing at each other, holding hands. Anything going on? And she's wearing red. That color is supposed to be only for Jesus.

All doctors, think they're smarter than me. Maya Maguire should be home becoming a Mother like God intended instead of saying my methods aren't as skilled as Ivins. But they chased me around the state for months, not even seeing I was there. Maybe they deserve something special.

Dec. 8. Figured safer with all the coverage and SWAT teams to skip the state for now.

Mailed #6 from Gallup in different envelope to Latinos Unidos. Complaining that their population will grow by 200 percent but less than 2% of funding from charities. My whole complaint in a nutshell. Need to stop their growth. So here's my humble contribution.

<u>Dec. 9.</u> Last letter in Albuquerque mailbox to Phoenix National Organization for Women. Supporting abortion and birth control. Trying to kill us off in the womb. Not gonna happen.

Not safe to keep going this way. No more new announcements. Intercepting my mail? Could've changed method but they got cameras, handwriting analysis. Knew this couldn't last long. Even Ivins had to stop. They didn't figure him out for years. That's gonna be me too.

But I got one more job. Hardest of all. Take me back to my roots. Me versus my Uvalde federale compadre. We'll see who's smarter.

THIRTY-FIVE

A glistening frost dusted Phoenix lawns on December 12. As the sun pierced the glowering gray clouds, Maya peered through the window to see FBI Agent Laura O'Brien dozing in her black sedan outside the ranch home.

Dr. Bingham was polite. Pink housecoat wrapped around her broad body, she knocked on the foggy windshield to wake up the agent and invite her to join them at the dining table. She boiled water for tea, brewed strong coffee, and microwaved a large bowl of creamy oatmeal, serving them with milk, creamer, sugar, and honey.

"Agent O'Brien, if you need to continue environmental testing in our offices, we'll cooperate. But you can't restrict Dr. Maguire's movements without arresting her."

Maya kept fixating on the *Internal Affairs* movie when she looked at the agent. Who played Andy Garcia's assistant? Laurie Metcalf. Of course, *that* Laurie Metcalf. The sister on TV's *Roseanne*. Movie *Lady Bird*. Her brain still didn't work in a straight line. Stress or lack of sleep? Probably both.

Agent Metcalf—no—O'Brien looked uncomfortable and appeared to deliberate a long time before responding. Maybe she didn't agree with her boss.

"You're required to wait for Agent Gomez. Here's the deal. If Dr. Maguire cooperates, we have no reason for legal actions." She pinned Maya with pinched brown eyes.

"You have nothing to lose by going along with us. We're starting our investigation in all directions and don't want to bring charges at this time. We can resolve this without anything official. Agent Gomez will be here shortly, and I'll fly with you to Albuquerque. After the New Mexico testing, we won't bother you again."

Maya ate her breakfast in silence, although Dr. Bingham attempted small talk about the unexpected chilly weather.

"I'm going to clean up, and then I'll be ready to go." Maya turned the shower all the way on and ran it as hot as she could stand. Her tense muscles relaxed.

She understood the agent's argument. None of them wanted to blow this up into a public spectacle. Just like in science, proving a negative might be challenging. How could she help the FBI rule her out from any part in the anthrax attacks? They wouldn't have any evidence she was in all the right areas at the right times. How long would it take to prove she *wasn't* there if they thought she had an ally to do the dirty work—Dave.

Her USDA colleague had agonized about Homeland Security's warning and the trauma any investigation would bring to his family. They must be in total meltdown. Eventually, the FBI should find enough information to eliminate them from having a role in this. But with anthrax lasting for decades in the soil, the contamination could have occurred at any point. How far back would they need to provide documentation on all their movements to prove neither of them had been in those areas? Proving a negative was close to impossible.

Last night, she'd been in shock and unable to think about contacting her family. But she needed their help, even if it flipped them out. She would turn her monumental mom loose on finding a good lawyer.

She stepped into the hall and Dr. Bingham hastened to join her, closing the door when they were both in the bedroom.

"Maya, I'll call Dr. Jaworski at CDC. They have attorneys to represent their employees when there are legal concerns. You should do what Agent O'Brien says and go with them to New

Mexico. I'm sure you want to return home and it wouldn't hurt to be cooperative."

"I'll go down in EIS history as the first officer brought up on felony charges. We can't avoid letting CDC know. I appreciate you making the call."

Dr. Bingham straightened her jacket. "It will be fine, I'm certain."

"There's issues CDC lawyers can help with and others they can't," Maya said. "With this being a criminal problem, they might not get involved. As soon as I can, I'll ask my mother to find a private attorney."

They looked out to see O'Brien open the door for Agent Gomez. "Dr. Maguire, I trust you got some rest?" he called out.

She couldn't accept him at face value anymore, not after remembering the movie. But maybe she was recalling only the fanatic features of the Andy Garcia character.

"The sooner this gets straightened out, the sooner I can get back to work," she said.

"Agent O'Brien will go with you. Dr. Bingham, we need to review the files on your network computer today."

. . .

She went through the motions of saying thank you to Dr. Bingham, riding to Sky Harbor with O'Brien, waiting for the plane, flying to Albuquerque, and exiting the gate at the Sunport. With climate change, experts always talked about the need to become more resilient. Maybe all the stress of the past few months did that for her, too.

Another FBI agent picked them up at the airport. O'Brien said they were going to the Runnels Building in Santa Fe—Dr. Grinwold. This bad news couldn't be avoided.

When they entered the State Epidemiologist's office, he said Dr. Bingham had called. His grim expression indicated he was upset. With her, or them?

"I'm sorry we need to inconvenience you and Dr. Maguire."

A state away from her supervisor, O'Brien seemed more embarrassed about the direction of the investigation.

"Can I meet with your IT person to review Dr. Maguire's network files and hard drive? We have her laptop. This agent will do the inspection and sampling of her office, and we'll disrupt you as little as possible. Dr. Maguire needs to wait here."

She was dropped off with Erika, who hugged her in greeting. After nodding to the two FBI agents, Erika closed the door and grilled her for a summary of the situation.

"Fucking unbelievable. You bust your butt, jeopardize your health working 24/7 for months, and that's how they treat you?"

Maya dropped into the guest chair. "I'm not thrilled, either."

"How can I help?"

"Can I use your phone to call my parents? The FBI doesn't want me calling anyone, but what the hell."

"Of course, should I step out?"

"Nope, they don't want me unsupervised, plotting my escape."

Erika busied herself on the computer and the phone was answered on the third ring.

"Mom, there's a bad development with anthrax."

"You're not sick, are you?"

"Sorry, no, nothing like that. FBI's trying to determine who sent the anthrax letters, and whether they're also implicated for the other infections. With Dave and me so heavily involved, they just want to rule us out."

Her mom's voice thundered through the phone. "Rule you out? As suspects? Are they out of their minds?" Erika glanced up, smirked, and went back to her computer screen.

"Probably a formality, but I need a lawyer with jurisdiction in Arizona and New Mexico to help in the negotiations."

"Dad's at the store. We'll find someone and call you back."

"They took my phone so call the office. Ask for Erika and she'll know how to find me. The 2001 attacks were a government scientist, so they need to cross us off the list. Don't freak out."

She decided to follow her own advice and not worry. But first, she had to reach Dave. She tried his cell—no answer. Nothing at his direct office line either, just voice mail. A secretary at the USDA number took her message.

Moments later, Stephanie knocked and entered. "You're the talk of the office."

Not what she wanted to hear, but Stephanie offered to bring back salads and drinks.

Maya restlessly paced the small carpeted floor area. "I want to call Manolo. You like him now, right?"

"Yeah, he's been good to you." Erika put her hand on the door. "I should leave you two alone."

"No, you can vouch I planned nothing nefarious. I don't want to be arrested."

She had his number memorized. "Manolo, this is Maya. I'm calling from Erika's office."

"Querida, what happened? I've been trying to contact you."

His concerned and comforting voice brought her to tears. She wiped them away, turning her chair to face the corner. She didn't want to cry in front of anyone.

She repeated the story. "I'm worried about Dave and can't reach him. They took my iPhone. Can you find out what's going on?"

"Por supuesto, cariña. But I'm coming to Santa Fe."

"No." She took a breath and switched to her political, persuasive, tone. "They'll investigate you, even though you didn't visit all the contaminated soil places like me and Dave. Have they called?"

"Gomez left a message."

She tried to assuage both their worries and find some humor. "You won't reveal any of my deep, dark secrets, right?"

They agreed to stay in contact as much as possible. *I love you* almost slipped out as her goodbye. She never told him that—couldn't trust feelings forged in the heat of extreme moments.

Stephanie returned with their lunch. "I talked to the agent tearing apart your office, and offered to let you stay with me."

"Sure you want to get mixed up with this?" Stephanie grinned and Maya said, "You're a life saver. Crossing my fingers that we'll put this behind us soon."

. . .

Her mom found an attorney experienced in rogue government employees. As Maya feared, Dave was also under investigation. He was allowed to stay with his Albuquerque in-laws while they tore apart his home looking for physical evidence and spores.

They both had a major setback when the FBI got positive results for anthrax on December 13—Maya's boots, Dave's truck, and his home garage. The attorneys argued those findings were expected given their months of work on it. Yellow pads of the same type as the letters were found at the New Mexico Health Department. Neither of their writing samples matched the letters, yellow pads were ubiquitous, and the investigation of travel histories was incomplete.

Both of them had alibis for most of the dates when the anthrax letters were postmarked. She didn't fly to Arizona until after the first three letters were mailed. It was shakier for Dave because the seventh letter was mailed from a northwest Albuquerque post office not far from Bernalillo.

Dr. Bingham reached her through Stephanie's cell phone early Monday, December 17.

"Bad news—all the lab testing is complete. What Agent Gomez said has been confirmed. Every single anthrax specimen from all the incidents and your property matches Texas Triangle soil."

"Dave hasn't been home since last Christmas. I don't think he was lying. He doesn't have close family there, just old friends."

"As you know, anthrax can stay in the soil a long time. So who knows when it was taken from there."

Unbidden tears of frustration clouded Maya's eyes. "How can we prove we didn't visit all the contaminated places beforehand? We'd have to be superhuman with a sophisticated team of bioterrorists to pull off all the locations plus the mail drops when we were in plain sight so much of the time."

"I know, Maya. I asked around. You both retained the best attorneys money can buy. Time spent focusing on you and Dave means fewer resources for other potential suspects. Someone at the FBI will wise up and realize that."

With agents rotating outside Stephanie's house, Maya worked on her drumming anthrax article and EIS presentation through Wednesday, when a compromise was hammered out. The FBI in conjunction with Homeland Security would continue their investigation and present any evidence to a grand jury for review. In the interim, she and Dave were free to return to their jobs and normal lives. The public posture would be that anthrax was still under active investigation.

She recovered her confiscated property and tried not to feel guilty at her privilege of good legal representation. Her parents weren't wealthy. She'd find a way to pay them back someday.

Although she became closer to Stephanie during her stay, she relished the time to herself when facing the dismantled apartment. Why couldn't the agents fit the stereotype of buttoned down, neat, and orderly? Taking environmental samples for *Bacillus anthracis* was like looking for a needle in a haystack, so they had to be thorough. She was happy they didn't find spores anywhere else besides her boots. At least once she cleaned up, she could breathe easy and not worry about inhaling bacteria.

Back in the office, she generated the first drafts of her anthrax deliverables on the office computer. On Thursday, she alternated getting feedback from Dr. Grinwold and making edits to the written report and draft slides. He rewarded her dedication by approving a long pre-Christmas weekend with Friday and Monday off work.

She agreed to meet Manolo in Chaco Canyon. Thursday evening, they completed the arrangements on the phone.

"Maya, I'm counting the hours. Two weeks since we've seen each other. You still all right with camping? It'll be cold."

"Getting out anywhere will be fantastic. Finding spores on my boots was unnerving, so I scoured my place nonstop. I'm so tired. Hopefully I'm not coming down with something."

"Anyone would feel lousy after what you've been through. But soon you can have your favorite doctor check you out."

"Probably just rebounding from extreme stress," she said. "What time will you arrive at Chaco?"

"Around two. We can check in by cell."

"I'll visit Dave in Bernalillo on my way over. Haven't been able to see him since this blew up."

"Querida, I'm envious he can see you before me. But I'll get over it when I can hold you again."

"Drive safe." She settled for a conventional goodbye, but came close to those dangerous three little words.

. . .

December 21 was crystal blue, a classic northern New Mexico winter day. Puffy white smoke plumes streamed up from the kiva fireplaces.

She pulled into the Bernalillo ranch gravel parking area by eight before Dave headed to his office, and greeted him on the front porch with a long hug. The bosque twinkled with glancing rays of the early morning sun sparkling through the frost. The neighborhood woodsmoke hugging the hills tickled her nostrils.

"Dave, I'm so happy to put this behind us."

"Not entirely over. Wish it was."

"But I have a few days in Chaco with Manolo. I feel reborn."

They headed out back to join his family at the corral. His two daughters, only four and five years old, looked like junior horsewomen cantering the ponies while everyone enjoyed the dazzling day. Emilia held hands with her husband until he excused himself to invite Maya to the porch bench. He grabbed a worn, wool blanket and tossed it across both their laps.

"Your girls are comfortable in the saddle given their ages."

"Been around these horses all their lives, but just in the pen, no trail riding yet."

"How are you feeling about our FBI predicament?"

"Eventually they'll stop considering us." He stretched out his legs, boot heels on the rough porch planks. "Why would we do it—just to get more research funds like Ivins? We don't need extra money to keep our jobs. It's clear this was perpetrated by a bioterrorist, maybe more than one."

She shivered, pulling her end of the blanket to her chest. "How many domestic terrorist attacks involved more than one person?"

"The Oklahoma City bomber had an accomplice. No one else is coming to mind, although family members or friends sometimes get roped in to help."

"If the letters were mailed by a scientist with access to a lab," she said, "they would use pure anthrax. It's a lot easier to infect someone with purified spores than contaminated soil."

"Seems impossible they could accomplish all this," he replied, "especially contaminating the heroin. Somehow they must have filtered the soil to contaminate the drugs. Smart enough to research all these ways to spread it. And who knows what they tried that's not detected yet."

He traced fingers through his streaked brown hair, and the gesture caught her attention. He was only thirty-one—couldn't be turning gray.

"What do you think about the Texas Triangle connection?" she asked.

"No human cases there, despite our heavy year for animals. Whoever's doing this must have pinpointed areas with lab-confirmed animal cases to collect soil loaded with spores. Must be someone with knowledge of the situation in Texas and access to the affected ranches, plus vaccination and PPE to head off infection."

"Did you talk about that with the FBI?"

"Sure. Whatever they're doing with the information, they're not telling me."

"I hope I'm not stereotyping," she said. "But the FBI has to be concerned about a white nationalist, and a religious fanatic, given the rhetoric in the letters and the type of attacks."

"The heroin could have infected any drug user, not certain groups. And why poison the petting zoo in Flagstaff? Another piece of evidence against me is my LDS background, with several of the letters citing the Book of Mormon. Plus, the Bible passages are from the King James version, which is favored by LDS."

Wind chimes of laughter mingled with barking dog as the girls raced around the pen. "Papa, look at this." Teresa, the older one, shouted and waved as she brought the pony to an abrupt stop.

"You're getting better control." He stepped to the edge of the porch and waved back. Emilia gestured for him to join them, but he held up two fingers. Maya understood he was asking for a few more minutes, but knew she should wrap it up.

"It's been quiet for a couple weeks since the last letter was mailed on the ninth." She gazed out at the crisp winter scene, trying to stay focused on a few beautiful things in life.

"May have been scared off, now that we know this is due to a bioterrorist," he said. "If it gets out we're under suspicion, they might be emboldened to attempt something else if they think the focus is elsewhere. Or if someone else is getting credit for their genius."

"I know," she sighed. "This whole pattern has been a week or two of intense activity with a new route of exposure. They need time in between to research and execute a new method of attack. Are there any they didn't try yet?"

"Well, there's one major species not hit in Arizona—cattle. The surge of cattle cases in Texas might be related."

She recalled an earlier conversation with shock. "Remember around Labor Day when you and I drove back to Phoenix from the refuge with Ben? He mentioned the Arizona National Livestock Show. Isn't that soon?"

"Between Christmas and New Year's. I went last year—a big

deal, lots of activity and security. Can't imagine how anyone could do something there. I'll touch base with Ben about it. Wouldn't hurt to beef up surveillance, make sure we have cameras, and check IDs."

She walked to the corral and said goodbye to his family. The girls were brushing their ponies and Bo yapped at mourning doves on the posts. "I'm grateful you all are home."

"Sorry not to cook a proper breakfast inside where it's warm. Will take us a few days to undo the FBI mess," Emilia said.

Maya remembered scrambling to organize her apartment before she left—papers, clothes, and books strewn on the floor, kitchen utensils all over the counters. Emilia and Dave had a much bigger house.

"I feel horrible our work is having this huge disruption on your personal life." Maya collected her purse and phone. "It shouldn't be happening."

"Ben and I will follow up on what we talked about," he said. "Chill out with the good IHS doc for a few days. Forget about anthrax."

"I'll give it a try," she promised.

HOST

What is it about livestock? Placid, domesticated, stupid. All adaptability bred out. If any animal is a host, that's it.

Harbor an uninvited guest, provide nourishment and shelter. Sounds so benign. But a host is essential. Ultimately, can't survive without it.

Too smart to kill the host, but sometimes can't help it. Things get out of control.

THIRTY-SIX

She spent too long relaxing at Dave's ranch and sorting through the anthrax news. It was five months since she drove to the park. Clouds moved in from the west, so she took the longer paved route via Crownpoint.

As her Prius bumped over the rutted dirt in the final miles, her heart sped up in anticipation of meeting Manolo at the Chaco campground. She couldn't be sure of his reaction if she was late. He was usually warm and friendly, but on rare occasions, he'd let slip a more temperamental, controlling side.

She brushed loose hair back under her cap and shoved the sunglasses higher on her face, trying to focus and speed up without sliding off the slick sand. She never dated. What was she getting herself into?

At the park entrance booth, she turned right toward the campground and spotted a splash of Corvette red before she saw him looking down the gray graveled road. The tall rock formations provided a terracotta backdrop for a small ruin, fenced off from the campsites. But her vision was filled with his brilliant smile.

"¡Mi corazón!" They enveloped each other with stroking arms and deep kisses. He leaned back on the Corvette, holding her. "I was sick with worry about you being under suspicion, unable to help."

Her heart continued to race, but was slowing with his reaction. He was happy to see her, not starting their weekend in anger. She stole his hat and dashed around the other side of his car, giggling and daring him to catch her. When he did, she apologized. "I'm sorry, really sorry, that I kept you waiting."

He reinstalled his hat and grabbed her shoulders. "I was afraid to call or text, not wanting to distract you from these bad roads."

"It's been hard to stay calm with the FBI investigation. They're so encompassing in their scope, I was freaked you'd be targeted for working with me and Dave."

He lowered his hands to her waist. "Gomez talked to me for quite a while. They tested my boots because we walked around the Pow Wow, but didn't find anthrax. He mainly asked about you two, seemed less focused on me."

Caressing her cheek, he casually inquired, "How's Dave doing, by the way?"

"Regretting his Texas connections since they're tracing the anthrax there. He's concerned about the Arizona National Livestock Show. Might be an obvious target for someone who seems to be outdoing himself with all the anthrax exposure routes."

"Publicity probably scared whoever is doing it into hiding. At least if something happens at the Show, the Ag vets can handle it."

"Dave recommended I forget anthrax over the next few days. Thank goodness the FBI didn't restrict my travel and keep me away from here."

"I'm thankful he advised you to put work aside. I was less happy imagining you with him instead of me."

Disturbed, she pushed back from his embrace. "You can't be jealous. He was with his family."

"Sorry, I have an impatient streak. And maybe some Latin temper."

He took her hand. "Let's set up camp and visit Una Vida before sundown."

His blue backpacking tent took only minutes to assemble on the tarp, finishing with stakes into the hard, brown earth. They parked at the Visitor Center and began a stroll up the steep trail through the hills.

Planned for multiple stories, the Chacoan Great House ruin was unroofed with masonry walls in decay. But original door and window openings allowed them to imagine the ancient structure when it had been fully built and operational. Before heading back, they took a short hike up a talus slope to see the petroglyphs.

"Unique animals, Dr. Maguire. Recognize any of them?"

"Beyond four legs, horns, and long tails, no." She laughed. "And how about this strange rectangular person with the spiral shield, Dr. Miranda? Do you think he's looking healthy?"

"Can't be as healthy as me, Dr. Maguire." He pressed himself against her. "Are you feeling better since we talked on the phone last night? Still need a checkup from your local physician?"

Her whole body reacted with happiness. No tension, just cocooned in warmth and safety. But she couldn't relax completely into the sensations, and pushed him away. "I'm doing great. We'll be cooking in the dark if we don't get going."

The sun turned the horizon a deep vermilion as they got back to the campsite. He dug the stove out of the backseat. "Tested this out last night, so should be able to use it."

She found the lantern and got it lit. While he cooked mac and cheese, she poured cups of red wine from a box. They sat side-by-side at the picnic table, savoring the simple meal and exchanging stories about childhood pets.

Temperatures dropped toward freezing, so they slipped on warmer jackets before washing dishes and putting all the equipment back in the car to avoid animal visitors. He pulled out two down sleeping bags and tossed them into the tent.

They stopped by the restrooms to clean up, then strolled back with fingers intertwined. The stars sparkled horizon to horizon, wide swath of Milky Way sweeping the sky. The carpet of brilliant gems was more beautiful, and comforting, than any city lights.

He unzipped the tent flap and shook out the sleeping bags. "We can keep these separate or zip them together. Your preference, Dr. Maguire." His tone was relaxed, humorous.

She allowed herself a brief moment of native caution. Were they ready? Then she buried it. "As you said, Dr. Miranda, it's going to be a cold night. I think the healthiest option is to put them together."

He lifted her chin, and she couldn't duck his perceptive eyes.

"Are you sure, Maya?"

She pushed past her embarrassment to return his intense gaze, and brushed the hair from his forehead.

"I didn't accomplish enough during the week of FBI imprisonment at Stephanie's house. But I did check with my doctor. She gave me a clean bill of health, and oral contraceptives."

"Same with me. Nothing for you to worry about." He clasped her fingers as he led her into the tent and zipped it back up. She watched as he joined the two bags into one. They stripped off boots and jackets before he held the double bag open, and they crawled in together.

With his legs wrapped tightly around hers, she nestled against his chest. They breathed in synch as the surrounding air heated up, and he slipped his hands under her blouse to stroke the skin of her back. He traced his lips and tongue across her eyes, ears, and throat. One hand slipped down under her belt to pull her closer. Although his touch paralyzed her with pleasure, she reached for the top button of his shirt.

"We'll be warmer without our clothes on," she said. "Scientific fact."

. . .

Faint sunlight peeked under the tent flap when she awoke in a warm embracing spoon. Rolling over to face him, she studied his tanned skin and long, dark lashes. His breathing was peaceful. She traced the hollow areas below his cheek bones, his aquiline nose, the bony ridges of his eyebrows. When she brushed his lips, he stirred. His forearms tightened around her bare shoulders, increasing their contact. His legs again encircled hers.

"Sorry, Dr. Miranda, I need the restroom." She grabbed her

clothes and pulled them on. The air was brisk and visible with each breath as she crawled out through the tent flap. She heard him groan and the rustle of a search for his own clothes.

A few minutes later, she found him dressed and waiting against the stuccoed wall of the restroom. This time, he didn't let her escape, hugging as he roamed strong fingers through her hair. The kiss was deep, mirroring their passion of the previous night.

His eyes opened and captured her own. "How are you doing?"

Chilled by the frosty morning, she nestled tighter into his warmth. "Muy bien, gracias, ¿y tú?"

"Seriously, Maya. This was a life-changing step for both of us. But especially for you—your first time—and after that awful experience in college. I want to know how you're feeling."

Her face grew hot, and she tried to answer. "I'm good, more than good." She unzipped his jacket and pressed even closer. He responded by enveloping her with his coat flaps.

She squirmed, unable to relax. "So tell me, how was I?"

"Sweetheart, you're the best thing that ever happened to me. We'll discover what we want together, over time, as leisurely or as fast as we both desire." From her belt buckle, he slipped his hand lower again, and she melted.

"Up for some morning delight?" he asked.

An hour later, she stretched like a cat as he kissed the scars on her inner thigh and hips, then moved up her spine. When his fingers stroked her breasts from behind, she grabbed the roaming digits and squirmed around to face him. "Your sister called you Mano. Spanish for hand. Kind of appropriate, considering how competent you are with them."

He circled her nipples with slow, gentle strokes. "Not complaining, are you?"

"Your touch has always inflamed me, from the very beginning," she admitted. "Overwhelming at first."

"Promise to let me know if I push beyond your comfort zone."

She answered by nuzzling his upper lip and they both dozed off.

As the full morning rays illuminated the blue tent walls, he kissed her shoulder and grabbed for his shirt. "I suppose you want breakfast now, too."

"Sí, si puedes."

"Whatever your heart hankers." He threw on his clothes and went out to the car for supplies.

They spent Saturday exploring nearby ruins, never letting go of each other's hands. Her favorite was Casa Rinconada, the largest excavated Great Kiva. Standing together down in the middle, she gazed up to tall, intricate masonry walls surrounding them in a massive circle. There were four large pits that originally had roofs.

"Can you imagine being here with thousands of people to participate in a religious ceremony?" He pointed out the underground passage that might have allowed performers a dramatic entry.

"Summer solstice is supposed to be special," she said. "A beam of light stretches across to illuminate a niche in the opposite wall. Maybe designed that way, or added during reconstruction."

"Everyone's always arguing over the truth, aren't they? For my truth—this is my favorite place in the world." He grabbed her hips, drawing her closer.

She held his collar, giving into the embrace and burying her face in the masculine scent of his neck. "I'm in complete agreement, with a p value of less than .05, so you can count on it."

He laughed out loud at her statistical reference. "Come on now, you promised to leave work behind."

After a dinner of canned beef stew, they cuddled on the picnic table and talked about all the places in the world they'd like to see. With years of schooling, neither had time nor money to venture outside the U.S. except for her childhood return trip to China and his infrequent visits to distant relatives in Puerto Rico.

"Africa—we should go there first," she said, "for a safari."

"You with the animals. But that sounds good to me. Let's make sure we go. Can you take a break when your EIS program is over in 2020?"

She answered by tracing her fingers along his pants leg from his knee up to the button at his waist. He threw the dirty dishes in the car and steered her into the tent.

. . .

They rose at dawn Sunday morning for a ten-mile round trip hike to Peñasco Blanco with its three great kivas and pictograph believed to record a supernova in the year 1054.

For dinner, they soothed aching muscles with hot chicken noodle soup, then collapsed into their combined sleeping bags and dropped into peaceful unconsciousness, merged into one.

She awoke first again, and stroked his chin where the hair was growing in. "You look even more like Lin-Manuel."

He tickled her bare waist. "If the PHS didn't require us to shave, I'd have a goatee like his just to keep you interested."

"We need to hit the road," she reminded him. "The campground will be closed over the holiday. Christmas Eve in Santa Fe is mystical, according to Stephanie."

While admiring for a final time the artistry of the sandstone backdrop and small ruin next to the campground, they disassembled the tent and packed supplies into the Corvette.

"We didn't see enough," she complained.

"Once a year, we'll come back," he said. "I can never get enough exercise and spiritual sustenance."

"And camping." She smiled and leaned against him.

"Next time, let's camp in a thunderstorm. That's when I'm really excited by nature." He winked and traced kisses along her jaw.

Christmas Eve in Santa Fe was as magical as Stephanie described. With an evening warmer than Chaco, down vests were sufficient as they meandered down the art studio-lined Canyon Road with the farolito candles fluttering in paper bags on roofs and adobe walls. Maya bought a necklace of twinkling lights for each of them.

They stopped in galleries, sipped wine and spiced cider, and sang Christmas carols in Spanish and English at the luminaria bonfires on the street corners. Piñon woodsmoke hugged the ground and wrapped them in a warm embrace.

The re-enactment of Las Posadas had started when they returned to the Plaza. On flat, projecting first story roofs of the surrounding buildings, Mary and Joseph stopped under second-floor windows, singing a request for shelter. Everyone received a candle and joined the procession snaking at street level. Until Mary and Joseph were granted a place for the night, red and black Devils danced around the rooftops, scaring them away but delighting the crowd.

They ran into Erika and Rolf. Maya gifted Kyle the two blinking necklaces, and he imitated the dance of the devils. Maya didn't share his joy over the rooftop antics. The demons conjured too many dead anthrax patients, Camino del Diablo border patrol frights, and Day of the Dead breakup with Manolo.

Pageant complete, they encountered Stephanie walking to the bus stop. "About time you brought him around again." Stephanie's crinkled eyes took the edge off her words and she invited them to her home for a Christmas breakfast of posole.

"Traditional Mexican soup with hominy, chiles, pork, and corn tortillas. Perfect antidote to a cold New Mexican morning. Supposed to have snow tonight."

. . .

They woke up Christmas Day to six inches of white powder on every adobe wall and rooftop. Facing the small fenced patio, the bedroom window was streaked with frosty fractals. Manolo crawled out from under the down duvet to step over to the braided rug. He pulled Maya naked to stand tight in front of him and they both appreciated the Hallmark view. His right arm fondled her breasts and the left tightened around her hips, keeping her slightly warmer.

"I love spellbinding nature," she said. "So we could grab the blanket and keep standing here, or I have another idea for celebrating the holiday." She pivoted to face him without loosening his embrace and detected his answer.

By midmorning when they arrived at Stephanie's apartment for the promised posole, she greeted them with a roaring fire in the kiva and red chili ristras hanging from the plastered entry hall.

"Not far to drive today," he noted. "Roads aren't in ideal condition for my Corvette."

They finished their first helping of the colorful soup and lounged in front of the fire. Stephanie took her hyacinth macaw out of its floor-to-ceiling cage which filled much of her study. "Quetzy and I have been through a lot over eighteen years. My husband and I adopted him when an elderly neighbor couldn't care for him. Now he's all I got."

Her eyes watered, then she went on. "My vet said they can live seventy years in captivity. They're endangered now in South America. We don't know how he came into this country."

Maya reached out her arm protected by the red corduroy shirt and Quetzy hopped over. She stroked lustrous blue feathers on his head while he swayed, pinning her first with one eye, then the other.

"Quetzy reminds me that I considered moonlighting in a vet clinic on weekends to keep up my clinical skills. But it never happened. Too busy doing anthrax field work."

"Yeah, you've been really goofing off." Stephanie put him in the cage and adjusted the opaque tarp as Quetzy screamed "Bye."

Manolo clinked his spoon on the empty stoneware bowl. "I've tasted great posole in my day, but this is the best. The Hatch green chiles add just the right amount of heat. Mind if I have seconds?"

"I could ask for the recipe," Maya said, "but I'd never get around to cooking it."

While they worked more slowly on a second course, Stephanie reminisced about times with her husband before he died of lung cancer. She described with amusing detail one of their fights during a long trip driving two cars as newly engaged teenagers.

"Before GPS and cell phones, if you got separated on the highway, it was tough to reconnect."

"My folks have some doozies, too." Maya poured another cup

of hot peppermint tea and tilted the pot toward Manolo. "But they love and cherish each other."

He lifted his cup for the pour. "I know from my parents' relationship, the quality of time is most important, not the quantity."

Maya remembered his mother's early cancer death but didn't feel it was her place to mention it without Manolo's lead.

Midafternoon, when Stephanie brought leftover posole to the homebound neighbor next door, they headed back to cuddle on Maya's couch with cocoa.

Her iPhone chimed with a call from Dave. "Ben let Dr. Bingham know we're planning extra surveillance at the Livestock Show and she wants you to come back. I can take you."

Maya returned to work mode. "Manolo can give me a ride. He's here in Santa Fe."

"Good for you. How was your rendezvous in Chaco?"

"Fine. I'll get back to you with my schedule."

"What was that about?" Manolo asked as she hung up.

"State Ag and USDA are establishing protocols for safeguarding the Livestock Show. Dr. Bingham needs me, too."

"Maya, you deserve a long break. Fred was generous in giving you a couple days now, plus some for Thanksgiving and the Grand Canyon. Doesn't make up for extraordinarily long days and weekends, but maybe he's aware you need a personal life. From the medical rumor mill, he and Nancy find a way to have one together."

He clenched his fingers in his lap. "But more important, I'm not comfortable with you risking an encounter with a madman at the Show."

"I've been in the middle of this from day one." She quieted his restless hands. "So have you, for much of it. We can't opt out at this point. No one else has such a deep understanding for what's happening."

For once assertive, she straddled his legs and held his shoulders, forcing his full attention. "I sensed the background explanation for cases wasn't accurate from the beginning. Possibly law enforcement was suspicious, but we never saw them until the drug cases. Even then, they never said it was a bioterrorist until the letters."

Hoping to calm her own fears, she took a deep breath. "Maybe they were preventing public panic. And even if we realized all this was due to one person or one group, I'm not sure what we could have done about it. They're shaking everything up, always something different in a new area."

"But now you two think you can predict the next attack." He pushed her off to the side and poured another cup of cocoa.

She watched him with concern, not wanting to get at cross-purposes again. "We're trying to think like this guy, whoever he is."

"Livestock shows are all over, in different places throughout the year." His tone indicated he was still troubled.

"This unknown bioterrorist has it in for Arizona." She joined him next to the kitchen counter. "Other than an unusual number of animal cases in the Texas Triangle this year, it's been quiet for anthrax except in Arizona. There were heroin-associated cases in other states, but tied by genetic fingerprinting to the Southwest."

He stopped her fingers stroking the hair on his chest above the V-neck of his shirt. "You're staying with me, not a hotel."

"Sí, mi amor. No argument."

When she reached Dr. Bingham, the older public health doctor warned, "I assume our zealous FBI team will be there."

"Fine with me," Maya said. "Manolo and I will be less nervous if the feds are watching over everything. They could be our protection in case something goes down."

"See you soon. Think about how you're going to do surveillance for spillover to people."

. . .

Maya and Manolo returned to his Phoenix apartment in the early afternoon of December 26, and Dave gave her a ride to the livestock show. She was surprised to find such a large venue with seventeen hundred animals from more than twenty-five states in the central part of the city, two miles north of the state health and ag departments. Ben indicated the property was used at other times for the state and county fairs. The gates had been open a few hours for early check-in.

At each entry point, gatekeepers compared identification with names on the checklist, and animals had to match their registration materials. With the surge in Arizona anthrax, the show added a last-minute recommendation for vaccination, but not all the owners pulled it off for their animals in time. Ben pointed out the cameras in the corners of the rafters.

"These go to the FBI and the EOC—Emergency Operations Center—where agencies gather whenever an emergency is declared. Each has an assigned table with connected laptops and multiple large-screen displays hanging down from the ceiling for different feeds. We didn't open it up during the previous anthrax incidents, so you didn't see it?"

She shook her head.

"The State hasn't declared an emergency, but we're using it, just in case."

"How late will the fairground gates be open today?" Dave asked.

"Only until five for those setting up. But the Staging Lot is open again at midnight for the Junior Exhibitors, kids between eight and twenty-one. They can enter beef, sheep, goats or swine."

"Health has extra surveillance," Maya said. "We have a system to monitor sales of over-the-counter antidiarrheal medicines in drug and grocery stores. A run on Pepto-Bismol is a clue something g.i. is going on. We've also alerted the health care facilities and private laboratories again. We'll do targeted notifications to certain groups, like dermatologists for the cutaneous anthrax lesions."

She left the Ag vets to continue their inspection of the grounds and exhibit buildings. Manolo texted he was at the front gate. She noted he'd kept his scruffy, Lin-Manuel look.

"Dr. Miranda, you look familiar. Didn't I see you someplace before?"

He hugged her to him, fingers slipping below her waist. "Still can't get enough of this."

"If you were in uniform, you might get reprimanded for that hug."

"Decided to let you have your Broadway star for a few more days. I asked for time off until January second."

"The FBI might be watching us right now," she cautioned.

"I apologize—just too ecstatic we're together."

"Can you drop me at the health department and bring over sandwiches in a couple of hours?"

"Like October? I loved being your delivery boy and chauffeur. Happy to do it again."

THIRTY-SEVEN

<u>Dec. 27.</u> Everything's fallen into place, just like I planned. Quieter yesterday afternoon before it officially opened today. Assholes from the press conference looking at all the entry points. Think they're so smart, better than me with all their fancy schooling.

And the cute Chink vet, still hot to trot. Not wearing red, but met spic doc in red Corvette. Why does she let him touch her? Girls always go for slick Latinos with their accents. Making babies right and left, turning Arizona brown.

FBI agents think they're not obvious with their little earbuds and microphones. They're not blending in, and never noticed me.

Guy from Uvalde happy to sign me on as extra hand. Come and go as I please, not gonna catch me with bad entry docs.

Why the hell are kids up at midnight to check in livestock? Working 'em to death. Cold nights, no moon. Just the bright glare of fairground towers and building fluorescents. No problem strolling unobstructed through the shadows.

Learning to sew while watching Mother paid off. And I know how to protect myself. Back to work. Risky, but when you've cheated death once, all a piece of cake.

THIRTY-EIGHT

"You young'uns may be able to survive on limited sleep, but this body is past the sell by date."

Ben adjusted a wool cap tighter on his bald head when Maya met her veterinary colleagues shuffling to stay warm outside the Youth Building. After spending most of Thursday at the health department and the Emergency Operations Center, she was eager to get back to field work. A few months ago, that reaction would have shocked her. Working through physical and emotional challenges was possible, and rewarding.

Dave raised his steaming coffee cup. "Dr. Smith, we haven't had this much fun since our last vesicular stomatitis outbreak."

"It's heartwarming to see the kids with their animals," Maya said. "I need to remind myself we're here to prevent another anthrax attack."

"Where's your protector-in-chief?" Dave asked. "He was glued to your side yesterday morning."

"Sleeping in. He figured someone should be rested and alert to watch our backs."

"Hanging with us while not on the government dime must mean he's got some strong motivation?" Dave arched his eyebrows but she could tell by his smirk he was making a statement, not asking a question.

Embarrassed, she ducked her head. "Chaco was inspiring."

"I'm gratified you're giving the guy a break."

"*Intelligence is the ability to adapt to change.* A Stephen Hawking quote from my mom. Guess I'm getting adaptable."

She sipped the hot tea. "By the way, you can be nice to Manolo. I realize he's not as smart, only specializing in one species. But he's trying to keep up."

Dave laughed. "Maya, if he could hear you now."

"Back to business at hand." Ben reviewed his notes. "When we checked Certificates of Inspection as the animals were dropped off, they got the brucellosis, tuberculosis, and trichomoniasis testing we require. Plus, the *Brucella* vaccine. Most Texas cattle got anthrax vaccine due to exposure risk and we have some coverage of Arizona cattle with the recent dairy concerns."

Maya stood straighter, brightened by the news. "I'm glad you could pull off vaccinations so quickly with the owners."

While swigging coffee, Ben thumbed his cell phone. "Animals from other states—too little time to work out that requirement, so we don't have full protection throughout the fair."

"Let's chat with staff working the show and see how things are going with animal health," Dave said. "If bad guys are trying anything here, it's probably too early to detect."

They completed several hours of quick look-overs for the animals and checked with exhibitors and staff. Maya opened a text from Manolo asking for their location. Outside the bull barn, he strolled up, scruffy and relaxed in worn frayed jeans, a black flannel shirt, and Yankees baseball cap. Nothing like the polished professional when clean-shaven in uniform.

"Dr. Schwartz and Dr. Smith." He shook their hands. "Mind if I tag along?"

"I'm freezing cold and headed to the office." Ben turned for the back gate. "Good luck with the sleuthing."

As he disappeared around the corner, Dave grinned and winked at Maya. "Dr. Maguire said you might join us today."

Holding her breath, she hoped he didn't mention the joke about veterinary superior intelligence. But he led them to the food stands.

They settled around a wooden picnic table with tacos and tortillas as the two men bonded over football. "Dallas plays the Giants Sunday," Dave said. "I'm pulling for my Cowboys, how about you?"

"More of a baseball fan," Manolo replied. "Caught a Giants game in New York, but I pick up Arizona Cardinals games on the radio driving to my hospitals."

Her muscles relaxed. She didn't realize they were tight in anticipation of possible conflict. Manolo was over any jealousy, or did a good job of hiding it.

While ignoring most of the sports discussion, she admired Manolo's enthusiasm with others. He admitted to some dark moments of the soul from his mother's death and his divorce, but his warmth put everyone at ease. Maybe some of that would rub off with time. She hoped to replace uncertainty and panic with calm, unpretentious confidence. Given all she handled and opened herself up to over the past few months, perhaps she was partway there.

"All quiet on the western front, in line with my favorite war novel." Dave gathered their paper waste. "I propose we meet back here at six for the evening dedication and reception."

"Surveillance or relaxation?" Manolo asked.

"Maybe for a few hours," Dave said, "we can let the FBI do their job all alone."

Her nostrils filled with a greasy odor, and she glanced over to the next picnic table. Brown ooze dripped over the plates. Chocolate-covered bacon? Then she looked up to the couple gingerly fingering the gloppy, fried strips into their mouths. Cowboy hats, colorful cotton shirts, crisp denim pants, ginormous silver belt buckles, and patterned leather boots. "I can't meet the standard of western wear," she complained.

"Don't worry, I'll wear my best hat and represent," Dave said.

On the drive to Manolo's apartment, she phoned Nancy Bingham and got approval to be off-duty. "With your working the weekend, you can certainly enjoy yourself tonight," the State Epidemiologist assured her.

In the garage, they dropped off their manure-encrusted work boots and jackets. He led her to the bathroom.

"Let me help you out of these dirty clothes." Pulling the baseball jersey over her head, he brushed his fingers against her bare skin.

"Yikes, you're cold," she squealed. "Turnabout's fair play." She stroked her own chilled hands on his abdomen when helping him undress.

He turned the water temperature to hot as he coaxed her under the steamy spray. Her brain turned to mush while he slowly massaged her head with gentle fingers and she inhaled the citrus scent of the shampoo. His hands slipped down as he caressed her back, holding her pressed to his body.

She rested her head on his shoulder and danced her tongue along his neck up to his mouth. "This is heavenly."

"Conserve water by sharing." He smiled. "See that on environmental brochures?"

He knelt on the tile floor in front of her, stroking the soap bar over her legs and feet. His lips soon followed. She leaned back on the wall to keep from collapsing, until she finally sank to the tiles with him, satiated.

As he tried to help them rise up together, she instead pushed him to a standing position. "Taking turns," she grinned.

The water heater emptied and her skin dimpled under the colder spray. She tugged him to the rug and toweled him off. "I'm happy you're off the clock and can keep this goatee. I like the way it looks *and* feels. Although you're also very handsome in uniform—I noticed it the first day we met."

He grinned back. "I guess we were both doing some noticing." He scooped her up and she wrapped her legs around his waist as he walked to the bedroom.

"Still not enough?" She couldn't believe she was encouraging him again as he lowered her to the bed.

"For someone new to this, you're rather insatiable. But I'm not ready for round two. I'd like a quick nap before we head out."

She lay down on top of him and pulled the covers over. "Me, too."

. . .

Arriving too late for the dedication, she spotted Dave in the corner of the reception area talking to a man who looked a bit like him, but thinner with lighter hair. The man was dressed as a working cowboy except for the stained leather bag slung over one shoulder. Why did he look familiar?

"Maya, Manolo," Dave greeted them. "Meet Sam Demille. He helped me out with the ranch while I was in vet school."

Manolo extended his hand but Sam shuffled his feet and didn't reciprocate. His hands looked roughened and red, and he avoided their eyes. "Honor to make your acquaintance, ma'am." The words were almost imperceptible.

They picked up the music of a country-western band in the corner. "Garth Brooks' *The Dance*? Even I recognize that one," Maya said.

"Care to tango, mi amor?" Manolo grabbed her around the waist and headed to the crowded wood-planked floor, leaving Dave to his Uvalde reminiscences.

"Another first for us?" She flirted, twirling her colorful skirt. "Believe it or not, my mother was an amateur dancer, and I know a few moves."

"By all means, take the lead." He pressed his lips to her cheek, fingers tightening around the small of her back. She melted into his body until she spotted a redheaded, buzz cut FBI agent in a dark suit near the door, tracking their every move.

THIRTY-NINE

<u>Dec. 28.</u> Fuckin cunt, knew she was doing that spic. Uvalde buddy not so bad, but his LDS kicked us out, said we can't go to celestial heaven with plural marriages. With that mark of Cain vet from Satan again this morning. Don't want to be here, send 'em back to Africa.

Plan perfect, they don't have a clue, not even those frickin G-men. Lots of time today to spread everything around. On my hands and clothes when we met? But couldn't abide touching them, especially the slut.

Gotta score Mexican crystal energy to keep going. Tomorrow's another day—another opportunity. Planning something personal for certain people who think they're better than me.

FORTY

Need U ASAP.

She read Dave's message at six-thirty Saturday morning while pulling on comfortable corduroys and a plum long-sleeved shirt. As Manolo drove the Corvette to the fairgrounds, Dave texted he was at the Junior Cattle Barn preparing for the Cattlemen's Day show.

"I'll drop you and park where nobody can hit my car with their doors."

She smiled, reminded that Manolo's optimistic temperament belied a few strong emotional quirks.

Within ten minutes, she located Dave taking the temperature of a heifer convulsing on the straw. "Febrile."

Another twitched beside him, and in the next stall, a third was dead with blood draining from its bodily openings.

"Somebody's taken their first shot. God, I hope we catch this son-of-a-bitch."

She spotted kids mucking out the waste and brushing down their animals. But in the back corner with the bloody, dead heifer, an elementary school-age boy curled up in a ball, crying.

"Shush." She yanked her right index finger up vertically against her lips to make Dave shut up, and pointed with her left hand to the whimpering child.

Dave looked flustered, but continued examination of the two dying animals. She opened the stall and knelt down.

"I'm a vet, can I help you?" She held out her hand and the dark-haired boy allowed himself to be guided away from his dead animal. "Are your parents here, can we call them?"

Shaking between his jerky breaths, the boy tugged a phone from his jacket. His thumb slipped over the password and *A-my dad* as his first contact, then pushed the phone toward Maya.

A thin, tenor voice answered. "Roy, what's up? I'm on my way back with the funnel cakes."

Roy opened his mouth but nothing came out.

"Sir, I'm Dr. Maguire," she said. "I'm a vet with your son outside your heifer's pen. Roy's fine, but we need you to meet us right away."

Within minutes, Manolo arrived a few steps behind a short, lean man with brown hair escaping from a feedstore cap.

"I'm Rich Edwards. What happened here?" Roy hugged his dad's legs.

"Not sure yet." She projected calm concern. "Dr. Schwartz is assessing these two ill animals, possibly associated with your own animal's death."

"Worked with cattle all my life and never seen that." His arm waved toward the bloody body.

"We're still investigating, but it might be anthrax."

His tone squeaked up. "Like at the dairy?"

She nudged loose hair back out of her eyes. "We'll do some tests. The bedding could be contaminated."

Catching Manolo's supportive gaze, she introduced him. "This is my colleague, Dr. Miranda. He's a physician and can talk with you about risks to people."

He escorted them to the barn door. She breathed out, grateful that he arrived so quickly. After calling the front office for more help, she slipped on gloves and stepped into the pen with Dave.

With FBI agents monitoring, Ben came back in and mobilized his team according to plans developed over the past week. He closed the barn and canceled the morning show. Dave packaged animal, bedding, and soil samples for transport to the lab. Ben identified other staff in full protective gear to move the three ill and dead animals to the Ag department's pathology unit and clean the stalls. Other nearby animals were moved farther away, pending final decisions based on anthrax results.

Maya updated Dr. Bingham that Manolo was talking to other families displaced from the barn. He let them know about anthrax symptoms and asked them to call the health department if they had questions or concerns. Dave and Maya toured the rest of the show grounds to make sure there was no other evidence of anthrax, then met up with Manolo near the breeding bulls.

"Beautiful animals," she said, glancing around the cavernous area. "Sure you want to keep this part open?"

"Too much going on to close it for a few heifers in another barn with clinical signs and no lab confirmation," Dave said.

"Some people were irate when you restricted access to the one barn and canceled the earlier show, until they heard anthrax," Manolo said. "They were more cooperative when reminded of the potential serious outcomes. Many were aware of other cases over the past few months, but it becomes more meaningful when it hits closer to home."

"Dave, I think we'll head to the health department," she said.

"No problem, let's touch base in a few hours."

By late afternoon, they completed a check of the surveillance systems, with no suspicious reports of unusual cutaneous lesions or a run on anti-diarrheals. She planned to engage with the Laurie Metcalf clone. Was the FBI agent as jovial in real life as the actress she resembled?

"Agent O'Brien, I'm here with Dr. Miranda." Her iPhone rested on the computer table with the speakerphone on. For a moment, she thought she was back at the fairgrounds instead of the empty state health building—cows were mooing. "Do you have someone looking at the show's camera footage?"

"Of course, you think we're idiots?"

Maya grimaced when looking up at Manolo. O'Brien was definitely not as agreeable as the *Roseanne* star.

"Any chance we could review some of it? With all our time at the show, maybe we can spot something."

Manolo had a hopeful look on his face when he jumped in. "We're on our way to the gas station. Can we grab you some sandwiches and sodas?"

The agent's bland midwestern voice softened. "I guess we could use your help, and I'll be with you every minute. So sure, come on by."

Except for O'Brien and a technician, the FBI office was deadly quiet on the weekend. Gomez was nowhere in sight. Maya's tailbone protested the moment it touched the metal folding chair—perhaps chosen to keep staff awake during tedious desk work.

On the laminate table, Manolo spread out chicken, turkey, and ham sandwiches on white bread and set down the two-liter bottles of Mountain Dew and Diet Coke. At first bite, Maya flushed with embarrassment. The sandwiches were stale but their bribe already got them in the door.

Sounds of bleating sheep emanated from a speaker under the monitor. The technician returned with a pitcher of ice and empty red solo cups. Maya filled hers with Coke.

"Could we start with the Junior Cattle Barn where we had the downed heifers? Wednesday when they started unloading animals."

"Three and a half days of footage." The agent's sarcasm was back.

Manolo again played mediator. "High speed is fine to start."

An hour into the review, Maya's phone flashed with a call from Dave, and she picked it up to answer. "We're at the FBI office, can I put you on speaker?" He grunted assent. She set down the phone and hit the button.

"Three heifers confirmed with rapid PCR test. Waiting on soil."

Apparently still not a FBI fan, Dave hung up. O'Brien poured another cup of Mountain Dew. "For someone who could be spreading anthrax around, he sure is quick to find it."

Maya flushed. "Shouldn't that tell you something?"

Clutching her forearm, Manolo pulled her back down.

O'Brien also settled down, but continued. "As my boss says, a hundred firefighters are convicted of arson each year." Then she waved at the technician who restarted the footage.

Several hours later, Maya muttered, "I'm not seeing anything." Like a slow cooker, she still simmered from O'Brien's remarks about Dave.

"Well, you're in there multiple times," O'Brien said.

With her tan face and protruding dark eyes, like one of the livestock show's impassive Brown Swiss, the FBI agent peered out under squared-off bangs. Was she accusing them, or being ironic?

Maya's aching body eliminated her efforts to be congenial. "Look." She slapped the table and snarled. "We walked through on our inspections, including early Thursday morning when the kids unloaded the animals. Did you see me do anything suspicious?"

She was unsettled—never questioned authority or lost her temper. Manolo touched her arm and gave her a look. She took it as reassurance and caution to stay on the FBI's good side.

He pointed to the screen. "Remember the man from Uvalde with Dave at the reception last night?" Huddling with the technician, he helped him scroll back through the recording.

Maya hurried around the corner to the restroom, eager for a break. When she returned, the tech still scrolled for Manolo.

"I should have stopped the replay earlier. His behavior in the barn was strange, then I put it together with the reception when he wouldn't make eye contact, hardly spoke, and kept watching us."

Maya called Dave and put him on speaker. "The Uvalde guy you introduced last night, what was his name?"

"Sam Demille—why?"

"Manolo saw him near the heifers. Might not mean anything, there's lots of people." She glanced at the FBI agent. "Including us."

"Dave, what do you know about him?" Manolo asked.

"He's part of a splinter group that maintains polygamy. Grew up in Arizona, but moved to Texas doing construction and ranching."

"Do you remember who hired him for the Show?" Manolo persisted.

"I'll check the records."

The technician was ready to review the film again. Maya wasn't sure if she would recognize Demille. She'd been preoccupied with her dancing date.

Manolo spotted him first in the Thursday morning video, after the youth had finished setting up their stalls and went home for a few hours of sleep before school. Blue flannel shirt under a half-open long brown coat, boots, cowboy hat, and leather bag all matched their memories. He strolled back and forth through the barn, reaching inside his coat. Frequently he shook one leg as if kicking away an annoying dog. O'Brien directed the tech to note the date, time, and location for each moment they saw him.

Dave called back. "Demille works for a Texas bull breeding outfit. Their animals are up-to-date on all the requirements and vaccinations, including anthrax."

"So why did he spend so much time in the Junior Cattle Barn?" Maya asked. "He's got kind of weird body movements."

"Things are winding up here at the show," Dave said. "They don't require photos for the crew, but we can help the FBI keep an eye out for him tomorrow. He was always a little standoffish, but you think he looks suspicious?"

"We'll tell you more when we review the footage from other cameras," Maya said. "Probably a long Saturday night."

FORTY-ONE

<u>Dec. 29</u>. Risk and work paying off. A few sick and dead heifers from the junior barn. No people, always fuckin slow to announce those. Didn't even close the fucking fair. Good for me, more opportunities.

Can't risk going out through the gate. Find an empty quiet stall somewhere to crash. Carry Moroni with me just for this, in case it's not safe to move in and out easily. Brought in soil hidden under animal feed, so I've got a stash.

Damned pimples itching. Rough hands from working outside. Too much roofing tar, barbed wire. Mother rubbed cream before they got broken in. Vaccine's always held so this couldn't be anthrax. Tired, busting my butt to pull this off.

When this is over, I can take a break, check out Patriots protecting the border. Or head south to help those under siege from the cartel. Wish Jacob was here. But he was headed in another direction with college. How would things be now if he hadn't been a jerkoff and grabbed that wrench?

Cell phones and libraries are incredible. All my research, all my arrangements. Mailed Christmas gifts. Nothing like letting those near and dear know you're thinking of them in the New Year.

FORTY-TWO

Maya propped her head with both hands at four AM on Sunday. O'Brien took a break and ran Sam Demille's name through their database, but came up empty. When Maya called Dave, she could tell by the muffled, vague tone that she woke him up.

"Sorry, you're on speaker again with the FBI. Rapid review of camera footage didn't identify a smoking gun, but we found Demille multiple times at numerous places. Still tugging his coat, the weird walk, and shaking his leg. In the last shots before the shutdown last night, Sam was scratching at his hands, and they looked more reddened. Hard to see clearly with those cameras up in the corners."

Agent O'Brien appeared more attentive and alert than Maya felt. "I called in another tech to review gate cameras. Demille arrived and left multiple times the first three days, Wednesday through Friday. Yesterday, he came in and out early until we lost him on gate cameras. But we still saw him in the grounds and buildings."

"Don't tell me you're coming around to someone else being the perp besides me and Maya?" Dave's voice was sleepy and sardonic.

"Might be," the FBI agent said, matching his joking tone. She ruffled her bangs. "I'm headed for bed. My boss is taking over." She directed a steely gaze to Maya. "You guys should be gone before he gets here."

O'Brien turned back to the cell phone. "There's still no criminal record for Demille. He was hospitalized at twenty-five in St. George, Utah. Fell off a roof doing construction. Had brain damage and his nineteen-year-old brother was killed in the same incident. We have no information that he attended any public or private school."

"He was younger, early twenties, when he took care of my ranch for me." Dave sounded like he had fully awakened. "I remember his brother, smart kid. Have you interviewed the ranchers in Uvalde? Sam worked for a lot of them. And the breeder who hired him to help with the bulls?"

"In process. Dr. Schwartz, we'll send over a sketch artist to the Show in a couple hours. Seems like you know Demille more than anyone else, and we need something to work with. We're trying to find a camera shot with his face, but he always had his hat down and the video footage isn't ideal."

After Dave hung up, Manolo turned toward the agent. "Does this mean Maya and Dave are off the hook?"

Maya stretched her back, standing next to him. O'Brien shifted in her seat. Uncomfortable going beyond the party line?

"Circumstantial evidence on Demille—time and opportunity. Similar to Drs. Schwartz and Maguire."

"¡Cabrón!"

Maya didn't remember ever hearing him swear before. She took his tensing fingers in her own.

"Look, they were never arrested." The agent's tone was terse. "Others thought we should consider it, but I put in a word to let them keep working, and they have damned good attorneys. So stop complaining."

Maya rested her hand on his bicep—hard as a rock, ready to punch. She never saw him lose his temper. Perhaps, even more than her, he had a slow fuse with a big bang if he was provoked.

"Let's get some rest," she suggested as she pulled him toward the door. There was still so much to learn about each other, and Arizona anthrax.

· · ·

Mountains of dead bodies, human and animal, dripped blood

out of every orifice. Hyperventilating, she struggled to find a way around. She crawled over them, slipping down on her stomach as her nose inhaled the sickening scent and her skin burned with fluorescing red fluid.

A loud ring from her iPhone broke the spell, and she groped over Manolo's back to the end table. Her eyes squinted open enough to recognize the number. "Dr. Bingham?" She caught a glimpse of faint low light from the winter sunrise peeking through Manolo's curtains. Her macabre nightmare was over.

"Based on your email update, I know you had a long night with little sleep, but we might have human cases connected to the Livestock Show."

Maya propped two pillows behind her and reclined against the headboard, keeping her voice quiet to avoid waking Manolo. "Who are they?"

"Teenager and child with animals in the Junior Cattle Barn. Cutaneous lesions, both hospitalized, and labs pending. I called Dr. Jaworski, and they're sending antitoxin. She offered to provide more CDC experts to help, but I said we have it under control. Tomorrow being New Year's Eve, the show will be over, and the animals and people will head home."

Maya rubbed her eyes. "Do you want me in the office or interviewing patients?" Then she remembered the sobbing child and prayed it wasn't him. "Roy Edwards is the kid who owned a dead heifer. Is he one of them?"

The harried voice continued. "That name doesn't match the suspect cases. Maya, enhance human surveillance at the show. If these are confirmed, I'll talk to Dr. Smith about closing early. The area where they were exposed has been closed since yesterday, so I don't know what we gain."

Maya felt a gentle caress on her thigh. "Manolo is still giving me a hand." She caught his dark gaze—he was awake and listening to her end of the conversation.

She grasped his wrist to stop his movement. "We'll work with the gate crew to keep an eye out for skin lesions in those coming or going. I think we can do it without scaring people."

Pausing, she weighed the next idea. "Should we check temperatures like airlines when they worry about infectious disease?"

"Too much alarm," Dr. Bingham said. "If it comes to that, we'll shut it down."

Maya completed the call and Manolo traced her lips with one finger. "I'm giving you a hand? How about more than one?"

"Manolo, you could hear we need to get going." His mouth replaced his finger, feathering her lips with hot breaths as he tugged her back down flat on the mattress.

"Okay," she groaned. "Gonna have to be quick."

"I think I can oblige," he answered.

. . .

Dave texted he was at the Junior Sheep and Goat Barn.

"Two and a half hours of sleep doesn't cut it." She yawned as they headed to meet him. "I'm so fried, I might walk into a wall."

"He may have managed more rest than we did." Manolo took her arm and they supported each other.

"We're not getting old and feeble, are we?" she joked.

"I wouldn't say so. Would you?" He nuzzled her ear.

She stepped away. "Manolo, no public displays of affection."

"You're right, I won't distract you. If anyone's watching, my clone is hiding out from the NYC hordes with a spectacular chica."

"You impersonate him and he'll get pissed off."

"I met him once—he has a sense of humor."

Dave spotted them as they entered the building. "Five sheep down."

She grabbed the nearest fence to keep from passing out. "I can't believe it. Why are we always a step behind?"

"I canceled the Lil Buckaroo rodeo, four to six-year-olds riding sheep."

"Kids that young do rodeo?" Manolo asked.

"They wear safety helmets and vests, and staff look out for animal welfare. Doesn't matter, we closed the area."

Maya felt for the gloves in her pocket. "Need help in taking samples?" All she could do was be useful, even if the continuing cases rocked her sanity.

Manolo touched her elbow. "Do you want me to advise animal owners again about possible symptoms?"

Her phone pinged. "It's Dr. Bingham." She scanned the text message. "In addition to the two hospitalized suspect cases with heifer contact, one more had contact with sheep late Saturday. Or soil in the sheep pens."

A movement along the opposite wall of the building made her eyes flash up. With heart pounding, she pulled on Dave's sleeve and pointed. He glanced up, frowned, and called out.

"Hey, Sam, howya doing, buddy?" He began to stroll over.

She heard heavy footsteps behind them. Agent Gomez sprinted past Dave. Sam's slight smile faded, and he broke into a run for the building door. Manolo turned to follow, pulling a reluctant Maya by her clammy hand. When exiting the building, Manolo's head swung back and forth as they tried to determine which way the others had gone.

Agent O'Brien grabbed each of them from behind. "Heard about the sheep and came in. Stay out of our way. We don't want things to get squirrelly."

Across the alley, Dave threw open the doors to the bull barn with Gomez close behind. O'Brien let go and headed to a different entrance. Maya and Manolo ran to the first door, and she tripped over her feet in sleep deprivation despite the surge of adrenaline. When they entered, Dave and Agent Gomez stood motionless.

"Lost him." Dave mouthed the words.

Gomez slammed Dave against the door. "You were stupid to try and approach him. Let me handle it from here."

"I know him, maybe he'd talk to me."

"Mr. Demille, FBI," the agent shouted into the large area,

ignoring Dave. The few people cleaning or checking their animals glanced up, startled. Gomez waved his arms and guided them nonverbally to his exit door. Agent O'Brien at the far end of the building helped others out. Maya watched carefully. She didn't see Demille among them, and O'Brien knew what he looked like, too.

When the barn emptied of people, it was eerily quiet. All she could hear was the heavy breathing and restless movement of the massive show bulls, until she sneezed from earthy molds in the hay and heavy dust dancing in the few rays of sunlight streaking through the high windows. The sound echoed off the wooden walls. Agent Gomez jammed Maya's shoulder against the door and gave his demonic Andy Garcia glare, then turned to scan the stalls.

"Mr. Demille, we're checking with anyone working with Texas cattle to help us solve a case. Can we talk?"

A flash of black caught her peripheral vision as a monstrous bull bucked into the air. A scream echoed when the animal ceased its spin and landed. Gomez led the way racing down the row of stalls, weapon drawn. Maya, Manolo, and Dave followed at a safe distance. When they caught up to Gomez, Agent O'Brien was on her phone calling in backup.

Demille writhed and moaned in agony amidst the straw and manure under the hooves of the fifteen-hundred-pound animal. With cautious steps, Dave opened the gate and distracted the bull with a pacifying tone. Two barn workers and Gomez leaned in, stretching their arms to wrench Demille out of the pen before Dave locked the gate again.

Maya withdrew fresh gloves from her pocket for Manolo. He knelt to feel for a pulse. Blood oozing from Sam's mouth and nose flashed Maya back to her morning nightmare. His blue eyes were teary and unfocused, but he was conscious and seemed aware of their presence. His vacant gaze drifted from face to face, finally settling on her shoulder-length hair.

"Mother?" A reddened, vesicled hand snaked toward her.

Cutaneous lesions? Still in disbelief that the culprit could be

Dave's friend, she glanced at her clear gloves on Manolo's hands. With her clinical training, how could she refuse comfort to someone in extreme distress? She was vaccinated and anthrax didn't spread between people. There was no risk.

She cradled Sam's cool, grasping fingers between her own, trying to avoid the draining lesions. He released a slow, lengthy breath as his eyes quivered, clear fluid leaking from the corners. Those pale penetrating orbs—his hand locked hard on hers. She had bumped into him at the Pow Wow.

EMTs from the standby ambulance rushed in. "He was stomped by the bull, probably has a crush injury," Manolo told them. "We need to make sure he's tested for cutaneous anthrax, too."

Sam kept his death grip on her. The attendants agreed when Manolo asked if she could join them in the ambulance. Gurgling moans emerged from his throat with a word she could barely hear—"Maroney."

The abrupt movement of the gurney into the back of the vehicle and the blare of the siren seemed to jar him awake. His eyes darted between the two of them. He continued to clench Maya as a paramedic started an IV line in his other arm.

"You don't belong here, neither of you." His words seethed out in a grim whisper from strawberry popsicled lips. "*White* lives matter. We set foot on the moon, built the best cities, conquered the world. Only courageous people like me will live forever in the celestial kingdom."

She yanked away to free herself, then turned from the drowning blue of his eyes and took comfort in Manolo's dark ones.

The EMT shouted, "He's not breathing—let's get him intubated!"

As the paramedic worked on his patient, Manolo pulled her back into his arms until the engine stopped and the back doors flew open, staff unloading what looked like dead cargo.

Dave and Agent Gomez greeted them in the waiting room.

"Did he say anything helpful?" Gomez asked.

"I heard Maroney," she said. "Somebody important to him?"

"Not clear to me," Manolo added. "I've had an occasional patient call me a moron."

"Moroni is the angel who gave Joseph Smith the golden plates, source material for the Book of Mormon," Dave said. "An angel blowing a trumpet is an unofficial symbol for LDS."

"Maybe he was praying?" she asked.

"You stay here, I'll see what's happening," Gomez ordered. They heard him on his phone as he raced down the hall.

Maya perched on a bench like a dog with foxtails in its toes, until Agent O'Brien arrived ten minutes later.

Dave leapt up to confront her. "You minders can't leave us alone for a second, can you?"

O'Brien stretched to her full height and met him chest to chest. "This isn't about you," she barked.

Maya drew him down to an acrylic chair bolted to the wall. "We're all wired," she apologized.

The agent dug a pen and black notebook out of her suit jacket pocket. "Tell me what you saw." Maya mentioned the brief exchange on the ride to the hospital and her previous contact with Sam at the Pow Wow. Dave recalled Sam's skill with his Texas longhorns.

Then an older male physician hurried into the waiting area with Gomez close behind. The doctor stripped off his surgical cap and ran gnarled fingers through the shock of white hair. "Dr. Miranda, the patient coded in the ambulance and we couldn't get him back. Looks like pressure on the heart from a compressed rib cage."

Maya's body flushed hot and cold. She couldn't interpret her feelings. Relieved or regretful that they might not get more clarity?

"Is anthrax testing underway?" Gomez interjected. "It's vital for our case."

"Yes, we got it started. He also has track marks, so there are lab tests pending on what he was using."

She slumped in shock while Dave leaned against the wall. She was saddened by the loss of someone trusted by him to take care of his ranch. But she was angry. Sam's words in the ambulance seemed to provide a possible motive for terrorism. How could he have done it?

Manolo sat down next to her and touched her sleeve. She welcomed his closeness as they absorbed the morning's revelations. A stream of questions swirled through her mind.

"Do you remember the film footage we reviewed?" she asked.

Manolo and Agent O'Brien nodded.

"Sam wore a shoulder bag. At the Pow Wow, he grabbed it away when I tried to pick it up."

Dave's somber appearance brightened. "You're right, he had it when we talked Friday night."

"I wonder what he used it for," she said. "He didn't wear it this morning in the sheep barn or when we found him with the bull."

"I saw it in the footage. We'll put a team on it," O'Brien replied.

"Good idea," Gomez said. "With no more information from Demille, we're at a stalemate. Dr. Maguire, are you sure it was the same guy more than a month ago at the drumming event?"

Who could forget those chilling eyes? "I'm almost certain."

Gomez pressed his phone to his ear and waved O'Brien over. A few moments later, they returned. "We just heard from Dr. Smith," Gomez said. "The lab confirmed anthrax in the soil from another letter."

"It's been several weeks since the last one," Maya said. "This is number eight?"

Dave grabbed the Agent's arm. "What's the connection with Ben?"

Gomez looked around the waiting room and motioned them to a quiet corner. "This one was dropped in a Tempe mailbox Friday night. Addressed to NAACP Maricopa County Branch, but intercepted before delivery."

"What did the letter say?" Maya asked.

"At the top, it cited the NAACP criminal justice fact sheet that African Americans constitute thirty-four percent of the correctional population. Next it said, 'Ben Smith, you and other slaves need to obey your masters, then your people wouldn't be in jail,' and Colossians Chapter 3, verse 22. A final scribble said, 'You don't deserve the name of our Prophet,' referring to LDS founder Joseph Smith."

Dave punched his fist on the wall. "Dammit—why now? None of the other letters mentioned somebody specific like Ben."

Gomez shook his head. "Just the first one to our new Senator. Others were groups, no personal names. Don't worry, we'll give him extra security. If it's Demille, this could be over. But we're not sure who or how many are involved, or what else might be in the pipeline."

Maya's body sparked with a burning pain. She scraped her legs and arms to stop the uncomfortable sensation. None of them had been targeted as individuals before. But despite the disturbing news about a letter centered on one of her team members, adrenaline from Sam's death subsided. She could barely hold her head up.

"Sorry, I don't think I'll be good to anybody today." She looked over to Manolo. "I need to go to bed before I fall over right here." He put his arm around her but she brushed it aside and called the health department to make sure the human surveillance plans were in place.

Dr. Bingham said she'd send a nurse to the Show to work with the gate attendants on monitoring. "Get some rest, Maya. Don't want you getting sick."

Dave paced in front of them, but the steps were uncoordinated. His deeply lined face and narrowed eye slits indicated he was wilting, too.

"Guess the state staff and fair crew can handle things without me for a few hours, after I talk to Ben." He swung his arm in the air again, this time avoiding the wall. "If they're coming for him, they're going to have to deal with me, too."

FORTY-THREE

Her eyes fluttered awake to a shadowy room. It was sundown. She crawled out from the scattered covers and found Manolo in the kitchen scrambling eggs with tomatoes and cheese. A voicemail waited on her phone—Dr. Bingham had called.

"You should have woken me up," she chided.

He circled his arms around her waist. "You needed it."

She lowered herself to the kitchen chair while he put a Yankees mug of hot green tea in front of her. On the return call, Dr. Bingham told her that the three human cutaneous anthrax cases from the Show had been lab-confirmed, as well as Sam Demille. As soon as she set the phone down, Dave texted. *Soil +, show open/closed??* followed by a frowny face.

Manolo put a plate of food in front of her, but she shoved it aside as she called the State Epidemiologist again. She rubbed her temples and struggled to keep a measured tone. "USDA says the soil is contaminated, which we expected from the animal and human cases. And somebody was killed, probably a bioterrorist. Are you going to let them stay open?"

She heard Dr. Bingham's long exhale. "Interagency debate, governor's weighing in. Ag will allow the show to finish on time tomorrow since the contamination was restricted to the two closed areas. The public can decide whether to attend tomorrow's events, and the animals will be gone by New Year's anyway."

"Are you supportive of that?" Maya pushed up hard from the

table, knocking over the chair and tossing a couch pillow across the room.

"We have to weigh the benefits of public health decisions against the costs of taking action. As long as the public and participants are informed, I need to defer on this one."

Maya gave a curt goodbye and tossed the phone on the table. "Fuck" exploded from her lips before she cut herself off. She never swore out loud.

Pulling back the plate of scrambled eggs, she sat in the chair Manolo had uprighted. "I don't know if I'm cut out for bureaucracy."

He stroked her cheek and smiled. "Everyone chafes at times, but somebody's got to do it."

After a quick kitchen cleanup, they fell back into bed and slept until New Year's Eve morning.

. . .

At the press conference near the show entrance gates, the team watched on the sidelines, relieved to be out of the TV cameras and questions. The number of reporters and cameras was small. Nobody wanted to be up early on a cold, gloomy day. But the local police and FBI made themselves visible.

"The Governor wants to thank the community for your tremendous support of our famous Arizona National Livestock Show." Dr. Smith had his gung ho, rah-rah face on, not showing any impact from the Friday letter attacking him, which hadn't been made public. "We got started in 1948 and the show highlights our $12.4 billion Arizona agriculture industry."

He removed his custom ball cap with ANLS on the rim and waved it, triggering some tepid cheers by the patrons shifting from foot to foot to stay warm, eager to enter.

"Y'all know that Texas has shared some of their anthrax with us this year." He winked at the State Epidemiologist who had gone to medical school at Baylor.

"We had to close the junior heifer and sheep barn this weekend because of some sick animals. The lab has now confirmed anthrax for them."

The local NBC affiliate anchor raised his hand, but Dr. Smith continued. "The Governor was proactive and we recommended cattle vaccination before the show, so the problem is limited. Let me turn this over to Dr. Bingham."

He passed the portable microphone down to her, and she took it with a wan smile. "Whenever there is anthrax in soil, there can be risk to people. We've confirmed three human cases of cutaneous anthrax, two who displayed heifers and one who brought sheep. All are recovering and should be released from the hospital soon."

More hands shot up, and some members of the public darted anxious looks between the speakers and their families. Ben took back the microphone. "Yesterday was not our lucky day. One of the cowboys working with the bulls got careless and was killed in an accident. His information will be released following notification of relatives."

Maya stretched up to Dave and whispered. "Nothing about Sam's connection, or the last letter?" He shook his head.

"Is the show staying open?" shouted the CBS reporter.

"This is our last day and animals are typically removed by tomorrow. That schedule will stay the same, but the two closed areas remain off-limits. In an abundance of caution, our attention shifts tomorrow to the Horse Show. We'll do everything we can to assure safety for our patrons and their animals."

The reporters crowded in, interrupting each other for details of the animals and people. Kids dashed for the open gates while parents jerked them back and headed for their cars, children complaining.

With the unknown worker's death and anthrax fear, crowds were light. Owners began hauling their animals out. The team monitored their animal and human health surveillance sources until the grounds were largely empty except for an awards banquet. At a nearby Italian restaurant, they met for a quick dinner and New Year's Eve toast.

"Here's hoping it was Demille and we won't be facing something more coming up, like at the Horse Show." Dave lifted his glass of champagne.

"Still can't reconcile the earnest young man who helped me on the ranch with someone distributing anthrax. Not sure how I missed a guy with that amount of rage and hatred."

"How will they work out the answer when he's dead?" Maya asked.

"We'll know if these weird, spaced incidents keep happening," Manolo said.

"I want it solved, so I can return to Santa Fe and a normal EIS officer life."

Manolo's face darkened so she stroked his thigh. "Not saying I want to be away from you."

"Get a room." Dave left money for his part of the bill. "Got a wife to sweet-talk 'cause I'm not home for New Year's Eve."

"Dave, if things stay quiet for the next twenty-four hours, I'm flying back to New Mexico and will be in my office day after tomorrow. I assume you're staying longer?"

"Few more days, making sure all's quiet with the Horse Show. Hope to find more information on Demille."

She reached out to touch his sleeve before he left. "I'll catch up with you at some point."

Manolo put both of his hands on either side of her face. He was flushed and his dark eyes narrowed. "First I'm hearing of you heading home."

"I'm sorry, should have told you first."

His face scrunched as he appeared to struggle with control. "I know you two need to coordinate."

Her nerves raced. She was surprised how difficult it was to coordinate her professional and personal relationships.

"I want to spend more time with you but I'm always in Arizona. I need to do justice to my primary assignment in Santa Fe."

He stretched an arm around her again and pulled her close.

"You're right, I admire your diligence. IHS is expecting me back to work, too. I don't want our time together to be over, even when it's this insane."

She didn't want to reinforce his sense of possession. When leaning in for a kiss, she shifted up to buss his nose. "Let's get back to your apartment and make the most of our New Year's."

Despite having slept so long the night before, she faded when they got back. She sipped chamomile tea and snuggled in his bed. He turned on NBC's Toast to 2018 with Carson Daly and Chrissy Teigen. Then she flipped the channel to PBS with Renee Fleming and the New York Philharmonic.

At 9:45, he lifted the covers and caressed her breast with one hand while stealing the remote with the other. "Can't miss the ball drop," he reminded her.

The brief moment of glitter, flashing jumbotrons, and screaming reawakened them. "Ever see one of those in person?" she asked.

"Once, in elementary school. It was more manageable without the extra security before 9/11." His thumb made lazy circles around her ear. "Want to do it together sometime?"

She shook her head. "Not sure about the crowds, but we'll think of other traditions." Clicking the remote, she turned off the TV. Cuddled against his naked, warm skin, she wrapped his arm around her. Making it to midnight was impossible.

"We'll celebrate in style next year," he said before they fell asleep embedded like a knot.

· · ·

New Year's Day dawned with torrential showers. They hibernated in bed, distracting themselves from the anthrax crisis and upcoming separation. With French toast and orange juice, they toasted 2019.

In the early afternoon, she phoned Dave and Dr. Bingham about her flight and to verify no new anthrax revelations. She texted Dr. Grinwold that she'd be in the office the next morning.

"Leaving Phoenix this time is harder," she told Manolo when pouring him a third cup of coffee.

"First time you're leaving after staying here. Is it feeling like home?" He clasped her body through the red bathrobe and dusted her lips with his own. Hawaiian Kona coffee breath, warm and comforting.

A storm watch pinged his phone. "Snowstorm is on its way, I'd better get you to Sky Harbor."

Outside the security line, he held her tight—too tight. She was conscious of crowds and curious eyes.

"More than a week of making love with you, I'm addicted," he growled in her ear.

She pushed back on his chest to separate them so she could breathe. To dampen the lonely, lost little boy sadness in his eyes, she stroked the dark whiskers on his chin. She wouldn't see his Broadway star look again when he shaved for work.

"We've got a three-day weekend coming up soon for Martin Luther King," she said. "Make a date?"

He loosened his grip and gave her a quick but deep kiss. "Sí, mi alma." My soul.

FORTY-FOUR

The first day back at the Runnels Building in Santa Fe was brightened by a short text from Manolo. *THX 4 gift!* with a heart emoji. Her brow furrowed. Gift? Her chest tightened with a pang of guilt. She didn't buy him anything for Christmas, there wasn't time. Could he mean the glorious goodbye in bed all morning before the flight?

Dr. Grinwold interrupted with a suspected mumps case. Her parents had it as children and nobody batted an eye about it. Since its inclusion with the MMR vaccine, cases were rare and Dr. Grinwold said contact tracing was an emergency. CDC had just issued guidance a year ago recommending a third dose for persons at risk during an outbreak.

She set the iPhone down and went back to work. She'd talk to Manolo when she got home.

At eight in the evening, she brushed snow off the FedEx box on her apartment doorstep, then used a knife to open the package. A beautiful piece of reindeer horn on a leather necklace nestled in a bed of straw. She sneezed when taking the jewelry out of the box. Probably just her allergy to the straw, aggravated at the Livestock Show. The card from an online art marketplace said, "Happy New Year, and many more. From your Manolo."

Maya kissed the small oblong pendant and fastened it around her neck. She and Manolo didn't plan for the future, other than camping at Chaco again and an African trip at some point. She flushed with guilt, remembering she still hadn't said she loved him, even though her attachment grew stronger every day. He said it to her several times, but didn't pressure her to respond in kind.

Settled into bed, she called Manolo, but he didn't answer. She snapped a selfie to text with a smiley face.

. . .

Thursday morning, Dave emailed that they were disposing of animal bedding in a fire pit. Maya connected with him by midday.

"Dave, get home to your family or Emilia will lock the doors."

"She doesn't like it, but she's come to terms with it. There's a ton of contaminated straw and dirt to contend with."

Maya envisioned the scene in the numerous barns. "Are you being thorough with PPE? Sounds like a hazmat site with all those spores."

"Never faced indoor contamination like this before, but I keep up with my vaccine boosters. I'll be fine. By the way, the FBI tracked down Sam Demille's vaccination records. In recent years, he was the go-to-guy for burials of infected animals in Uvalde."

"So he had previous experience with anthrax," she said. "If vaccinated, how could he get infected?"

"No vaccine is perfect, immunity can wane, and he was overdue for an update. Hasn't it been six months since you helped me out in Keams Canyon after your first vaccine? Check with the hospital to see if you can be boosted."

She squirmed in the chair—almost forgot the third dose. "Thanks for the reminder."

"The FBI has moved Demille to their lead suspect for anthrax at the Show. He ditched his coat in a corner of the barn and it had dozens of pockets sewn into it for dirt samples. They're testing it today. They believe he carried the dirt in through the jacket and opened those Velcro pockets to let it fall to the ground. Had to shake his leg with dirt falling in his pants and shoes. He got a heck of a dose over those four days."

"Are we off the hook? Do they think he orchestrated all the anthrax attacks?"

"Still speculation," he said. "If the coat tests positive, along with the surveillance camera video and his own infection, he's responsible for the Livestock Show. But nothing connects him to the earlier incidents, other than your spotting him at the Pow Wow."

She rested her head on one hand, drooping again. "I wish we knew for sure. It makes me uneasy to think someone might still be out there, maybe someone working with him, planning another attack. There's no new human cases and no hits with the BioWatch air monitors in various classified locations around Phoenix."

"Glad it's limited, like most of our incidents except for the heroin. Got to wrap this up and get home this weekend."

Next, she tried to reach Manolo without success.

At home while cleaning up her kitchen, she got a return text showing him wearing a similar but larger necklace, with a question mark. He still didn't answer the phone. At eight-thirty, he called.

"Maya, I got your text and phone messages before getting in the shower. Sorry you couldn't reach me. We had an unusual spike in infants with invasive pneumococcal disease among the White Mountain Apaches. Drove up to Whiteriver yesterday and just got back. There was poor cell coverage and no time to contact you until now."

"I can't imagine anything worse than having a sick baby. I hope you get it under control." She shifted the phone to show off the necklace. "I want to thank you for this, it's beautiful."

"I'm confused, it's not from me. I was going to thank you for mine. The package was wet yesterday morning from the freak snowstorm, but I found my sister's old hair dryer and got everything dry before heading out of town. I've been wearing it, thinking about you."

"Manolo, is yours from EcoAnimArt?"

"Sí, querida. The back of the card says the artist enjoys using earth and nature to create unique gifts."

"Manolo, I didn't order jewelry for you." She tried to keep from panicking. It had to be a mistake. "Someone's trying to punk us. My only connection to reindeer is Holiday Home, but if they were trying to scare someone, it should be me and Dave. He didn't mention anything about reindeer jewelry, although he's still not at home."

"Maya, I'm wiped from my trip. Not as young as you, guess I don't bounce back as well as I used to. Feels like the flu, although I got my flu shot. Can I give you the tracking number to my package and you can ask your new friend Agent O'Brien to look into it?"

"Not really a friend," she said.

"Maybe she's not all bad. She stood up for you and Dave when her boss wanted to lock you up."

"I'll give her a try, and we should stop wearing the necklaces." She yanked it off and tossed it to the end table. Her breathing slowed when she saw Manolo do the same.

"Te quiero, talk to you tomorrow."

"Manolo, I don't want to tell an ID specialist what to do, but you know flu shots aren't perfect. You should check it out—might need an antiviral."

He agreed and promised to call her in the morning.

She reached Agent O'Brien and provided both tracking numbers for the packages. "How long does it take FedEx to deliver them?"

"Depends on amount paid. Cheaper shipment means longer delivery times."

"Holiday Home in Flag sold reindeer jewelry," Maya said. "They were unhappy over financial losses when Rickie Sanchez died. Maybe they used EcoAnimArt as the intermediary to hide the source. But they reopened and business is booming over the holiday."

"We should consider Sam Demille, too," the agent warned. "He died on Sunday and didn't leave the Livestock Show after Saturday morning, but he could've sent the jewelry before then. Maybe he saw the Holiday Home press and got the idea of reindeer necklaces to spook you."

Maya pulled the duvet tighter as she began to shiver. "Let me know when you trace the packages. We both have the necklaces, in case you need to see them."

. . .

Dave called early Friday morning. "I planned to fly home today but found Demille's bag partly buried in the dirt of one of the barns. The FBI has it and there was a diary. Angel Moroni on the front with his name. They're analyzing it now."

"Maybe it will confirm if he's connected to the earlier cases?"

"I got a quick look at the last page before they took it. Something about Christmas gifts, mail, making sure to let people know in the New Year that he was thinking of them."

She dropped to her kitchen floor. "Did Emilia get any FedEx packages for you?"

"Don't think so. She didn't say anything."

"Manolo and I both received reindeer horn necklaces on Wednesday, supposedly from each other. Agent O'Brien thought it could have been Demille showing he knew our team was at Holiday Home. The diary entry that you saw appears to confirm it."

"Why didn't I get one?"

A flood of heat flashed through her body and the room turned black—precursor for a full-blown panic attack.

"Dave," she managed to eke out. "Manolo's not answering me. Last night, we thought he might have the flu. I'm probably being paranoid, but can you swing by his place before you leave? Just want to see if he's all right."

"Not a problem. I'll let you know if I find him at home."

"Thanks, I don't know what I'd do without you."

Dave called back in forty minutes. "Maya, you gotta get out here. I texted, I called, and when he didn't answer the door, I spotted him through the bedroom window. He didn't wake up when I banged on it, so I broke it open and crawled in. He was unconscious. Ambulance is on its way to Phoenix Indian Medical Center."

FORTY-FIVE

She flew down La Bajada Hill from Santa Fe to Albuquerque. It took all her will power to stay focused on the highway and not start screaming. Driving too fast focused her attention on the road instead of Manolo's health. After her flight landed in Phoenix, Dave opened the truck door for her at the arrivals curb just before noon.

"Tell me what's happening." She evened out her voice tone.

He eased into traffic. "He regained consciousness briefly but is still sleepy and disoriented. On the positive side, he has no skin rashes or ulcers, no obvious necrosis. No signs of liver damage."

"All good." She took an enormous breath, and continued. "What's the bad news?"

Dave flicked her a quick glance. "Fever, difficulty breathing, lung infiltrates and widened mediastinum. Sputum has pus but no blood."

She rubbed her eyes, hard. Too much like some of those earlier cases. "Is anthrax one of the differentials?"

"I mentioned it to the EMTs. He's at Phoenix Indian Medical Center, his hospital, so they know he's been working on it."

"Did you contact Nancy?"

"She's already there."

Between Dave and Nancy, they wouldn't be alone. "Manolo's family?"

"It'll take most of the day for them to arrive from New York."

The truck paused at the hospital main door.

"He's in the ICU. Can you go in on your own while I park, or should I walk with you?"

She couldn't make a simple decision with her overtaxed brain. He located a spot in the parking lot and led her in.

Entering the front door, she flashed back to early August. She had flown out to meet Manolo and investigate Danny Koopee, who died of anthrax the next day. Manolo had been in uniform, greeting her at the door with warmth and humor despite the tragic circumstances.

This time, it was Nancy who welcomed her to PIMC. Their relationship had always been formal and professional. But now, Maya welcomed the comforting cocoon of someone who was patient and strong.

"I feel so guilty," she sobbed. "He didn't want me to leave Phoenix, but I insisted. He was under the weather last night, and I didn't push hard enough for him to get checked out immediately."

"Maya, sit down with me." Nancy pulled her to the padded bench. "You're panicking. Hold my hands and breathe. Use your abdomen and count. Three breaths in, three out. Now push out your abdomen and suck in air. One - two - three. Hold your belly, tighten those muscles, and push the air back out. One - two - three. Let's keep going."

They repeated the slow breaths for several more minutes. "See, you do have control over your body." Nancy looked at Dave. "Can you find Maya something to drink?"

When he returned, she drank the water and her brain kicked over into higher functioning mode. "I assume they're looking for anthrax. Anything else?"

"As an ID specialist, Manolo gets exposed to many different organisms," Nancy said. "He's handled a lot of flu cases recently, and pneumococcus this week. We're one of the highest states for hantavirus and plague. Both can lead to pneumonia. Lab tests are underway."

The room swam in front of Maya's eyes. "Manolo didn't do soil testing and animal handling like Dave and me. He wasn't considered at enough anthrax risk to get vaccinated."

"Don't get ahead of yourself. Tests are pending. We'll know what we're dealing with soon."

"Can I go in now?"

"Let's check with the doctors. He hasn't been coughing, but they're using droplet precautions because of the rule-outs."

When the doctors approved her to sit with him, she donned a gown, mask and gloves. Last time she used full hospital PPE was when he'd brought her to see Danny Koopee, in this same ICU suite.

As she pushed open the door, a tear slipped down her cheek. He was asleep but stable. Only an oxygen mask, no ventilator, so when he woke up, she could talk to him.

She sat alone in the hard plastic chair next to the bed and picked up his hand, the one without the IV in his arm.

"Mano, I'm sorry I ever cost us time. Should've focused on us, everything wonderful we have, and not on your past."

She gently fondled his fingers and tried the deep, slow breaths she practiced with Nancy.

"My anxieties and fears get in the way of embracing life to the fullest. You deserve someone more mature and stable."

She was spiraling into a self-defeating cycle, and shook out her limbs. "But I've learned and gotten stronger. We were able to talk about the future—not let my worries destroy us."

He had shaved again for work. She stroked the line of his jaw under the lips that were so persuasive, then brushed back his soft, dark hair.

"Mano, I don't know why I was too shy to admit it, but I love you."

He stirred and groaned. Could he hear? His eyelids fluttered but he didn't waken. The chief resident bustled in. "Dr. Maguire, we need to do a spinal tap, collect a cerebrospinal fluid sample."

She went out to the hall and disposed of the PPE. Ben was there and held out his hands. "We've been down a long road together since August. I'm praying Manolo fully recovers." He led her to the long bench seat, then bent forward and recited quietly, "Sweet Jesus, show us miracles of healing like never before." His quiet authority calmed her mind.

Within the hour, the chief resident came by again. "CSF was cloudy. The gram stain found many WBCs and gram-positive bacilli, singly and in chains. Appearance is not consistent with *Listeria*. Could be *Bacillus cereus* or *subtilis*, but given his history, we're assuming *anthracis*."

Nancy got up and came over to Maya, holding her in her arms. Voices drifted in and out, including the stentorian bark of Agent Gomez. Where had he come from?

"O'Brien updated me about the jewelry theory," he said.

"He could have been infected from soil at the Show," Dave replied. "Manolo walked around in it for several days, like plenty of people there. Maya and I are protected. You need to analyze the reindeer horn necklaces—here's Manolo's key. I saw his on the bed stand and the box and straw packaging on the kitchen table."

Gomez approached Maya. "Dr. Maguire, the necklace you received through FedEx, where's yours?"

Handing him her keys, she said, "Your New Mexico agents are familiar with my home." She caught Dave's smile at her mild attempt at sarcasm.

Later in the evening, after Ben and Agent Gomez had left, she was back in Manolo's room, holding his hands. Anthrax, her worst fear. At least she was at no risk of catching it, so she pulled down her mask and kissed his eyes, hoping they would open. But his body remained immobile, with quiet, shallow breathing.

"What animals do you want to see on our safari?" she asked. "Big cats are first on my list. Smaller species would also be incredible. African wild cats, caracals—"

"Maya." Nancy touched her shoulder. "The blood culture confirmed *Bacillus anthracis*. He's been on IV penicillin G and antitoxin since the CSF tap. This won't change anything, just reinforces the plan. Dave's at the airport picking up his sister and father."

Her head collapsed on his arm. Anything but anthrax—it was only supposed to be in a few Texas cattle and deer. This was a bad dream she'd wake up from.

. . .

The Mirandas arrived at midnight, and Nancy's instructions filtered into the room. "Anthrax isn't spread person to person. So they're not requiring protective equipment unless you would feel safer or if you have anything contagious. We wouldn't want to give him another infection." Maya no longer wore PPE, avoiding the claustrophobic barrier between them, feeling his warm skin with her own.

As his family rushed into the room, his muscles contracted in a generalized grand mal seizure. When Maya didn't let go of his hand, the nurse pried her fingers away and shoved them out. They watched through the window as his team adjusted medications through his IV lines. Ramona and Maya began to cry, and Sebastian drew them close, tears also tracing his skin.

Maya paced, unable to sit still. Nancy and Dave visited with Manolo's family until the doctors said he could have visitors again. The staff added a vasopressor drug to stabilize his blood pressure and began dialysis with signs of renal failure. Maya and his family took turns at the bedside, never leaving him alone. He worked at PIMC—he was one of their own. She knew he was getting the best possible care and tried to reassure his family.

But he was getting worse, and she couldn't talk with him. His temperature remained elevated, up to 104°F despite the antibiotics. Holding his hot and sweaty hand increased her own hot flashes of anxiety. The hospital added a cooling blanket under his sheets. Seizures stopped, but he was not waking up. Every time his limbs twitched, she buzzed for the nurses.

She didn't meet Sebastian Miranda at Thanksgiving. In less than twenty-four hours, his lined face and pony-tailed gray head bent over his son was comforting to her, too. His devotion reminded her of her own father, who consoled on the phone. When she answered one of the frequent calls, she told him not to drive down from Flagstaff. She needed to spend every moment with Manolo in case they lost him.

Throughout Saturday night, although he didn't regain consciousness, they talked to him. Ramona leaned close to his ear. "Remember that time when you dragged me on the Coney Island Cyclone and I was petrified, but we laughed hysterically afterwards?"

With anthrax dominating their time together, Maya didn't know about Manolo's Bronx childhood. Baseball games at Yankee Stadium, playing hide and seek in the Cloisters, fishing in Van Cortlandt Park. Sebastian and Ramona had warmhearted family stories.

Maya hadn't slept in forty-eight hours. Sebastian napped on a nearby cot. She lowered her head to Manolo's bed and drifted off.

· · ·

Bright rays shafting through blue nylon, giggling under soft, white cotton sheets, warm, gliding skin, sexy, sibilant Spanish. A noise startled her awake. *Not voices, but something . . .*

Rubbing her eyes, she spotted Ramona on the other side. Her vision was still fuzzy. "Did you hear him? Did he say something?"

They studied the pale face. Under the oxygen mask, his lips were moving. Ramona hit the call buzzer and the nurse rushed in.

The chief resident updated them with his evaluation. "Might be a sign he's regaining consciousness, but could also be involuntary movement." He paused, then gave a smile of encouragement. "He's stable—still critical—but hanging on."

Despite her admonishments, her parents arrived Sunday afternoon. She greeted them with a grateful hug and didn't argue over their presence. Nancy and Dave were again in the waiting room to provide support. Dave had met her parents in Flagstaff and tried to distract them with amusing stories of veterinary field work.

She rejoined Manolo's family in his room. At 3:40 PM, she was holding both Manolo's and Ramona's hands. The heart monitor alarm went off and she flashed to her cardiology class. Ventricular tachycardia? Hospital staff prepared the defibrillator as others propelled them out the door.

Maya leaned on the window but nurses yanked curtains. A shout of "All clear" was audible before loud thumping shock sounds. In the movies, she told herself, they're always saved.

She slumped to the floor and began shivering uncontrollably. Grabbing at her throat, she gasped for breath. "Tongue swelling, can't breathe," she croaked.

Her mom alerted a nurse and her dad helped her to a gurney. They wheeled her into the nearest available room where a junior resident took her vitals. He grabbed a warm blanket and wrapped it around her. "She has panic attacks." Her dad's voice was worried and she wanted to calm him, but couldn't speak.

The resident reassured them with the blood and EKG results. "Carbon dioxide levels are low, indicating hyperventilation. Her heart has a normal but rapid rhythm. Given the circumstances, I'll give her an injection of Ativan for a panic attack. Dr. Maguire, do you understand?"

She tried to get up.

"Nothing you can do. They're working on stabilizing his heart and lungs. Let's get you in better shape."

The injection spread a warm relaxation from her toes to her scalp. Not enough to pass out, but muscles slackened into the hospital bed and she lost track of time. She touched her fingers to her throat, maybe relaxing. Until she heard a strangled cry—Ramona?

On unstable feet, she leapt from the bed despite grasping hands and shoved aside the curtain. Ramona was sobbing, supported by her father.

"I'm sorry to startle you. We did almost lose him," the ICU chief said. "But we re-established normal rhythm and he's showing very brief signs of some awareness, which is great news. He fought the trach tube so we pulled it and he's breathing on his own. Despite the crisis, his prognosis is currently more promising."

Maya's knees buckled and arms braced her fall. She perceived her dad's reassuring voice but didn't understand the words. Finally she comprehended the physician who stood between her and his family. "You and Dr. Maguire can stay with him for a few minutes."

Ramona's eyes caught hers, and Maya nodded. Her parents helped her to the hospital bed to wait. As she rocked and cried, *Hamilton* lyrics about death not discriminating between sinners and saints drowned out all the other voices. That almost came true, and she couldn't let go of the fear. Within fifteen minutes, Dave drew aside the fabric barrier. "Ramona said you should go in, Maya, if you're up to it."

Her parents helped her to Manolo's door, where Ramona and Sebastian held her in a long embrace before she stepped into his room, alone.

He looked so much improved over the past two hours. Her eyes were glued to the gentle rise of his chest with each slow breath. He was still and pale, but beautiful.

Maya caressed the curl that was always falling over his forehead despite the military haircut requirements. After lifting his hand, she pressed his fingers to her breast. Then she rubbed her lips against his fingertips, unresponsive but still warm.

She set his hand back down and feathered his eyelids with soft kisses. When would she see again his deep, loving gaze?

As she pressed her mouth to his ear, she whispered his name, hoping to inspire a similar response. It would kill her never to hear his voice, so sweet and silken, it could melt an iceberg.

Careful of the oxygen mask, IV fluid lines, dialysis equipment, and tubes still draining his chest, she nestled her head next to his as tears rolled down her cheeks.

"There are things I still have to say," she repeated like a mantra.

Someone gripped her shoulder—Ramona. "They want to run more tests."

Maya turned back for one more look. He'd only needed a ventilator for a short period after the arrhythmia and he was stable. It wouldn't be a final look. She knew she had to keep their happier times at the forefront of her mind, but couldn't help wanting to remember this, if *Bacillus anthracis* claimed another life.

. . .

Hospital staff stopped by to check on him and meet his family. Flowers accumulated at the nurses' station. Dave brought in trays with multiple cups of coffee. Maya was numb and nonresponsive but no longer shaking and hyperventilating. Her parents held her and shook their heads whenever someone came near.

Within another two hours, Nancy was back with the preliminary report. The volume of fluid drainage from his chest had reduced, but the lymph nodes remained enlarged. His temperature stayed below 100°F for three hours. The conclusion was meningitis and septicemia due to primary inhalation anthrax. Staff were concerned about his lack of response to most stimuli due to brain and spinal cord inflammation, and they said he remained in critical condition.

When Nancy finished her summary, Ramona knelt next to Maya's side.

"You know we consider you family. I don't think Manolo had a chance to talk with you, but he mentioned last week he was planning to propose marriage."

Tears began to flow. Why was she so conflicted? She almost lost him forever, but the mention of marriage was mind-blowing. She never could have said yes, only two weeks since they first made love. And just a year older than he was at the start of his failed marriage.

Agent Gomez returned and interrupted Ramona's surprising words. After he reconnoitered the waiting room, he sat next to Maya. Only Manolo's family and friends were nearby. He looked around one more time, then started speaking in a quiet voice.

"I thought you'd want the lab results on the necklaces. The straw inside both boxes and the jewelry leather cords had anthrax. The lab concluded Dr. Miranda was infected and you weren't for several reasons. You were vaccinated; he was not."

She groaned and buried her head.

Ramona cried out, "No, no."

"Second, spores were more dispersed in his kitchen, compared to your apartment. We found a hair dryer there. Is that something he used?"

A haunting thought filtered out of Maya's frozen brain, and she forced out the words. "He said the package was wet, and used the hair dryer to dry it out."

"Makes sense," Gomez said. "He may have aerosolized more spores, leading to a greater chance of inhalation."

Ramona cried out again and leaned her weight on her father. "The hair dryer is one of mine. I left it when I was here, and forgot to remind him to bring it at Thanksgiving."

Appearing uncomfortable with the emotional outburst, Gomez shuffled his feet under the chair. "We concluded Sam Demille was the sole bioterrorist. He ordered the reindeer jewelry after our December 7 press conference. Necklaces were FedExed from Tempe on the twenty-eighth, the same date he mailed the NAACP letter. Should have used FedEx for that to avoid detection. Perhaps he intended Ben to hear of the threat sooner, hoping to scare him into shutting down the show."

The cold chills when clutched by Sam had been justified. And she had met him earlier at the Pow Wow when she knocked the bag off his shoulder. If she hadn't been so fixated on finding Manolo that day, maybe she would have noticed something suspicious. An opportunity to interrupt his deadly attacks, and she missed it.

Dave added, "Another reindeer horn package was addressed to me but never sent. Our prior history, chat at the reception, or shared LDS background might have changed his mind."

"We analyzed the diary and talked to Demille's family," Gomez said. "Real closed group, disinclined to cooperate, but we confirmed the general outline of what Demille wrote. Tough life. Sexual abuse in extended family from their Prophet, who died in prison recently. Demille was kicked out as a teen and struggled to raise a younger brother on his own."

Dave continued. "Things went haywire for Sam from the construction accident that killed his brother. He had residual effects from the head injury, and focused on groups he thought impacted his life—Native Americans, migrants, women's rights groups."

She interrupted with a tug on his arm. "But it doesn't make sense. His religious group expelled him. Why would he defend them in such a warped way?"

"It's not clear to me either." He shrugged. "For example, the Flagstaff petting zoo wasn't directed at anyone specific. Apparently he was trying out different sources of anthrax exposure based on what he found on the internet."

Nancy shook her head. "I still can't believe someone with no scientific training, no education, could pull all this off alone. And why Arizona? This was his original home."

"We found pamphlets and manifestos he carried in his bag," Gomez answered. "The attacks were motivated by changes Arizona is experiencing—becoming more 'purple,' electing a Democratic woman to the Senate. His experience with anthrax was in Texas, which became a safe haven. He was angry about Arizona, resentful of the church and his family who went back to Arizona after they excommunicated him."

"My fuckin' fault." Dave slammed a fist against his leg. "I was the one who recommended him for anthrax cleanup at an affected ranch. That's when his experience handling contaminated soil started."

"But wasn't that before his brain injury?" Maya asked. "It's not like you could have seen anything wrong and thought twice about training him that way."

"He was already a lost boy when I met him," Dave said. "No one knows how many. Kicked out into the big, bad world because elders reserve the girls and women for themselves. There are some social support groups trying to help, but many fall through the cracks, never adjusting. Doesn't mean they'll go down Demille's path. He 's a unique case of brains, unusual trauma, and twisted ideas."

She straightened up from elbows resting on her knees. "Why was Danny first?"

"Probably accidental," Gomez said. "Demille stumbled on the encampment while wandering and planning a trip back home. Didn't like his music—Michael Jackson. He was sensitive to male sexual abuse, hearing about boys attacked by the Prophet."

"Wrong place at the wrong time," she mused. She pushed her father's arm away and stiffened. "But not for me and Manolo. We were targeted."

"Apparently so," Dave said. "Demille was pissed off by the anthrax letter press conference. He saw us there. Wherever he turned, we were close behind."

"But we weren't tracking him," she said. "We didn't even know he existed. So why would he feel threatened by us?"

He grimaced. "Give yourself more credit. With our responding so quickly to each outbreak, he was forced to change his plans. Manolo was caring for patients and not involved in our field work, but close to you."

"According to the diaries," Gomez said, "Sam noticed your connection with Manolo at the Pow Wow and press conference about the letters, then stalked you at the livestock show."

"I remember how distracted he was at the reception when you arrived and started dancing," Dave added.

"Manolo's life hangs in the balance because of me," she said, numb in her grief.

Dave glanced over to the Mirandas who were rigid with shock. "That's not what I said," he snapped, but continued more gently. "You can't in any way think this was your fault."

"In a way, this was a cosmic fluke," Nancy said. "Anthrax is lurking in many places in the soil, but it's hard for people to get. We don't spend our lives with our faces in the dirt like livestock.

Bioterrorists spread anthrax with purified spores, not contaminated soil."

"My Texas colleagues are still shaking their heads over this," Dave added. "Demille had an area in Uvalde where he stored soil he'd been collecting for years from all the anthrax hot spots. What's the chance he could locate enough spores to successfully infect animals and people with them? Mix the dirt with heroin to spread the spores but still have it injectable?"

Maya sagged in the chair and closed her eyes, lips barely moving. "One in a billion chance he could pull this off, but somehow he did."

FORTY-SIX

A week after his hospitalization, Manolo opened his eyes. His father and sister did a quick salsa to celebrate, and hugged Maya. But he didn't react to their joy. Although his condition was stable, with no remaining signs of anthrax infection, he still couldn't speak or coordinate his hands to write.

The physicians were concerned that the seizures and brain infection left him with residual neurologic damage, and discharged him to a rehab center. Ramona flew home to NYC to help her husband with child care. Manolo's apartment was professionally disinfected, so Sebastian and Maya stayed there to supervise the daily physical, occupational, and speech therapy at the clinic.

All she got was a slight smile when she and Sebastian came for the treatment sessions. Did Manolo know her? Her coworkers donated unused sick leave for another week off work, but she had to get back to Santa Fe.

Overwhelmed with guilt, every detail of the past few months chugged through her brain. If Manolo hadn't met her, he wouldn't have been exposed to anthrax. A tiny part of her rational mind understood the flaw in that perception. In an alternate universe without her in it, Danny would still be his case. And without their teamwork dogging Demille's steps, how many more people would have died?

On New Year's Day, when she flew home before his collapse, they promised to see each other on the Martin Luther King holiday.

Instead on that weekend, she was leaving him, not alone, but in limbo. He couldn't communicate when or if he wanted to see her again.

Her parents offered a ride home to Santa Fe by way of Flagstaff.

"I should understand more about Sam Demille and the environment." On the treadmill next to her dad in his local gym, she tried to reactivate her brain.

"What do you mean?" He hit the pause button on his machine.

She wiped moisture from her neck with a towel. "A single human contaminated Arizona, but wasn't implicated in the Texas cattle cases. So why is there so much animal anthrax in Texas if it wasn't Demille? Initially we blamed warming soil and bad weather stirring up the spores. Even though Arizona cases were Sam's attack, climate change increases our risk of diseases from animals and insects."

"There's a lot you might never figure out. Remember the Florida guy you told me about who got anthrax? All he did was visit some parks. Let's take a quick drive. I want to show you something."

At the public library, she relaxed with the *New York Times* until her dad returned with two books. "You said you were near Abbey's gravesite."

She looked at the title—*The Monkey Wrench Gang*.

"Heard of monkey-wrenching? That's from this one. A group of misfits plan to restore the natural balance by blowing up a dam. And in the second one, *Radio Free Vermont*, Bill McKibben imagines Abbey admirers stumbling into a Vermont secessionist movement to establish a climate- and local-friendly homeland."

She smiled. "Dad, were you a hippie activist?"

He ran fingers through short hairs on the back of his head. "I had more plumage and was into the environment, like many of my generation. But a hippie? Your serious mom wouldn't have looked at me twice."

On Sunday, after an early phone call to Sebastian and Manolo, she headed out with her dad from downtown Flagstaff for fresh air. It was crisp and cold at the base of the San Francisco Peaks, sunlight glistening off snow crystals. The powder was fresh and deep as Maya broke trail on the golf course.

The only sound was the slippery slush as each ski slid forward. She spread them in a V to scamper up a small hill and paused at the top to catch her breath. The blue-green ponderosas looked like they were sprinkled with confectioner's sugar, dusted with a new foot of snowfall.

Her dad caught up, panting heavily. Snow dropped with intermittent plops off the branches to the white carpet below.

"I glanced through the books last night," she said. "Those authors were passionate about preserving beauty like this. But Abbey was a rebel until the day he died. He would have hated this manufactured nature for idol rich guys hitting a ball around the greens."

Her dad elevated one ski and banged the pole against it, knocking off snow stuck to the fishscales on the bottom. "Bit too radical for you?" Then he lifted and knocked the other one.

She followed his example with her skis. "Guess I'm a 'look before I leap' gal."

Blue wings flashed, followed by a startling, harsh wah-wah. A Steller's jay flitted between the towering trees looking for conifer seeds. Humans, animals, and the environment in perfect harmony on a spectacular January morning. *One health*, she remembered from school. And her motivation for becoming a veterinary EIS Officer.

. . .

When her parents dropped her off at the Santa Fe apartment, her mom trotted out another Stephen Hawking quotation. *However difficult life may seem, there is always something you can do and succeed at.*

Of course they wanted to refocus her attention to work. She'd come too far in handling the challenging demands of public health. But after closing the door, she curled up on the couch for the daily call to Phoenix. Her personal life had progressed, too—remaining stuck in first gear would be tragic.

"Maya, ¿qué tal?" Sebastian's accent brought back poignant

memories of Manolo's phone greetings. "I have great news. Mano walked the complete length of the double-bar exercise route. Hanging on for dear life the whole time, but one foot swinging in front of the other. If he continues with this progress, they said he can go home to his apartment. I'll stay with him, of course."

"Damn, I wish I'd been there." She wasn't comfortable with swearing, but Manolo freed up her impulses and she was more spontaneous in multiple ways. "Hold the phone to his ear."

It was a gaping void on the other end, but she pushed ahead in hope that something went through. "Mano, your Dad said you're doing great at walking. Keep at it and I'll visit as soon as I can. Or maybe he can bring you to see me here."

Sebastian's voice came back on. "The doctors are not sure what he's processing cognitively. I don't know what, or who, he remembers." Trying to assuage Maya's guilt about leaving? But the effort didn't work.

She slammed the phone to the end table in anger over what Sam took away from them. But then she checked it for damage and settled back to the cushions. She should do more for Manolo. And she should have done more to prevent this.

On Tuesday morning, her first day back at work, Dr. Grinwold for once was sympathetic. "Sorry I was short with you at times. I have diabetes. My insulin and blood sugar are sometimes unstable."

"Thank you for letting me know. Your patience these past few weeks has been incredible, and I really appreciate it," Maya said.

Stephanie was supportive when she poked her head into Maya's office and found her slumped over the desk in periodic descents into loneliness, guilt and regret.

Maya overnighted with Dave and his family at their Bernalillo Ranch on the first weekend in February. That turned out to be even better medicine than indulgent parents. She helped care for the animals, cooked dinner with Emilia and Dave, and played with the kids. Before bedtime, he brought out his guitar and serenaded the family with country-western tunes.

A lot you don't know about somebody until you live with them, she reflected. She remembered her brief seconds of doubt about his possible role with Arizona anthrax, and deflected the thought with loud applause for his performance. After placing a call to Phoenix, she held the phone so Manolo could hear some of the concert, too.

On February 12, she drove back to Flagstaff to be with her parents. The next day, she relaxed in the family's Chevy Volt as her dad drove them down to Tucson. When passing through Phoenix, her breath caught with regret that they didn't visit Manolo. But her parents committed to a stop on their way back north. At five o'clock Tucson time and 8 AM February 14 in China, the family of four sat together at her grandmother's kitchen table.

"Happy twenty-sixth birthday, Maya!" Her Irish family cheered as Hypatia yowled along with the loud singing.

They celebrated again on Valentine's Day, her official U.S. birthday, with a drive east of the city to Saguaro National Park for cake. As they shivered on the cold concrete picnic table benches, she drank in the beauty of the towering multi-limbed cacti and thin, spindly spikes of ocotillo, all frosted white on the north side from the rare snowstorm that spread down off the mountains to the desert valley below.

But the serenity was disturbed. She had made no Valentine's Day plans with Manolo. A holiday for love—what would they have done to celebrate? It was only a tiny bit easier day by day to stop the *what if's* and enjoy the memories of their limited time together, before Sam Demille and anthrax destroyed the beginning stages of their romance.

As promised, they visited the rehab center to touch base on the way back to Flagstaff. Was it her imagination, or did his smile become broader when she walked into his room? As she approached him on the bed, his hand reached a few inches toward her. Sebastian grasped his son's arm, which was no longer tanned but still muscled from the daily PT.

"Mijo, do you recognize this beautiful lady?"

She studied his face for any hint of awareness. Even in complete repose, he still resembled Lin-Manuel Miranda. She yearned for his energetic, animated expression. But there wasn't a blink of response when she leaned in to kiss his cheek.

. . .

As Maya struggled with her focus, Erika recommended the female psychiatrist who helped her cope with her sexual harassment complaint. "She's Asian, like you. Korean, I think. Not sure how she got to New Mexico. You guys are as rare as hen's teeth."

There were no major disease outbreaks, but Maya had so little control of her emotions that she feared bursting into tears at the slightest stress. Therapy might help in transition back to a functioning life, so she scheduled an appointment for Friday, February 22 at the end of the school holiday week.

On Thursday, she gave Dave and Emilia a day off by taking the girls to the Indian Pueblo Cultural Center and the BioPark Zoo, as she had promised in the fall. She and Manolo had talked at Halloween about how they both wanted children. Unlikely for that to happen, but she could be a great honorary tía.

Emilia took the kids for dinner with her parents and Dave picked up pizza, asking Maya if they could talk alone. They sat on an old porch swing in the enclosed back patio, looking out at the setting sun coloring the frosty grass a hazy pink. An electric space heater glowed, warming the area. The girls fed the ponies before they left, and a few contented whinnies drifted over from the nearby stable. Bo, Dave's black Lab, curled up at their feet.

When Dave remained silent, Maya asked a question, one that preoccupied her since the FBI told her more about Demille's diary.

"You knew Sam when he managed your ranch during vet school. Did you ever get a hint that he was a racist fanatic?"

He shifted the black cowboy hat that rested next to him on the seat.

"We don't talk religion or politics while castrating cattle."

He was right. Everyone paid attention to the job at hand when outside on the ranch, other than some ribald humor. She deflected the tension by reaching down to scratch Bo's floppy ears. But she couldn't drop her concerns.

"Does it bother you that Sam used his religion—your religion—in some kind of justification for what he did?"

"Fuckin' pissed. Gives some people an excuse to vilify Mormons. But Sam was unique in his pathology."

She thought back to her own feelings of being an outsider. Despite her broad, southwestern accent, some still assumed she was not American. "Sam hated everyone who was different—maybe self-conscious about his own differences, not being able to fit in."

"Something was off when I met him again at the Livestock Show reception. He was no longer the eager young man I knew years ago, trying to make a life for his brother. He let slip mourning Jacob's loss, but I didn't find out more than that. I hope all his hatred was from the brain damage in his accident, not something deeper inside of him."

She touched his arm. "You seem to care about him."

He brushed her away. "I didn't share everything they found out about Sam. Not easy for me to say, and don't know how you're going to take it."

Usually calm and rolling with the punches, he looked older than his thirty-one years. His face was haggard and he appeared guilty, eyes darting to her and then away.

"What's wrong? Did you find out something new today?"

"FBI told me a couple weeks ago." He rubbed his eyes. "With your psych appointment scheduled tomorrow, I hope you're in a place to hear this."

Her heart raced. What could he wait weeks for? "Just say it."

"Until college, I lived with family in Texas. My dad and I managed our ranch together. But everything went downhill after that."

"I wondered what had happened." She shifted her legs and grabbed a blanket to reduce her involuntary shivering.

"He was an alcoholic. Without me around to be on his case, he got drunk and killed himself in a car accident my first week of vet school."

She clutched his hand. "My God, Dave, I'm so sorry. How did you ever get through it?"

"No choice. Being a vet was my dream. Besides, his death was a long time coming—it would have been cirrhosis or liver cancer."

Talking about the death of loved ones was difficult. Manolo's vanishing into his own mind felt like the person she loved had died, even though his body was still recovering in Arizona. But she needed to be supportive for Dave like he was for her. She needed to know it all.

"What about your mother?"

Tears swelled in the tidepools of his eyes before he wiped them away. "Sorry, been so long, shouldn't affect me like this. He lied and told me she was dead."

In a breathy voice, she asked, "What happened?"

He swallowed. "The FBI did extensive interviews in Texas and Arizona. They were tracking down Sam's contacts and family, including the time when I hired him and helped him find other work at Texas ranches."

"What couldn't you say until now?" She grabbed a second blanket as her shivering increased.

"Sam talked a lot about his mother in the diary. She had plural marriages. Turns out she was married before she moved to Arizona, to my father."

Shock chilled her to the bone. "Dave, what are you saying?"

His tears started again, and she held his hand tighter.

"Dad was abusive to her—she was afraid of being killed. They were LDS but he fell away. She tried to escape with me, but he dragged her back. Finally, she disappeared on her own, to hide out with their sect when I was a year old."

He turned away and pummeled the hat. "I didn't know about any of this."

She couldn't believe what she was hearing, and tried to piece it together. "She . . . married there and had Sam and other kids? And Sam was your half-brother?"

Leaping up and rocking the swing, he exploded. "Maya, you were beating yourself up for Sam targeting Manolo. It was my fault, everything that happened to you, Manolo, all those people who died of anthrax. Why didn't I know? Why didn't I sense he was my brother when I met him during vet school? That was before his accident on the roof in St. George. I might have changed the course of history."

She touched his forearm. "You're no more at fault than I was, even though we both feel guilty. How could you possibly know who he was or his intentions?"

"I should have sensed a connection with Sam and Jacob. Their life paths would have been different if I realized it."

How to console him? "Can you establish a relationship with your mother and siblings now?"

He shook his head. "She told Gomez she didn't want to see me."

"When they've recovered from the blow of what happened with Sam, you can reach out to them."

"They'll just blame me for not helping him and Jacob."

"Dave, you don't know that. Give it time, like you told me. We can support each other." She dragged him back down to the swing. "Have you told Emilia?"

"Not yet. I owed it to you first. You and Manolo were the ones affected by my ignorance."

"She'll be your rock, and you have her family. Doesn't make up for what you went through with your dad, and now with your mom and siblings. But Emilia's family can be there for you, like my parents were there for me when my biological family couldn't be."

With the two friends settled again, Bo snuck in from the kitchen. They sat quietly, petting and scratching him. He rolled on his back and thumped his leg as Maya rubbed his belly with gentle strokes. Nothing as soothing as pets, even if they couldn't erase the pain.

The next day, Erika brought her to Rancho Viejo, a Santa Fe suburb, to meet her psychiatrist who reinforced lessons of cognitive therapy and prescribed clonazepam, an anti-anxiety medication. Maya told herself she was ready for baby steps to fully embrace her new life, despite its uncertainties.

Dave's revelation weighed on her soul, but helped drag her out of desolation. It was a stark reminder that others were suffering. She wasn't alone—maybe she'd try the group therapy sessions the counselor recommended.

Inspired by Reverend Tompkins, the Unitarian Universalist minister and first Tucson anthrax case, she took Erika up on an invitation to stop by the UU Santa Fe church for Sunday service.

The minister offered her use of the piano during quiet evenings, and she took comfort in music each night for an hour after the daily call or FaceTime to Phoenix. When focusing on fingers gliding over the keys, her mind was absorbed in the timeless themes of love and longing from *In the Heights*. But her heart slipped too easily from the Miranda who wrote the musical to his look-alike maybe distant relative whom she loved.

FORTY-SEVEN

Maya fell back into the routine of daily consult calls. Knowing the ability of *Bacillus anthracis* to survive for years in the soil, she kept in touch with Nancy and Dave to monitor for new human or animal cases. Demille had spread his poison in rural areas except for the livestock show fairgrounds, which were thoroughly cleaned.

Work kept her mind occupied during the daytime, but at night, Sam's vile words in the ambulance still haunted her. She didn't belong here because she was born in China. And Manolo, too, just because his parents were immigrants from Puerto Rico. After repeated pleadings, Agent O'Brien snuck her an electronic scan of the diary.

The animosity against people of color, including her personally, pierced her psyche. She had to talk to someone, and called Dave.

"Did you ever see the full diary?" she asked.

His quiet breathing seemed to last for minutes. "Yeah."

She took deep inhalations herself, determined not to get angry with him for withholding something again. "You never told me that. O'Brien finally gave it to me."

"You were distracted with Manolo. I didn't want to upset the apple cart."

Why was her colleague protecting her like a fragile flower? Sam was her real enemy. It wasn't fair to get sideways with Dave because of the biological connection. Her innate reserve kicked in and she stayed focused.

"Sam was mad that we kept showing up to the crime scenes," she said, "causing him to go somewhere else and try a new method. But his hatred of me, Manolo, and Ben—it was race. And for me, a double whammy. I'm a woman, not behaving like a Mother should. His overall rantings were bad enough, but when he mentioned us by name . . ."

"Sure you want to talk about this over the phone? It's rough."

She heard the ponies neigh behind his voice, and realized he must be near the corral. The bosque lured her back, but she was stronger now, not dependent.

"I'm dealing with it," she said. "He just changed so much. In the early diary entries, he was an innocent boy, although the indoctrination was already having its effect."

A gate clanged, then Dave's strained voice continued. "It weighs on me, whether I could share any of his perceptual predispositions. I hope not. But he spared me, because I was white and he remembered me from Uvalde. Doesn't feel right."

Her back complained, stiff without support, and she adjusted the couch pillows. "I told you before, it's not your fault. But his words reinforce my never quite fitting in, anywhere. That I'm over my head, into things I shouldn't be."

"Maya, if I was standing right there, I'd throttle you." His voice was harsh, but with a tinge of sarcasm. "I'm not gonna let my insane half-brother murder your morale."

"Just more to work on in therapy. I hope you'll do the same. Don't define yourself by him."

Hanging up, she reminded herself that Sam's legacy was over, at least for new anthrax cases. But she also knew that for her, Dave, and Manolo, the impact might be lifelong. They'd have to help each other find shoots of new growth out of the manure of Sam Demille.

. . .

In March, the promise of spring tantalized in her personal and professional life. Days lengthened and snow melted from the Sangre de Cristo peaks, visible from her living room window. Sebastian confirmed that Manolo's eyes brightened when she contacted them by FaceTime. His therapists approved his living back home in his apartment with Sebastian, and Maya flew to Phoenix the first weekend to help with the move. But Manolo's face was always a blank. He didn't seem to recognize her.

As they dropped her at Sky Harbor on Sunday night, Sebastian hopped out of the driver's seat to grab her bag.

"I'm sorry I can't stay longer or fly out more often," she said, twirling her hair in frustration. "I used up all my vacation and sick leave when he was hospitalized."

"I understand, hija. It isn't clear what he understands. Considerable therapy is scheduled, and it's not a problem for me to be here." He pulled out a scrap of paper from his shirt pocket. "But Mano wrote this while you were packing your things this afternoon."

She unfolded the wrinkled piece of envelope. It was hard to read, but her name was faintly scribbled in pencil. She jerked open the front passenger door to show it to Manolo. "I'm so happy you're thinking of me." She leaned in for a kiss. No response.

Back in the office on Monday, Dr. Grinwold restarted reviews of her slides for the presentation at the EIS conference in Atlanta. "You won't have any problems. Remember all the public engagement and press conferences you did for anthrax? This will be your peers. Piece of cake compared to what you went through."

She hoped he was right, but he still didn't know about her anxiety disorder. Nancy planned to recruit for Arizona her own two-year EIS Officer at the conference based on the visibility of Maya's work. Dr. Bingham would be at a disadvantage, not having been EIS herself. Maya didn't want to be the cause of any new officer interpreting the Arizona assignment as a poor one, based on her presentation performance or interactions.

. . .

After the early Sunday flight to Atlanta on April 28 and leaving her luggage in the hotel, she strolled through Centennial Olympic Park toward the aquarium. The popular spray fountains were off, but laughing children chased around the giant green fan sculpture of running athletes, blackened by shrapnel. Their joy was in sharp contrast to the 1996 domestic terror bombing. Arizona wasn't the first or last target.

Random rushes of anxiety about her presentation dissipated as warm rays filtered through the gentle, pale blue sky and heated her bare skin. Strong daffodil stems thrust up out of the bright green carpet. Brilliant yellow frills, deep orange centers, and yellow-white double clusters swayed at their tips. Azaleas splashed golden yellow, salmon, and violet swashes along the streetsides. With deep breaths, she inhaled the moistened, hyacinth-scented air and embraced life moving on.

On Monday morning in the Sheraton Atlanta Grand Ballroom, she took a quick swallow of water and began her anthrax talk. The twenty minutes for her presentation and questions sped by as she relied on her go-to tricks of a knee on the chair and Manolo's good luck, bear claw earrings.

When she rejoined the podium table, Lila Becker, her California colleague who preceded her on measles, gave her a thumbs up. "Bet you surprised yourself. That was fantastic." Maya beamed, and the CDC director shook their hands at the morning break.

"Unless someone like you cares a whole awful lot, nothing is going to get better. It's not." Dr. Mona Hanna-Attisha began her guest lecture on Wednesday with that quote from *The Lorax*. Maya sat in the front row, entranced by the Iraqi immigrant who inspired the nation with her work on the Flint, Michigan lead poisoning. She felt Dr. Mona looking directly at her as the physician exhorted the audience to be stubbornly persistent when lives were on the line, even in the face of severe challenges.

The number of personal interactions was intense during the rest of the week. Sometimes she escaped out the back door of the conference area for a quiet moment to ease the demands of conversation. She met many of the sixty-six new EIS Officers, including all seven veterinarians, and shared information about their upcoming training.

"Some people think Atlanta assignments are more prestigious, but states are where the action is. We're all spread out but become close when we work together like on the injection anthrax."

Despite the nonstop conference schedule, Nancy made time to take Maya out to dinner and share her own impressions of Manolo's progress based on several visits to the clinic and his apartment. Then she thanked Maya for talking up the Phoenix assignment. "My fingers are crossed that you'll have a colleague next door in early August."

Last August, less than a week on the job, she had met Manolo and Danny Koopee, the first anthrax patient. That event took her life down an unexpected path, with challenges she didn't know she could master. And now, nine months later, she was a speaker at the EIS Conference, providing well-received scientific analyses of one of the year's most newsworthy infectious disease outbreaks.

. . .

Back in the state health building on May 6, she finally put the months of tension and preparation for the conference behind her. Although average New Mexico temperatures were warming in recent years, frost could still surprise at the beginning of the month. Tiny violet snowdrops poked through the dirt outside her office window—new life always emerged—and she answered a call from Nancy, pleased about her match with a young male internist from Massachusetts.

"Enzo Russo. Do you remember him, Maya?"

She frowned. She didn't have a favorable impression of the tall Harvard-trained Boston Brahmin who tracked her down during a poster session.

"Dr. Maguire, I need you to review for me, after rodent exposure, the specific distinguishing features in the respiratory signs, radiologic exam, and chemistry panel between hantavirus infection and primary plague pneumonia."

"Dr. Russo, maybe if you put that Harvard degree to good use in Arizona, you'll find out."

He reminded her of the snooty bully from Harvard on the phone during the first week on the job. Or maybe it was only a Columbia/Harvard public health rivalry. The EIS officer designated for Phoenix was young, attractive, and intelligent like Manolo. Assigned to adjacent states, she was required to work with him. But there was no comparison—Manolo had been warm and welcoming, whereas this new colleague was arrogant and abrupt.

There'd never be anyone in her life like Manolo, no matter what their future might bring. He had willed himself out of despair when his mother died of cancer. Now Dave was coping with a deceased sibling-bioterrorist and a mother he never knew who wanted no contact. Both provided outstanding examples of courage and persistence. She would not throw away her shot.

. . .

Northern New Mexicans reveled in a heat wave. Spring flowers caught up to Atlanta. After an unpredictable winter, residents and tourists crowded the streets and trails.

Sebastian drove his son to Santa Fe in celebration of his progress using a wheelchair, although communication skills lagged far behind. Maya was dismayed that he still couldn't speak or write except single words, but his desires sometimes could be discerned through body language.

She persuaded Sebastian to relax and explore the City Different while she managed Manolo alone for a day-long excursion to Taos. As she reached over from the driver's seat to stroke the frown lines near Manolo's mouth, he grinned broadly and she fastened his seat belt. After dropping Sebastian at the Plaza, she pointed the Prius north toward vermilion hills painted for perpetuity by famed artist Georgia O'Keefe.

In the late afternoon, she peered down six hundred feet to the narrow strip of the Rio Grande River, fingers of her right hand gripping the overlook's metal rail and fingers of her left holding Manolo's as he rested in the wheelchair. A gleaming silver box had a small blue label:

CRISIS HOTLINE
THERE IS HOPE
MAKE THE CALL.

"You are someones why" was written in red marker at the top above a red button next to PUSH TO CALL.

The Gorge Bridge northwest of Taos was the site of numerous suicides, on average two per year. The light temperate wind and spectacular high mesa view made her dizzy, but sorrow over what might have been didn't tempt her to throw everything away. She leaned over to kiss Manolo. He didn't respond with passion like he used to, but his hand stroked her hair as it feathered his cheek.

In the morning, they had driven along the meandering, tree-lined High Road to Taos. At its outskirts, they took a tour guided by a Taos Pueblo college student of his thousand-year-old multistoried adobe home. Manolo was able to climb out of the vehicle on his own, but when the guide offered to push the wheelchair, they accepted.

As she offered enchilada bites at the Hotel La Fonda Taos restaurant, he knocked her fork aside and took his time bringing the food to his mouth while she admired the floral murals on the wall. After lunch, they escaped the strong sun on one of the benches under the Plaza gazebo. He dozed in a postprandial nap while she made up stories about the strolling tourists and locals.

A young woman close to her age approached, holding an infant wrapped in a light blue blanket. Maya smiled, and the mother and child smiled back. "How old is your baby?" she asked.

"He's four months," the woman answered.

Same age as her adoption. She ached to hold him but didn't want to freak the mother out. Instead, she gestured to the bench and left them to relax.

She maneuvered the wheelchair through narrow streets back to the car, then drove a few miles northwest to the Millicent Rogers Museum with its Native American and Hispanic art. They stayed only a short time in the small artifact-filled galleries. The flashbacks were too vivid of the Halloween visit to the Palace of the Governors in Santa Fe, when they started their journey into love before multiple life events derailed them.

At the Rio Grande overlook, the other pedestrians buzzed with excited conversation. Cars zoomed across the bridge, creating a slight vibration she tried to ignore.

Six months earlier, they stood together at a similar vantage point in Arizona, looking down at the tiny Colorado River in the Grand Canyon. She recalled his laugh and the strength of his body keeping her calm from the anxiety-provoking height.

At the New Mexico river, she felt no anxiety even if Manolo's disability reversed their roles of helping each other. While bending down to squeeze his hand, strengthened by hours of therapy, her body was jolted by lightning flashes of joy.

They completed the first slow traverse from east to west across the bridge, then the iPhone rang. As she answered from the viewing platform, the setting sun warmed her back like a heating pad. The department's off-hours service gave her two messages. The first was from Nancy and she quickly returned the call.

"Sorry to bother you, Maya. I know your weekends without work are rare. A Yuma woman was in bad pain from a skiing accident a couple years ago. She had trouble functioning on prescription drugs and three days ago injected heroin that she secreted away last fall. She was admitted to the hospital this morning but died of massive hemorrhaging. Initial tests of urine and blood indicate *B. anthracis*."

Maya glanced down at Manolo, resting with his eyes closed. Sebastian had warned her that he tired quickly.

"Do you need me to come out? Manolo and Sebastian are here in New Mexico. If Dr. Grinwold approves it, I could catch a ride to Phoenix with them."

"No, I promised Fred we would oversee any of our anthrax from now on. Prior to her illness, the patient visited friends in Flagstaff. We're checking to see if she also visited Holiday Home. Could be some residual contamination there. Probably it was the heroin and not the petting zoo, but Dr. Schwartz is on the way to take soil samples."

Dave to the rescue again. He was always available to respond to anthrax. She wondered why it ever crossed her mind, even for a millisecond, that he could have been associated with the outbreak. Sure, his half-brother was responsible, but Dave hadn't known they were siblings. The suspicions had been initiated by Vanessa. The Homeland Security vet was paid to be paranoid.

Manolo struggled with the water bottle in his lap. "You okay, Mano? Are you okay?" She opened it and gave him a drink.

What was next? The on-call operator had provided a number for the Jicarilla Apache Clinic in Dulce near the Colorado border. If her mental map of northern New Mexico was correct, she was only a couple hours away from Dulce. She vaguely remembered a beautiful lake, but it might not have any water left. Drought had hit hard in recent years.

After cupping hands over her ears to reduce noise from wind and car traffic, she called the clinic back. The nurse reported six family members with fever, headache, body aches, and rash. Initial lab tests had ruled out measles and chickenpox. The youngest girl, only four-years-old, had bloody forearms from scratching.

The nurse asked, "Dr. Maguire, we don't know what this is. Do you?"

She touched a bear claw earring and glanced down to the rapids sparkling bright against the black basalt canyon. Palpitations tweaked her chest. "I'm sorry, I don't have any idea."

A moving spot of white against the dark wall caught her

eye—a bald eagle, surfing the wind currents. She delighted in its graceful, unhurried movements, going with the flow. What did the young waiter in Española say about the eagle? Courage, wisdom, strength—a leader among men. Manolo had added, "and women."

Inhaling a deep breath, she got back to her phone call. Her voice was calm and confident. "But working together, I'm sure we'll figure it out."

She dropped the phone into her bag and crouched down next to Manolo. He had maneuvered his wheelchair closer to the river view and his forehead was beaded with sweat. Always hot when they were together, and not just from global warming.

Discovering the white handkerchief in the left front pocket of his jeans, she pulled it out to dab his brow. "Is that better?"

He nodded. For the first time, his dark gaze appeared to capture hers with full awareness, like the old days, and his lips turned up into a smile. The hand in his lap struggled toward her and she reached to hold it. The third and fourth fingers were bent to his palm, while the others remained straight—American sign language for I Love You.

CODA

Diversity is the key. Not all are so robust, or spread directly through contact. Some need other creatures to help—ones that are only too willing. Blood sucking isn't a choice.

Author Notes

Who are your favorite fictional medical detectives? Now you can include veterinary epidemiologists and public health veterinarians.

The MayaVerse at https://drmayamaguire.com/ offers entertaining, educational, and enlightening insights into microbial mysteries. **Please join the Reader List on the main page for updates on new publications in e-book, print (including large print), and audio formats**.

Public health veterinarians are broadly trained and contribute to One Health across the spectrum of health impacts. Additional materials including disease references are available at the MayaVerse. Secondary characters have prequels or side stories in short works, with some published and available free-of-charge from links at the website.

Maya Maguire is a fictional character, whose life journey is experienced through an alphabetical, twenty-six novel series. But she's inspired by children from China including my daughter Lian Henderson. Thanks, Lian, for your close review and unvarnished feedback!

One adoptive parent said that these girls will be "kick-ass and change the world." These children who found new homes should write their own stories. But I hope the experiences of a fictional one will resonate. The diverse character viewpoints and backgrounds, including health challenges, are informed by the lived experience of the author, who supports #ownvoices authorship beyond her own.

The career arc of Dr. Maya Maguire is modeled on the passion and integrity of my veterinary epidemiology mentors: Drs. John Reif, Suzanne Jenkins, John Emerson, O. J. Rollag, Jim Martin, John Freeman, and F. T. Satalowich; and my veterinary public health contemporaries: Drs. Faye Sorhage, Mira Leslie, Catherine Brown, Mary Grace Stobierski, and Jeff Bender.

The exciting journey of a veterinary epidemiologist, including work at state health agencies and training through the Centers for Disease Control and Prevention (CDC) Epidemic Intelligence Service (EIS), is based on my lengthy and rewarding career.

Additional information about anthrax or the CDC EIS Program was provided by Drs. Allison James, Bruce Akey, Peter Mundschenk, Van Brass, and Heather Venkat. Provision does not imply endorsement by those employees or agencies.

Anthracis was polished with recommendations from Tom Henderson, audio engineer for Maya Maguire Media. I am proud to serve the Burlington (Vermont) Writers Workshop as its Secretary and workshop leader. Particular thanks for early edits go to Dr. Kate Connell and Liz Teuber, as well as BWW workshop leaders Stephen Kastner, Dick Matheson, Vicky Phillips, and their workshop participants. The genesis of the MayaVerse was fostered with Professor Philip Baruth and his University of Vermont class.

I'd like to thank the University at Albany, University of Vermont, and Champlain College for library resources and support of my life-long learning. Book cover microorganism photomicrographs are from CDC and other photographs are the author's.

Although *Anthracis* is informed by fact, it is a work of fiction. Descriptions of events, locations, agencies, or Native American Nation staff and functions are intended to anchor the microbial threats in real life, but are used for fictional purposes.

Email feedback is welcome for any works in the MayaVerse at drmayamaguire@gmail.com. Scientific consultants are particularly encouraged to share their experiences and insights. Please join us in the MayaVerse community!

Anthracis Discussion Questions

Book groups interested in discussions with the author should email <u>drmayamaguire@gmail.com</u>.

    Anthracis crosses genres, with multiple themes in the framework of a zoonotic disease. The following questions may help in thinking about and discussing the novel.

1. The genre elements include mystery, thriller, women's fiction, and romantic suspense. How do each of these elements contribute to the overall arc and your enjoyment of the story?

2. The main character is a young Chinese American woman adopted as an infant by an Irish-heritage family living in the Southwest. What elements of the character's background enrich the story?

3. How do issues of immigration play into plot and character development?

4. Characters have strong diverging views on immigration and race, some informed by religion. How are these diverse viewpoints developed and justified?

5. What are some biological, regional, cultural, and religious influences on our perceptions of 'the other'?

6. How does the theme of disability influence the story?

7. The Southwest is intended as a character in itself. How does the geography and history influence the story?

8. What are differences between public health and health care? How should our society achieve a balance supporting both?

9. Does the novel's style increase engagement with the characters, alternating first-person diary entries with Maya's third-person point of view?

10. Zoonotic diseases are those in common between humans and non-human animals. How is transmission, investigation, prevention, and control more complex for zoonotic diseases than those infecting only humans?

11. What is the role of climate change in the story and for zoonotic diseases?

12. How can someone with a veterinary medical degree contribute to disease investigations?

13. Like *Anthracis*, the television series *The West Wing* and its subsequent podcast http://thewestwingweekly.com/ illuminate government service. How do the challenges and rewards differ depending on career, training, background, and character?

14. For authenticity, writers often rely on personal experience, while protecting privacy of those sharing life events with the author. Writers also use research and close consultation with others to create characters, plot events, and settings not their own. As a reader, do you have a preferred balance of work informed by an author's imagination, research, and representation of their background?

About the Author

MILLICENT EIDSON is the author of the alphabetical Maya Maguire microbial mysteries. The MayaVerse at https://drmayamaguire.com includes prequels, "El Chinche" in *Danse Macabre* and "What's Within" in *Fiction on the Web*, and a side story, "Pérdida" in *El Portal Literary Journal*. Awards include Best Play in *Synkroniciti* and Honorable Mention from the Arizona Mystery Writers.

Dr. Eidson's work as a public health veterinarian and epidemiologist began with the Centers for Disease Control and Prevention and continued at the New Mexico and New York state health departments. She is a public health faculty member at the University at Albany and the University of Vermont. An author of over a hundred scientific papers, articles, and book chapters, she discusses public health communication through creative writing on the podcast: https://www.drchhuntley.com/post/episode-194.

With formative years in the Southwest, Millie enjoys family trips to Arizona and worldwide, but has settled in Vermont with her husband Tom Henderson and daughter Lian Henderson, inspiration for Maya Maguire. Millie's creative writing is supported by the Burlington Writers Workshop, Alliance of Independent Authors, Authors Guild, and Sisters in Crime. She can be found on Twitter, @EidsonMillicent, and Instagram, @drmayamaguire.